P9-DDP-925

Thunder Rise

THUNDER RISE

G. Wayne Miller

ARBOR HOUSE
WILLIAM MORROW
New York

Library of Congress Cataloging-in-Publication Data

Miller, G. Wayne.
Thunder rise / G. Wayne Miller.
p. cm.
ISBN 1-55710-045-4
I. Title.
PS3563.I3775T48 1989
813'.54—dc20 89-33909
CIP

Printed in the United States of America

First Edition

1 2 3 4 5 6 7 8 9 10

BOOK DESIGN BY NICOLA MAZZELLA

To Alexis

ACKNOWLEDGMENTS

Many helped; many lent support. I'd especially like to thank: Liza Bakewell, Brown University; John Castellucci; the Centers for Disease Control; David Conboy; Jane Dempsey, R.N., Women & Infants Hospital of Rhode Island; Alison C. Guinness; Kelly Howland; Dave Silva; Mary Wright, R.N.; Irene Wielawski, medical writer, Providence *Journal-Bulletin;* and the rest of the PJB crew, who have always been supportive of my writing, no matter what kind.

PART ONE
NIGHTMARES

CHAPTER ONE

Sunday, August 3

MAUREEN MCDONALD, Susie and Hank McDonald's five-year-old, was the first.

Unlike June and July, when it had been unbearably hot and drought had ruined the corn, the weather that Sunday afternoon was a vacationer's nemesis—drizzly, unseasonably cool, with no promise of quick improvement. The Red Sox and the Mets, who might have brought some color to the gray, had both been rained out; TV programmers had substituted an old western and a bad Bogart. Even the annual Berkshire Crafts Fair across Thunder Rise in highbrow Lenox had been postponed, according to Ginny Ellis, who'd called Susie just before lunch to commiserate. The weather had put such a damper on things that Susie had actually toyed with the idea of cranking up the wood stove, cold and dusty since jonquils had pushed through the ground back in early May.

At the approximate moment the Mystery Disease (as many would later call it) gained its first toehold inside Maureen, her mother was sorting socks.

She was in the living room, sitting on the couch, three drawers of the damn things heaped in front of her on the floor. Hundreds of them, Susie thought. Easily hundreds. In a family where the telephone bill was a monthly argument, how could such a wealth of socks possibly have accumulated? she wondered idly. How, with so many permutations, were there so few mates? One of the burning issues of our time, she thought self-derisively. She sighed, once again contemplated firing up the wood stove, and then opened a new line of debate: whether 2:20 P.M. was too early to crack a beer or whether a cold one was just what the doctor had ordered.

Hell of a way to start a vacation, thought her husband, a millwright at General Electric in Pittsfield, as the western flickered across the twenty-five-inch TV he'd given the family last Christmas. Along about one o'clock he'd waged—and quickly settled—his own beer debate. He was nearly through his third Pabst Blue Ribbon now and glad he had most of a case left on ice.

When you get only a week, is it too much to ask for decent weather? he mused as he went to the window. *It's like somebody up there has it in for the McDonald family. Last year, rain. The year before, that crazy tornado. The year before that, cloudy every single day and so cold your balls were turning blue. Every year, nothing but crap. It's like being cursed or something.*

The weather hadn't made any noticeable impression on Maureen.

Dressed in her favorite orange slicker, hood up and tied, she'd cheerfully spent the better part of the morning playing some child's secret game on the lawn by the edge of the woods. Yankees down to their very soles, the McDonalds owned twelve acres of God's good green earth and considered it the best investment they would ever make. It was a mostly wooded spread, with an inconsequential stream licking across it, hidden away at the end of a twisting gravel road halfway up Thunder Rise. The nearest neighbor was Ginny Ellis, a quarter of a mile distant. Next to her it was Old Man Whipple, that crazy coot, almost a mile away.

The beauty was that Thunder Rise was mostly state forest, with a goodly portion of it belonging to the Pittsfield watershed, a restricted zone. Translate: no development. A century ago it had been quarried and mined by tough-talking entrepreneurs from Boston and Albany and Hartford. No matter how deep they'd gone or how furiously they'd dug or fervently they'd prayed, they'd found no mother lode of copper or granite and not even a trace of the gold an Indian legend promised was deposited inside the mountain's innards. One by one the companies had gone bust, and the workmen had drifted away to better places and times, leaving behind only rusting machinery and crumbling shafts.

Through the living-room window Maureen's parents had kept an attentive but not overbearing eye on her—the way parents do when their kids have coexisted with the wild since before they could walk. These were people who recognized the outdoors as a trusty companion, who valued its quiet and simple order, who respected its rules, admired its beauty. They found peace in nature, the McDonalds did.

A few minutes after lunch (grilled cheese sandwiches and reheated canned clam chowder, an economical choice that did nothing to raise Mommy and Daddy's spirits), Maureen waded through the living-room socks and asked Mom if she could go upstairs and nap.

"Tired, pumpkin?" Susie asked.

"Yes, I am," Maureen answered languidly. Her voice was an echo of Susie's, soft and undemanding, but not without a modest authority. Her voice wasn't all she'd inherited from Mom. Physically she was a miniature replica of Susie, as people meeting the two of them never failed to remark: same black hair; same green eyes; same long legs; same perfectly sculpted hands and neck. About the only gene Dad seemed to have gotten in the pool was the one for noses: Father and daughter had identical sharp, oversize noses.

It had been two years since Maureen had volunteered to nap. Still, nothing to be alarmed about. Kids naturally get exhausted on rainy days, Susie reassured herself; the dampness sucks the energy straight out of them.

"Do you feel all right, honey?" The standard precautionary question.

"Well . . . my stomach hurts," Maureen said. *Stomach,* Susie thought with a sudden tightening of her own insides. *Oh-oh.*

"Does it hurt bad?"

"Kinda bad."

"Show me where, sweetheart."

When they were children, Susie's sister had almost died of a burst appendix. The experience—the crying, the crazy telephone calls, the ambulance arriving, that long wait with a baby-sitter, the touch-and-go recovery—was all seared into Susie's memory.

"Here," Maureen said, rubbing her lower abdomen.

"Right in the middle?"

"Yeah."

"Not over here," Susie said, lightly kneading her daughter's right side just below her rib cage.

"Unh-unh."

"It's not tender where I'm touching now."

"Unh-unh."

"You're sure."

"I'm sure. It's down here," she said, indicating her lower abdomen again, "and it feels squishy-like."

"Probably something you ate, honey," Susie said, trying to convince herself. *At least it's not her side,* she thought. *That's when the red light flashes.*

"Maybe it was the chowder," Maureen said. "It tasted real old."

"Could be. Sometimes chowder doesn't settle right."

"What's 'settle right' mean, Mommy?"

"It means your body hasn't been able to digest it properly. Digestion is what your body does to food so it can run itself. Sort of like how a car uses gas."

"Am I going to throw up, Mommy?"

"I certainly hope not."

"I don't like to throw up. I think it's yucky."

Susie laughed. "It *is* yucky."

"Mommy?" Maureen said, her eyes widening a bit.

"Yes?"

"Do they let you take naps in kindergarten?" *Can't be anything too serious,* Susie thought, the relief starting to take hold, *if she's got her mind on kindergarten.*

All summer kindergarten had been on the front burner of family discussion. It was only another month now before she would start. They were sensible folks, the McDonalds, and they wanted their child to be in love with learning (she'd not attended nursery school; this would be her all-important first taste of the classroom). Since June they'd kept up a drumbeat of talk of new clothes, a new backpack, a Rainbow Brite Thermos, slews of Popple stickers, and her very own set of click ball-point pens. Maureen and her friend Jimmy Ellis, Ginny's son, were going to ride the bus together to the Morgantown School. As it was turning out, that bus ride was going to be the biggest thrill of all.

"Sure they let you take naps in kindergarten," Susie said. "Little ones. I think they call them quiet time. Now come on, pumpkin. Upstairs with you."

"OK."

"I'll get you all snuggly under a blanket," Susie said as they threaded their way through the tangle of socks. "The calendar may say summer, but it sure feels like fall."

"Yeah, it does. I hope I didn't get a bug playing outside, Mommy."

"I hope so, too, sweetheart. Now, come on. Say sweet dreams to your father."

"Sweet dreams, Dad," Maureen said.

"Sweet dreams," Hank said. The last five minutes he'd been half listening to his family, half listening to the TV. "I'm sure you'll feel all better after a little rest."

Mother and daughter were one step shy of the top stair when Maureen began to scream.

"OWWWWW!" she wailed.

"What is it, honey?"

"MOMMY, MY STOMACH! MAKE IT GO AWAY! PLEASE, MOMMY! I DON'T WANT A BUG! I WANT IT TO SETTLE RIGHT!"

The color in Maureen's cheeks had drained away, and she was on her knees, doubled over and sobbing. For one frightening second Susie was afraid she was going to lose her balance and go crashing down the stairs. Somehow, she managed to catch her. Maureen clung to her and clawed the stair rug with her perfectly formed fingers.

It's burst, Susie thought with a dread that made the inside of her skull swirl.

Her appendix has burst, and we're twenty-five miles minimum from the nearest hospital, and half of those miles are potholed gravel and dirt roads, and it's been raining buckets, and the mud's a foot deep if it's an inch, and the car's going to get hopelessly stuck in that mud, I just know it is, and Maureen, my little baby Maureen—my only little pumpkin who I love with my heart and my soul a million times over—is going to die before we can get her there, and it's all because of our pigheaded insistence that our closest neighbors be the fucking birds and bees and flowers and trees.

She wrapped her arms around Maureen, but that did nothing; the child continued to wail without interruption, without even stopping to catch her breath, already dangerously short. Susie felt helpless, completely and utterly and terrifyingly helpless, helpless the way someone newly afflicted with spinal paralysis must feel helpless when he tries to move his legs the first time.

So she did what any good parent does when she's over her head and going down for the third time: She yelled for her mate.

"Hank!" she shouted.

No immediate answer. The sounds of a western brawl in the background.

Susie shouted again. Louder. Longer.

"HANK! HAAAAANNNNNKKKKK!"

Hank had heard that tone only once before, and it was drilled into his subconscious. It was when Maureen had been an infant and she had the croup, at 2:00 A.M.

He came tear-assing across the house, sending socks flying, beer spilling. On the TV the crackling sounds of a gun battle ricocheted about.

He was too late.

As quickly as it had started, Maureen's fit—the white intensity of it—had passed, leaving her whimpering but otherwise unharmed.

"What in hell is going on?" Hank said.

"She—she had a pain in her stomach," Susie said as she soothed her daughter, whose crying was subsiding into sniffling. "Oh, Hank, I thought it was—"

"Appendicitis."

"Yes."

"I . . . feel a little better now, Mommy," Maureen said weakly. "I feel better, Daddy."

Together her parents carried her to bed, kissed and hugged her, then watched over her while she drifted off. Susie waited in pins and needles for a recurrence of the pain, but there was none; whatever it had been *(the chowder, right? it was the chowder, wasn't it?)* was gone as suddenly as it had come.

It was two forty-five by the time Maureen was deeply asleep.

It was three-twenty when Dr. Bostwick returned Susie's frantic call. "Highly unlike appendicitis," he allowed, "but for caution's sake, watch her carefully and call back the second there's any change. My guess? Too early for flu. I'd put my money on that chowder," he'd said good-naturedly just before hanging up. "Never forget, dairy products spoil more easily than one might imagine."

It was three thirty-two when the McDonalds felt an insignificant tremor, as if something down there in the earth were grumbling; it passed in less than five seconds. Neither thought much of it, and it was doubtful either would have remembered it an hour later. There often were tremors in the earth around here; they lived near a fault line, or something like that. Nothing at all like the one that ran through California, they'd been assured. This one was harmless.

It was five thirty-five when Maureen tossed off her down comforter and stretched herself awake.

The nap seemed to have done the trick. Until bedtime Susie and Hank watched her like a hawk, but there were no more complaints, not that night or the next day.

Not for more than three weeks.

Not until her first nightmare, which featured a giant bear.

CHAPTER TWO

Thursday, August 7

"WHY DO I want to leave New York?" Brad Gale repeated.

"Yes. Why would an editor at *The New York Times* making, let's see"—the middle-aged man behind the mahogany desk glanced at Brad's letter and some notes he'd scribbled on it—"making seventy-three thousand dollars a year want to work for a newspaper where a cat stuck in a tree overnight once was page one news with a banner headline and a three-column photo? For barely a third of what he's earning now? You do understand, Mr. Gale, that twenty-eight-five is nonnegotiable?"

"Yes, I do."

"And quite unlikely to increase in the very near future. Western Massachusetts doesn't have the economic base to support heavy advertising, which means our salaries of necessity are low. Livable, certainly, considering what things cost up here—especially compared with New York—but low by almost any other standard."

"I understand."

"You also understand that the editor's position is a salaried one. Not a penny of overtime, not even during your seventy-hour weeks. And you will have plenty of those, I can guarantee you. At my newspaper those are the rule, not the exception. We're not a large operation here."

"I'm prepared for that kind of schedule."

"You will have six reporters, including one in sports; four copy editors; a city editor; one full-time photographer; and a minuscule budget for stringers. Our circulation, let me remind you, has hovered around the twelve thousand mark for years."

"I understand."

"You do it all."

"Yes."

"Doing it all has meant, on more than one occasion, delivering to a disgruntled subscriber when the paper boy was sick," Dexter said, not entirely truthfully. In the twelve years since his father had died, turning over control of the paper to him, that had never happened. But it fitted the image he was trying to project.

"As a former paper boy myself, I would consider the duty an honor," Brad responded.

The man behind the desk, Paul D. Dexter, publisher and owner of the Morgantown *Daily Transcript,* studied the four-page résumé in front of him. Frankly he had been very, very surprised to receive it in the mail. Those salaries—it wasn't every day you had someone like this Gale fellow banging down the doors for a position at the *Transcript.* Mostly the paper got applications from college kids who'd done dissertations on media ethics but couldn't write a compelling feature on cats in trees, not if their button-down-collar lives depended on it. Either them, or alcoholic burnouts who hoped to wind down their careers in the Berkshires, where the needle on life's meter usually stayed a few degrees lower than almost anywhere else in the Northeast.

This Gale fellow was something else again.

He wasn't an alcoholic; a couple of discreet inquiries to old friends Dexter had in the business had confirmed that. No college kid either. This was a thirty-six-year-old thoroughbred who had a good chance of winding up in the newspaper hall of fame if he played his cards right. In his fourteen years in print journalism he'd won damn near every award in the book, including everything the Associated Press had to offer, the Hillman and a Penney-Missouri. He'd been runner-up for the grandest slam of all, a Pulitzer. Number two man in the *Times* Washington bureau for a while. A stint in Beirut before the shit really began to hit the fan in that crippled corner of the world. Then, like many reporters catching their first whiff of the middle age that's headed their way, he'd chosen to become an editor—and done well in his two years at it. Awfully damn well. Dexter's friends at the *Times* spoke of him as having the potential someday of running the shop, and that was praise not easily pried from such crusty veterans.

"So please tell, Mr. Gale," Dexter said. "Why does a gentleman who's headed straight to the top want to run a little backwater paper like ours?"

"Company line or the truth?" Brad asked, wishing like hell he could have a cigarette. In the six years since a growing fear of cancer had broken him of a two-pack-a-day habit, he couldn't recall wanting one so badly.

"The truth, Mr. Gale."

"My ex-wife," Brad said earnestly, "is a cunt."

He honestly hadn't intended to use that word—"bitch," "jerk," "idiot" had actually been uppermost in his mind—but there it was, happily popping out on its own. *Good going, idiot,* he thought glumly. *I want this job so bad I can taste it, and what do I do? Fire away with the filthiest entry in the* Dictionary of American Slang. *Not that the word isn't accurate. I'm not the first one to call her that, nor do I expect to be the last. But for all I know, this Dexter character is a card-carrying member of the Moral Majority.*

"I see," Dexter replied. Brad thought he detected the precursor to a smile on his face, which to this point had been neutral, business-like, but it must have been his imagination. Wishful thinking. "A . . . *cunt,*" Dexter said pensively.

Brad didn't need a weatherman to tell him which way the wind was blowing. "Excuse my candor," he explained lamely, "but you said you wanted the truth. And it *is* the truth. If you had the misfortune of knowing her, I'm sure you would agree, although I'm equally sure your choice of word would have been more respectable."

"I appreciate candor," the publisher said, with no further clues to his reaction. "Candor makes for good newspapermen. While you're being so candid, Mr. Gale, why don't you tell me some more about your wife?"

"Well," Brad stumbled, "there's not much to say."

"Say it anyway," Dexter insisted, none too politely. "As one man to another."

"Well . . . she's an actress. Once upon a time a quite successful one. She's attractive in a plastic kind of way. She has the emotional maturity of an eleven-year-old. She drinks too much and has a soft spot for cocaine. We were married almost five years. All but the first were hell. The last was worse than hell. We had one child, a girl. Our divorce took nine months; I figure I've put her lawyer's kid through college, with a BMW to get home on the weekends. On top of everything, there was a very ugly custody battle, most of it behind the scenes, that I eventually won. For that, you can thank my lawyer. He's the best."

"How old is she?"

"My ex-wife?"

"Yes."

"Thirty . . . thirty-three."

"And your daughter?"

"Almost five and a half."

"A very nice age," Dexter said appreciatively. "Very nice indeed. I have three children myself, two girls and a boy, and I recall that stage quite fondly. Please continue."

"That's about it." Story selection, photo display, graphics—these he'd rehearsed on the drive up this morning. But not his personal life. It wasn't a chapter of the book he liked to open anymore. All those confrontations and depositions had exacted their price.

"She's made it rocky for you?" Dexter prodded.

"Rocky—ha! Since February, when the order was issued, she's made my life unbearable. My daughter's, too. I'll spare you the gory details, but suffice it to say it's time to pull out of New York, much as I love the place."

"I see."

"But that doesn't mean I'm coming here out of desperation," Brad added quickly. "For a long, long time I've wanted to have my own paper. It's always been a dream of mine. And if I may be immodest for a moment, I think I have the credentials to do an excellent job of editing the *Daily Transcript.*"

Dexter shifted his considerable weight, reached to the ashtray for his pipe, and filled it from a fresh pouch of custom tobacco. He tamped it to his satisfaction and leaned back in his leather chair, his right hand clutching an embossed gold lighter. This was a man who took himself very seriously and expected others to do the same. This was also a very wealthy man, if Brad had to guess; his newspaper was probably only the tip of the iceberg. He was probably heavily into real estate, too, or timber, or banking, or pork futures. Something more than small-town publishing to give him the right to gold lighters and leather-back chairs.

A minute passed, and then a second minute, and then a third. Dexter wasn't saying anything. Just comfortably settled into the depths of that wonderful chair, seeming to go over every inch of Brad's face with a fine-tooth comb. One of Brad's talents was reading people, but he couldn't seem to get a line on this one. Inscrutable, his face a Rosetta stone.

It must be the obscenity, he thought. *He's the goddamn publisher, and what's he think he's got in his office, trying to worm his way into the number one slot? A loose cannon, that's what. Somebody who'd get right to work bringing the whole house of cards down in some bloody libel suit.*

"A . . . *cunt,*" Dexter said slowly, as if deriving some secret pleasure from pronouncing the word.

"I'm sorry about using that word," Brad said, "it's just that—it's just that the last year isn't ever going to make the top ten on my hit parade."

"There's no need to apologize," Dexter said. "Having experienced now for many years the privilege of one myself, I can relate to your appreciation of ex-wives. Ones who are . . . I can't be quite as candid as you, Mr. Gale, you understand . . . but ones who are, shall we say, irascible? My only hope is that you didn't get nailed as badly as I did on the alimony."

"Believe it or not, there isn't any," Brad said.

"You must be as brilliant as they say," Dexter remarked, finally lighting off his bowl. The aroma was pungent, outdoorsy, but not sweet; it conjured up an evening by a roaring fire, a glass of brandy in hand, a golden retriever at the feet.

"I don't know about brilliance," Brad said modestly. "It could merely be luck."

"I trust you would show better judgment in the use of words you would choose to publish," Dexter said, ignoring him. He ran his fingers through Brad's résumé again. "Judged by this, you would."

There is *a god in heaven,* Brad thought with relief, *and he's chosen this second of this hour of this day to smile down on me.*

"Oh, God, I would," Brad said hastily. "Don't worry about that."

"We *are* a family paper. And events really do move at a different pace up here. We simply don't have most of the big-city problems, thank the Lord—the drugs and crazy people running through subways with guns."

"Of course."

"Not that it's all cats in trees in Morgantown. That's just my idea of a little joke. We do have our controversies. We do have our issues, many of them the identical issues people everywhere in this great land of ours are facing. Life may have different rhythms, but there's no such thing as a truly backwater community anymore. Not in America. TV, the telephone, and the automobile have long since seen to that. Mr. Gale, would it surprise you to learn that AIDS education in our schools is emerging as the issue of the year?"

"No."

"Not a single recorded case of AIDS in the town, perhaps three, if that, in all of Berkshire County, and yet some of our parents believe now is the time to start if we are to protect our children long term. Naturally, an equally vocal contingent believes that we would be bringing Sodom and Gomorrah one step closer by simply mentioning AIDS in the classroom context."

"All the ingredients of a classic imbroglio."

"Then there is me. Before he handed the reins over, my father instilled in me the grave responsibilities of a free press according to his interpretation of the First Amendment of the United States Constitution. I have embraced that philosophy in its entirety, and so, while we seek primarily to entertain and inform, we also believe in slaying dragons when it is within our modest power to do so. We may not have mass circulation, but we do have an impressive insurance policy and a Boston libel lawyer, also a personal friend, who happens to be one of the best in the business. We do not shy away from the big stories, Mr. Gale. As an example, I would point to the county corruption story we did three years ago. Two people are still serving sentences as a result of our work. I believe I mailed you a photocopy."

"You did. It was a fine piece of journalism. Worthy of a Pulitzer."

"That's your territory," Dexter said, smiling.

The publisher paused, ruminating. Again, Brad didn't have the faintest clue to what might be going through his mind. And Brad wasn't about to be a brave little boy and ask, the way he might have had the tables been turned—he interviewing Dexter. No, Dexter was the kind of man who took his good time and expected to do so without challenge. For the second time in under an hour, Brad wished he had a cigarette. Dexter's pipe smoke had filled the room with a pleasant bluish haze, which Brad found very inviting.

"Just one of the many battlegrounds with my ex." Dexter chuckled emotionlessly, his free hand stirring up the smoke. It was as if he'd been able to read Brad's mind. "It used to drive her absolutely batty. I've always thought that's precisely what turned me into the incorrigible smoker I am today, her endless hounding."

Brad laughed in understanding.

"Mr. Gale," Dexter said, pulling himself out of the depths of his chair.

"Please call me Brad."

"OK, Brad. When could you start?"

"You mean—"

"That I'm hiring you just like that? Yes, I am. I had fully expected to offer you the position before you arrived. That is, if, after meeting me and seeing our little shop, you're still interested."

"God, yes," Brad said, feeling somehow silly, reduced.

"When could you begin?"

"Yesterday wouldn't be too soon," Brad said, "but realistically, I'll have to give two weeks' notice. The *Times* has been good to me. I owe them that at least."

"Naturally."

"Let's see," Brad said, fumbling around inside his blazer for his calendar. "If I were to phone this afternoon, that would put my last day there the twenty-second. Then I'd need a week to find a place to live."

"If you have trouble, you would be most welcome to stay with us," Dexter offered, "you and your little girl. What did you say her name was?"

"Abbie."

"Abbie. And you needn't worry about the, ah . . . ex. She's long since out of the picture."

"Thanks for the invitation. I hope I won't need to take you up on it. Anyway, I could start . . . let's see . . . Monday, September first."

Dexter looked at his appointments book. "You're certainly welcome to start then"—he chuckled—"but I'd just as soon give you it off. You may be in for seventy-hour weeks, but you also get a few holidays off. September first is Labor Day."

"You're right, it is."

"How about Tuesday, the second? That'll give your little girl a few days to get the hang of Berkshire County. School doesn't start until Monday, the eighth."

"Mr. Dexter?" Brad said, rising. He extended his hand. "You've got yourself a deal."

CHAPTER THREE

Friday, August 8

JIMMY ELLIS, Maureen McDonald's friend, was the second.

It began for him five days after Maureen, when he wandered away from his backyard the way five-year-old boys with a spirit of adventure and a good set of legs have forever.

It happened while he was clandestinely playing Rambo, a game his mother had outlawed for reasons he didn't buy. She said it had to do with guns being bad and there being altogether too much violence in the world—especially America, where two Kennedys had been ass-sass-inated, which he understood to mean killed in a particularly bad way. Jimmy felt plenty sorry for the Kennedys, even though he had no clear idea who they had been, but Mommy's patient explanations still didn't cut it. Couldn't she see Rambo was just a game? Nobody got ass-sass-inated with toy guns. If you got shot, all you did was lie down, count to ten, then get back on your feet again, as good as new.

He was in the backyard, on the far side of the garage.

Mom couldn't see him here, couldn't see the supersophisticated rocket launcher he'd assembled with a board, nails, and an unusually enterprising imagination. She couldn't see the submachine gun, either, or the ammo, or the grenades, or the minitransmitter, or the bow and arrow that had gotten him through a week in the jungle. She couldn't see how cleverly he'd camouflaged himself (although she would when it was time to wash up for lunch). She couldn't see the bullets being laid down by the enemy copters that filled the sky, couldn't hear the sharp *whiz-thwack* of lead all around him, the *bam-boom-bam* of explosives as they tore up the earth.

And there was absolutely no question she couldn't see the piles of enemy soldiers he'd ass-sass-inated. But there they were, in twisted piles, littering the battlefield.

The ground assault was coming from the woods. Until now he'd had no trouble holding it off. He was good, Rambo was. A machine-gun burst here, a grenade there, not a wasted slug or rocket anywhere. How else could you survive alone against such odds?

But in the last ten minutes things had deteriorated. They were crazy, these enemy soldiers, and now they were pouring across open territory in one fearless human wave. On and on and on, with no end in sight. It was as if they had a factory for them back there in the woods, and they'd cranked the assembly line up to full.

He dodged behind a rock, then sat, trying to catch his breath. The blood was heavy in his head, and he felt it pounding behind his temples; when he closed his eyes, he could see stars. In a boyhood filled with hard playing, he couldn't recall ever being so energized. He was afraid he might explode if he wasn't careful.

He looked up.

As bad as it was on the ground, the aerial developments were much worse. In the last half hour they'd brought in those deadly helicopter gunships. Using infrared technology and some pretty advanced electronic snoopers, they'd found him with no problem.

Of course, this target was no wimp. This was Rambo, and until now Rambo had managed to keep the copters at a distance—long past the time a lesser soldier would have bitten the dust. But not even Rambo could hold out forever. His ammo was low, and he was going to have to find new cover until reinforcements arrived. He'd radioed for support but been unable to get through. His best bet would be to get to higher ground, where the reception was better.

Things were desperate.

He looked back toward the house, where his mother probably was still washing dishes or talking on the phone. He looked around the house, at the woods abutting the yard. A whisper of breeze laid its fingers upon his face. The weather had finally cleared after drizzle and fog that had seemed to last forever, and the morning was warm but not humid. Sunny, with birds chirping, the forest enticing—the kind of morning you wish they all could be.

For a moment the attack receded, and he ruminated, almost angrily: *Bet they don't let you play like this in kindergarten. Bet the smelly old teacher is just like Mommy, thinks guns are bad. Probably do nothing but coloring, sissy stuff like that.*

A bullet zinging by his ear, so close he could feel the heat as it parted the air, jolted him back.

They were closing in. It was now or never.

Taking a huge breath, he struck out from the safety of the rock. Through the gate, into the field, hitting the deck when they started in with the shoulder-launched rockets. He slithered on his belly, to make himself as inconspicuous a target as possible.

He plunged through the briar into the woods and ran madly, his breath coming in shorter and shorter gasps. Prickers grabbed at his clothing, branches snapped at his face, the undergrowth tried to get a hold on his feet, but he was too determined to let that slow him any. Deeper and deeper he went, the canopy of leaves blocking out the last glimpse of his house, sealing out the goodness of that incredible summer day. This new world was not only dim but cool and damp from the rain earlier in the week, and the earth had a distinctive rich smell, the smell of freshly sprouted mushrooms and crawly creatures under rotted logs.

He wasn't supposed to come in this far.

How many zillion times had his mother told him that? How many lectures had she laid down about the dangers of Thunder Rise? As long as he could remember, she'd been lecturing him about the place. The woods were fifteen miles thick if you went straight up and over the rise, she'd warned—fifteen miles of uncharted deadfalls, bears and snakes and who-knows-what-else. But that wasn't the worst of it. Not only could you get lost up there, maybe lost overnight, but you could stumble into one of those caves that honeycombed Thunder Rise. Caves and crumbling mine shafts and water-filled quarries, the legacy of fools a hundred years ago who'd thought they could strike it rich. Only two years ago little Bobby Fulton had wandered up here. A week later they'd found him floating facedown in one of those deep, dark quarries.

Of course, Dad was the real reason she was so paranoid.

Dad had died on Thunder Rise. He'd been hunting that sparkling fall day, and he'd bagged his limit of grouse, had them in a feathery heap in the back of his Jeep, in fact, when it flipped—throwing him, then following behind a microsecond later in a perfectly matched trajectory. He'd bled to death, trapped there underneath his machine. Bled from a crushed skull, his blood matting the leaves in an ugly crimson splotch that had dried to a flaky crust by the time rescue workers pried his body free. Jimmy had just turned one, too young to know that Dad, seatbeltless and full of Jack Daniel's, had been gunning that vehicle past fifty on a trail where ten would have been reckless.

Jimmy didn't remember his father, didn't remember ever remembering him, as far as he could tell. Dad was only half a plastic-framed wedding picture Mommy kept in a drawer.

Jimmy took cover behind a tree. The enemy was everywhere.

He could hear them crashing through the underbrush, breaking branches . . . only a few yards behind him . . . got to radio for reinforcements now, Rambo, or you're gonna get yourself cap-chured . . . and you know what horrible things they do to you when you're cap-chured . . . things with bamboo shoots and razors. . . .

He ran, squeezing off rounds of his submachine gun.

A half mile into the woods.

He could hear them, louder.

Without warning, he was into the clear. It was a road, a logging and mining road from another century. To Jimmy, it was a supply route for the enemy. And while there was a certain risk in traveling it, he could make better time.

He started up the road. Faster he pushed on, fancy-stepping to avoid rocks, deadfalls, twisting gullies left by the rain.

Suddenly another sound.

A roaring kind of sound.

At first he didn't differentiate it from his game. Didn't realize that he was hearing, not imagining, it.

A roaring.

From over there. Over there, by that ledge.

He stopped, frozen. The game was suddenly over, the helicopters and shoulder-launched rockets and enemy soldiers disappearing in an instant, chased away by a new feeling of fright.

That noise. Not exactly a roaring. More a growling.

Just the wind.

Or a black bear.

Rambo had flown the coop, leaving behind a little boy who right now was probably the biggest scaredy-cat in Berkshire County. Jimmy felt something in his gut tighten. Felt a tingling in his nuts, as the big boys called what was between his legs.

For the first time he realized he was lost.

Don't ever go up there. You do, and you'll get the licking of your life. He could hear her words now, as clearly and loudly as if she were standing next to him.

Lost.

That terrifying word, "lost."

Lost, the way Bobby Fulton got lost before they pulled his body out of the quarry. They said it had gotten dark on him all of a sudden. They said he'd wandered directionlessly then, crying the whole time, sobbing for his mommy and daddy, getting colder by the minute, not seeing the quarry (how could he, in the moonless night?), not knowing he was approaching the edge of it, not knowing he was about to drown when he stepped off into space. . . .

The growling brought him back. It was louder now, more vivid, closer, probably just around the side of that ledge. It was definitely not his imagination. It was definitely not part of the game. It was real, as real as his fright.

What is it?

It came to him in a flash.

Old Man Whipple and his dog.

Old Man Whipple, who eats little boys for breakfast.

Whipple was the only person who lived higher on Thunder Rise than the Ellises. No one knew what he did anymore; since his sister's death in May, the only time he was seen was driving her beat-up Jeep on weekly shopping trips. But there were all sorts of rumors. According to one, he'd taken up devil worship. Another, started by the McDonalds—who claimed to have heard it from the horse's mouth—had him digging in one of those mines, drawn by the old Indian legend about buried gold.

The most frightening of all was the one the big boys told. Like all the other rumors, that one had Whipple crazy as a loon—but this loon carried a shotgun loaded with rock salt, which he was only too willing to discharge at anyone foolish enough to venture within range. At the Y Jimmy knew a kid who swore he'd been fired at when he was riding his dirt bike on an old logging road.

This logging road, Jimmy thought with dread.

"M-M-Mr. Whipple?"

Nothing. Only a sound like panting.

"M-M-Mr. Whipple?"

He tried to remember the dog's name. It wouldn't come.

"Here, doggy, doggy, doggy . . ."

Panting.

"Mr. Whipple, I was only"—his mind was racing fast now for an excuse—"I was only looking for *my* dog!" It was a lie, but he hoped Mr. Whipple didn't know he didn't have a dog.

"He ran off and—"

The sound again, closer.

Jimmy tried to finish his sentence. "M-m-m-m . . ."

And then it was there, staring him in the face, its moist nose twitching as it savored his little boy's scent.

A wolf.

It stood there, eyeing him, nostrils twitching excitedly at the fresh smell of fear. Almost casually the wolf opened its mouth. Two rows of perfect white teeth, each as sharp as Rambo's knife. Two gums, black as the nights on Thunder Rise, a driplet of saliva from one corner, the leftover of its last meal . . .

Jimmy didn't remember running.

He didn't remember the paralysis that had frozen his legs thawing, and then his stumbling, falling, getting up, continuing on, cutting his face, scraping his elbow, his only navigation luck and the fact that it was easier to run downhill than up.

He only remembered his mother bending over him, looking into his face with eyes that finally could register relief.

He was on the living-room couch, where Ginny had carried him after he'd come screaming into the yard, then collapsed near the garage. For an endless terrifying moment, the period of his hyperventilation and eyelid-fluttering, she was sure he was dying. They had gone through her mother's mind with frightening speed, the entire catalog of possible afflictions: seizure; rattlesnake bite; allergic reaction to bee sting; heart attack. Heart attack. She'd read in *Good Housekeeping* once about a boy her son's age who'd died from one. Extremely rare, but it happened.

Please God, she'd prayed. *Not him. He's all I have left.*

Jimmy tried to raise his head.

"It's OK," she said, gently forcing his head back to the pillow. She smoothed his brow again with a towel, moist and still cool from the ice cubes.

Jimmy looked at her, his eyes glassy.

"It's OK, sweetheart."

He struggled to speak. She put her finger to her lips, then his. "Shhhh," she whispered. "Don't say anything."

But he had to.

It was coming back now, coming back in all its three-D, full-color horror. It—it . . . He had to warn her. It was still out there. For all he knew, it had followed him and was outside the house this very instant, watching, waiting. Stalking.

"W—"

"Shhh."

"It was a wolf."

"Shhh," she repeated. "There are no wolves in Morgantown."

"But I saw it. Big . . . teeth . . ." His eyes filled with tears.

"Jimmy, it must have been your imagination."

"It wasn't my 'magination," he said.

"There haven't been wolves in Berkshire County since the Pilgrims," Ginny said patiently.

"But I *saw* it, Mommy," Jimmy insisted. "I—I know I wasn't supposed to be up there, but I was. I'm sorry, Mommy, but I got lost, and—and I saw it. I *saw* it."

"OK, sweetheart," she said. "OK."

"It was a wolf."

It had to have been a dog, Ginny decided, its size and ferocity magnified by Jimmy's imagination. Probably Whipple's dog, the old fool. Last she knew, he had some kind of mutt . . . a mangy cross between a German shepherd and a collie, wasn't it? Jimmy was lucky he hadn't been bitten.

"You probably saw a dog, sweetheart," she said gently.

Jimmy did not answer. A tremor, barely discernible, was passing through the house, and he could feel the couch rattle, ever so slightly. Ginny did not notice, or if she did, she thought it was only her son, his body momentarily reliving a nightmare.

In three seconds the tremor had passed.

Wolf, Jimmy thought, his fear catching in his throat.

Wolf, and he's gonna get me. Mommy, too.

As his mother painted his elbows with Mercurochrome, he started to cry all over again.

CHAPTER FOUR

Monday, August 25

"DAD?" the little girl in the Mustang said to the driver. She was a five-and-a-half-year-old, large for her age, with curly brown hair she kept tamed (temporarily, at least) with matched barrettes.

"Yes, hon?" Brad answered as he shifted into fourth. He checked his watch. Ten-thirty A.M. Right on schedule. He'd chosen this time in hopes of avoiding the worst of Manhattan's rush hour. Judging by the traffic on the Henry Hudson Parkway's northbound lane—steady, belligerent as always, but moderately light—he'd been successful. Throw in an hour for lunch and gas, and they'd be in Morgantown by four, no sweat.

"Can I have a pet?" The childless yuppie who owned their apartment building hadn't allowed them.

"You sure can, honey," Brad said. "Any kind of pet you want."

"How about a... *camel?*" Abbie laughed. For some reason, she thought camels were the funniest-looking animals.

"One hump or two?"

"Two!"

"You've got it," Brad said. "We'll keep it in the living room, how's that?"

"But how would we get him in the front door? Camels are *very* big. They're the most hugest animals you ever saw." She knew, having made three trips to the Bronx Zoo in the last year, once with her nursery school, the other two times with Brad.

"You're right," he said, pretending to sigh. "We'd have to keep him on the front lawn, I guess. Or on the roof."

"That's silly, Dad. Maybe we could get a barn."

"Maybe."

"Then I could feed him and ride him to school."

"I doubt seriously they'd let you have a camel in kindergarten."

"Yeah, I guess not. What I'd really like is a dog," Abbie said enthusiastically. "I was only kidding about the camel. Can I have a dog, Dad?"

"Oh, I don't think so," he said, teasing her. The truth was, Brad was New York's biggest sucker when it came to his daughter. And Abbie knew it.

"Please?"

"Well . . ."

"Please-oh-please-oh-please?" If she hadn't been buckled into her seat, this was when she would have thrown her arms around him, successfully concluding the preacquisition ritual.

"Well . . . I think a dog can be arranged," he finally said. It was already near the top of the agenda, right after shelter and school.

"Thanks, Dad! Thanks millions!"

"You're welcome, hon."

"You know *why* I want a doggy?"

"Why?"

"Because dogs are smarter than cats. I think it's because they have bigger brains, don't you?"

"Could be. Dogs are more loyal, too."

"What does 'loyal' mean?" she asked thoughtfully.

What your mother wasn't, he thought with sudden, surprising bitterness. So she wasn't so very far from his thoughts after all. "It means they're your best friend," he said. *What your mother isn't.*

"Oh. Well, I think I'd like a collie. I saw one on *Mister Rogers.* Are collies loyal?"

"Very. You've seen *Lassie,* haven't you?"

"Yeah, but I don't like it. It's in black-and-white."

"That used to be one of my favorite shows when I was your age. All the shows were black-and-white then."

"Collies are awful big." Abbie cut him off.

"Bigger than you, Apple Guy," Brad said, calling her by nickname, which had evolved from her eighteen-month-old attempt to pronounce her full name, Abigail. No one else, not even her mother, ever used it. Hearing him say it almost always made her feel special inside.

"Probably eat as much as a camel."

"Almost." He smiled.

They were quiet for a while after that. The Mustang was packed to the dome light with stuff you'd be crazy to trust to the movers—his word processor and printer, the TV, the VCR, bank documents, his leather flight jacket, the best china, a milk crate of Abbie's most treasured books and dolls. Tucking a Popple under one arm, she busied herself with her favorite volume, a Little Golden Book about dinosaurs. Abbie traveled well, had since she was an infant. If she got tired, she wouldn't complain. She'd put her head back and snooze. Despite what she'd been through . . . what *they'd* been through . . . she was an easy kid. A great kid. Brad loved her with an intensity that sometimes frightened him.

To this point the morning had been a whirlwind of activity, none of it particularly pleasant. Final instructions to the movers. Last visit to the bank. A phone call to the *Times.* A phone call to Dexter. A phone call to the woman who ran the bed-and-breakfast where they'd be staying. A phone call and a final shouting match with the landlord, this one over the security deposit, which Brad knew he could kiss good-bye. He'd been with lawyers too much lately to fight there for it, even if it was thirty-five hundred dollars. Let the yuppie have it, the asshole. And may his next tenants amuse themselves with chain saws.

Abbie traced her fingers over the words of her book. For the first time since breakfast, Brad was alone with his thoughts. With more effort than it should have taken, he reminded himself what today was supposed to be: a clean slate. The big Square One. The First Day of the Rest of His Life and all that jazz. A day to march bravely into the future with chin up, shoulders back.

And he did feel some of that, at least superficially.

There *was* a whole new life awaiting them in Morgantown, Massachusetts, as trite as it sounded. Such beautiful countryside, the Berkshire Hills. A part of New England where many of the basic rules of modern living—the ones governing anxiety and stress—seemed to have been suspended. What better place to bring up Abbie, who, Brad was starting to worry, already was showing the first signs of the jadedness that eventually sours every native New Yorker. And his new job . . . the responsibilities . . . the challenge. He honestly couldn't have hoped for better, salary notwithstanding. Dexter, the old boy, may have been a tad on the constipated side, but all in all, he seemed a good sport. Brad sensed strongly he was the type who would go to the mat for his staff—and it wasn't every day you could say that about a publisher.

But no matter how hard Brad tried to be forward-looking, he found his mind wandering to the past, to his ex-wife. Especially while Manhattan's skyline still filled the rear view.

She was an actress. Once, in those heady days when the bloom had still been on the rose, a very fine actress. There had been whispers in some very high places that Heather Pratt might be It—the next supernova from the same galaxy that had produced Faye Dunaway, whom she resembled physically, if not temperamentally. Heather'd had several leading roles off-Broadway, some respectable supporting roles and understudies on Broadway, had landed a small part in a forgettable detective movie filmed in New York. She'd done summer stock in Williamstown. Panty hose commercials for TV. And when times were really slow—and that was only twice since she'd come to New York from Ohio at the age of nineteen—she'd dipped into fashion modeling, winding up in *Mademoiselle* in the process.

Brad had met her then, at the height of the hype. Six years ago. Heather's career had already achieved apogee, but no one would have guessed that then, certainly not Heather or the artists and writers and actors and directors in her circle. Everything was still looking up. Rocket Heather. Watch her leave gravity behind. She was twenty-six, and she was so damn good-looking, so fair-skinned and blond-haired and long-legged and green-eyed, that the average man lost his tongue within seconds of saying hello to her.

Not that Bradford T. Gale was any slouch himself. Rutgers undergrad, a year on a weekly out in California, a master's from Columbia, a quick stint at the Boston *Globe,* and then on to *The New York Times,* where he quickly established himself as resident wunderkind. The guy had Pulitzer written all over him; it was merely a matter of time. Everyone knew it. And while he wasn't giving Tom Selleck stiff competition in the looks department, he wasn't your basic street corner troll either. Heather wasn't the first woman to get turned on by his looks—the horn-rimmed glasses; button-down shirts; L. L. Bean loafers; the three-day growth long before Don Johnson made it fashionable.

They met at a party in SoHo. Brad didn't lose his tongue when they were introduced. He launched directly into a discussion of the hazards of nuclear waste disposal, his latest project for the *Times.* What did she think about it? Was the government to blame? She liked that kind of talk. Liked the intelligence and biting humor that came with it. Most of all, she liked a man who didn't seem to give two good shits about her looks and her plays but who actually professed interest in her worldview. *Who actually seemed interested in* her, *not what she had become.* That night they smoked two joints, drank six glasses of white wine between them, giggled like high school sweethearts.

"I want to fuck," she whispered in his ear.

They were still making love in Brad's Upper West Side apartment when the sun came up over Central Park.

There was no stopping them then. Their early relationship was a crazy and passionate thing, one that would have done F. Scott Fitzgerald's heart good. Spring, with magic in the air. There were lunches at Mama Leone's. Parties in the Village. Opening night for an off-Broadway production of a Tom Stoppard play, in which she had the lead. A week on Nantucket, where one midnight they swam naked in the Atlantic, then made love under the moon.

Two months later they discovered she was pregnant.

Brad figured it would be easy. A quick abortion, and let the show go on.

Heather's decision blew him away.

Never the most careful female where fertility was concerned, she'd twice gotten nailed, twice opted for abortions. A third was out of the question, she told Brad. She'd wanted a child since she was one herself, had read that more than two abortions raised the chances of miscarriage astronomically, and so this was it. She would have the child. If Brad didn't want to get involved—well, this was still a free country, last she checked. He could go the fuck back to his nuclear waste and never hear from her again.

It was his first taste of another side of Heather, the acid side.

Of course, that wasn't what he wanted. He loved her. Over dinner at the Tavern on the Green, he asked her to marry him. She said yes. The ceremony was the Saturday after Thanksgiving at her parents' Long Island summer home. It was a very small affair, only a few relatives and close friends and almost no one from New York.

Abbie was born eleven months, three days after they'd met, on April 16.

It was a textbook labor and delivery, relatively quick, without complications; baby and new mom came home two days after admission. (Despite Brad's protest, Heather still insisted on calling her Abbie, after her grandmother. "Abigail Gale is redundant and silly," he said, rehashing the running battle they'd had in the last months of her pregnancy. "I think it's cute." "She'll get laughed at at school." "You're paranoid, Brad." He gave in.) There were immediate life-style adjustments for both parents. The sleepless nights. Croup. All the standard horror shows. But overall Brad was surprised at how well it was going. Goddamn if everything didn't seemed to be meshing. They both thought they had been too young for this, but now that they were neck-deep in it, they were doing OK.

Abbie was an incredibly cute baby, all dimples and Ivory Snow skin and smiles. Brad liked her immediately. Love would take longer, but from the instant he saw the top of her head wedged between Heather's stirrup-bound legs, he was fascinated by her—and far prouder than he'd imagined he would ever be. This was his own flesh and blood. His personalized investment in the future of mankind. He and Heather had done something remarkable. Created a perfectly formed human being, virtually from dust. It was an awesome feeling, and he didn't know exactly what to make of it on the philosophical level. He only knew that on the gut emotional level, he could be terribly proud.

The first jolt came from Heather.

Flush with new motherhood, she'd taken six months off from acting. Six months was exactly how long it had taken for the thrill to be gone. Changing diapers went only so far toward nourishing the artistic soul, she discovered, and it did nothing at all for an ego used to constant public feeding. That fall she was making the rounds of producers again. She thought it would be easy picking up where she'd left off—a matter of presenting her calling card—but she was wrong. There was nothing big out there open for her, she was told politely. Telling herself it was only a temporary measure, she did cattle calls. Nothing doing. After a month the best offer she had was a role in an off-off-Broadway production.

Brad hadn't seen enough of it yet to understand the actor's ego. He was only worried by the woman he was coming home to every night—an increasingly short-tempered and depressed woman. He tried to be encouraging. Tried to tell her that any career has its normal ups and downs, and so long as the wheels keep turning, nothing could remain the same for long.

He was wrong, she said. Dead wrong.

Something had changed. She could see it in the directors' faces, hear it in their voices at auditions. She could feel herself becoming yesterday's news.

At first she didn't blame Abbie. She blamed Brad. Brad had never been supportive of her career. Brad really wanted her to stay home with Abbie. Brad had married her only for her looks. Brad was self-centered. Brad was this. Brad was that.

It went on like that through the winter and spring. Anger and arguments, and increasing alcohol consumption by Heather. That's when Brad had his first glimpses of the treacherous current that swirled beneath her fair-skinned exterior. A consummate actress, she'd been able to hide that part of her for almost two years.

Soon after Christmas Heather finally landed a small part in a soap opera. It was not a headliner role, wouldn't stretch her acting abilities to the limit; but it was full-time, and it was decent-paying in a town where three quarters of her peers were waiting tables and clerking at Macy's. She hated the role immediately. She complained to her producer, and it was there on the set of that soap that the word began to leak out: Heather Pratt is a pain in the ass. Heather Pratt isn't worth it, folks.

A month into the soap, she quit.

That's when she started to focus on Abbie. If it hadn't been for the time off . . . if it weren't for the care now . . . if . . . if . . .

In their arguments, which more often than not degenerated into bitter shouting matches, Brad recited the litany of actresses who had had children while simultaneously powering their careers to the top. Carol Burnett. Joanne Woodward. Lucille Ball. *What the hell do they prove?* Heather would shout back. How many hundreds or even thousands of other actresses with children never made it? Was he such a Cro-Magnon that he missed the feminist issue here?

The line was being drawn. Heather on one side. Abbie and Brad on the other.

Heather turned twenty-nine. Abbie took her first steps, spoke her first words. Brad was a Pulitzer runner-up for investigative reporting. Heather turned thirty. There were parts, but it was two-bit work, pocket change. Where once the people who counted left messages on her answering machine, now they did not return her calls.

Brad's rising salary allowed them the luxury of baby-sitters. And so Heather would leave Abbie, head downtown to SoHo, the Village, all the old haunts. There were enough has-beens and almostweres from the good old days still kicking around to provide her with a support network. She could commiserate with them. She could drink and do lines of cocaine with them. It soon developed into the old story: Aging actress-artist comes screaming up on the big three-oh only to find the road she's on isn't taking her around the wall, but head-on into it.

The top finally blew almost exactly a year ago, when Heather, drunk on red wine and high on God-knows-how-many joints of marijuana, slapped Abbie across her face. Not hard enough to hurt her seriously, but enough to open up a river of blood from her nose. Enough that an emergency-room visit had been necessary.

The next day Brad was in a lawyer's office.

That afternoon he was in a Realtor's office, signing the lease to a furnished apartment on the Upper West Side.

That evening he took Abbie and moved in.

They were in Yonkers now.

They'd left the Henry Hudson Parkway, the Manhattan skyline had disappeared from the rear view, and they were heading north at a smooth sixty-five miles an hour on the Sawmill River Parkway. He knew it was only his imagination, but it seemed it already was ten degrees cooler. After a rainy start August in New York had finally lived up to its reputation the last couple of weeks.

"Dad, where are we going to live?" Abbie asked, looking up from her dinosaurs book. "Are we going to have a whole house?"

"I sure hope so, Apple Guy. That's the plan."

"What's it look like?"

"Well, we haven't found it yet," he said. Hadn't had time to grapple with the central issue: whether he could afford to buy or would have to settle for renting. "We'll be staying at a bed-and-breakfast while we look."

"What's a bed-and-breakfast, Dad?"

"It's like a hotel, only smaller. Sort of like an inn. They have a lot of them in New England. They're very nice."

"Oh. Do they give you breakfast in bed?"

Brad laughed. "Not usually. You usually have to come downstairs. But I've been told that they almost always have doughnuts."

"Sugar doughnuts?" she said excitedly.

"That's what I hear."

"Oh, boy!"

Abbie thought a moment.

"Dad?" she said.

"Yes?"

"When we find our house, can I have a swing set?"

"Of course you can."

"Of my very own?"

"Of your very own."

"Thanks, Dad."

Abbie was quiet again. She did not return to her *Brachiosaurus, Iguanadon, Tyrannosaurus rex.* Looking over at her, Brad could see the lines in her face deepen. Even when she'd been a toddler, her face had been an accurate reflection of her moods. Mostly they were happy-go-lucky moods. She was also capable of deep brooding. Living for so long with so much background tension, Brad thought, had done that to her.

He had learned long ago to read her face. He was reading sadness now.

"What's wrong, honey?" he said.

"Nothing," she answered unconvincingly.

"You sure?"

No answer.

"Is it your mother?" Since long before the divorce he'd been unable to refer to her as Mommy. That was Abbie's word. It would never be his. "Mommy" implied affection. "Mother" described a biological connection.

"Yes," she said, sniffling. "I think I'm going to miss her."

"Of course you are," Brad said. This was not the first time they'd played this scene out over the last two weeks. But moving away from New York at sixty-five mph gave it a sting it hadn't had before.

"Will I ever see her again?"

"Of course you will." He stifled the urge to say: "Not if I had the final say in the matter." The truth was, Heather had visitation rights that, should she decide to exercise them, gave her the opportunity of weekly visits. Brad sincerely doubted she would, but it remained to be seen.

Abbie's eyes filled with tears. Green eyes. Her mother's eyes.

It ripped him apart, seeing her like this.

"Oh, honey," he said. "Would you like a hug?"

She shook her head yes. Brad pulled the car off the road, leaned over, and put his arms around her. The tears fell freely. Her body shook with her sobs.

It took a couple of minutes for her to calm herself.

"Listen, you Apple Guy," he said, wiping the tears with his fingers.

"W-what?"

"You sure you're listening?"

"Y-yes," she sniffled.

"Because I have something very important to say."

"OK."

"As soon as we get our house, I promise you can have a dog. Any kind of dog you want, OK?"

"OK." Her face was brightening.

"Now let's stop the tears and get back on the road. We have a long drive ahead of us."

"Dad?" she said.

"What, hon?"

"I love you."

"I love you, too, Apple Guy," he said, hugging her again.

CHAPTER FIVE

Monday, August 25
Afternoon

THE MAN leaning into the pay phone at Harrah's Casino in Reno, Nevada, had a bucket of newly won quarters, $156.75 in all. The operator told him how many he needed for fifteen minutes. He followed her instructions, put the phone to his ear, and waited for AT&T's computers to find him a cross-country circuit.

Someone seeing him might have guessed he had Native American blood; that guess would have been right. Someone hearing him might have guessed he was raised back East, probably in New England; that guess, too, would have been correct. He was a tall man, with broad shoulders, a pockmarked face from a losing battle with teenage acne, dark, unblinking eyes that were no windows to his soul. He looked to be about forty, although it was possible he was five years older or younger. His hair was long and black and done up in a carefully constructed ponytail. Like many of the gamblers in the background, he was dressed in working western: Levi's; flannel shirt;

denim jacket with sunglasses slipped into the vest pocket. Not a man you would want to meet in a dark alley under anything but the friendliest of circumstances.

A female voice at the other end said: "Hello?"

"Is this my favorite little sister?"

"Charlie!"

"How are you, Little Sis?"

Little Sis. Ginny Ellis couldn't remember a time her half brother had ever called her anything different. She loved the affection written into that name. It seemed to say about their relationship: "This one is special. This one is the real thing."

"I'm fine. The question is: *How are you*?"

"Same as always," Charlie Moonlight said. "Getting by."

"Where are you? I can tell by the line it isn't Morgantown."

"Reno."

"I should have known," Ginny said, without recrimination. "Low on money, so you decided to go to the well."

"Can't fool you, Little Sis."

"And you're winning, right?"

"You could say that," Charlie said, fingering the quarters.

That brimming bucket was only the tip of the iceberg. It had been a good two days—not a record, but damn near one. He'd been plugged in. That was what had counted. Tapped into a conduit he'd never tried to define, never dared to, a conduit he only knew as a repository of luck, both good and bad. At every table, at every machine, he'd felt it inside him: a familiar involuntary tightening of all his muscles, a sensation similar to butterflies in his stomach. In his head he could see them: the blackjack dealers' cards, the winning sequences on the one-armed bandits. Since arriving Saturday morning, he'd cleared more than twenty grand—money he'd immediately deposited in the bank. He'd been plugged in, all right.

"You know," Ginny said, "one of these days that great luck of yours is going to run out and you're going to get burned. Burned bad."

"When I'm plugged in," Charlie said matter-of-factly, "I can't lose. And when I'm not plugged in, I don't play."

"You'll run up against the wrong character at some poker table and you'll find yourself—"

"Now, before you deliver one of your lectures—"

"No lectures, Charlie. I'm glad to hear from you."

She meant it. They were only half siblings, but they had always been tight. Ginny believed the age difference had helped make that possible. Charlie was eighteen years her senior, and they had never lived under the same roof, except for short spells. No chance to develop the rivalries of closely spaced siblings. No chance for turf wars, or bitching over what's on TV, or who's doing the dishes, or who's got the car Friday night, or how long Sis has been in the bathroom, or how late Brother got to stay out, or any of the other nonsense that gets blown out of proportion in the standard family. What they'd had were time and room to feel each other out on their own terms.

But there was more to it than that.

Almost ten years ago Charlie had introduced Ginny to his best friend, and that best friend and Ginny had taken an immediate liking to each other, and that liking had quickly turned to love, and before you knew it, they were married, had built a house in the woods, and had brought a son into the world—a beautiful blond-haired boy, Charlie's godson. And when Jimmy Ellis, Sr., had killed himself in his Jeep that fall afternoon on Thunder Rise, Charlie had been the first to find him. Charlie had been the first to tell Ginny. Charlie had sat next to her at the funeral, his arm around her, cushioning her sobs. Charlie was a wanderer, but then . . . *then, when she'd needed someone most* . . . he'd been there. And he'd been there since, whether by phone or his trips back East. Been there for her and for her son.

"I'm sorry I haven't called earlier," Charlie said.

"It's only been three months," Ginny chided. "You could have been dead and buried for all we knew."

"You worry too much."

"No. Not me. But Mother does. She'd never say it, of course, but she's been pretty concerned. Three months, not even a postcard. Mothers worry about that kind of thing, Charlie. You ought to know that by now."

"I thought you said no lectures," Charlie said lightly.

"I did," Ginny said. "Just a gentle reminder about family responsibilities. Are you still living in California?"

"Yes. Just across the border from Reno."

"Don't tell me you have a job."

"Not exactly," he said, and now an eavesdropper would have sensed he wasn't hot to continue this line in the discussion.

"Well, *I've* got news on the job front. Guess."

"Let me see . . . last I knew you were at a printshop. In Pittsfield, right?"

"Correct."

"And . . . you're not there anymore."

"You got it."

"You're working in Mother's place."

"The bed-and-breakfast? Be serious."

"I give up."

"I'm *teaching*!" she said proudly. "At Morgantown Elementary!" Since graduating with her certificate from the University of Massachusetts six years ago, she'd had her name in for a job at Morgantown. But it was a small school (as Abigail Gale and her father would discover when she enrolled there) with virtually no turnover. The kind of school where teachers automatically become institutions, where the institution on retirement automatically merits a banquet, a gold watch, and a posed picture of both banquet and watch across the front page of the local rag.

"Congratulations, Little Sis. What grade?"

"Third."

"Too bad."

"Why bad?"

"You won't have Jimmy. He starts kindergarten this year, doesn't he?"

"Indeed, he does."

"Is he looking forward to it?"

"Why don't you ask him yourself? He's right here. Want to speak to him?"

"Does the sun set in the West?"

"Hold the line a second." In the background, she yelled, "Jimmy! Telephone!"

"Hello?" the young voice said after a bit.

"Is this my favorite nephew, the one and only James Ellis?" Charlie asked.

"Uncle Charlie!" the small voice said excitedly.

"Pardner!"

"Are you coming over?" It was always the first question.

"Not today, pardner. I'm pretty far away."

"Are you in another country?"

"I guess you could say that," Charlie said. "I'm in Nevada."

"What's Nevada?"

"It's a state. Like Massachusetts, only much bigger. All the way over on the other side of the country. Your mom can show you on a map. So, how've you been, pardner?"

"Good." Already the excitement in his voice was slipping away. It wasn't like Jimmy. He could usually get a couple of days' mileage out of a call from Uncle Charlie, at the very least.

"Only good? I hear you're starting kindergarten next month. You must be excited."

"I guess."

" 'I guess?' That doesn't sound like the guy I know. The one who loved nursery school. Remember how much fun nursery school was?"

"Yeah."

"Well, kindergarten is even better. Believe me."

There was silence while Jimmy looked to see where his mother was. She'd gone into the bathroom. "Uncle Charlie?" he whispered.

"Yes?"

"Did you ever kill any wild animals?"

"You mean, like deer? You know the answer to that."

And he did. One of the most fascinating things about Uncle Charlie was his knowledge of the woods. More than once Jimmy had listened spellbound as he'd spun tales of stalking deer across the snow-blanketed wilderness. More than once he'd taken his nephew into the woods behind the cabin he kept in Morgantown to show him firsthand nature's secrets and wonders.

"Not deer," Jimmy said tentatively. "Bigger animals. Wicked fur-oshus ones."

"Like moose?"

"Yeah, but even more worse."

Charlie was picking up on it now. Not Jimmy's tone, but something just beneath the surface. Charlie could feel it there, hiding in his nephew's words. For a second he thought it must be related to the prospect of kindergarten. He dismissed that almost immediately. Something was troubling Jimmy, but it was more serious than butterflies about school.

Before Charlie could speak again, a computer voice interrupted.

"Please deposit seventy-five cents for each additional minute. . . ." it droned.

Charlie quieted the voice by feeding it enough quarters to reach Hong Kong for the rest of the week.

"You still there, Jimmy?"

"Yes."

"Is something wrong with my pardner?"

"No." Jimmy wasn't convincing.

"You sure?"

"I'm sure."

Charlie screwed his eyes shut, blotting out the casino's incessant flashing and buzzing. There was a sensation in his mind, fleeting, a dark shape . . . there evanescently and then completely gone. It had moved like . . . like what? *Like an animal. A large animal. A wicked fur-oshus animal.* He could get no more of a fix on it than that. If he had been plugged in, the way he was when he was on a roll at the poker or blackjack tables, it would have come to him. A Kodacolor-perfect image of what was bothering his nephew, just like pictures of the dealer's cards. But he wasn't plugged in. Couldn't make himself be either. His talent wasn't large enough to plug in on demand.

"You know, you can tell your uncle Charlie," he said softly. "I won't tell anyone. I promise."

"Well . . ."

"Tell me, Jimmy," Charlie said firmly.

"Well, in the middle of the night there's something in my room."

"Nightmares."

"That's what Mommy says. She thinks it's from watching too much TV. But it's not a nightmare. It's real. In my room." Jimmy's voice threatened to break.

"What's in the room, pardner?"

"The wolf. The same one I saw in the woods."

Wolf. A large animal. A wicked fur-oshus animal. The words echoed in Charlie's mind. It was an uncomfortable echoing.

Jimmy gave a summary of what had happened in the woods. Now that it knew where he lived, he said, the wolf was stalking him. It was a patient and very clever wolf, a ferocious and completely evil one, and it was taking its sweet time. Waiting for the right moment to pounce, a moment Jimmy could only guess. Just like Uncle Charlie tracking a deer across the frozen wilderness.

"I thought maybe you could kill it for me," Jimmy said, and it was then that his courage dissolved and he started to cry.

They talked another five minutes, Charlie reassuring his nephew that there weren't any wolves left in Massachusetts—and even if there *were,* no wolf would come within miles of a human being, just as no wolf could ever climb up the outside of a house to a second-floor bedroom. Jimmy didn't sound convinced, but he had composed himself by the time his mother was through in the bathroom. For good measure, before Ginny got back on the line, Charlie promised to look into things the minute he was back East in the fall. If he found a wolf . . . of course, he would kill it. Instantly.

In the ensuing minutes Ginny gave her own version of the woods episode. She verified that the nightmares had started soon after and were occurring perhaps every third night. Her theory was that the threat of school was responsible. True, she agreed, Jimmy had gone to nursery school without apprehension; but that had only been two days a week, and she and her friend Susie McDonald had car-pooled to bring their children. Kindergarten was a Much Bigger Deal: five days a week, in the same school as the big kids, delivered to and fro every day on a regulation-size school bus. Give him a week, Ginny said, and Jimmy would feel right at home. The nightmares would naturally pass.

The conversation covered several other topics before ending with Charlie saying he planned to be back East by Halloween, please be sure to tell Mother.

Charlie was oblivious of the casino's glitter as he returned the phone to its cradle, took his remaining quarters, and headed for a cashier's booth. He was not plugged in anymore; it had been ready to pass before the phone call, he'd felt it clearly, and now there wasn't a trace left. He knew better than to risk even another half hour. He'd done that once—gambled when he wasn't plugged in—and he'd wound up fifteen thousand dollars in the hole. Never again, he'd vowed.

After changing his quarters for bills, Charlie got in his Cherokee and started the two-hour drive over the mountains to the trailer he'd been renting since coming to northern California last spring from Morgantown.

Wolf.

The word haunted him as he drove across the state line into the rugged beauty of the Sierra Nevadas, which rose from dynamited ledges on both sides of the interstate. Normally, breathing the evergreen air here, seeing these mountains—so unlike the gently weathered hills of his home state—had a profound effect on him. The inevitable aggravations and tensions of a trip to the city would fall off him, like a snakeskin, as he traveled deeper and higher into the rock.

Now he was oblivious.

And not simply because of what his nephew had said, although that was unsettling enough. Hearing the word "wolf," having it register—*thinking it as he was now, dark and disturbing, like thunderclouds overspreading a blue mountain sky*—had struck some deep ancestral chord. Had somehow ricocheted back through the centuries, back through his genes to the tribe of his father, a full-blooded Quidneck, a faint trail leading back, back to . . .

. . . he didn't know what to. Only that it wasn't anything good, that it didn't concern only Jimmy.

More than that wouldn't come. Not for several days.

CHAPTER SIX

Monday, August 25
Evening

BRAD SAT in an overstuffed chair, the comfortable one in the corner by the front window of their second-story room, and watched the sun go down in a blaze of crimson. The final rays flirted briefly with the rose-print wallpaper behind the bed, and then they were gone, leaving the room amber. The evening breeze had carried away the heaviness of the afternoon, and now it was bringing back the strong, cool smell of pine.

Brad was relaxed—maybe too relaxed, the part of him that had been running on nervous energy the last two weeks kept saying. He took another sip of his beer, second from a six-pack of New Amsterdam he'd purchased in New York and kept chilled in a Styrofoam cooler. A mini-celebration was in order. It wasn't quite so simple, he realized, but as he sat there with his feet up, slaking his thirst, it really did seem as if his head had cleared since he'd left New York. With some careful engineering on his part (more puppy talk, mostly), Abbie's mood, too, had swung around long before they'd arrived in Morgantown. And the Boar's Head Inn, the unlikely medieval name Mrs. Fitzpatrick had given her bed-and-breakfast, had turned out to be one of those rare places that surpassed their travel guide reputation. It was typical of New England inns built a century or so ago, offering large bedrooms crammed with ponderous old furniture, a sprawling living room, and a location that would make a New York developer drool. It was a mile outside town, nestled in woods at the base of the Berkshires. From either of the establishment's two porches, you were afforded uncompromised views of the hills.

Abbie was on one of those porches now, a floor below Brad.

He could hear her voice, animated and high-pitched, and he could hear an older voice talking back. It belonged to a woman he'd noticed in the dining room earlier. Not just another background person, but a woman with looks: long brown hair; large eyes; perfect white teeth that formed a high school sweetheart's smile. Any way you sliced it, a cut above your average woman. She'd been sitting alone, and through soup, salad, main course, and dessert, she hadn't stopped reading an oversize hardcover book. He couldn't see the title, but if forced to guess, he would have put his money on a best-seller. Maybe a Michener or a Krantz. After dessert she'd closed her book, taken a last sip of coffee, and gone onto the porch. On his way up to their room Brad had seen her out there, still lost in her reading.

From their bedroom Brad tried to catch her conversation with his daughter. They weren't loud, and something buzzing out there (cicadas? crickets?) was drowning out most of what they said. Here and there he caught a word or two, but no complete sentences. Still, he caught enough to know that it was an amicable exchange. Whoever she was, she seemed at ease with children.

Time—he could not guess how much time—passed. For a while he wondered idly about the woman—where she was from, what she was doing here. From the woman his mind wandered to the new job. It lingered there awhile, going over the same issues yet again, and from the job his thoughts moved along to the inn and the sixtyish woman who owned it. In the course of these thoughts he opened his third beer. As he finished it, the amber tint to the room gave way to light gray, the light gray soon enough to dark gray, liberating the shadows from their daytime hiding places. The room, so cozy in daylight, now had more than its share of mysterious spots. Someone more in tune with the supernatural might have expected to hear soft footsteps.

Brad was turning on the lights when Abbie bounded in. His face lit up. Here she was, the little girl who always made him catch his breath, the only person on earth he was crazy for, the bouncing, smiling, outgoing girl with her endless stream of questions. The girl with the personality, intelligence, and looks to take her places when she blossomed into womanhood—some mighty big and exciting places, he'd bet. The girl who had her old dad exactly where she wanted him, wrapped tightly around her little finger.

"Well, if it isn't my favorite Apple Guy!" Brad greeted her.

Abbie hugged him, kissed him on his cheek, then touched his chin as if she wanted it on the record that she'd noticed all the stubble but understood why it was there. She scrambled onto his lap. Getting up, she accidentally dug a knee into his crotch. It hurt like hell, but Brad swallowed the pain and the instinct to yell out. It was funny in a way, but any references to their respective "private parts," as he'd taught her to call them, always made him uncomfortable. Unless there was absolutely no way around it, he didn't mention them—certainly not in any casual context. Maybe he was just being old-fashioned. Maybe his parochial school upbringing was surfacing after all these years of trying to bury it forever. But he didn't think that was it. He thought it had everything to do with the near hysteria Americans had developed for anything that smacked of child abuse. As a journalist he was only too aware of cases where ex-spouses had used the charge of sexual abuse in attempts to ruin their former mates. No question, Brad was paranoid, but the last year had taught him paranoia could be an extremely useful survival tool.

"Know what, Dad?" Abbie asked when she was comfortable.

"What, pup?"

"There used to be Indians around here!"

"Indians?"

"Yup. A whole big tribe of 'em."

"You're kidding!"

"Nope. They lived in tepees and huts, and they used to catch fish and trap animals, like rabbits and squirrels. I think that's icky, eating squirrels, don't you, Dad?"

He thought of the wonderfully tame creatures that would eat peanuts out of your hand in Central Park. "I sure do," Brad said.

"But that's what they did. Honest."

"Just how'd you find all this out, Apple Guy?"

"That lady told me on the porch. She said Indians lived all around here back when it was just woods, and no white people like us. That was before the Pilgrims, I guess."

"I bet you're right."

"She said there are still some Indians here, only they don't live in tepees anymore. They live in houses just like we do and have regular jobs and things like that. She said you might not even know they were Indians unless they told you, because they talk the same as us now, too."

"And how does she know all this?"

"Well, she had a book about Indians. But there weren't any pictures," Abbie said, sounding disappointed.

"Did she say what she does when she isn't reading?" he asked.

"She said she studies Indians. At a brown college."

Brad had to ponder that before it clicked. "Do you mean Brown University? That's the *name* of a college, not a *kind* of college."

"Yeah, that's it," Abbie said, shaking her head in agreement.

"Did she say anything about a degree?"

"A degree?" The lines on Abbie's face deepened.

"It's what you get after you've graduated. Older people like her often are going for their Ph.D.s."

"For their what?"

"Their P-H-D. It's a kind of degree you get after years and years and years of work. Some people are my age or even older before they get them."

"Wow," Abbie said with awe. She didn't exactly think her father was *old,* but she understood quite well that he was *a lot older.* "I don't remember if she said anything about a P-H-D."

Brad took another hit off his beer. "Can I have a sip?" Abbie asked. "Please?"

"Just one."

Abbie raised the bottle to her lips, sending one damn fine swig down the old hatch. Brad pulled the bottle away. Abbie patted her stomach in appreciation, then belched softly. Abbie had it down pat, the whole beer-quaffing ritual. Brad secretly liked to think he'd been a good model.

"Say 'excuse me,' " he reminded her.

"Excuse me."

"And no more," he said firmly when his daughter reached for it again.

Abbie went to the window and looked out into the night, which had settled completely over them. You couldn't even see the purple outlines of the hills anymore. The wrought-iron lamppost at the end of the drive was on. A great flurry of moths was congregated around it, their wings fluttering so crazily that she could hear them over the background of crickets. Abbie watched, fascinated. Where they lived in New York, there were occasional mosquitoes (they laid their eggs in Central Park, Brad had told her), and there were plenty of cockroaches—some very large and nasty specimens among them—but moths and butterflies were infrequent visitors. Abbie knew them mostly from books and *Sesame Street.*

Except for the moth convention, the porch was empty. The woman had gone.

"Did she say what kinds of Indians, Apple Guy?" Brad asked when Abbie had returned. Indians might make a nice feature story for his paper.

"No."

"No names of tribes?"

"No. But she told me her name. It's Thomasine."

"Do you mean Thomasina?" he said, emphasizing the final vowel.

"Oh, no. She said that's what everyone always thought, that it was Thomasina, but it really wasn't. She said she was the only one she knew with her name. Do you like that name, Dad?"

"I guess so," he answered. "It certainly is different. Did she say her last name?"

"Unh-unh. Only her first one."

Abbie tugged at his beer. Brad gave in, allowing her a small sip.

"Dad?" she said earnestly when her throat was clear.

"Yes, hon?"

"Are you going to have a date with her?"

He wasn't surprised at the question. She'd asked it, or one very similar, before about women with whom he'd come into contact. He knew that the issue of divorce and the great uncharted territory that followed had been discussed—surprisingly frankly and effectively, he thought—on *Mister Rogers.* And he knew she was old enough to understand that in most cases both Mommy and Daddy after the divorce eventually got around to going out with Someone New (the kid never had much of a say in who it would be, Mr. Rogers had said; you just had to trust Mommy and Daddy's judgment). Just like big kids, most divorced mommies and daddies went out on "dates."

"No, we're not going out on a date," Brad said. "I don't know her, Apple Guy. You have to know someone before you ask her out on a date."

"Maybe you *should* know her," Abbie said. "She's very pretty. And I think she's very smart, too. I liked her, Dad."

"I'm glad you did. But I'm still not going to ask her out on a date. Now I think it's time for this young lady to go to bed. I want you to brush your teeth and get your PJs on, and then I'll read you a story."

"*Two* stories? *Please,* Dad?"

"Well . . ." He teased her.

"Pretty please with sugar on it?"

"OK, as long as there's sugar on it."

"Goody! I want the dinosaur story and *Rainbow Brite.*"

"Did you bring them in from the car?"

"Yup."

"OK, you got it. Two stories. Now go brush your teeth."

Abbie padded off into the bathroom. Brad listened to the sounds of water being drawn, brushing, rinsing, and gargling. Finally, he heard her voice—so much a little girl's voice, he thought, like some kind of baby songbird.

"Dad?" she called to him.

"Yes, Apple Guy?"

"Can we leave the light on tonight?"

"Are you scared?"

"No . . ." She hesitated. "Well, it's a *little* scary, that's all."

"Of course we can," he said as Abbie padded back to where he was sitting, dinosaur book in hand.

CHAPTER SEVEN

Tuesday, August 26

"MOTHERFUCK," Harry Whipple swore through sixty-eight-year-old toothless gums. "Motherfucking fuck."

His kerosene lantern had blown out, he'd forgotten the flashlight he'd been reminding himself to carry, and now it was darker than the inside of an asshole. Whipple groped inside his coveralls for his hip flask. He took a swallow of whiskey and belched, leaving an acid taste in his throat.

"Motherfuck," he repeated. He was cocked to the gills, but that was no front-page news.

Just where the Christ had a gust of wind like that come from, anyway? he wondered. Here, a good quarter of a mile inside this disintegrating old mine? He'd felt it clearly—more substantial than a draft, cold, clammy, raising the hairs on the back of his neck as if someone invisible had lightly touched him there. It wasn't the first time he'd felt air stirring in this hellhole, but it was the first time it had been strong enough to extinguish a Coleman lantern.

There'd been a noise, too. A low rumbling, coming from underneath and to one side of him, back where he'd been digging three months ago.

"Fuck."

He dropped the pick he'd been swinging. The metal hit rock, sending up a sharp echo that seemed to pierce his eardrums. The lantern and wooden matches were a good twenty feet away. Twenty feet of rotted timbers, small boulders, rocks, dirt, broken bottles, all the assorted crap that had piled up in two months of backbreaking work in this spot. *A man could get seriously hurt trying to find his way through that mess in such total blackness,* he thought. *A shit-faced man could get himself killed.*

Somewhere on him he had a book of matches. Or a Bic lighter, he couldn't remember which. But he remembered he'd been wearing these pants the last time he'd allowed himself the luxury of a cigar, two or three days ago, and he figured whatever the hell he'd used to get the thing going had to be in one of his pockets. The question was which one. With both hands he started exploring. Jesus, these pants had a lot of pockets. He couldn't recall ever knowing just how many. Pockets in the rear, pockets on the side, pockets on the front, pockets down the leg. Pockets inside pockets. There seemed to be something in each of them, too. Keys. Several varieties of change. A penknife.

Matches. Where were the matches?

"Piss," he swore.

Finally, success. He found matches in the watch pocket, closest pocket to his underwear, which was permanently stained a rusty color from the sweat and piss that got to percolating in there when he was working and drinking at full steam, as he'd been most days all summer. The cover of the book was soggy. Whipple opened it. He struggled to separate a match. Christ, was it stuffy in here, gust of air or no gust of air. More stuffy than usual—and the usual was like a greenhouse with the sun blazing and the vents shut. Maybe that was because he'd been at it since eleven, and it was going on three now. Time to call it a day, once he got his lantern lit.

The first match sputtered and died. So did the second. So did three, four, and five. He was swearing up a storm now, cursing the darkness, dead niggers, his dead sister, the punks on their dirt bikes, the Indians who were supposed to have discovered gold here but refused to tell the white man exactly where.

The sixth match held. He cupped his hand around it and prepared to move toward the lantern.

That's when he saw it.

Something moving through the shadows.

An animal? Whatever it was, it looked fifteen feet long.

"Fuck," he swore.

Animal.

No, that couldn't be. Weren't no goddamn animals in North America that big, let alone western Massachusetts. You didn't need Marlon Perkins to tell you that.

"Shit."

The match sputtered and went cold in his hand, which was shaking badly.

Since May he'd been at work in this abandoned mine.

May, the month his only sister had died, leaving him a house and more than one hundred acres of land a half mile up Thunder Rise from the closest neighbors, the Ellises. She'd been a spinster, Marjorie Whipple had, meticulous and efficient in everything she'd done, and when a cerebral hemorrhage quietly claimed her in her sleep at the age of eighty-one, her affairs had been in order. A lawyer had witnessed her will, and her burial policy was paid up, and her place in the family plot at Morgantown Cemetery was properly reserved. She'd even selected an undertaker—there really was only one to select, Jake Cabot—and expressed to him her wishes regarding her final rites.

Harry's inheritance wasn't his because Marjorie had any particular fondness for her younger brother ("an accident," her dear mother had confided to her before she'd passed on in 1952); in fact, quite the opposite was closer to the truth. While Marjorie had carved out a modest niche for herself as a county court clerk, Harry, in the grand scheme of things, had successfully developed into the classic loser. He'd had a succession of failures as short-order cook, garage monkey, school janitor, painter, woodchopper, assembly-line worker at the GE plant in Pittsfield. In Marjorie's eyes, her only sibling was a lazy sot who'd so far come to nothing and now, in the twilight of his drunken existence, certainly never could. But there were no other relatives, and Marjorie had been too frugal to be big on charities, so Harry Whipple had inherited all: the land, the house, the furnishings, a rattletrap Jeep, and a paid-off mortgage.

He was living on his meager Social Security in an apartment over Morgantown Hardware when the assistant at Kelly's Funeral Home brought word of her death. "That's too bad, isn't it?" He said, and those five words were the extent of his grief, public and private. He was, however, somewhat surprised to learn that Marjorie, being of sound mind and body, had named him her heir. But he didn't ponder that one any too long either. According to his calculations, after sixty-eight years of the bad stuff, it was about time his luck changed for the better. After packing his clothes into a single suitcase, he moved in the afternoon she was planted.

He'd always loved her place, despite having been invited to visit on only three occasions he could recall (the day of their mother's funeral, the day Marjorie returned from the hospital after an attack of kidney stones, and a Christmas too many years ago to remember). Loved the location. Loved the house, a bungalow with two bedrooms, kitchen, living room, and bathroom. And to think it was his now. To think that he'd outlived his stuck-up, holier-than-thou, old-maid sister. How it did his heart good claiming her bed, cooking on her stove, eating off her dishes, taking his daily craps in her once-spotless toilet. Irony wasn't a concept familiar to him, but if it had been, he would have attached the word "supreme" to it. Here was a place where he could close out his account the way he most desired: by peacefully drinking, unencumbered by constables or Bible-toting sodality ladies out to save his soul. All courtesy of dear departed Sis, a Christian woman who to his certain knowledge had never touched so much as a drop of the stuff.

He hadn't planned to dig.

In the grand tradition of bachelor lushes, he'd planned to eat frozen dinners and Dinty Moore beef stew and kick his dog, Eddie, when the damn thing was in need of it. With his shotgun he'd planned to keep the punks at bay and shoot the woodchucks getting into his meager garden. Once a year or so he planned to put on his Sunday best and make the trip to Albany, where, in the privacy of a room at the Days Eaze Inn, he would get his dong pleasantly sucked by an aging whore of many years' acquaintance. He planned to watch the Red Sox games in the summer, the Bruins games in the winter, and he planned to have just enough leftover energy to keep the road plowed with his dead sister's Jeep. In this way he would ensure himself a steady supply of booze.

But he hadn't planned to dig.

Hadn't any intention whatsoever of spending his days inside a crumbling-down shaft some band of pie-eyed dreamers not remarkably different from himself had bored into Thunder Rise over a century ago. In fact, he almost certainly would have followed Marjorie to the grave without the knowledge that it was there, barely a ten-minute walk into the woods, if not for the phone call one morning a week after he'd moved into his new home. But the phone did ring, and Whipple did answer it (it was destined to be the last call before he had the phone disconnected for good), and a very official-sounding man did identify himself as an officer of Pittsfield National Bank. Marjorie Edith Whipple, God rest her soul, had maintained a safe-deposit box with his bank for many years, the officer said. As sole designated heir, whatever is in it is legally yours, Mr. Whipple. If you could clear this matter up at your earliest convenience . . .

That afternoon Whipple drove his Jeep into town. He would have been hard put to say exactly what he was expecting to find. On the one hand, his sister had been one of the all-time penny pinchers, so there was reason to hope she'd squirreled something valuable away—jewels, maybe, or a second life insurance policy. On the other hand, she'd been an awfully queer bird, and so, he reasoned, there was probably a much greater chance she'd used it to store items without any worth to him—family photographs, for instance, or something of Mother's. Marjorie had always been soft for Mother, the whore.

It seemed the second guess was closer to the mark when he started emptying the box. Birth and baptismal certificates, pictures of young mother with baby daughter (none of middle-age mother with young son), a ring that might be worth a few bucks, a dried corsage (she'd never been married; had she ever been to a formal?).

The map was at the bottom, tucked away inside a yellowed envelope. It was an elaborately drawn document, lettered in an old-fashioned hand with old-fashioned ink, and it was dated 1867. Actually, there were two maps on the single piece of parchment. One showed Thunder Rise. It was labeled "Gold???? Give 'em Hell!!!!" The other was the crude floor plan of a mine that had been bored into the mountain with human and horsepower. Attached to it was a note in Marjorie's handwriting. It told of discovering the map during a cleanup of one of the basement storerooms at the courthouse where she'd clerked. To clear her conscience, it also told of her attempt to find its owner. Having failed, she'd felt free to take it. Her supervisor had approved, or so the note said.

It did not occur to Whipple then, and it would not once occur to him in the thirty-three days he now had left to live, that the map might have been his sister's idea of a joke. Not the document—that looked authentic, and had an expert examined it, he would have concluded that it was indeed well over a hundred years old. No, the joke wouldn't have been the map itself but rather the idea of leaving it where it would surely be discovered by her useless brother, Harry Whipple, one of the great dreamers himself before booze had taken over. A dreamer who just might be tempted into dreaming again after seeing that word that has so teased and tormented mankind over the centuries: gold.

Whipple knew, and Marjorie knew he knew, of the Indian legends. In the whole county you would have been hard pressed to find a native who hadn't heard one or another of the tales about gold being buried inside Thunder Rise. If you had gone to the Berkshire Historical Society and nosed around in the card catalog under "GOLD, MORGANTOWN," you would have found a dozen articles chronicling a dozen failed attempts over the centuries to see if there was anything behind that old Indian legend. You would have come across the only verified strike, by an independent prospector into a lode that had yielded several pounds of the precious stuff before running dry in 1861. That modest strike, never duplicated, had touched off a rush culminating in the formation of the Berkshire Minerals Company, that firm of pie-eyed dreamers that had bored a half mile into the mountain before going belly up in June 1868.

For three months Whipple had been digging. Sixty-eight frigging years old, looking at least ten older, and what had he come down with but a case of gold fever—and a bad case at that. After seeing the map, after pondering it a few days, after recalling the legends, he'd been unable to shake it. Not that he had grandiose plans for what he'd do with his newfound riches, should he beat the odds and happen on the mother lode that was rumored to be in there. He didn't have a place in Florida in mind, or his own private jet, or a million-dollar yacht. Maybe he'd buy his favorite whore a brand-new Cadillac and go riding with her down Main Street, hooting and hollering at the assholes. Maybe he'd just hoard the stuff, fill his cellar with it, his chest of drawers, his linen closet, bathe with it, eat it for dinner, shit it away down his virgin sister's toilet.

He had gold in his blood, and there hadn't been a day since late May that he hadn't rolled out of bed, pissed last night's whiskey out of his system, swallowed his morning ration of Alka-Seltzer, fried himself three slices of bacon and one greasy egg, then trudged through the underbrush to the mine with a fresh flask of Heaven Hill in his hip pocket.

It had been no walk in the park, his new career.

The rock had been harder than he'd expected, although not impenetrable, the air stuffy and difficult to breathe. Every evening his muscles had ached and his lower back felt as if it were going to snap. Still, he'd made progress. The pains had never entirely gone away—at his age they never would—but most of them moderated in direct proportion to how much booze he downed. He'd gotten the knack of it pretty easily. It was, after all, only digging—a grown-up version of what keeps a tot in a sandbox smiling for hours on end. Dynamite would have helped, but Harry Whipple wasn't going to risk an arm on explosives. Not in here. The timbers were already shaky enough. The last thing they needed was a good top-to-bottom blast.

He'd spent the first two weeks clearing a side shaft off the main mine, some three hundred yards in. Judging by the way the shaft had been drawn on the map—in what appeared to be darker ink—Whipple had a hunch this had been the last area of the mine to be worked. Probably this was where they'd run out of money, here in this shaft (maybe, he prayed, when they were very, very close), and just before pulling out, they'd filled it back in to spite the next guy. Gold diggers down on their luck would have been like that, Whipple thought. Yes, sir. Grade A prickheads, just like their modern-day cousin here. Anyway, it seemed a good place to get the hang of things because it was filled with rubble, much easier to work than the solid rock at the end of the main shaft. Once he'd gotten a wheelbarrow in on the act, he'd been able to advance nearly a foot and a half a day.

He'd gone perhaps twenty feet, was at the point where he was seriously questioning the integrity of the timbers and wondering just how he was ever going to replace them, when he punched through into empty space. There was nothing behind that rock he'd removed from up top there. Nothing at all. He'd stuck his shovel through, waved it around.

Nothing, only moist air that seemed a good fifteen degrees colder.

Fragments of a short story he'd read years ago in school flashed through his mind: something about a man bricking his worst enemy up inside a wine cellar. Had he opened up a grave? Was it one of the gold diggers the others had wanted out of the picture for some reason? Was there a skeleton, the fingers scraped away as he'd gone mad with hunger and fear? Or was there gold in there, enough to make him the wealthiest man in Berkshire County? He took a healthy tug on his whiskey. Suitably bolstered, he crawled up and loosened a few more rocks until he had a hole big enough to get his shoulders through. Then he shone his lantern, drew a breath, and looked.

He was looking into a cave.

"Motherfuck." His words had no echo at all.

Nature, not man, had been at work here. That was his immediate reaction. The walls were dark, smooth, moist from water that had been dripping for centuries, and they shimmered iridescently in the lantern's glow, shimmered as if they were the source of the light, not a reflection of it. It was not a wide cave; with your arms outstretched, you could almost touch both walls. Maybe "cave" wasn't the right word. Maybe "chasm" was better.

Whipple squinted into the distance. He could see the ceiling—it was only ten feet or so above where he was—but he could not determine where the cave ended. It did not seem to end. It seemed to penetrate deep into the mountain's bowels, winding and curving past the limit of his vision.

He repositioned the lantern and looked down.

His heart skipped a beat. For an instant he was afraid he was going to pass out.

There was a bottom all right; you could just barely see it—a hundred feet down, at least. He tugged desperately on his flask, but booze didn't have what it took to level this one out. His head was swimming, the way it always did whenever bottom was greater than the distance from his eyeballs to his feet. Whipple was an acrophobic. A very serious one. Ladders, tops of roofs, even attics—you wouldn't find him that high to save his life. And those were small potatoes compared with bridges or skyscrapers or, God forbid, planes.

He inched backward—back toward the safety of the shaft. No wonder his nineteenth-century brethren had stopped digging here. He was goddamn lucky he hadn't toppled into that abyss himself. In his one glimpse he'd seen that the drop to the bottom was sheer cliff, not a foothold anywhere. The only way down would have been by rope. Not this gentleman. He had gold fever bad, but there were limits. He'd just found his.

The noises had begun the next day, a day in early June. Soon enough they'd become part of the background, nothing more, nothing less. They were low, rumbling kinds of noises, as if large parts of the earth had gotten restless and were slowly shifting position. He'd heard them before, of course. Most of Morgantown's old-timers had. Not nearly this loud, he had to admit, but the same distinctive groaning—like a giant grinding his teeth, as schoolchildren were fond of saying.

They were called the Morgantown Noises, and since the white man had settled the region, two generations after the *Mayflower* had anchored off Plymouth Rock, there had been a running record of them. They were not continuous. Decades had passed when no one had heard them, and then there had been spells of a year or two when they were heard monthly or even weekly. The Quidneck Indians, who'd been the original settlers of this part of the Berkshires, believed they were restless evil spirits. The white man had a less romantic explanation. The seismologists who had studied them—at least three since 1900 had—had concluded that they were almost certainly caused through the mechanics of plate tectonics, the natural shifting and rearranging of plates within the earth's crust, the identical process that, on a far greater scale, was responsible for California earthquakes.

Since his childhood Whipple had heard the Morgantown Noises several times. Once they'd been accompanied by a trembling that had shaken the dishes in his mother's china closet. The seismologists had described that incident as an earthquake, very low-powered and harmless, as most earthquakes in New England and New York had been since records were first kept. Mostly the noises had been muffled, lasting five or ten minutes until they were gone.

It did not puzzle him that the noises this time were louder. Of course, they were louder. He didn't know diddly-squat about seismology, but he had enough neurons still firing to reckon that whatever caused the noises, it had to be louder the closer you got. And he was inside the goddamn ground, wasn't he? And when he wasn't, he was living closer to the mountain than ever before, wasn't he? So what did you expect, that the noises would be quieter here?

He did not reseal the side shaft. He simply determined not to go down there again and went to work at what he considered the next most likely spot for gold, the end of the main shaft.

The noises, like the cave, had soon enough receded to the background.

His hand was trembling, but he managed to get another match lit.

It was still there, the thing in the shadows.

"Motherfuck," Whipple swore under his breath.

It was moving. Not at him, but out of the mine, back toward the entrance and the side shaft. Faster, as if it had crept up on him and now did not appreciate being seen.

"I'll be a goddamn son of a bitch."

A bird.

No, a dinosaur.

Goddamn if that wasn't what it looked like, a dinosaur with wings. Just like in that documentary the faggot public TV station had shown sometime last year. A baby *Rhampho*-what's-its-name. A foreign-sounding word. One of those Latin jobs.

Dinosaur.

Oh, man. If ever he needed proof he'd been hitting the sauce too hard, here it was, in Panavision color. Seeing dinosaurs. That beat everything. He almost laughed, it was so crazy. The urge grew suddenly, and then he *was* laughing, an uncontrollable belly laugh that shook his frame.

The match smoked and went out. Whipple got another going on first try.

It was still there. Whatever it was, it had stopped in its tracks. Almost as if it had decided to . . .

. . . to catch one last glimpse of him before scooting away.

The match went out.

Oh, man, Whipple thought. *You oughta ease up on the sauce, old boy. At least switch to something lower octane.*

He lit another match, expecting this time to see the next creature in the series—a giant bunny rabbit, maybe, or a giant talking lizard. But this time there was nothing in the shadows. No movement. Nothing lurking. No goddamn dinosaur returned through millions and millions of years to personally stalk and devour Harry Whipple. Whipple moved falteringly toward the lantern, reached it before the match burned out, and held the flame to the wick. The Coleman flared to life with an intensity that hurt his eyes.

Compared with match power, the lantern lit the mine like sunshine. Just for argument's sake, Whipple stumbled over to the far wall of the mine. It was as he thought: no footprints; no signs of disturbance of any sort; only the rubble he'd kicked up inside a mine abandoned a century ago.

CHAPTER EIGHT

Wednesday, August 27

BRAD WAS poring through the Morgantown *Daily Transcript,* drinking black coffee and making his notes on a yellow legal pad.

Abbie sat across from him, fiddling with her spoon. The Boar's Head Inn was a pretty neat place, she'd decided. Three—count 'em, *three*—cats, each appreciative of petting, and a big friendly hunk of a sheepdog, called Champ, that seemed to do nothing but snooze. Lots of places to explore, both indoors and out. Really neat things to eat, too. Cheerios and pastries and toast with grape jelly and everything for breakfast, with that really nice Mrs. Fitzpatrick not minding a bit filling a special order for chocolate milk (after Daddy reluctantly had given the Big OK). About the only losing point was how spooky some of the corners of their room got after dark; but Daddy had determined through close examination that nothing was hiding there, so that wasn't really so bad after all.

Brad's mind had locked on to the paper. He wanted to go in Monday with a real zinger of a game plan, something that would impress Dexter and motivate the troops right off the bat. He'd finally decided on one. He was going to initiate weekly writing seminars. If he'd uncovered one major weakness in all the back issues he'd gone over, it was the paucity of quality feature writing. When it came to flair, the *Transcript* was very gray indeed. With work, that could be turned around. It might never reach *Times* level, but he'd seen some pretty small papers turn out a damn good product. They could do it here.

Brad made a note about a new reporter named Rod Dougherty—of the entire staff, Dexter had mentioned in a lengthy letter, his stuff seemed to have the most potential—then took his nose out of the paper and put his pen down. The last fellow breakfaster, a middle-aged man who had arrived last night, had finished, and now he and Abbie were alone in the dining room. Like every room in Mrs. Fitzpatrick's inn, this one seemed to whisper: "Feel at home. You're among friends now. The world turns a little more slowly inside these four walls." The dining room was blue: light blue wallpaper, a more substantial blue on the upholstered chairs and rug. The ceiling-to-floor windows were crowded with hanging plants—philodendron, Swedish ivy, Christmas cactus, African violets, many in full bloom. And that amazing fireplace. With mantel and associated brickwork, it took up most of one wall, and it was no inconsequential wall. Brad imagined settling in by it some fall afternoon, a brandy in his hand, a hardwood fire blazing . . .

. . . and he was surprised to find himself thinking about that woman Abbie had been talking to, Thomasine.

She hadn't come down for breakfast this morning, or if she had, she'd eaten and gone before he and Abbie had arrived. He hoped she hadn't checked out. For two days he'd wanted to talk to her. Wanted to find out some more of what she—a woman of her age and *(there, you've said it, you chauvinist pig)* good looks—was doing in the Berkshires. On the basis of what Abbie had said, he was intrigued. Indian research. Hmmm. Probably she was involved in some kind of archaeological dig. Could be a story. He wondered if the *Transcript* had already done one. He'd have to have Dougherty or someone check into it.

Mrs. Fitzpatrick startled him from his thoughts. She backed abruptly through the kitchen's swinging doors, a portly bundle of good cheer. She was carrying a coffeepot in one hand, a wicker basket in the other. In the basket was a confusion of brochures, newspaper clippings, and scribbled notes.

"More coffee?"

"No, thanks," Brad said. "Any more and my teeth will float."

Mrs. Fitzpatrick laughed—the high, thin laugh of a woman who turns beet red at dirty jokes, while secretly relishing every word. She put the pot down on the server and returned to the table with her basket. She sat down. Unconsciously her free hand reached for the plate of Danish, still half full. She grabbed a raspberry pastry, generously buttered it, and took a large bite.

"I almost forgot these," she said when she had swallowed. "Spent half the evening getting them together, and here I've almost let you slip away without them. That would be just like me."

Abbie surveyed the basket. "What is it?" she asked.

"Real estate ads and flyers. You know, the ones addressed to resident and occupant and so forth. Plus some notes I made on the phone with Wilfred Smith. He's a dear old friend, has an agency over in Pittsfield. I know how hard you've been looking, so I thought I'd get my two cents worth in. 'Course, don't feel obligated to do a blessed thing with it. You do as little or as much as you like."

"That was awfully nice of you," Brad said.

"If you're going to be an editor, you're going to need a place fit for an editor to live. Not to mention the fact that you've got the sweetest girl in the world, and we wouldn't want a peach like her living in any dump."

Abbie giggled.

"You *are* a peach. Reminds me of when Ginny—that's my daughter—was her age, Mr. Gale. Lord, it seems so long ago," she said thoughtfully.

"Say 'thank you,' Abbie," Brad prodded.

"Thank you, Abbie," she mimicked. It was a trick she'd picked up in New York from one of the big kids who lived down the hall.

"Abbie . . ." Brad scowled.

"Thank you, Mrs. Fitzpatrick," she managed before giggling again.

"I'll let you paw through this on your own time," Mrs. Fitzpatrick said, "but do you mind if I make a recommendation? Might save you some trouble."

"Not at all."

"This isn't in any of the papers. That's why I don't have a picture. Wilfred told me about it. New listing, hasn't had a chance to get it into his flyer yet. You jump right on it, and I bet you'll be the first to see it."

She rustled through the basket and found her note, written with a lazy hand. Squinting, she scrutinized it. Her lips moved slightly, as if she were asking herself some weighty question. Then she tapped her forehead with the palm of her hand. She'd obviously remembered something.

"That's right," she mumbled. Turning toward Brad, she said: "Before I get your hopes up, let me ask you a question."

"Shoot."

"Do you need furniture?"

"Not really. We've got five rooms of it sitting in a warehouse in New York. The movers can have it here in a week or less. At least that's what they say. I just have to give 'em the word."

"Good," Mrs. Fitzpatrick said, the creases in her brow loosening. "Because according to Wilfred, this doesn't have a stick of it. Not even a refrigerator. Do you have a fridge?"

"No, but I could buy one."

"Double good. This is Harold McGuire's place. Harold senior. Went to school with his son a million years ago. His name was Harold, too. We called him Junior. He made it big out West somewhere, St. Louis, I believe it was. Became an accountant. Anyway, when the old man died last year, he came into the place. Sold all the furnishings, Wilfred says. Beats me why he didn't get rid of the house, too, but that's people for you."

"Maybe it was for tax purposes," Brad offered. "You can get screwed on capital gains."

"Most likely that was the case. Anyway, he's decided to rent it, but who's to say he won't change his mind in a year or two and decide to sell? You did say you were interested in either renting or buying, didn't you?"

"Yes. It all depends on the price."

"Well, you can't beat this price. I don't know whether Junior's got fluff between his ears instead of brains, but all he's asking is five hundred a month. Course, you pay utilities, but wait'll you hear what you'd be getting. This is a Victorian, three full stories. Never been in it, but Wilfred says it's got five or six bedrooms, three baths, fireplaces, pantry, library—you could take your editing home to that nice and easy—porch, full-size attic. I can see your little peach up in that attic now, rummaging through old trunks or playing with the dollhouse I know you're going to build her."

Abbie's eyes had been widening, and now they were huge. She'd never been in an attic (unless you counted the top of the Empire State Building, but that wasn't a *real* attic, no matter how high and scary it was), but she'd read enough about them to know that they were very special, very magical places. Once all the ghosts had been cleared out, of course, a task she'd leave to the resident spook chaser, Dad.

"I bet you'll like the area, too," Mrs. Fitzpatrick continued. "It's up at the base of Thunder Rise."

"That's the hill with the wonderful view, isn't it?"

He remembered it from the drive they'd taken yesterday on their initial house-hunting expedition. The highest peak around, he recalled. They'd driven up it to the end of the paved road, stopping to stretch their legs. From this vantage point, perhaps halfway up the mountain (he'd already learned the natives called these peaks mountains, not hills), you could sense the full majesty of the Berkshires, stretching north toward Vermont and south toward Connecticut like some gentle occupying army. After Manhattan, it was hard to believe any place could be so serene. The only sounds had been songbirds and the faint drone of a propeller plane, miles and miles away.

"That's it," she said.

"Beautiful area."

"Indeed. Still pretty wild. Of course, you give the damn developers a few years, and it'll be all paved and sewered." She sounded angry.

"I doubt that," Brad said congenially.

"They doubted that about Apple Hollow a few years ago and look what happened. You take a ride by there today and you'd swear you were in Albany."

"Are there any dinosaurs on Thunder Rise?" Abbie piped up.

"She's fascinated by dinosaurs," Brad explained. "She's got all the books about them."

"I would never go near a meat eater," Abbie said. "Like *Gorgosaurus* or *Tyrannosaurus Rex.* He's the king of the dinosaurs. But plant eaters might be OK. They had tiny teeth. Maybe you could pat one if you were careful."

Mrs. Fitzpatrick winked at Brad, as if to acknowledge his daughter's obvious brilliance at being able to pronounce such big words—correctly, as far as she could determine. "Well, meat eaters or no meat eaters, there's no need to worry," she said. "There haven't been any dinosaurs on Thunder Rise for millions and millions of years."

"Are there any deer?"

"As a matter of fact, there are, sweetheart. If you keep your eyes open, why, I bet someday you might even run into Bambi up in those hills."

"Really?"

"Really and truly."

"Wow! Did you hear that, Daddy?"

"I did."

"Deer!"

"Once upon a time," Mrs. Fitzpatrick went on, "there were even Indians living up there."

"I know that," Abbie said, the wonderment in her voice evaporating abruptly.

"And how do you know that?"

"Thomasine told me."

"I see. Well, that is her field."

"I know it's none of my business," Brad said, "but did she check out this morning?"

"As a matter of fact, she did. It couldn't have been much later than seven-thirty. I was in the kitchen—"

"Oh, rats," Abbie said. "You know what I forget to ask her, Dad?"

"What?"

"If the Indians wore feathers in their hair. Do you know, Mrs. Fitzpatrick?"

"Sometimes they did."

"And they hunted with bows and arrows?"

"Yes."

"*Real* bows and arrows?"

"Real ones. They trapped and fished, too."

"You seem to know something about Indians," Brad said.

"I should. I married one. A Quidneck, the tribe that lived all throughout this region. The stories he would tell . . . I never knew whether to believe the half of them."

"Is he still alive?" Brad asked.

"My goodness, no. George died when Charlie was still in school. That's all of thirty years ago now."

"Charlie?"

"I'm not being very clear, am I?" Mrs. Fitzpatrick said. "All this talk of Charlie and Ginny and George, God rest his soul. George—what can I say about him? He was my husband, and I loved him with my whole heart, even if my family didn't. We had one child, Charlie. Charlie must be . . . let's see, now . . . must be going on forty-five now. I'm showing my age now, aren't I?"

"Not a bit," Brad said. "You don't look a day over sixty."

"Go on now," Mrs. Fitzpatrick said, flattered.

"Does Charlie live here?"

"Not too often."

Brad's face showed his puzzlement.

"What I mean is he stays in a cabin he owns out in the woods. That's when he's around, which isn't enough to suit me. He's out California way now. Lord only knows where he'll be next year at this time. Charlie doesn't like roots. Never has. Says roots are for trees, not people. His father was like that. How I ever kept him as long as I did will be a mystery eternally."

"Ginny is your only daughter," Brad said.

"Right. She's quite a bit younger than Charlie. Her father was Mr. Fitzpatrick. He . . . left us. A long time ago. I haven't heard from him in years. Decades." Brad could see that she had opened the family closet, revealing a very prominent skeleton inside. She did not sound embarrassed, but that was clearly all she intended to say on the subject, now and probably ever. Close closet door and lock it.

"I understand," Brad said, a certain comfort and understanding in his voice. It had been second nature, but now he recognized what he'd been doing: subtly drawing the woman out. It was a veteran newspaperman's absolute worst trait—the inability to leave the interview in the newsroom.

"Ginny's almost twenty years younger than Charlie. Has a son Abbie's age. He starts kindergarten this fall."

"They'll be classmates," Brad said, patting Abbie's hand.

"And very good friends, if I were to have to predict. Jimmy's a very sweet little boy."

"Does he like dinosaurs?" Abbie asked.

"As a matter of fact, I believe he does."

"Goody!"

"Where's *she* live?" Brad asked.

"Up on Thunder Rise—not all that far from that house Wilfred was telling me about, in fact. Speaking of Wilfred, would you like to give him a call? Or would you rather thumb through the rest of this?" She rustled through the wicker basket. "We seem to have gotten lost in gab."

"I think we'll try Wilfred," Brad said.

"I thought so. Here's his number. You go into the other room and give him a buzz while I clean up here. Tell him I referred you, and there shouldn't be any problem. He ought to be able to meet you over there with the key."

"Thanks, Mrs. Fitzpatrick."

"Go on," she ordered. "Phone. The morning's getting away from you."

Brad took a last sip of coffee and went through the living room to the front desk.

"I know what you want," Mrs. Fitzpatrick whispered to Abbie when he had gone.

"What?"

"Another glass of chocolate milk."

"Can I?"

"Only if you don't tell your dad. He'll think I'm spoiling you. Promise?"

"I promise!" she whispered back, thrilled that Mrs. Fitzpatrick had let her in on a big conspiracy. Mrs. Fitzpatrick's place had turned out to be very nice, Abbie thought, but Mrs. Fitzpatrick had turned out to be even nicer.

"Then let's go into the kitchen. Come on. Quick. Like a bunny."

CHAPTER NINE

Friday, August 29

IN THE HOURS between midnight and dawn both Maureen McDonald and Jimmy Ellis had nightmares. They were similar in certain key respects, but they were not identical.

In Jimmy's, the wolf reappeared.

The same wolf that had vanquished mighty Rambo up there on Thunder Rise, the same razor-fanged black-back wolf that had already visited him several times here in his room. Visited repeatedly, almost nonchalantly, as if staking a personal claim on the room and the terrified, wide-eyed little human it always found there, lying under a single sheet on an oaken twin bed.

Jimmy was not sleeping when he saw the wolf tonight. He was certain of that, even if he could not convince his mother.

Not that he'd been awake the whole night—although he had intended to be. Jimmy had been relatively calm tonight, unlike the other nights this week, when bedtime had been A Major Crisis. He'd summoned up all his courage and even made a joke or two about the wolf, a development that had brought a tangible feeling of relief to his anxious mother.

He could laugh because he'd thought and thought and thought, and now he finally had a plan.

The plan was to stay awake until the sun had returned to the eastern sky. There was a chance, by being so vigilant, he would be able to hear the wolf coming and somehow be able to scare it off before it got into his room. How, exactly . . . he hadn't gotten to that yet.

But there was a more overwhelming reason why he was going to stay awake all night, no matter what it took. He had a secret weapon. A camera. His mother's old Instamatic, which he'd stolen from her closet and hidden under his pillow. He was going to take a picture of the wolf. That was the beauty of his plan. That was why he couldn't miss. A color snapshot, for all the world to see. Even if he couldn't scare it off, he would have proof it existed. A picture would be something his mother couldn't ignore.

He had not told her. Unh-unh.

He knew what her reaction would be: anger and, if not outright anger, another dose of disappointment that Mommy's son was still a long way from getting over This Ridiculous Thing. She hadn't said anything that cruel to his face, of course, but he could sense it clearly. Mom was frustrated and more than a little ashamed. Because Jimmy was Having His Problems. Turning into a Nervous Wreck. God forbid, maybe even in need of Outside Help. That was the gist of certain telephone conversations she'd been having when she thought he wasn't listening. Conversations with other mother friends. A conversation with the family physician, Dr. Bostwick. Even the tail end of their most recent long-distance conversation with Uncle Charlie. One way or another, "this nightmare thing," as Mommy called it, had been hanging over them the better part of two weeks, like a spell of bad weather that refused to lift.

So he'd been on his best behavior all day (playing quietly in the yard and not telling his mom he'd been on red alert for the wolf). Supper, no sweat. An hour of TV. Then the bedtime ritual, nice and orderly. The story, quietly. His teeth, without protest. His bedside prayers, his head bowed and hands clasped. His mother checking under the bed ("Nothing here, big guy!" in a big cheerful voice), checking in the closet ("Nothing here, either!"), checking out the window ("All's clear!"), then kissing him good-night and leaving the hall light burning bright. As she moved down the hall to the stairs, he could sense what she was thinking, so clearly she might as well have been shouting it: *I think he's finally Getting over It.*

Long before midnight he'd drifted off. Despite his best intentions, drowsiness had crept over him like a blanket of fog, and he'd been dragged under, under, under, to a place where there was crying and danger around every corner. The place where the wolf lived.

He was dreaming about the wolf when a sound from outside his sleep disturbed him. He opened his eyes, and there it was, at the foot of his bed.

This time it didn't just stare him down. Didn't only breathe on him and flash its teeth. Didn't wait for the inevitable collapse, Jimmy reduced to tears and calling out for his mommy.

It spoke to him.

A deep, growling voice unlike anything he'd ever heard. Half person and half animal.

"It takes time, Jimmy," the wolf said.

So it knew his name. That scared him more than its being able to talk, the fact that it seemed to know him so well . . . so very, very well . . . seemed in some incomprehensible way to consider him its buddy. A wolf who liked it here in his room had no intention of ever staying away, not for good.

"It can take weeks or even months, what I'm going to do to you."

Something in Jimmy's stomach flipped.

"I might have to go away for a while. I could, you know. I'm very busy. I might go away until you thought I was gone for good—until you thought I had been only a nightmare, like that silly mommy of yours says. It could even become a little game, couldn't it? A little game of hide-and-seek. It might seem as if I'd be gone for good, but I'd be back. I promise, Jimmy.

"And when I did, maybe I could lick your hand. Then maybe I could give you a little nip, like playing with somebody's doggy. Then a little harder, a little higher, eating your wrist, and your forearm, and your elbow, and your shoulder, all the way until you were gone! All gone, Jimmy! All gone!

"Nothing but bloody little scraps of you left!"

Jimmy's breath was catching in his throat, and he was trying—trying not to cry, not again, not four nights straight this week.

But the tears were forming, and he knew in another few seconds he would be powerless to stop them. His body was trembling, as if he were outside in December without a coat.

But it wasn't December. It was August, and he was lying under a single sheet, and the room was hot, too hot, and it was slowly closing in on him. He could see the walls, feel them, surrounding and compressing him.

"Are you listening, Jimmy?"

He fumbled beneath the pillow for the camera, his fingers all thumbs. The camera would save him. The camera would give him

Proof. Just click the shutter and Mommy would believe him. And if for some reason she didn't, surely Uncle Charlie would take care of the wolf when he came back.

He couldn't find the camera. The pillow seemed to have swallowed it.

The wolf trotted casually over to the side of his bed, and it was then and there—close enough that Jimmy could feel its body heat, could see its matted fur—that he noticed it had undergone some strange transformation. It wasn't a wolf's face anymore. There was human in its face now, too. Human eyes. A human shape to the mouth and nose, surrounded by all that black fur. A red face, lined with capillaries.

"You know what, Jimmy?"

His stomach flipped again, and there was acid in his throat.

"Your mommy can't help you. She won't be able to save you. No one will. Because they don't believe I'm here, do they? Grown-ups think I'm just a troubled little boy's nightmare, don't they? Oh, yes, Jimmy. I know all about grown-ups. I know all about moms. Silly mommies. Thinking they know what's best for a little boy. Well, we know what's best for a little boy, don't we?"

Jimmy's fingers contacted the camera.

He grabbed it, pulled it out, didn't bother to focus through the viewfinder. There wasn't time. The wolf—it was moving again. Toward him. Jimmy drew his knees to his chest and retreated crablike toward his headboard, a crab in panicked retreat.

Jimmy held the camera in the wolf's direction and pressed the shutter.

There was a click.

And no flash.

The panic was sudden, all-encompassing, nose to toe in a millisecond. He'd loaded a new cartridge in the camera, but he'd forgotten to check the batteries.

They're probably dead, he thought. It was the most horrible thought he'd ever had.

His finger bore into the cold metal camera again.

This time the room exploded in light—the most wonderful, incredible flash of light—then went dark. The image of the wolf was burned like an X ray onto Jimmy's retinas. The first bulb must have been bad.

"What's this, Jimmy?" The wolf sounded surprised. "A *camera?*"

He pressed again. Another explosion. Another X ray on his eyes.

"Why, it looks like Mommy's camera. Yes, that's exactly what it is. Does Mommy know you have her camera? I bet not. I don't think she would be very happy if she knew you had taken her only camera, Jimmy. I think she would be very upset. I think probably she would have to punish you, Jimmy.

"I'd better take that camera for you, Jimmy. For safekeeping. We wouldn't want anything to happen to Mommy's favorite camera, now, would we?"

And with that, the wolf reached out and took it. Took it with its paw—but not really a paw. A paw that had fingers, gnarled and twisted, and fingernails as black as a wood stove.

Jimmy covered his eyes and screamed then. His bladder control, which had been tenuous, gave out completely. His urine was seeping into the mattress when Ginny came tearing in, her eyes wide and red.

She was too late to see the wolf.

Camera and all, it was gone. It always was by the time Mommy came.

Out the window, the door, through the walls, through the floor—Jimmy never saw it go, just as he'd never seen it come.

Maureen's nightmare concerned the bear.

It completely filled her bedroom, leaving barely space for Maureen and her furniture. It must have been magical to be able to be so big and still get into the room. Magical, like things that could only happen in *Alice in Wonderland* or a fairy tale.

And that's why when Maureen opened her eyes in the middle of the night that first night and saw it, she was more fascinated than afraid. She was sure she must be dreaming. A dream about visiting a zoo with mommy and daddy and happening upon the largest, most amazing bear in the whole wide world . . .

. . . sitting safely in its cage.

Dreaming. She was sure she was.

Until the bear breathed on her. She felt that breath, hot and moist on her cheeks, and she smelled it. The smell was incredibly foul. It was like Daddy's bad breath the morning after he'd been eating pepperoni pizza and drinking beer, a sweet-sour smell like tomatoes rotting at the bottom of the refrigerator vegetable bin.

That's when, smelling that awful smell, she knew it couldn't possibly be a dream. It was *really there,* a real bear, a real monster bear, waiting to eat her, just waiting to gobble her bit by bit, inch by inch, until there was no trace of her but a bloodstained sheet.

Go away, she silently urged it. *Please, please don't hurt me. Just go away. I promise I won't tell anyone you were here if you'll only go away.*

It did not go away.

Maureen closed her eyes, thinking that might help, but when she opened them again, it was still there, smelly and black-furred.

And it was grinning. That was the most awful thing. It might even have been better if it had been growling, but it wasn't. It was grinning—its huge mouth open, its huge teeth sharp as the knife Daddy used to carve a Sunday roast.

She closed her eyes again, and a strangled squeak escaped her.

It was not loud, but against the perfectly still backdrop of the night, no wind stirring, no dogs barking, no owls in the distance hooting, it was loud enough to wake her mother, a notoriously light sleeper.

There was nothing in the room by the time Mom was there, hugging her.

Of course not, Maureen thought. *A bear that big that could fit into a room like hers had to be very smart. Knew when to be seen, when to hide.*

Like Jimmy's mother, Susie McDonald was brimming with explanations. It was only a shadow. You were only half awake. The mind can play funny tricks like that when it can't decide if it's awake or asleep.

It was Maureen's first nightmare that year, although it would not be the last. It occurred almost a month after that vacation Sunday she'd been sick.

CHAPTER TEN

Tuesday, September 2

ALMOST TO the halfway mark of his first day, and so far things had been going—to quote an otherwise forgettable colleague—swimmingly.

He'd spent the first half hour with the publisher, shooting the shit about Labor Day, about the recent spell of fine, summery weather after all that rain and cold, about Brad's house hunt. Dexter seemed pleased but surprised they'd found something so nice so quickly, but when Brad told him Mrs. Fitzpatrick had been involved, he nodded understandingly. Mrs. Fitzpatrick belonged to that most respected of small-town species: the community pillar. Knew everyone and everything. Most important, Dexter averred, knew how to get things done. A good one to have on your side.

Dexter also showed him a dummy of the editorial page for this afternoon's edition. It had three letters from readers (one about AIDS; another about the upcoming agricultural fair; the third complaining of poor mosquito control in the years since Big Government banned DDT, which said writer still considered God's gift to insecticides), an Oliphant cartoon (making light of George Bush's presidency), and an editorial Dexter had penned, cautiously backing AIDS education in Morgantown schools. That would be another of Brad's million and one duties, personally proofing the editorial page, even contributing editorials when Dexter was on vacation or otherwise indisposed. Brad smiled when he saw that the masthead had already been changed to reflect the new leadership. There it was in black: "Bradford T. Gale, Editor." No managing or executive or deputy qualifier. Just "editor." The title had a country flavor that made Brad beam.

At nine Dexter had brought him around to meet the staff. All four copy editors were in today, as were the city editor, full-time photographer, and five of the six reporters, including Rod Dougherty, the paper's newest acquisition. He'd been out of college four years, had cut his teeth at a group of weeklies, but he still looked about sixteen years old, all bright-eyed and bushy-tailed. That surprised Brad, who had seen elements of maturity in the writing samples Dexter had mailed him in New York.

Brad pumped hands and traded small talk like a politician on election morning, dumping everyone's name into the old memory bank, knowing damn well it would be days before he had them all straightened out. He was great with faces, not so great linking them with names. For some reason, his brain needed extra time to hack the right pathways through that neuronic jungle.

"Read your nuclear waste series," said Lisa Radeke respectfully. At thirty-one, she was one of the paper's senior reporters. "Very impressive, Mr. Gale."

"Thank you. And call me Brad."

"It nearly won the Pulitzer!" Rod Dougherty said.

"Did you read it?"

"No," Rod said unapologetically, "I don't usually read the *Times.* But I heard about it. You don't have a reprint, do you?"

"I could probably rustle one up somewhere."

"That'd be great."

"I'd like one, too," said Lisa.

The rest of the morning he'd been more or less an observer. That was what he'd penciled in for this week—aggressive observation. In other words, poking his nose into everyone's business, the better to get a line on how the machine really was put together. He considered himself lucky to have the luxury of a week or two to figure things out. But the *Transcript* had been without an editor for two months now, and the city editor, a pleasant-mannered sixtyish man who'd neither wanted nor sought the top job, had the daily drill down pat. As Dexter had reminded Brad over coffee, he hadn't been brought in to rebuild the machine. The nuts and bolts were already securely in place. He'd been signed on to make the sucker soar. Brad's words, not Dexter's.

It was noon now, and Brad was standing at the head of the table in the conference room, conducting his first budget meeting. Going over the day's events, coming up with a rough idea of what tomorrow's paper would look like.

In the world he'd left, budget meetings were hush-hush affairs, held behind closed doors by invitation only to the paper's top editors and publisher (if he so desired, and he rarely did). An exclusive club. Only after his last promotion had Brad been allowed in. He never got beyond his initial impression that a Pentagon war room drill couldn't match a *Times* powwow for gravity and solemnity. It was as if the *Times* crew believed it was deciding the fate of mankind for the next twenty-four hours.

Brad wanted a limited democracy at the *Transcript,* believing he could reap benefits by involving everyone. And so he'd issued a standing invitation for the entire staff to attend budget meetings. About half of them were on hand for the initial session. A good turnout, even if their numbers would dwindle as the novelty wore off.

He started with an unfortunate—but he felt unavoidable—rendition of a Rotary Club speech. He told everyone how pleased he was to be there, how many good things were in store for him and them and their paper, how his proverbial door would always be open to each and every one of them. He said that while he reserved the final say on news decisions, as a good editor always must, he expected them to contribute fully to discussions leading up to those decisions. Almost unconsciously he ended his pep talk with the inevitable sports analogy. "We're all on the same team," he said, "driving toward the same goal, playing for the same crowd. . . ."

Then it was on to the news. The selectmen's meeting tonight. The board of canvassers' meeting. A follow on a car accident that had injured three this morning. District court. The police blotter. A crop update (it had been a crazy season weatherwise this year for hay and corn, the county's biggest crops, and rumor had it more than one farmer would be belly up by Columbus Day). An advance on next week's Miss Berkshire County contest, which had a record number of entrants, eleven. A preview of Regional's cross-country team, which last year had had four all-staters. Nothing to set the world on fire, but a respectable enough first budget for a first-time country editor.

"Anything else?" Brad asked before breaking up the meeting.

No one said anything. He decided to interpret that as a positive sign. A compliment on how thoroughly he must have conducted the meeting.

"OK, class dismissed. Remember," he said cheerfully, "this is *our* paper. And that's not just some happy horseshit from the new boss. I mean it."

The staff trickled out, leaving Brad to erase the blackboard.

"I did have something I wanted to talk about," Rod Dougherty said when everyone else had gone.

"Why didn't you bring it up at the meeting?" Brad wasn't scolding, but he was puzzled. It seemed too early in his tenure to be having heart-to-heart chats. "That's the idea, a chance for us to bounce ideas off each other. Sort of like group therapy."

"I—I wasn't sure if it was a story or not. I guess I wanted to talk to you alone about it first."

"What is it?"

"The noises." He pronounced the words solemnly.

"The *what?*"

"The noises. The Morgantown Noises."

"You've lost me," Brad said, shaking his head.

"That's right, you've just moved here," Rod answered quickly, as if just remembering. "They're sounds. Deep in the ground. A rumbling, as if an earthquake were coming. Anyone who's lived here any time has heard them or heard about them. Heck, I've been here only six months, and I've heard them myself. If you didn't know any better, you'd have thought it was a jet taking off somewhere. Only there isn't an airport big enough for jets within forty miles."

Brad was becoming intrigued. "They can't be constant. I've been here a week, and I've never heard them."

"Oh, no. They're pretty irregular. Maybe once every week or so. It all depends, I guess—on what exactly, I don't know, and apparently no one else does either. I'm told years and years have gone by without a peep, and then there'll be a period of a month or half a year when they're rumbling every week, which apparently has been the case since early June. There doesn't seem to be any pattern. Not that I can figure out anyway."

"How long have people been hearing them?" Brad asked.

"Again, nobody knows precisely. Hundreds of years at least. And probably as long as people have lived in this region, which is probably a thousand years or more. I've been doing a little research down in the morgue and at the library. The noises were a part of Indian legend long before the white man settled this area. That was in the 1700's. The Indians told the Puritans it was evil spirits getting angry."

"It's like people today telling their kids that thunder is God bowling," Brad said.

"Right. In fact, that's apparently how Thunder Rise got its name, from one of the early settlers, listening to the Indians. They believed it was evil spirits, trapped inside the rise. According to the Quidnecks—that's the name of the tribe—they make noise because they're pissed they can't get out. Somehow they're able to shake the ground. Probably by stamping their feet or shaking their spears. Whatever evil spirits do to make noise."

"Interesting," Brad said. It was turning out to be quite the history lesson. A sprinkling of geology and folklore, too. One thing Rod wasn't was a dope . . . the way Brad already suspected a couple of his fellow reporters were.

"I thought you'd be interested," Rod said triumphantly.

"So there are caves around here," Brad said with sudden enthusiasm. As a boy he'd been fascinated with caves. For an entire summer, after visiting Howe Caverns, he'd wanted to be a speleologist. Until now he didn't know the conditions needed for caves extended this far east.

"A few, yeah, way up on the rise. But not so far up that a Cub Scout wasn't able to wander off from a camping trip after dark and get stuck for the night. That was in July, before you got here. Page one story. They had the bloodhounds out, and there was talk of bringing in the National Guard when it ended. Lucky for him they found him. Alive and uninjured, although scared out of his wits. Claimed to have been stalked by a wolf all night. Of course, there are no wolves anywhere near here."

"Sounds like a good story."

"It was."

"Did you write it?"

Rod nodded.

"I'd like to see it. I'm reviewing everyone's recent work."

"Sure. That's when I first got interested in the noises, when that Cub Scout got lost. A fire fighter who's lived here his whole life filled me in on the legend. According to the Quidnecks, the evil spirits were driven into a cave centuries ago during some megabattle with a great Indian warrior. He sealed the entrance. When they couldn't get out, they started raising hell. After raising hell awhile, they quieted down. A few years later they'd be back to raising hell. They go in cycles, sort of."

Brad finished erasing the blackboard and sat down at the table. "My daughter would love this," he said. "She's really into Indians."

"How old is she?"

"Five and a half."

"It's a good age to be into Indians," Rod said. "I was into them myself when I was that old."

"So was I. When I was growing up, that's all we played. Cowboys and Indians. Once in a while, for variety's sake, Cops and Robbers. Or Army. No Masters of the Universe back then."

"Or Rambo."

"I take it your research has come up with the real explanation for what causes the noises."

"Yes. According to several scientists who've studied them—and believe it or not, there have been several, including one from Cornell who published an article in *National Geographic* about ten years ago, and another guy from the Weston Observatory—the noises are caused by the natural movement of continental plates within the earth. I'm no seismologist, but apparently, when the shifts are big enough, when these plates collide, you get earthquakes. That's not unusual in some places. California, for instance, which has the San Andreas Fault and earthquakes all the time.

"What seems unusual, at least to me, is having fault activity so slight that only noise—no broken china or shattered windows—is produced. That's more or less what we have here. On the basis of what I could find in the library, although there have been several earthquakes recorded over the years in this area, only one—in the eighteenth century—was strong enough to do any damage. It wasn't serious damage either; a couple of chimneys fell down, a bunch of farmers were terrified, and that was about it."

Earthquakes in New England—it didn't surprise Brad. He'd read somewhere that the region was actually one of the livelier ones in the country in terms of earthquake activity. But as Brad had noted, almost all the activity was very mild, discernible only through instrumentation.

"By the way," Rod continued, "we're not the only game in town, so to speak. There's a place in Connecticut with similar noises. Moodus, it's called. South-central part of the state, near the Connecticut River. Its noises are much more famous than ours. I remember reading an article about them when I was living in Boston right after college. The *Globe* magazine did a big takeout. I bet even the *Times* has done a piece."

Brad leaned over the table. "Let me ask you something," he said.

It struck him again, his face three feet from Rod's, just how young the kid was. How goddamn *curious* he was. Ideas and new things still fascinated him, still could get the adrenaline flowing; you could see it in his eyes. What a refreshing change from the newspaper denizens of New York and Washington, jaded places both. Rod reminded Brad of himself at that stage of his career, full of the wonder and enchantment of the world. Seemingly full of the same piss and vinegar that had driven Brad.

"Shoot."

"If the noises have been around so long," Brad said, layering the slightest edge onto his voice, "and you've just told me they have, why should we do a story now? What's the news peg?"

"The news peg," Rod said, sounding the tiniest bit pissed, not enough to be surly, but enough to show that he wasn't cowed, "the news peg is that the noises this summer have been unusually loud. I'd be the first to admit they sounded pretty low-key to me when I heard them, but I'm relatively new here. I don't have anything to compare them with. The people I've talked to have, and they say the noises have never been this loud."

"Do they conclude from this that we're about to slide into the sea?"

"No, I don't think anyone's alarmed or anything, but that doesn't mean they're not talking about it. They are. I've had half a dozen calls, maybe more. The folks at Town Hall are yacking about it. It even came up at a selectmen's meeting. Mostly as a joke, but it still shows there's a lot of interest in it. Something doesn't have to be bad to be news, does it?"

"Jesus, you sound like one of our old-lady readers," Brad said, laughing. " 'Does it have to be bad to be news?' The answer is no. Something doesn't have to be bad to be news. Didn't they teach you that in J school?"

"I didn't go to J school."

"Good. No evil habits to drum out of you. Now about these noises—"

"What I had in mind was talking to some of the old-timers, maybe a few newcomers in town who haven't heard them before, then getting into some of the Indian legends. I already have a lot of that background stuff. Then I could call a seismologist, maybe luck out and track down one who studied the noises before. It would be a feature story and a news story, all in one. That's what I was thinking, anyway," he said, trailing off.

Brad did some quick mental calculations. "I'm sold," he said after a moment.

"Really?"

"Really."

"Thanks, Mr. Gale."

"Brad."

"Thanks, Brad. I was really hoping I could convince you. Some of them"—he gestured toward the newsroom—"some of them think if it isn't a meeting or an accident, it isn't a story. I think that's the legacy of the guy you're replacing. I don't mean to bad-mouth him, but . . . well, let's just say he wasn't the most imaginative guy I've ever met. I think some of that rubbed off."

"And between the two of us, I'm here to rub it away. The publisher is explicit on that point. He wants more pizzazz in his paper, and he's left it to me to figure out how to do it. Now, I want you to take a couple of days and give me the best story anyone's ever written about the Morgantown Noises."

Rod was incredulous. He'd never had two days to do any story. The news hole, as the space that wasn't advertising was called, was a devouring beast. It kept reporters churning out an almost unbelievable volume of stories—five, six, even seven or eight of them a day.

"What about tonight's board of canvassers' meeting? I'm down to cover it."

"I'll try to get a stringer," Brad answered, "and if I can't, fuck it. It won't be any different from the last three million board of canvassers' meetings. No one will miss it. I want you to follow your game plan. It's a good one. Talk to some of the people who have been hearing them, call a university or wherever you can find a specialist in these things, go back over the clips, go to the library, whatever."

Rod sat looking at his new boss. He wore a peculiar look, as if Brad were some kind of green-skinned Martian who'd just landed his spaceship in the parking lot. Two days, one story . . . yeah, he must be a Martian.

"Well?" Brad said.

"Well what?"

"What the hell are you waiting for?"

By two-thirty, when the pressmen got the presses cranked up, the newsroom was almost completely empty. Brad finally had a few minutes for lunch. He sat at his desk, stuffing his face with chicken tenders and a double cheeseburger he'd bought from Burger King, located across Main Street from the *Transcript.*

The Burger King had come late to Morgantown and still seemed an anachronism, an unwelcome one in the minds of many. It had been open two years (the zoning board meeting at which permission was finally granted had been a tumultuous affair, attended by more than two hundred people, all but a handful—the lawyers and the board chairman—hopping mad), but old-timers still marveled at it, much the same way their grandfathers had been all atwitter when the town's first movie theater had opened eighty years ago.

Few other national chains were represented downtown. Western Auto had long been a fixture, as had the IGA and T. J. Miller's Ford, the county's oldest dealership. Those and the Mobil station, which stubbornly continued to display the winged-horse logo, and the Exxon station (where a grease- and soot-stained Esso sign still hung next to a Playboy calendar over the garage workbench) were the only trademarks an out-of-state visitor would have recognized.

The rest of Main Street was taken up by businesses that were jealously owned and operated by local families, businesses which, like the *Transcript,* had been passed down through the generations. Zeke's Hardware Store, named for one of the town's most colorful nineteenth-century characters, Ezekiel Brown. Today Ezekiel's great-great-grandson was behind the counter. Burton's Seed and Garden Shop. Nat's Plumbing and Heating. Paul's Diner—open only for breakfast and lunch since Paul Bouchard had hit seventy-five. The Oak Tree Tavern, where the hot-stove league was in residence every winter. The office of Dr. Mark Bostwick, family practitioner. Bostwick was thirty-seven, and he'd had a practice for eight years. He, too, was from an old Morgantown family.

Throw in the Civil War monument, a branch of Pittsfield National Bank, St. Mark's Episcopal Church, the First Congregational Church, and the bandstand where the American Legion staged its annual Memorial Day program, and that was it for Morgantown's commercial district.

No malls. No video arcades with stoned-out punks in leather jackets scratching their balls as they take on Darth Vader and fantasize about getting laid tonight in the back seat of a GTO. No mile-long parking lots with Rows A through Triple Z and half a zillion orphaned shopping carts. No K Marts with nineteen-year-old clerks wearing blue eye shadow and chewing Juicy Fruit gum you can smell on your clothes an hour later. If you wanted that side of contemporary American culture, you made the fifteen-mile drive into Pittsfield, where the local townspeople had actually gone out of their way to attract such ventures—establishing a Mall Commission ten years ago to lure back business lost to Albany. It was a commission that had more than done its job. Today there wasn't just one mall in Pittsfield. There were three, and a proposal by a Boston developer for a fourth.

Brad finished his last chicken tender, wiped his fingers, and picked up the phone.

A small voice answered hello. "Is this a certain Apple Guy?" he said.

"Hi, Dad!" Abbie fairly shouted. Brad breathed a bit more easily. It sounded as if her first day without him were going better than he dared dream.

"You being a good girl?" The automatic question.

"Sure. You know what we did this morning?" Her voice was in the mode that could just about make his spine tingle, all bubbly and little-girlish. *Daddy's* little-girlish.

"Let me guess. You . . . took a ride on a submarine."

"Nooo! Guess again."

"You . . . made a pet out of a dinosaur."

"That's silly, Dad. Dinosaurs have been ex-stink for millions of years."

"You . . . built an airplane."

"Daaaaaddddd . . ."

"I give up." He sighed deeply.

"We baked pies!" Abbie exclaimed.

"You did?"

"Yup! Three apple pies and four rhubarb pies."

"I can't believe it."

"Well, we did. Mrs. Fitzpatrick let me roll the crusts. Then we baked tarts. Two tarts. One for you and one for me. You know what, Dada?"

"What, honey?"

"I really like Mrs. Fitzpatrick. Can I always stay with her?"

"Always? Does this mean you want to leave me?"

"Oh, no. I mean after kindergarten. You said I have to stay someplace after kindergarten because you'll be working."

"That's true, Apple Guy." It was the first sour note of the day—the day-care issue rearing its ugly head again. Mrs. Fitzpatrick had agreed to take Abbie for Brad's first week of work, the last week before Abbie's kindergarten started, ostensibly to give Brad time to find a more permanent arrangement. With everything else going on, he hadn't had a chance to look for someone else. And he'd forgotten to place an ad. Even if he placed one the second he hung up, he would only make the deadline for Friday's paper.

"Maybe I can keep coming to Mrs. Fitzpatrick's. I think I'll ask her."

"No, no," Brad admonished.

But Abbie did, right after hanging up the phone.

And Mrs. Fitzpatrick, without having to think twice, said yes.

"You can be part of the staff," she said. "The afternoon staff."

"Goody!" Abbie said, and gave the portly, good-natured woman a great big bear hug.

* * *

Mrs. Fitzpatrick had been right on with her tip about the house.

It was a Victorian, built with care and pride, impeccably maintained except for the last few months, when it had been vacant. Brad's only reservation was its size—twelve rooms, guaranteed to be a pig to heat. Abbie saw no such drawback. All those rooms—they were like foreign countries waiting to be explored. And that attic. That huge, drafty attic with the two giant windows that let in enough daylight to chase away any lingering scariness. It was just what Mrs. F. had promised: a private little paradise, seemingly designed and built with an adventuresome young girl in mind.

That night Brad signed the lease.

The next morning the moving van arrived.

The next evening they were settling in.

CHAPTER ELEVEN

Thursday, September 4

BRAD LEFT work at five-thirty, ridiculously early by the schedule that would soon imprison him, and joined his daughter for dinner at the Boar's Head Inn. Mrs. Fitzpatrick had a full house, and the dining room was packed; but she managed to squeeze another table into a corner by the fireplace for "my favorite editor and my even more favorite little girl," as she called them.

Brad had a surprise for Abbie, but he didn't spring it on her right away. What kind of fun would that have been?

"I played with Jimmy today," Abbie told him over prime rib, which had been the Thursday dinner (absolutely no substitutions) at the Boar's Head Inn as long as Mrs. Fitzpatrick had run it.

"Who's Jimmy?"

"Jimmy Ellis. He's my age. Mrs. Fitzpatrick is his grandmother. That means she's his mommy's mommy," Abbie explained.

"That's right." Brad nodded. Ginny and Jimmy. He remembered her mentioning them now. They were the ones who lived not too far from them on Thunder Rise. One of these days Brad planned to drive up and introduce himself.

"You know what?" Abbie piped up.

"What?"

"He's going to kindergarten this year, too. We're going to be in the same class!"

"Really."

"Yup. And you know what else?"

"What?"

"You won't believe it."

"Try me."

"Mrs. Fitzpatrick is going to baby-sit for him, too. We're *both* going to be on the staff for her. Isn't that amazing?"

"It's incredible," Brad agreed. "Jimmy's mother's a teacher, isn't she?"

"Yes. But she doesn't teach kindergarten. She teaches the big kids in the third grade."

"I see," Brad said. "So tell me about your new friend. Do you like Jimmy?"

"Oh, yeah," Abbie said as if it were a foregone conclusion and could only have been raised by someone stupid. "He likes dinosaurs, just like me. He's got all the books. That's just like me, too."

"It's a match made in heaven," Brad said approvingly.

Abbie was baffled. "What's that mean?"

"It's a grown-up saying. It means you two are going to get along."

"Well, we do. The only thing is he doesn't like to play with My Little Ponies. He said that's for girls, not for boys. Is it really only for girls, Dad?"

The answer—as he would feel obliged to give it—could take upwards of an hour. Not tonight, Brad decided. Gender differentiation could wait until another day. "Let's just say some people think that," he offered.

Dessert was a hot fudge sundae with vanilla ice cream, real whipped cream, and a maraschino cherry on top.

"Wipe your face, honey," Brad said when Abbie had finished scraping her bowl. "We've gotta get a move on."

"Where are we going?"

"It's a surprise."

"A surprise?" she parroted.

"Yup."

"Goody! Are we going to get my puppy?"

"If I told you that, would it be a surprise?" Brad said, disguising the disappointment he felt that she had guessed right off the bat.

"Well . . . how about a clue? Just one itsy-bitsy clue. Please . . ."

"OK," Brad said, rising from the table. "Here's your clue: It's a *happy* surprise. Now that's it. My lips are sealed." He patted her bottom and fairly hustled her out of the dining room. As they left, he winked at Mrs. Fitzpatrick, who had been let in on the big secret.

"Come on, Apple Guy," he said, "let's scoot."

It was coming on seven o'clock.

Thunder Rise had already blotted out the sun, and the shadows were lengthening rapidly. They drove north on Route 6, across the residential belt that was tightened around downtown Morgantown. Through a traffic light, the last one for ten miles. Past the Agway store and the John Deere dealership and the milk cooperative. The ranch houses and Capes thinned and disappeared entirely, and they were into gently sculpted farmland. Unlike other parts of Berkshire County, where the agricultural economy of the last three centuries was slowly being transformed into one that was service-oriented, most of Morgantown's three dozen or so farms were still being worked—dutifully, if not profitably. Brad wondered how much longer they could be worked at all, even with the generous tax concessions he knew the Massachusetts legislature had recently granted farmers. There was a good story in it. Not an original story, but a worthwhile one. A community service story, the kind guaranteed to warm a publisher's heart. As soon as he got his head above water, he'd assign someone to take a few days and do it.

Route 6 paralleled the Misquamicut River, which followed the base of a valley glaciers had carved out twenty thousand years ago. The soil was black and rich here, with few of the rocks that normally characterized New England's user-unfriendly soil. Brad looked across the cornfields and the hayfields, past the dairy barns, over pastures dotted with cows, into the Berkshire woods. The trees were luxurious shades of green, but he could see reds and yellows already creeping into the foliage. He suspected this was the last week the trees would be so lush. Summer was on its way out. Brad felt it strongly for the first time. It had been an August-like day, but now, at dusk, there was a definite nip to the air. It was more like an

October night, with a real threat of frost, than the fourth of September, only three days after Labor Day. Christ. It had never been this cold this early in Manhattan. The Mustang's windows were up, and Brad was even tempted to turn on the heater, but he didn't. That was a concession it was much too early to make. It would soon enough be fall. Soon enough after, they would be locked in the grip of the long New England winter.

We'll cross that bridge when we come to it, thought Brad, who wasn't particularly fond of snow, certainly not the amount they got in these parts.

He reached into his pocket for the classified ad he'd ripped out of the paper, checked the directions he'd written over it with his distinctive red Flair pen, and concluded they were on target. Only another mile or two.

Abbie had her face glued to the window. He wondered what was going through her mind. Since leaving New York eleven days ago (was it only eleven days? It seemed like a year . . . a hectic but pleasurable year), Abbie hadn't mentioned her mother. No, strike that. She *had* mentioned her. Yesterday, when they'd moved into their new house, she'd observed how her mother probably would like the place. Unless Brad was forgetting some other occasion, that had been it. He didn't know if Abbie was internalizing her feelings, burying them in some part of her subconscious mind for recall later, or if she was simply too absorbed in mapping out her new world to have time for any other issues. Sooner or later, one way or another, Brad knew, Heather was going to surface.

And he would be ready, as best he could. But he wasn't going to bring the issue up, certainly not tonight, the night of the big surprise. Let sleeping dogs lie, so to speak.

Brad started singing their song. "Our Little Song," as they'd titled it. A song they'd composed together in dribs and drabs over the past two years. An original tune with highly original lyrics.

My, oh, my, she's my Apple Guy.
Give her a kiss, won't you try?
Give her a monkey, I don't know why.
Take her to a movie, but let's not cry.
Climb on a staircase, way up high.
Along with my favorite little old Apple Guy!

There were additional verses, dozens and dozens of them, with more being composed all the time, but Brad didn't get any farther this Thursday night.

There was the sign. He turned off the road.

"OK," he announced. "Here we are."

The sign said MORGAN'S FARM. PRIZE HOLSTEINS SINCE 1922. These Morgans, Brad had been told, were descendants of the town's founder, and for longer than anyone could remember they had been dairy farmers. They also bred championship golden retrievers, recommended to Brad as the best possible breed for children. There had been only one litter this year. Abbie could hear yipping and yapping the second Brad pulled into the drive.

"My puppy!" she hollered happily. "We're going to pick out my puppy!"

"That we are," Brad said.

"Oh, Daddy!" Abbie kissed her father on the cheek.

And then she was out of the Mustang, barreling down the drive toward a makeshift chicken-wire pen.

"You must be the Gales," said the broad-shouldered sixtyish man heading toward Brad's car. Brad noticed he was wearing a wool coat. Brad took a deep breath and exhaled. His breath came out in a cloud. It had actually dropped several more degrees in the twenty minutes since they'd left the Boar's Head.

"Brad Gale," Brad said, extending his hand.

"Henry Morgan. Spoke to you on the phone. Have any trouble with the directions?"

"Not at all."

"Good. I see the little one can hardly contain herself." He sounded pleased.

"She's wanted a puppy for years," Brad said.

"And you've been holding out on her this long?"

"Oh, no." Brad quickly corrected him. "We lived in New York, in an apartment where pets weren't allowed."

"That's downright criminal, but it sounds like New York," Henry said disdainfully. "Only good thing to ever come of that place is the Yankees. Before Steinbrenner, that is. You're better off out here in the country, believe me."

"Dad? Can I go in?" Abbie begged at the kennel gate.

"I think we should ask—"

"You go right ahead, young lady," Henry said, unfastening the wire hook. "You just be careful you don't step on any of the you-know-what. I haven't had the chance today to clean it up."

"Anyone I want?" she said, sounding overwhelmed by the responsibility of choosing the *right* one.

"I'm afraid there're only three left to choose from," Henry said. "We're lucky to even have them. As I told you on the phone, Mr. Gale, that litter goes back to late spring. Not the cuddly little pups most kids have in mind. The good thing, of course, is they're both weaned and nearly housebroken."

While Abbie considered the dogs, Henry and Brad talked a bit, mostly about the weather, as farmers are wont to do.

"Is it always this cold on the fourth of September?" Brad asked.

"Lord, no," Henry said. "Been the craziest year for weather I can recall, and I've been eligible for Medicare longer than I'm going to admit. Heck, Dad don't even remember nothing like it, and he's nigh onto ninety years of age. The first part of the season was the drought. Oh, it was a wicked one. Lasted almost into August. Shriveled most of the corn up into stuff that isn't fit for a Halloween decoration. Then the rains came."

"You must have been relieved."

"We were, for about the first three days. That was enough to balance the register. Problem was, they didn't stop then. It rained on and off—mostly on—for another week. Ten days straight in all. Now this cold. If I didn't know any better, I'd say we were due for a frost by daybreak."

Abbie interrupted them. She was at the fence, a golden jumping and licking her face and wriggling like a reptile. Abbie's smile was a yard wide, and she was giggling uncontrollably. Brad couldn't remember the last time she had been so ecstatic.

"Is this a girl one?" she asked. "I want a girl one."

Henry checked. "And that's what you have."

"Goody! I want this one. Can I have this one, Dad? See? Isn't she cute? And she likes me! She really really likes me!"

"Is that one OK?" Brad asked.

"To be honest, that's the one we had planned to keep." Henry and Brad both saw Abbie's face drop. She looked crushed.

"However," he continued, "since she's going to such a good home, and seeing as how we've got another litter due any day now, she's yours, Abbie."

"Oh, thank you, thank you, thank you!" Abbie enthused as Brad began to write the check in the last light of day.

CHAPTER TWELVE

Friday, September 5

"Hi."

Brad looked up from his desk. It was Thomasine, the woman Abbie had gotten so friendly with their first night at the Boar's Head Inn.

"Hello," he said. His voice was uncustomarily scratchy. Finding her standing there—it had surprised the shit out of him, that's what it had done. Not that he'd spent every minute of the last eleven days fantasizing about her. But she *had* popped into his thoughts now and again.

Until this minute he'd assumed he would never see her again.

"She told me I should see you first."

"Who?"

"The woman at the front desk. I'm interested in an article your newspaper published this afternoon. This," she said, tapping Rod Dougherty's page one piece on the Morgantown Noises.

"Right. The noises. What can I help you with . . . Thomasine, isn't it?" His jaw muscles were starting to relax.

"Yes. Thomasine Lyons."

"And I'm Brad Gale. Father of Abbie, editor of Ye Local Rag," he said, attempting humor, achieving cornball. "I guess you already know that."

"I do," she said perfunctorily. "I had a question about that article."

Here it comes, Brad thought. *The opening piece of the New Era and already we're under attack.* "Fire away," he said politely.

"It makes repeated reference to Indian legend, and it quotes an expert in Indian affairs out of New York University—Mel Slocum, I'm familiar with his work—but it doesn't mention any Indians living in the area today. Do you know if your reporter talked to any?"

"No, I don't," Brad admitted. "I'd ask him, but he's out on assignment."

"Do you expect him back this afternoon?"

"No, but he'll be in first thing Monday morning. You could try him then. Excuse my nosiness," Brad said, "but why do you want to know?"

"I *expect* you guys to be nosy," she retorted. Brad couldn't tell if she was disparaging him. He decided to give her the benefit of the doubt. "I want to know because I'm tracking down Native Americans involved in a land suit here that ended eight years ago. The Quidneck tribe. The one your reporter mentioned. It was one of the original Indian claims in the Northeast."

"Did they win?" He'd heard of such claims, although not this particular one. He guessed it had been major news.

"No. That's what my thesis is about. How the Quidnecks have been impacted in the years since the suit ended and the U.S. Supreme Court refused to consider the appeal. If they'd won, they would have been millionaires."

"I bet."

"But they didn't. It demoralized them—in the tribal sense, that is. I have reason to believe it not only destroyed their tribal unity—their cultural identity—but deeply embittered them toward the white man. It was a white judge and jury, of course. But I've got a long ways to go before I can prove anything like that."

"Abbie mentioned you were a student at Brown. She called it 'a brown college.' As if it were the color of the place." He chuckled.

"Well, it *can be* a shitty school," she declared.

Hold it right there, Brad thought. As roughly as some of his female friends spoke, especially the New Yorkers, he'd never really outgrown the silly notion that vulgarity ("naughty words" his Irish Catholic mother had called it; close his eyes, and he could still hear her lecture him) was intended only for men. That it wasn't *ladylike,* as Mom had steadfastly maintained. Certainly not on first meeting someone.

"I take it you're not exactly . . . happy there." He fumbled for the words.

"Thomasine Lyons and Brown University don't always see eye to eye. My thesis, as a prime example. My adviser's a hard-ass. The way she's been holding me up, I figure to have my Ph.D. no later than the first quarter of the next century. But you don't want to hear all this."

"No—I do," Brad insisted.

"No, you don't," she said. "And besides, I'm not here to pour my heart out. I came because I happened to be in the supermarket and I saw your paper. This article caught my eye. As I said, I'm trying to track down members of the tribe still in the area, and at this stage I can use every lead I can get. Except for the fact that your reporter didn't mention any Native Americans today—something I would have done had I written it—it was a good piece. This guy Dougherty has a nice style."

The woman sure knows how to hand out a compliment, Brad thought sourly. "Thank you," he said. "Rod's one of our better people."

Thomasine peered around the newsroom. She seemed to be soaking up the detail, as if she'd never been in a newsroom before. As if it were a foreign land, which it probably was, Brad supposed, to an outsider. So many incredibly messy desks, the papers and reports and notepads and phone books piled to the ceiling. He could have guessed what she was thinking: *How in all this confusion can they possibly get the paper out day after day?* It was a question he'd asked himself, a question he couldn't always answer.

Brad seized the opportunity of her gazing about to do unobserved what he had wanted to do since Thomasine had walked in: stare at her. He'd thought it that first night at the Boar's Head, and he thought it again even more strongly now: She had his kind of looks. The same long brown hair, large eyes, small lips, and high cheekbones that had always sent a little jolt through his body. God, he liked how she looked. And dressed. She was wearing a white cotton blouse, chinos, track shoes, with a sweater tied around her shoulders. He was surprised at how pleased he was to find out she hadn't been simply passing through that night at the Boar's Head. To judge from what she'd said about her research, she'd probably found an apartment or a house to rent.

She turned back toward him.

Brad glanced quickly at the wall clock. Four-forty. He was already ten minutes late for his meeting with the publisher. Dexter was one man who didn't like being stood up.

"Look," Brad said apologetically, "I'm really interested in what you're doing. I mean, there might be a good story in it." *Jesus, does that sound like a line,* he thought.

"Oh, I don't know about that," she said. "Anthropology can be pretty dry stuff."

"It can also make for good reading when you've got an interesting project, and it sounds like you have. Which is something I'd like to discuss with you. Unfortunately I'm late for a meeting. Could we—could we maybe get together sometime, you know, whenever, for . . . lunch?"

"Lunch?" she said uncertainly.

"To . . . discuss . . . your research."

Boy, was he floundering. Brad Gale, prizewinning journalist, take-charge editor, was getting his tongue tied in a knot. Like a goddamned eighth grader asking his first girl to a dance. But it had been so very, very long since he'd asked a woman for a—no, he wouldn't consider it that. Because it *wasn't* a date. It was lunch, that's what it was. A purely professional function. Everything on the up-and-up.

Besides, he was sure she was going to say no. He wished now he'd never asked her.

"Lunch would be fine," she said agreeably.

"Really?"

She looked at him oddly.

"I mean, great." He was fumbling again. "Do you want to set a time now? Or how about if I call you?"

"I'll call *you,*" Thomasine said, "probably in a week or two. In the meantime, I can reach Mr. Dougherty here Monday morning?"

"Yes. You might even catch him this weekend if you're lucky. We work pretty long hours around here."

"Thank you," she said, and left.

CHAPTER THIRTEEN

Sunday, September 7
Night

IN MORGANTOWN eight young children had nightmares bad enough to wake them. That was twice the number of the week before. There were four villains in these nightmares: a bear; a wolf; a vulture; a snake.

Four children had stomach cramps so severe they cried out in their sleep.

Maureen McDonald threw up at quarter past midnight.

Jimmy Ellis slept soundly all night long, nightmare-free.

Three thousand miles away Charlie Moonlight slept hardly at

all. He could not ever remember having had a case of insomnia so bad. For some reason, he was dwelling on his nephew, Jimmy. Jimmy and Charlie fishing. Jimmy and Charlie having dinner with Ginny. All of them at Mrs. Fitzpatrick's Christmas morning. Charlie giving Jimmy a deerskin jacket for his fifth birthday. Charlie calling Jimmy from Reno, Dallas, once from Anchorage, Alaska. Jimmy as an infant, his father dead a week. A hundred memories of Jimmy.

Jimmy dead unless he did something.

Did what?

There was no answer.

Near dawn Charlie finally slipped into sweaty, restless sleep.

CHAPTER FOURTEEN

Monday, September 8

THE SKY was cloudless and blue, the morning warm enough for short sleeves. After a weekend of unusual cold the weather was seasonable again.

Abbie, Brad, and Maria, the new dog, were at the end of their drive waiting for the bus to take Abbie to her first day of kindergarten. Brad had his video camera balanced on his shoulder. Maria, named after Abbie's favorite *Sesame Street* character, was tied to a tree, straining against her clothesline leash. The star, dressed in a red jumper and white blouse, was carrying a Sesame Street lunch box and practicing her skipping.

"Don't get too near the road," Brad cautioned.

"I won't, Daddy," Abbie said.

The puppy whimpered.

Abbie heard something else. So did Brad.

"I think I hear it," he said.

"Is it coming?"

"I think so."

Abbie scooted toward her father and wrapped her arms around his legs for protection.

The bus appeared, model car size at first. It lumbered toward them, impossibly slow as it moved beneath a canopy of maples and oaks, tinged with the first colors of fall.

"Hey, I thought you were excited," Brad said, tousling her hair with his free hand. He was careful not to tousle too forcefully. He had spent half an hour getting her ready for the Big Moment.

"I *am* excited," Abbie insisted. "*Wicked* excited. But I never was on a school bus before."

"You'll love it, sweetie," Brad promised.

"Is the driver nice?"

"Very nice."

"Will it go fast?"

"Only fast enough."

The sound of rusty brakes, and the bus was there, just feet away, dwarfing them both. They could feel the heat of its engine, smell exhaust. The monitor, a gray-haired woman wearing a fluorescent orange traffic belt, alighted. She looked both ways once, twice, three times, then gave the go-ahead.

"OK, Abbie." She invited her to come on board.

"She knows my name," Abbie whispered to her father.

"You have a good first day, OK, Apple Guy?" Brad said.

"OK, Dad."

They embraced.

"I love you, sweetie," Brad said.

"I love you, too, Dad."

"Be sure to have Mrs. Fitzpatrick let you call the second you get back."

"OK, Dad."

They were still embracing.

"Bye, sweetie."

"Bye, Dad."

"Bye, Maria."

"Maria says bye."

"I'll miss you."

"Miss you, too."

"See you tonight."

"OK."

Now she was on board, her face tiny and inconsequential against the window.

She waved.

He waved back.

The bus that had kidnapped her disappeared around the bend.

She was gone, Daddy's little girl taking another of the giant steps that would whisk her into womanhood before either of them really knew it had happened. All morning he'd been fighting back tears, and now, now that she couldn't see him, now that he was alone with the fool dog she had come to love so desperately, so completely, he let them fall. They spotted his cheeks, and he wiped them away; but he was not ashamed they were there.

Brad put Maria into the pen he'd constructed by the side of the garage, got into his Mustang, and drove to the school. It wasn't enough that he'd seen Abbie off; he wanted to greet her arriving at school, too. Maybe that would make up for the fact that he'd be at work when she got through her half day.

Morgantown Elementary was on Elm, which intersected with Main near the commercial heart of the town. If Main was Morgantown's commercial district, Elm Street was its municipal locus—a row of six buildings: Town Hall; the district courthouse; the post office, served by the same postmaster for thirty-seven years; the fire-police station, the only one of the lot built after 1960; the Lucius F. Perry Library; and Morgantown Elementary. Until construction of a regional high school in 1965, the building had housed all thirteen grades. Across Elm was a park that bordered the Misquamicut River.

Like Town Hall and the library, which had been built at roughly the same time—the turn of the century, when it seemed one architect had a monopoly on America's municipal design—the school was constructed of red brick and capped with a slate roof, which in turn was topped by a copper-plated cupola with a rooster weather vane that still accurately indicated which way the wind was blowing.

Quintessentially New England, Morgantown Elementary. A charming place.

Except now as he stood on the front walk with a gaggle of other parents (who were all dangling cameras of one sort or another), waiting for Abbie, Brad wasn't thinking of either quintessence or charm.

He was thinking of asbestos and lead paint.

These goddamn museums are full of the poison, he thought with alarm.

He remembered a story he'd done roughly the same time he'd been up to his eyeballs in nuclear waste disposal research. It was about a quiet little all-American town in Delaware where, a major U.S. Public Health Service study had revealed, the rate of a little-known cancer called mesothelioma was triple the national average. Many of the cases had been traced to the community's pride and joy, its grammar school, where generations of townspeople had sat for twelve straight years innocently breathing asbestos fibers that had been used in construction of the building's walls.

He remembered what that school had looked like. Morgantown Elementary was a dead ringer for it.

As for lead paint, why, just talk to any child welfare worker about that.

Jesus, am I being paranoid or what? He chided himself.

Am I?

If his reporting had taught him one thing, it was that the modern world oozed poison. Day by day, minute by minute, on every continent, in every tiny hamlet and every city, mankind was generating an utterly mind-boggling volume of shit. Some of it was pretty tame—garbage and human feces and fertilizer, for example. But a lot of it was very, very dangerous shit. Slow-acting, carcinogenic, mutagenic shit. Lethal-with-just-one-swallow shit. Shit piled stories-deep in toxic waste dumps, slag heaps, ash pits, municipal landfills. Shit trickling invisibly and odorlessly through the groundwater. Shit in the rain, the soil, the ocean, nibbling away at the ozone.

The kicker was, those were only part of the threat. Because you could test water for toxics. With money and effort, you could clean up dumps and rivers and inner harbors and asbestos- and lead-laced walls of schools. You could pass laws and appropriate money for superfunds and clean water acts. You could fine the hell out of producers, send them to jail. Eventually you probably could even get nations to stop producing fluorocarbons. And while nuclear waste on first blush was the ultimate nightmare, it was not, on consideration, a never-ending nightmare. If you had faith in technology, and Brad still did, you had to believe science eventually could—no, *would*—find a way to render it harmless.

No, it wasn't the inanimate shit that petrified Brad. *Living* poison—that was the truly scary shit. The wide world of microbes, starring those wonderfully nasty little buggers: bacteria and viruses. Especially viruses. One need only look as far as AIDS to see how real that nightmare was. Throw antibiotics and vaccines at them—if your scientists can develop them—and they will be only too happy to mutate. Maybe that was how the world would end. Man brought to extinction courtesy of some bug.

Yeah, you're being paranoid all right, pal, Brad concluded, *but a little paranoia never hurt anyone. Like that dude said, it ain't paranoia if the bastards really are watchin'.*

The beauty about working for the fourth estate was that you could take action. You could get things done, a point driven home quite poignantly, Brad thought, when the feds had established a special nuclear waste disposal study commission in the wake of his *Times* articles. The *Transcript* would have to do a little digging, that's all, and discover if there had ever been asbestos or lead paint in Morgantown Elementary and what steps, if any, had been taken to eliminate the risk. If none—well, that's what editorials and page one stories were all about.

The bus arrived. He raised his camera.

First to disembark was the monitor. Behind her came a boy. Brad would later come to know him as Jimmy Ellis. Behind the boy was Abbie. They were chatting. Jibbering and jabbering, as his daughter liked to call it.

"Hi, Dad!" she called out, and she was smiles, all beautiful little-girl, tug-at-the-heart-strings smiles, as she walked up the steps into Morgantown Elementary.

CHAPTER FIFTEEN

Friday, September 12

"I WANT to make love to you, Brad," the voice on the other end of the line was saying throatily. "I want us to fuck our brains out, just like in the good old days. You were always so gooooood in bed."

Heather's drunkenness came through clearly. Whether this was her idea of a joke or if in some demented way she was expressing desire, Brad didn't know—and didn't care. He pressed the phone against his ear so tightly it almost hurt. Not because he was hanging on her every word, but because he feared the whole newsroom was going to tune in.

"Heather . . ." he began.

"I want to sink down on your big, throbbing—"

"You're drunk." He spit the words into the phone.

"And you're a cocky asshole." She spit back, her voice turning to ice, just like that. That was what had always frightened Brad, the split-second shifts of mood. From glad to sad in the time it took to snap your fingers. As long as he'd known her, he'd never been able to figure out if that was really Heather, an emotional seesaw, or a trick she'd picked up in acting class.

"Thank you," he said, "from the bottom of my heart."

"An emotionless cocky asshole who cares only about his fucking newspaper and his fucking awards and his fucking ego. You're a selfish prick, Brad. That's the worst kind of thing to be."

"And you," Brad hissed, "are one of life's all-time losers. Headlined any Broadway plays lately, Heather? Hmmm? Any TV movies of the week? Any *Cosmo* covers in the works, or aren't crow's-feet in this month?"

It was a low blow.

The kind of low blow that had greatly accelerated the decline and decay of their relationship during its final destructive months. He'd vowed once they were history, once the decree was signed, sealed, and delivered, that he would never stoop to that level (he considered it *her* level, just as she considered it *his*) again. And with a couple of notable exceptions (including one extremely ugly scene on the sidewalk of Park Avenue South), he'd kept that vow. But now—now, for some reason, it was too tempting.

His barbs were true, as were hers. That is what gave them such lethal impact. He knew what her career had degenerated to. He knew where her dreams had gone, melted into the ground. Waiting on tables while waiting for the big role that was going to catapult her to the top again—and knowing deep in her soul the chance of its happening was next to nil. If there had been a soft spot for her left in him, he might have acknowledged the real-life role she'd been forced to play and felt a degree of sympathy. Because the veer Heather Pratt's once-stellar career had taken really was a tragedy, in its own small way.

But time was long since past he could feel anything but contempt. He imagined it was the same for her.

"Up for a Pulitzer again this year?" she sneered. "I can't tell you how very, very proud we'd all be, seeing you rewarded for defending truth, justice, and the American way. You know, until you moved out, I guess I never realized how awesome it was to be so close to a real superhero."

His bile was up, and he wanted to swear. He wanted to call her the word he'd used in his interview with Dexter. That would have been very satisfying, but he couldn't. Out of the corner of his eye he'd noticed Rod and others watching him but pretending not to.

"Heather," he said, straining for control, "you have five seconds to cut the shit. If you don't, I'm going to hang up. Then I'm going to buzz the operator and tell her to hold my calls. And don't make this a test. I mean it. I don't have time for any more of your crap."

That had a sobering effect.

"I called because of Abbie," she stated flatly.

"What about her?"

Jesus, Brad thought. *Now we're going to get into the custody issue all over again. The ghosts don't go away, do they? And I thought I'd put enough distance between us. The North Pole wouldn't have been far enough.*

"Don't sound so hostile. I am legally entitled to have her once a week, you know."

Brad did.

That had been the settlement: Brad getting primary custody, with Heather having visitation rights on weekends and many of the major holidays. Considering how fathers usually fared, his lawyer had assured Brad, it was a remarkably good deal. Not that it had come cheaply or easily. Or without a little pretrial nastiness, mainly depositions and motions related to what Brad's lawyer was convinced they could paint in open court as Heather's alcoholism. In the end, that was what had swayed her: the threat of a public lambasting, one that surely would drive the final nail into her acting coffin. And so, just before the trial had been scheduled, she had given in.

"I know you're entitled to once a week," he said solemnly.

"Well, I can't take her this week, or the next couple, for that matter. Something's come up. It'll have to be October."

He'd expected this to happen. It had happened when they all still lived in New York, at most two miles apart. When it was convenient, when it fitted into her schedule, Heather took Abbie. But when there was something better on the horizon (something better in June had been the Poconos with her new beau, a doctor), she passed. There was no reason to think things would improve by their moving to the Berkshires.

"You can tell her yourself," Brad said coldly. "I'll say you're going to call."

"That's big of you, Brad."

Reluctantly he gave Heather their home number. Then he hung up.

CHAPTER SIXTEEN

Wednesday, September 17

THOMASINE AND BRAD were through lunch and were lingering over coffee when Abbie burst into the Boar's Head Inn with the big news about Saturday's fair.

For the better part of an hour Thomasine had been briefing Brad on her thesis. This was the field portion of her research, she explained, and she expected it to last at least into the spring; she'd taken a one-year lease on her Main Street apartment just in case it went over. Three quarters of her work would consist of tape-recorded interviews, with the other quarter devoted to library and court investigation. The plan was to focus on the core of about fifty Indians who had been centrally involved in the land suit. Find out where they stood today. Find out about their jobs, their incomes, their political affiliations, their children, their religions, their health insurance (if any), on and on and on. A soup-to-nuts profile of a shattered tribe.

That had been the plan. Executing it was turning out to be something else again.

She'd been in Morgantown going on a month, she lamented, and she'd managed to find exactly one Quidneck who was willing to talk. The bitch was that he was an older man, with a shaky memory and an attention that spanned no more than 10 of her 350 or so questions. As for the other forty-nine principals, tracking them down was turning out to be far more difficult than either she or her adviser, an accomplished academician, had imagined. They seemed to have become a migratory group, heading off to upper New York State for a year or two or five, heading out West for good, packing their belongings into the back of a pickup and riding off into the sunset without bothering to say good-bye or leave a forwarding address. Except for the older man, whose usefulness would be limited, the eight or nine she'd found wanted nothing to do with her or her research. There'd been enough grief during the trial, they told her; what kind of fool would want to go through that all over again?

So it wasn't shaping up as a stroll down easy street, Thomasine informed Brad. The best research never did.

Brad had been doing most of the listening and little of the talking. He was fascinated by this woman's work, by this woman, and he was impressed. For several years after college she'd worked as a stockbroker in Boston. Probably made a killing at it, although she didn't come right out and say that. But brokering wasn't for her. It was, she said, a profession overcrowded with assholes, an intrinsically greedy, shallow business where God was spelled BMW and heaven was two words, Club Med. The analogy she used—Brad almost choked laughing, it was so ridiculous, yet so on target—was Chinese food. Looked great, tasted great, and it passed through you in about an hour. About three years ago, when she was twenty-seven, she'd quit. No big apocalypse, no premature mid-life crisis, just "Good-bye, fellow brokers, I'm out of here." Going to study something that's intrigued me since I was a little kid hearing about the first Thanksgiving, and that's Indians—and what exactly happened to them in the centuries since that feast. And don't ask me to explain it any better than that, because maybe I can't."

Thomasine looked up from her coffee, and there was Abbie, bounding into the dining room. Thomasine and Brad had just struck their deal: She would consider being the subject of a feature story, provided he would first let her camp out as long as she desired in the *Transcript*'s library. She was hoping the morgue would provide some valuable leads.

"If it isn't the big kindergarten student herself," Brad said, embracing his daughter. He'd told her he'd be at the Boar's Head for lunch, although he hadn't said who would be joining him. Not being sure exactly what to say about Thomasine, he'd decided to let events unfold by themselves.

"Hi, Dad!" she said. Then, turning: "Hi, Thomasine."

"Hello, Abbie. You remember my name," she said affably.

The whole lunch had been like that—a surprisingly pleasant, relaxed hour that had more than lived up to Brad's expectations. That day she'd come into the paper, Thomasine had come across a bit uptight. Maybe she'd just been shy. Maybe that had been her business side. After dining with her, Brad could understand why Abbie had so taken to her that night on the porch at the Boar's Head.

"Sure I remember," Abbie said. "You're the Indian lady."

Thomasine chuckled. "I guess I am."

"That's what she's been doing," Brad said. "Filling me in on the Indians."

"They used to live around here," Abbie said.

"That's right. A whole tribe of them."

"And they used to wear feathers and they had bows and arrows, too. Sometimes they caught fish, and they cooked them on great big fires way out in the woods. Yup. That's what they did."

"What a smart girl," Thomasine said.

"Did you know they wore clothes made out of deer's skin? They did, you know. Mrs. Fitzpatrick told me. She was married to an Indian once. But I don't think he wore deer clothes. I think he dressed regular."

"I think you're right," said Thomasine, who'd heard Mrs. Fitzpatrick's life story the second night she'd stayed at the Boar's Head.

"Dad," Abbie said, pulling at his sleeve, "can we go to the fair? Mrs. Lincoln told us there's going to be a fair on Saturday." Mrs. Lincoln was Abbie's kindergarten teacher.

"So I heard," Brad said.

"I was supposed to see my mommy this weekend," Abbie explained to Thomasine, "but she called and said I couldn't come because she has a very bad cold. Isn't that too bad?"

"Yes, it is," Thomasine agreed. Brad had mentioned in passing that he was divorced and that his ex-wife lived in New York. Reading between the lines, Thomasine had concluded that she was not the most stable character.

"But she said she'll be all better next month, and I can see her then. Besides, I think the fair will be fun. I've never been to a fair. They don't have fairs in New York. Do they, Dad?"

"Not this kind of fair, honey."

Brad was livid all over again. *That bitch,* he thought. *That lying bitch.* Heather had called Saturday. Asked to speak directly with Abbie, not even a hello or how are you for Brad. Abbie'd been on the phone ten minutes. When she hung up, she told Brad what her mother had said: that she missed Abbie terribly, that she wanted desperately to see her, but that she couldn't for a couple of weeks, she'd come down with a terrible cold and not only wasn't feeling up to speed but didn't want her dear daughter to get it.

Brad knew it was a lie. He knew because she hadn't mentioned a word about any cold when she'd called him the day before. *And since when had Heather kept something that big a secret? Histrionic Heather? Melodramatic Heather, miss an opportunity like that? Please . . .* No, it was the worst kind of lie—an unimaginative and juvenile lie that might . . . just might . . . fool a five-and-a-half-year-old. And it wasn't the only lie she'd told. Abbie didn't know, of course, but Brad had picked up the extension and eavesdropped on their conversation. He'd heard Heather tell their daughter how many times she had tried to call since they'd moved, but there hadn't been an answer, or directory assistance didn't have the number, or it had been busy.

Lies or no lies, Heather's call seemed to have been therapeutic. It was the first contact Abbie'd had with her mother since leaving New York, and she'd been almost giddy over it the rest of the day. Abbie wasn't so young that she wasn't affected by the divorce and the separation—it would continue to take its toll, in ways that might not surface for years, Brad was sure—but neither was she old enough to be bitter or even angry, not the way he was so bitter and angry. He was beginning to suspect that Heather could treat Abbie like dirt or elevate her to queen, and it would not affect his daughter's gut feelings. Good mom, bad mom, indifferent mom, Heather was Abbie's only mom. Thinking of Heather's power made Brad sick.

"Can we go to the fair, Dad? Please? Pretty please?"

"Oh, if you're a good girl, I think it can be arranged."

"Goody! They're going to have cows and horses and pigs and even some baby lambs, they're so cute, and there's going to be rides, and games where you can win prizes, and candy apples . . . what are candy apples, Dad?"

"They're apples that have been dipped in caramel," he explained. "Very tasty."

"And very messy," Thomasine added.

"Jimmy Ellis says he's going, too," Abbie said breathlessly. "Maybe we could meet him there. Maybe you could come, too, Thomasine."

She hesitated before saying: "I'd love to, but I have to be in Providence this weekend. I have a meeting with one of my teachers."

"Oh," Abbie said thoughtfully. "Well, maybe the next fair."

"You've got a deal."

Abbie pointed at her father. "Block your ears, Daddy," she ordered.

"Why?"

" 'Cause I have to tell Thomasine a secret and you can't hear. Go ahead. Block them."

Brad did.

Abbie got up on tiptoes and whispered in Thomasine's ear: "Do you like my dad?"

"Yes," Thomasine whispered back. "I think he's a very nice dad."

"Goody!"

"Was that the secret?" Thomasine asked. Across the table Brad was keeping his ears covered. He looked comical.

"Nope. The secret is: I think my dad likes you, too. But don't tell him I told you, OK?"

"OK. It'll be just between us."

Thomasine looked at Brad, and for the very first time she had a fantasy about him. She wondered what it would be like to kiss him. Not a deep, lingering kiss, not a kiss that would propel them toward dizzying heights of passion, but something fleeting, a quick brush of lips and cheek, contact that could be explained away, if necessary, as merely an accident. Could it really have been two years since she'd kissed a man?

CHAPTER SEVENTEEN

Saturday, September 20

IF BRAD COULD have stopped the wheel of life from turning, if somehow he could have reached into the cosmic clockwork, ripping out the gear that would have stalled it forever, he would have chosen to stop it on Saturday, September 20. That was the day he and Abbie spent at the fair. Time could never steal a single detail of that spellbound day—from its beginning, when Abbie cooked Aunt Jemima pancakes and bacon for them both, to its end, with Abbie asleep on the couch, a red-coal fire crackling, and Brad slowly nodding off, a look of contentment spread wide across his face.

Except for the incident with Jimmy Ellis—a very minor blemish, or so it seemed then—that entire day was as close to perfect as they come.

The Berkshire Agricultural Fair had been a tradition for more than a century (NOT A YEAR MISSED SINCE 1878! the red, white, and blue banner fluttering over the ticket booths proclaimed), and for year-round folk, it ranked with Pittsfield's Fourth of July parade and Lee's Christmas tree lighting ceremony as one of Berkshire County's absolutely *de rigueur* events. Encompassing thirty-five acres of permanent fairgrounds in nearby Stockbridge, it had the proverbial something for everyone: animals, rides, games, crafts, fortune-tellers, funny-shaped vegetable booths, food, a dog track for the bettors, of which this God-fearing part of the world had more than its share.

They arrived at opening time, 11:00 A.M.

"Can we see the bunnies first, Dad?" Abbie asked as Brad pored over the program, fifty cents from the man on stilts. *"Please?"*

"Sure, pumpkin." He ran his finger along the map, found the 4-H tent, and briefly surveyed the fairgrounds before figuring out which way to head. They were just setting off when the Ellises, Jimmy and Ginny, found them. Abbie handled the introductions. Brad and Ginny shook hands and allowed as how they were very glad to finally meet, they'd each heard so much about the other through their children, who were fast becoming the best of friends.

"I didn't think we were going to make it," Ginny said after dispensing with the obligatory small talk about school, the newspaper, and the pristine weather today. "Jimmy was sick half the night. Threw up and had a fever."

"That's too bad," Brad said. Having been there himself, he knew there was nothing worse than being a single parent with a sick kid.

"Yeah, but I'm OK now," said Jimmy. He didn't mention nightmares. He hadn't had one of those for going on two weeks now, almost long enough to be ancient history . . . and certainly long enough that neither he nor mom would connect them with last night's episode.

"Just to be on the safe side, I took him to Dr. Bostwick this morning," Ginny said. "He has a Saturday morning clinic. He said he thought probably it was an upset stomach. A touch of a bug, maybe, or something he ate—and we did have fish, although *I* wasn't sick. Anyway, Dr. Bostwick gave him a clean bill of health. So here we are."

"Super," Brad said. He reflected momentarily and continued: "Bostwick's the GP, isn't he? Has an office on Main Street not too far from the paper?"

"Right. And he's a peach, trust me. A highly competent, wonderfully mannered peach who loves kids, including, presumably, the three of his own. In all the years we've been going to him, I've never had a complaint."

"So you'd recommend him."

"Oh, yes."

"We've been so busy settling in that I haven't had time to get a doctor. Some parent. I think I'll give him a go."

"I recommend him highly. I've had him since before Jimmy was born. He delivered him, in fact."

They chatted on like that awhile, the four of them strolling through sunshine and farm-smelling air. Against Brad's better judgment, they'd brought Maria. Overwhelmed by the myriad of scents—animals, plants, people, most of them new, all of them intoxicating—the puppy's nose twitched and twittered so noticeably that Abbie asked if she was going to be all right. "Yes, unfortunately," Brad said. Straining against her leash, the puppy tried to go a hundred different ways at once. Brad had all he could do to control the fool thing. She was going to be some powerful brute when she was full-grown, that was certain. Good thing retrievers were so gentle, so good-natured with kids.

They paused at the entrance to the rabbit tent. Bunnies were old hat for Jimmy—he'd even raised one one summer until a fox one night toppled the pen and made short work of old Bugs—but for city-slicker Abbie this might as well have been the Seventh Wonder of the Modern World. Row after row of caged rabbits—cute, contentedly brainless rabbits, maybe two hundred of them, maybe more than two hundred, each and every one chomping enthusiastically on pellets and lettuce leaves, as if they hadn't eaten in a month and had never seen anything more appetizing in their lives. Black bunnies. Brown bunnies. White bunnies. Long-haired bunnies. Short-haired ones. With tails. And no tails. Giggling, Abbie and Jimmy plunged into the tent, the parents following a few steps behind. Brad wondered how many seconds it would be before Abbie made the inevitable request: When could she have one of her own?

Only looking back would Brad realize that what happened next had been a portent.

What happened was that a 4-H student whose name tag announced her as Carla, and who had raised a dozen of the rabbits on display, and who was watching over her animals the way nervous mothers watch sleeping newborns, asked her two young visitors if they would like to hold one.

"Can we really?" Abbie asked breathlessly.

"You really can," Carla said good-naturedly.

"Goody!" Abbie yelled.

"Yeah, that'd be fun," Jimmy said, less keenly. Rabbits were rabbits were rabbits, he'd learned after about three days that summer.

Carla reached into one of the cages and withdrew a fluffy ball of black fur.

"Do they bite?" Abbie asked when Carla held the rabbit out. She would not extend her hands until she had a satisfactory answer.

"Oh, no," Carla said. "They're very gentle."

"Are you sure?"

"Domesticated rabbits are very tame, honey." Brad elaborated.

"OK," Abbie said. Hesitatingly she held her hands out.

"There," Carla said, depositing the rabbit. "That one's named Peter. Isn't he soft?"

"*Very* soft," Abbie said with amazement. She was even more amazed to discover how warm the rabbit was, how pronounced its heartbeat was, how its nostrils never stopped twitching. She liked everything about this animal. It was at this moment that yes, she decided she had to have one of her own.

"Here's one for you," Carla said, handing Jimmy a brown one. Jimmy was a pro at handling bunnies—all that experience before the fox had done its thing. He cupped his hands, and Carla lowered the rabbit into them.

The rabbit freaked.

It was as if making contact with Jimmy's skin had sent a jolt of strong current through its rabbit body, haywiring the neurons and muscles. First it squirmed, then it flailed its legs, then it hissed—*hissed,* like a reptile—and then it did what a million years of evolution have taught all mammals to do when under siege.

It bit him.

Jimmy screamed and dropped the rabbit. It hopped a couple of yards away and then stopped, frozen. Brad had to dig in his heels to prevent Maria from attacking it.

"Jimmy!" Ginny yelled. She rushed to her son and clasped his hand. There were teethmarks, but thank God the skin hadn't been punctured.

"Ow! Oooooow!" Jimmy complained. It hurt, the way a pinprick hurts a few seconds before fading away.

"Oh, I'm s-s-so s-s-sorry," Carla said. "She's n-n-never done that before. Honest. I don't know what got into her. Are you all right? Are you?"

"Yeah, I'm all right." Brad couldn't tell if Jimmy was holding back tears or not. Abbie watching so closely probably wasn't helping the situation any. Especially since she'd held her rabbit without incident.

"Are you c-c-certain?"

"He's fine," Ginny said.

And he was. But by silent consensus, that was it for the bunny tent. It was going on noon, and Brad suggested lunch. The vote was unanimous.

Ginny and Brad had hot dogs and beer. The kids had chili dogs, fried dough, candy apples, and root beers and would have gone for the cotton candy and Italian ices if parents didn't hold the purse strings. *If you thought the kid was sick last night, Ginny, my friend,* Brad ruminated, *just wait'll the encore tonight. After all this food they'll be hearing these two in Albany.*

The rides opened at one, leaving just enough time to stroll through the vegetable tent. Abbie and Jimmy couldn't have been less interested, but they tagged along uncomplainingly because the rides weren't open yet and there was nothing else they wanted to do.

Brad's fascination with vegetables was newfound. During his first three weeks on the job he'd discovered that up here in the wilds of Berkshire County there was an informal hall of fame for funny-shaped, oversize, off-colored, mutant vegetables. Just yesterday he'd remarked to Rod Dougherty that if he had a nickel for every warped squash some hillbilly had brought into the *Transcript* in hopes of a photo, he'd be a rich man. What was really bewildering was how these amateur agronomists claimed to have produced these marvels: by feeding them milk in eyedroppers; by tying them; by sweet-talking them; by applying fertilizer whose homemade ingredients were family secrets. A mighty strange hobby, Brad thought. It beat anything he'd seen in New York.

The tent didn't disappoint Brad.

More mammoth, misshapen vegetables than they were growing in Chernobyl these days. This year had been a disaster for the real farmers—the growing season had been fluky, with drought, a deluge, and then an early frost—but for some strange reason, it had been a banner summer for the current crop of candidates to the Mutagenic Veggie Hall of Fame. There was a 540-pound pumpkin, almost as tall as a man *(a 540-pound pumpkin,* Brad thought. *Jesus).* A zucchini squash longer than a hockey stick. Another zucchini squash with dual stems, like a two-headed Hydra. Potatoes shaped like human beings, complete with pimply faces and stubby limbs.

"Ay-yup," acknowledged a grizzled old coot whose pockmarked face bore an uncanny resemblance to the monster gourds he'd grown. "Been a heartbreak year for corn, but it don't seem to have hurt the gourds none. Nope."

Brad was preoccupied with a display of two-pound beefsteak tomatoes (each nearly the size of a basketball, grown by a correspondingly beefsteak woman wearing a button that proclaimed: I ♥ TOMATOES!!!) when Abbie asked what time it was. She and Jimmy had been growing impatient by the minute.

"My gosh, it's one o'clock," Brad said.

"Rides!" Abbie shrieked.

"You got 'em, Apple Guy," Brad said as they cleared the tent.

Abbie was no stranger to amusement park rides. She was, in fact, developing into a rides freak. Before she'd mastered walking, Brad and Heather had taken her to a merry-go-round, and she'd fallen in love immediately—whether with the up-and-down motion or the metallic beat of the calliope, or both, Brad was never sure. From the merry-go-round she'd graduated to bigger and braver rides until now not even a roller coaster was too much.

They rode for hours, with Brad and Ginny soon dropping to spectator status. The train. Copter Cups. Tilt-a-Whirl. The Ferris wheel. The Scrambler. The Roundup, a fiendish ride which even Jimmy refused to go on ("I think I'm still a little sick from last night," he explained, hoping that would let him off the hook with this rides-crazy *girl*). After a round of corn on the cob, Abbie had her fortune read by "Mother Rosetta, Gypsy" ("You will soon experience great changes," she predicted). On their way to the ring toss, they ran into Maureen McDonald and her dad, as well as Rod Dougherty, who was doing a feature for Monday's paper. Abbie came up short at the ring toss, but Jimmy won a Rambo poster (Ginny didn't want to raise a stink in front of the Gales, but she knew where that poster was headed the instant they got home).

After a trip through the House of Horrors (Abbie closed her eyes for most of it), it was five-thirty. Abbie was pooped. Jimmy was pooped. Brad and Ginny were pooped. But before the Ellises parted company with the Gales, Jimmy took his mother aside and whispered something in her ear. She grinned and nodded and reached into her pocketbook. She handed her son a dollar bill.

"Jimmy would like to give Abbie a present," Ginny announced.

"A *special* present." He corrected her.

"A special present?" Abbie said. "For me?"

"Yup."

They're still at the age, Brad thought with equal parts appreciation and relief. *Another six months to a year, and he'd be too embarrassed.*

"What is it?" Abbie asked eagerly.

"It's a surprise," Jimmy explained. "Come on."

"Can I go with him, Dad?"

Brad looked to Ginny. "They're just going to that tent," she said, gesturing toward the flowers display.

"Sure, pumpkin," Brad said. "Just don't be long."

"OK."

When the two children returned, Abbie was holding a red carnation and beaming. Jimmy had his hands behind his back.

"Was that your gift?" Brad asked.

"Yes!" his daughter exclaimed.

"That must mean you're friends."

"We are," said Jimmy.

"Good friends," Abbie added. "We have to be, or he wouldn't have given me a flower."

"And she wouldn't have given me one, too. See?" he bubbled, pulling his hand from behind his back. He was holding a carnation, too, identical to Abbie's. She'd spent her entire allowance on it.

Abbie placed her carnation in a vase and helped Brad arrange the kindling for the fire. Then they went out onto the porch. The sun was gone, but there was light left in the sky, still some leftover heat from the fading day, enough that sweaters weren't necessary. They sat together on the glider, their gazes fixed across the back field toward the summit of Thunder Rise, colored with a deepening purple. The moon, nearly full, was making its first appearance of the evening. Nature was putting on a show. Brad sipped on a beer, Abbie a can of Slice.

"Dad?" Abbie asked after a spell.

"Apple Guy?"

"Is the moon far away?" She pointed toward Thunder Rise.

"Very far."

"Like from here to New York?"

"Oh, no. Much farther. Thousands and thousands of miles."

"Is God in heaven that far away, too?"

"Not exactly . . . It's more like—"

"I think he *must* be very far away," Abbie interrupted. "Because when I talk to him when I say my prayers, he never talks back. I ask him to, but he doesn't. Why doesn't he talk back, Dad?"

Brad's mother, a devout Catholic (a "mackerel snapper," Brad teasingly called her, but only when she was in the very best of moods), had taught Abbie to pray. Brad had known better than to interfere with Mother's lessons. Abbie did not pray nightly, as Brad had as a child, but only as the mood swayed her. Brad neither encouraged nor discouraged the practice. Religion—even at five and a half—was a personal decision, he strongly believed.

As for this matter of God not talking back, Brad was stumped. It had been one of the mysteries of his own youth, too. One he'd never solved, along with why God, being so infinitely good, could allow war, famine, horrible car accidents, the leukemia that had claimed a fourth-grade classmate.

"I don't know why he doesn't talk back," he finally said.

"Maybe he can't *hear* me," Abbie exclaimed, as if struck by sudden inspiration.

"Could be."

"Maybe if I *yelled* instead of praying, he would hear me." It was kid's logic, simple and innocent.

"Maybe."

"Maybe the old man in the moon would hear me, too. Moon! God!" she yelled into the night. "Can you hear me? It's Abbie! I'm down here! See? Down here on the porch!"

She stopped.

"They don't answer," she said sadly.

"I think it's too far," Brad said.

Abbie waved. "Well, maybe they can see me wave," she said. "Hi, God. Hi, moon."

Soon it was cold and dark. They moved from the porch to the living room. Abbie brushed her teeth and got into her pajamas. Brad got another beer from the fridge and lit the fire. It caught nicely. Her two favorite Barbie dolls in hand, Abbie settled with Brad on the couch and he read her her good-night story. From a dinosaur book, of course.

"Dad?" she said sleepily when it was almost nine-thirty, well past bedtime.

"Yes?"

"I love you."

"I love you, too, Apple Guy."

"Good night."

"Good night."

Brad felt at peace with himself, here in the little corner of the universe they had claimed as theirs. In less than a month that universe would be turned upside down.

CHAPTER EIGHTEEN

Wednesday, September 24

"OPEN WIDE," Dr. Mark Bostwick said as he moved the tongue depressor into position. "Say 'ah.' "

"Aaaaaaaah," replied the little girl. Stripped down to her underpants, she was sitting apprehensively on the examining table. From her seat by the door Susie McDonald watched.

"That's a girl," Bostwick said as he shone a chrome-plated flashlight down Maureen's throat. "Keep it open. Wide. Wider. Nice. Thatta girl. OK. You can close now."

"Are you finished?" Maureen sounded as if she dreaded the answer. Dr. Bostwick had been going over her now for fifteen minutes. Seemed as if there weren't a part of her body he hadn't poked, prodded, or felt.

"Almost," the doctor said as he tossed the tongue depressor away. "Just want to have a look in the old ears. You won't even feel this."

Maureen was stoic as he probed one ear, then the other.

"OK, Maureen," Bostwick said. "What a good girl. You can get dressed now. And make sure the nurse gives you a lollipop on the way out."

Turning to Susie, he said: "Her ears are fine. Her nasal passages are swollen. She's congested. Her throat is inflamed. I don't think it's strep, but I took a culture just in case. I'll hear from the lab first thing in the morning. But I think it's probably a cold."

He wasn't sure he believed that.

Most of her symptoms fitted the typical cold pattern—the congestion, throat irritation, runny nose, general feeling of discomfort—but not all. The nausea she felt from time to time didn't fit. The sharp, sudden abdominal pains she'd been having occasionally didn't either. If it had been three months farther into the year, even two, he would have guessed she had some kind of lingering flu. But the Centers for Disease Control's Morbidity and Mortality Weekly Report, which he received, wasn't reporting a single case of the flu anywhere in the country yet. He seriously doubted this season's strain had chosen Morgantown, Massachusetts, to introduce itself to America.

"A cold for almost six weeks?" Susie said skeptically. It was her second visit to Bostwick in the last month, and she was concerned. Not in any big way, but enough to demand an explanation—something she was not in the habit of doing from doctors.

"The rhinovirus is a stubborn little critter," Bostwick explained. "I've seen colds linger for six *months.* I wouldn't be worried."

But he was. He was justifiably proud of his clinical skills, but experience had taught him even the best clinicians weren't perfect. What if he'd missed something? Maybe it was only one out of every thousand cases, but everyone misses. *Everyone,* no matter how brilliant. That's what reading biographies of all his doctor heroes and medical school had taught him. Was he doing enough with this kid? Should he be ordering other tests? An expensive battery of tests that in all likelihood would do nothing more than scare the child and panic the parents? Should he refer them to a specialist in Pittsfield? Or would that be overreacting, passing the buck, covering his ass in case of a suit, the way some of his colleagues did.

No, he didn't feel his usual confidence treating Maureen McDonald.

And she wasn't the only one.

That was the really unsettling thing. It had taken until now to realize it—to *admit* it, damn it—but he'd been shaky with several other diagnoses recently. Shaky as never before in his practice, which included hundreds of families from all over the county.

Since late August he'd seen a number of children with symptoms he'd diagnosed as "colds." So? It was no big deal, he'd been telling himself. Germs go around. In the closed environment of a small-town grammar school, they go around with lightning speed. Schools are like heaven for germs—so many warm bodies in such close contact with each other. *School's been open barely three weeks. Obviously some kid brought back a stubborn virus from summer camp, and now it's making its merry rounds. That's all. Nothing to call in the CDC about.*

And because he had always prided himself on how conscientious he was (he could honestly say he hadn't gone into medicine for the money), it was easy to be paranoid . . . at least fleetingly.

Until now he'd never tallied them. *Jesus,* he thought. *There must be a dozen kids with some or all of these symptoms. Maybe more than a dozen. If it were January, I wouldn't give it a second thought. But it's not January. It's September twenty-fourth, barely autumn.*

And there's something else here that doesn't look quite right either. None of the symptoms have been steady. Not with Maureen, not with the others. There will be a spell for a week or two, then seeming recovery. Then the symptoms again. Or new symptoms. All right, so there's reinfection.

But—but—

Bostwick didn't like all those buts.

He made a mental note to watch each case very, very carefully and to follow up in a week on all of them. And that wasn't all. As soon as the McDonalds left, he was going to have his nurse pull the charts of every child he'd seen over the past two months. He was going to spend the weekend poring over all of them to see what he could come up with . . . if anything.

He hoped it would be nothing.

"I want her to get plenty of liquids and rest. Keep her home from school if she doesn't feel up to it. For the fever, Tylenol. And Triaminic for congestion."

"Like before," Susie said dubiously.

"Like before. I'll call when I get the strep results. And I want you to call here in a week, even if the symptoms moderate. I want to know how you make out." Maureen was dressed now and was waiting by the door with her mother.

"I'll call," Susie said.

"Make sure you do. Because if I don't hear from you by next Thursday, I'll be calling you."

CHAPTER NINETEEN

Sunday, September 28

IT WOULD NOT be inaccurate to say that beef stew and his bowels killed Harry Whipple.

And it would not be inaccurate to say that it started with beer.

Whipple didn't ordinarily drink beer. Once upon a time he'd

been crazy for the stuff, but as his alcoholism had progressed, brew had lost its punch, and he'd moved on to the hard stuff. But it had been so damn warm the last two days—Saturday had set a record, eighty-eight degrees, or so the TV weatherman had said—and so damn stuffy in the mine that he'd gotten it into his head that nothing but ice-cold beer could quench his thirst. Yesterday afternoon he'd driven into town and bought himself a case of Genesee sixteen-ouncers.

It was gone by ten-thirty, the time he passed out on the couch. While he slept, the beer went to work on his intestines—went to work with a vengeance—and by the time he got up this morning, his bowels were gurgling. By midafternoon they were in a state of revolt. By the time he finally gave in and plunked his liver-spotted ass on the toilet, he was poised for the largest crap of his life—or such he adjudged it when, after much huffing and puffing, it was finally over.

It was like a sick infant's worst diarrhea. It bubbled and splattered out of him for what seemed an eternity, and there was so much of it that mid-movement, he was forced to flush the hopper for fear it would overflow. And oh, did it stink. Lord amighty. This was so bad that Whipple, who was not endowed with mankind's most delicate nose, actually thought he might throw up. When he was through, he threw open every window on the first floor.

Whipple settled onto the couch to have himself a nice tall tumbler of Seagram's on the rocks.

He'd worked an hour or so in the mine today, but slaving away in there was wearing very, very thin. Some days just lately he hadn't worked at all. It was slowly dawning on him that no matter what his dead sister's map promised, there was probably no gold—or if there was, a greater power than Harry Whipple was needed to get it out. Just what had convinced he'd be luckier than those fools who gone before him anyway? Another couple of days in there, he'd decided, and he was going to pack it in.

The whiskey went down smoothly, tumbler after tumbler of it. There were a couple of ball games on TV, but Whipple paid little attention. By late afternoon, when the worst heat of the day was starting to back off, TV was merely background. Whipple had slipped away to his favorite place, the alcohol ozone.

By six-thirty something vaguely resembling a hunger pang tore at his innards. Whipple hadn't eaten a thing all day, but that was hardly unusual. It had been years since he'd had a really big appetite, even longer since he'd eaten three square meals in one single day. Food just didn't have it for him anymore.

Still, he had to eat. Something to silence his stomach. It always came down to that. He got unsteadily to his feet, tottered into the kitchen, opened the cabinet, and rattled around inside with his free hand. Some selection. A can of tuna. Two boxes of macaroni and cheese. A half-full jar of horseradish, which, for the life of him, he couldn't remember buying. A dirty jar of peanut butter. A can of Dinty Moore beef stew. That was it, his entire larder.

He opened the stew and poured it into a blackened pan. He put the pan on the stove, turned the propane to high, nearly fell on his way back to the couch, took a slug of Seagram's straight from the bottle, thought about taking a piss, and passed out.

On the stove the stew was getting warm.

First it bubbled. In ten minutes the gravy had thickened considerably. In another ten minutes it was paste. Five more, and the water content had boiled away completely. The pan was getting very hot. Soon it was glowing. Smoke filled the kitchen.

Whipple's snoring was louder than the TV.

Outside, his dog had been sniffing this new smell. It wasn't a completely unfamiliar smell; the master had burned food before, many times. But this scent had an unusual intensity, a sharp bite the dog didn't recognize. Sniffing it almost hurt his nose. In an earlier era the dog might have gone inside to investigate. Seeing Whipple unconscious, sensing something was very wrong, he might even have barked or tugged at his pants leg to awaken him.

Yes, once upon a time, he probably would have done that.

But things had not been good lately between Whipple and Eddie. Ever since he had gone into that mine, there had been something different about the man. It was not something the dog could taste, or see, or smell. But it could be sensed, the way a cornered animal instinctively senses entrapment. It was a strong sense. A sense of badness. Of an enemy lurking in the shadows. It scared the dog, could actually make him shiver. Since late spring he had tried hard to keep out of the man's way. Mostly he had been staying outside or in the barn, where he slept nights now.

A sudden gust of wind blew down from Thunder Rise. For an instant the ground shook. Shivering, Eddie slunk off to the safety of the barn.

The pot was red now, its contents completely carbonized.

The stove itself was getting dangerously hot, too. Not once since moving in had Whipple cleaned it, and the accumulated grease had melted, was smoking now. Hotter and hotter it got until, just before seven-thirty, when it was dark outside, it flashed with a sound like air escaping an overinflated tire.

The fire might have been confined to the stovetop grease if every window on the first floor hadn't been open. It might have burned more slowly, penetrating Whipple's unconsciousness to sound an alarm. But the windows were open, and the wind was blowing mightily. The crosscurrents caught the flame, driving it against the wall, spreading it to the curtains of a nearby window.

In less than two minutes the house was engulfed.

Rod Dougherty was the first to spot the fire.

He was visiting at Brad's, was opening a beer in the kitchen—the room with the best view of Thunder Rise—when he thought he saw flames licking up out of the mountain.

"Brad, come here," he said excitedly. "Quick."

Brad came in from the living room, where Abbie was parked in front of the TV. A *Rainbow Brite* tape was on the VCR. Twenty more minutes, and she had an appointment with the sandman. Tomorrow was the start of another week.

"Look," Rod said. "On the mountain. I think it's a fire."

"I think you're right," Brad said after one look. "Shit."

"It's got to be pretty big if we can see it this far away. Are there any houses way up there?"

"A couple," Brad said. Then it hit him. "Jesus!" he nearly screamed. "Jimmy Ellis lives up there! The McDonalds, too!"

"Who are they?"

"Kids in Abbie's kindergarten class!"

"Should we chase it? I've got my camera in the car."

"After we call the fire department. You call. I'll get Abbie."

"Gotcha."

Rod got on the phone. Brad rushed into the next room, grabbing two coats from the closet on his way in. "Here," he said to Abbie. "Put this on."

"Where we going?" she said.

"Just get in the car," he said. He didn't want to take her, but there was no choice. He'd covered enough fires in his day to know that by the time he'd made baby-sitting arrangements, the house—if indeed it was a house—would be to the ground by the time they got there. And if it were the Ellises or McDonalds, they could be . . .

He refused to think of that.

Rod drove so fast that Brad was afraid a tire would blow out before they got there, but it was a chance they gladly took. Up Thunder Rise Road they went, first seeing the flames, then losing them behind the trees, then seeing them again. Past the Ellises. Past the McDonalds, both houses intact, Brad breathing two audible sighs of relief. Higher and higher they went, the fire brighter and brighter.

The fire department was already there, but it was too late. The house was on its way to the ground. By the time the engines had arrived, only the frame was still standing. The roof had collapsed, the walls burned through, taking some of the power out of the fire. The fire fighters' only job now was hosing it down so it wouldn't spread into the woods.

"Any idea whose house it is?" Rod asked.

"None," Brad said. "I don't even know if it was occupied."

The ambulance had arrived simultaneously with Brad, Rod, and Abbie. The EMTs took their time getting out. Brad had a pretty good idea what that meant.

"Stay in the car," he ordered Abbie.

"But, Dad—"

"No buts," he snapped. He hardly ever used an angry tone with Abbie, but there was no way she was going to see what they would be loading into that ambulance.

"Whose house was it?" Rod asked a fire fighter.

"His name was Whipple."

"He was a crazy old thing," added a man standing near them. "I should know. We're his neighbors."

"Who are you?" Brad asked.

"Hank McDonald."

"Maureen McDonald's father?"

"Yup."

"Brad Gale." He introduced himself. "*Transcript* editor. This is Rod Dougherty, one of our reporters."

"Pleased to meet you. Too bad it had to be like this. You're Abbie's father, right?"

"Right." He dismissed that line of conversation with a curt tone. "Was he home?" he asked.

"Yep," McDonald said. "Except for runs into town, he was almost always home, far as I could tell."

"Has anyone seen him?" Rod said. "I mean, maybe he got out."

The fire fighter pointed to Whipple's Jeep. A small crowd of fire fighters was gathered to one side of it. Some were on their knees, examining a dark shape. No one seemed to be moving urgently.

"Not alive," the fire fighter said. "We couldn't even find a pulse."

"Frankly, I'm not surprised this happened," McDonald said, in a surprisingly unsympathetic voice.

"Why do you say that?"

"Because he was a drunk, that's why. This for the paper?"

"Well . . ." Rod was taking notes.

"Hell, it doesn't matter. Everyone knows Whipple was a drunk. Everyone knows he was a crazy fool, too. Rumor had it he's been digging for gold somewhere up here the last few months."

"Gold?" Rod said. "He told you that?"

"Only once. It was the only time I ever talked to him. He was drunk as a lord, wandered into our driveway one evening, babbling on and on about how it was only a matter of time before he was filthy rich. 'Rich nuff to buy 'n' sell all you pisspots,' I believe is how he put it. I was set to call the police when he relieved himself on my lawn, then wandered back into the woods."

"Do you think he was really digging for gold?"

"Who knows? He was crazy, as I said. And it is an old Indian legend: gold buried somewhere under Thunder Rise. It's so much poppycock, of course, although it's true a hundred years ago a company went bankrupt digging for it. There's supposed to be an old mine shaft left up there. That's what they say anyway. I've never seen it. Not that I've exactly gone looking for it."

"Interesting," Brad said, and the wheels were turning.

McDonald filled Rod in on what he knew—about Whipple's sister leaving him the house, about the supposed search for gold, about some of Whipple's background. He'd been a drifter and a loser—exactly the type who might be mesmerized by the possibility of gold. It would make for a good story. Bizarre as hell . . . a natural hook for readers.

They left before the body was loaded into the ambulance for its trip to the county medical examiner's office.

"Did someone die, Dad?" Abbie asked as they drove home.

"Yes, honey," Brad said. "Someone died."

"Who?"

"Someone you don't know, sweetheart. An old man."

"Is he with God now?"

"Yes, sweetheart. He's with God."

Abbie looked out the window to see if the moon was up there, but clouds had moved in, and she could not spot it.

"I guess he didn't see the fire," she mused. "Because otherwise he would have stopped it, wouldn't he, Dad? Before the guy was dead?"

"Yes, he would have, honey," Brad said, unconvincingly.

CHAPTER TWENTY

Monday, September 29

BRAD CONSIDERED Rod's story, which led the paper the next afternoon, an outstanding piece of work, and he wrote a note to the publisher suggesting a raise might soon be in order for his star reporter. In twenty-five inches Rod had managed to capture the drama of the fire and—without insult or ridicule—the peculiar nature of the man incinerated in it.

Thomasine, who'd been holed up inside the *Transcript*'s library all day, agreed.

But her interest in the story was not purely journalistic. Her curiosity was piqued by these four paragraphs, which appeared at the top of the jump page:

> Whipple was said by neighbors and some longtime residents of Morgantown to have spent the last several months pursuing mankind's age-old dream of striking it rich by digging gold. Dating back to when Indians were the only residents of Morgantown, there has been a legend of gold being buried somewhere on Thunder Rise, according to Historic Society Chairman Elizabeth C. Fulton.
>
> "Near as I can tell, he was digging in an old mine shaft or something up there," said Hank McDonald, the deceased man's neighbor. "I guess it was left over from a long

time ago, when a company went bankrupt digging for gold."

Miss Fulton confirmed that gold speculators in the last century had dug a shaft, abandoning it when no gold was found. She said that there has never been any evidence that the old Indian legend of gold on Thunder Rise has any basis in fact, although she noted that has never stopped people such as Whipple from looking.

McDonald said that, to his knowledge, Whipple—like those who came before him—never found any gold inside Thunder Rise.

Gold.

Indians.

Interesting.

The legend didn't seem to have any obvious bearing on Thomasine's thesis, but that didn't mean somewhere down the line it might not be important. As any anthropology researcher worth her salt learned very early in the game, no scrap of information even remotely relevant to the topic at hand should be discarded. There was no telling when that scrap might become useful. Anthropologists, as her adviser was fond of saying, were the world's greatest pack rats—or damn well ought to be.

Thomasine cut the clip from the paper and filed it into a manila folder. That evening, during her daily session with the IBM PC she had set up in the study of her apartment, she entered a synopsis of it into a floppy disk, along with summaries of the other material she had gleaned from the paper's library. Through cross-indexing, she could find anything in her growing data base in a matter of seconds. When she was done, she tuned her stereo to a soft-rock station, poured herself a glass of cold chablis, and settled onto her couch with *The New York Times Magazine.* It had not been an especially fruitful day. A microfilm search was painfully slow work, hard on the eyes, but there was no way around it.

The one bright spot had been lunch again with Brad. Today was the fourth time they'd gone out for lunch or sat together in the paper's conference room sharing sandwiches.

She smiled. She was really getting to like this guy, divorce, child (she was a cutie), and all.

And she appreciated the pace. There was no pressure here, no expectations. If anything was happening between them, it was happening in its own sweet time. "If it turns out we're only going to be friends," his words and manner seemed to say, "then that's all right."

All of That was fine with Thomasine.

Her last relationship had been as doomed as his, and that was just fine.

CHAPTER TWENTY-ONE

Tuesday, September 30

THEY DID NOT know emotion. Did not know gratitude.

But they were almost happy. Were emboldened.

They could come and go now, unencumbered by the old fool who had set them free.

Not that he had ever been any serious problem. More an annoyance, the way mothers and fathers were an annoyance.

Now he was gone, chased away forever.

CHAPTER TWENTY-TWO

Wednesday, October 1

ABBIE REQUESTED, and automatically received, "dinosaurs" as her bedtime story.

What else for the past year? An occasional Berenstain bears book, or *Sesame Street,* or *My Little Pony,* but mostly it was dinosaurs she demanded on the last stop to dreamland. Brad approved; dinosaurs, he believed, were the perfect creatures to feed a child's robust imagination. They were huge ("Some of them were bigger than houses, Dad!"), they lived long ago and far away ("before there were even people"), and they were the mightiest animals that ever walked the earth ("Even a lion would run away from a *Tyrannosaurus rex*"). Most amazing of all, they had *disappeared forever* ("but you can still see their bones in museums and places").

He remembered how fascinated *he* had been at a similar age, and he was secretly pleased that his daughter was now, too (Heather had detested dinosaurs, another of their endless disagreements). There seemed to be something universal about the youthful appeal of giant, mythical beings. In some psychoanalytic sense, Brad supposed, dinosaurs and dragons and the like were healthy concepts. A medium through which kids could get acquainted with their fears—without risk of any real-life penalty.

Abbie sat in Brad's lap, absorbed in the color drawings as he read the text. Maria, who seemed finally to be housebroken, was asleep on the floor. Abbie knew them by heart, of course, all those Latin names, each about a yard long. Could pronounce each perfectly. It was only a matter of time, Brad surmised, before she could spell them perfectly, too.

Page by page, they went through the litany. *Brachiosaurus,* the largest dinosaur. *Diplodocus,* the longest. *Tyrannosaurus rex,* the king. *Brontosaurus,* the thunder lizard. *Trachodon,* the one with the bill like a duck. *Triceratops,* which compensated for its relatively small size with armor and three deadly horns. *Rhamphorhynchus,* a flying reptile. That was about the only one Abbie really didn't like. It reminded her of a vulture—a giant, scary bird she'd seen once on TV in some cowboy and Indian movie. Vultures were very bad, she'd concluded, because they liked to eat only dead things. Ick. Why, vultures had even eaten *people* after they'd died, like that poor guy in the movie who'd tried to cross the desert without food or water or a horse.

"I would never try to pat a meat eater," Abbie said when Brad closed the book.

She was stalling for time. Acting out her version of the procrastination drama that is featured nightly in homes across America. The moment of truth had arrived, and she didn't want to go to bed. *Well, let her stretch it a bit,* Brad thought. That was OK. He'd been working until seven or even later the last two weeks, and his weekday contact with Abbie had dwindled to a precious two or two and a half hours a day. He missed her, he realized. Until now he hadn't realized—or acknowledged—how much.

"And why wouldn't you pat a meat eater?" he asked.

"Because he might try to eat you. People are like meat to dinosaurs, you know," she explained. "They have very sharp teeth. They could swallow you in one bite, and then you would be gone."

"It sounds scary."

"Yeah, well, you would just have to stay away from them.

Maybe you could hide in a cave. A caveman cave. A little one, so they couldn't even get a claw inside. Then you'd be safe."

"Maybe you could pat a baby meat eater."

"Daaad," she groaned. "They're dangerous, too. The only thing is, their teeth are smaller. But they could still kill you. A baby meat eater is *this* big," she said, stretching her arms to the limit.

"I see."

"The only kind of dinosaur you could pat is a plant eater. If they were still alive, you might even be able to have one for a pet."

"What about Maria?" The dog's ears perked up, then flopped down again.

Abbie looked puzzled.

"Wouldn't she be jealous?" Brad said.

"No. I think they would be friends, don't you?"

"Yeah, I guess I do."

They talked like that until Abbie's eyes were heavy.

"Time to call it a day, kid," Brad said.

Abbie did not protest. Hand in hand, they went up the stairs. Abbie brushed her teeth while Brad fluffed her pillow and straightened her blanket, twisted into a heap at the foot of her bed, where Abbie had left it on awakening that morning. They were not into making beds in the Gale household. Brad had had his fill of hospital corners during his own growing up.

The house had six bedrooms. Six large, drafty bedrooms, each with its own turn-of-the-century steam radiator. Two of the bedrooms remained empty. Two were filled with unopened boxes and cartons that Brad knew in his heart of hearts he wouldn't unpack for months, years, maybe never (one of the boxes dated to his last week at college, when he'd cleared out his dorm). Abbie's room was on the other side of the bathroom from Brad's, far enough for privacy, close enough that he could hear her snoring if he listened closely and the house was quiet.

"Done, Dad," came her small voice from the bathroom.

"OK, let's get you in."

She bounded into the room, leaped onto the bed, pulled the blanket around her, snuggled her favorite Barbie doll, and announced: "You forgot my drink."

"You're right, I did," he said, heading for the stairs. "What do you want?"

"OJ."

"We're out."

"Ginger ale?" she asked hopefully.

"Don't have any."

"OK, water," she said, resigned. "With an ice cube. With *two* ice cubes."

"Do we say 'please' anymore around here?"

"Please? *Pretty please*?"

"That's better."

Brad went down the stairs.

Fleetingly, bitterly, he thought of Heather. He often did at Abbie's bedtime—more than any other time probably. And not for nostalgic reasons. In the last year of their marriage, the year the shit had hit the fan with its ugliest force, Heather had been home very few nights before midnight. At first she had her alibis; at first Brad believed them. Must-see plays. Casting that went over a few hours. Acting class, followed by inevitable but innocent drinks with the instructor. Slowly the excuses changed, finally dwindling altogether. She was with friends. She was in the Village. It was none of his fucking business. This wasn't Sicily or Louisiana or some Neanderthal place like that, where wives were the property of their husbands. She had her life. Her rights. *Her sadly sputtering career,* Brad thought.

So Abbie's bedtime ritual had fallen exclusively to Brad. It was one of the few bright spots on the domestic front during that hellish period.

"Dad?" Abbie said when he returned with the water.

"Yes, Apple Guy?"

"Can you check under the bed?"

"Sure."

He was surprised. It had been months since she had asked for that reassurance; he just naturally assumed she'd gotten over another of the standard childhood fears. Well, he wasn't about to dwell on it. Sometimes fears returned. Sometimes they never went away for good, only hid somewhere for a while, waiting for the right opportunity to pop back out. Sure. The mind was funny when it came to fear. At the *Times* he knew an editor—a forty-one-year-old editor—who still admitted to checking under his bed occasionally. It was a newsroom joke.

Brad got on his hands and knees. Nothing but dust devils.

"All set," he proclaimed.

"Thanks, Dad."

"You're welcome." He kissed her, then stroked the hair off her face. "Now you go to sleep."

She did, almost before he was out of the room.

Brad followed Abbie at ten-fifteen.

At eleven forty-five her screams jarred him awake.

In the seconds it took to jerk into full consciousness, he was sure there was a fire. He was convinced they were back in New York, still living with Heather, and she had stumbled in drunk after midnight and passed out on the couch with one of her goddamn cigarettes just the way he'd yelled at her a million times not to, and her fingers had relaxed, and the cigarette had dropped to the rug, and the rug had started to smolder, and then it was blazing, and toxic fumes were filling the apartment, and they were going to die . . . they're all going to die . . . *Abbie's going to be* incinerated . . . and it's *her* fault, all *Heather's* fault . . . Heather with her death wish and growing hatred for life. . . . *Goddamn egocentric loser psychotic Heather . . .*

"Daaaaddd!"

Brad flew out of bed, out of his room, into the hall, stubbing the toes of his left foot with bone-breaking force on the doorjamb. Later his foot would throb unbearably, two toenails would turn black and peel off, but there was no pain initially; his panic effectively blocked that. He could have taken a bullet right now and not felt it.

He passed the bathroom.

Fire.

Only now was it beginning to penetrate. There was no fire.

There was only Abbie desperately screaming.

He reached her door, which he'd left open a crack so she could see the bathroom light.

"Daaaadddd!" she kept yelling, her voice pure terror.

With his uninjured foot, he kicked the door. It banged into the wall and almost fell off its hinges. The knob punched a hole through the plaster into the slats beyond.

Abbie's bed was empty.

She's being kidnapped. After *fire,* that was his second thought.

The window.

That's how they came in. That's how they're taking her out.

The window was open. After kissing her good-night, he'd closed it and drawn the shade. He remembered that.

The shade flapped quietly in the night air.

Kidnapped. While she was sleeping, just like Lindbergh's son.

His mind rocketed into warp speed now. In a fraction of a second his brain had cataloged the options: Call the police, get a knife, follow them out the window, shout, threaten, scream, cry, turn on all the lights. . . . His brain was beginning to process the relative merits of each when he heard her again: "Daaaaddddd!"

The voice was terrified, close by. Brad raced to the far side of her bed, and there she was: on the floor, her legs drawn to her chest, her hands framing her flushed face, crying. In the sallow glow of the night-light, she looked pathetically tiny and fragile, like a porcelain doll in a dusty corner of an antiques shop.

"Oh, honey . . ." He wrapped his arms around her.

She was quivering. Any worse, and he would have believed she was convulsing. He tightened his embrace. He couldn't recall ever experiencing such a strong sense of how fragile, how dependent and *small* a child really is. Not even when she was a baby had the feeling been so powerful. He'd often thought he would lay down his life for his child. Until now he'd never realized how willingly he could actually do it.

"Shhhhh." He soothed her. His own breaths were coming in heaves. He was becoming aware of a ballooning pain in his left foot.

"It w-w-was there," she cried. "B-b-by the window."

"What, sweetheart?"

"A *R-r-rham-pho-rhyn-chus.*"

"It must have been a nightmare."

"But it w-w-wasn't. It opened the window. It was there. It had huge wings."

"A nightmare, honey."

"No. I saw it. It flew in and—and . . . started coming closer and closer. Right on my bed. I was trying to get away and—and that's why I'm on the . . . floor."

"But there aren't any dinosaurs anymore," he reminded her gently. "There haven't been any for millions and millions of years. You know that."

She could not be dissuaded. "But I saw it. And it talked to me. It said it was going to—to take me away. Not tonight, but someday. 'When it was good and ready,' it said. And I was going to . . . die. Daddy . . . please don't let it. . . ." Her crying, which had tapered off, returned with tidal force.

"Shhhh. Sometimes we *think* we see things, but it's only a dream. Dreams can be very real, you know. *Very* real. I remember when I was just your age, I used to dream that I could fly. I could see trees and roofs and cars and people, all very tiny way down there. It was cold up so high, and I could hear the wind rushing by, and I was sure I was flying. But then I would wake up and know it was a dream."

"Can dreams really be that real?" she said. Brad could see her conviction beginning to soften.

"Oh, sure. Good and bad dreams can both seem that real."

"But it looked just like it did in the book," Abbie said. "If I hadn't been so 'fraid, I could have touched it."

And maybe we'll just lay off that book for a few nights, Brad thought. "I can imagine," he said.

"Why did it talk, Daddy?"

"I think that's just more proof it was a dream. Even if there were some dinosaurs around today, which there aren't, you don't think they could *talk,* do you?"

The logic impressed her. "Nah, I guess not," she conceded.

"Come on," he urged. "Let's get you off this floor." She had calmed considerably. He helped her to her feet.

"Can I sleep with you, Dad?" she begged.

"Of course."

It was not a habit he wanted to get into—he could just imagine the child abuse investigation team knocking on the door after Abbie innocently let it slip at kindergarten that she'd been "sleeping with Dad"—but tonight, tonight was fine. After a stop at the bathroom, where Brad took a fistful of aspirin for his aching foot, and Abbie downed a tumbler of water, they crawled together into his king-size bed. Abbie curled herself into a ball. Brad pulled the covers over her, fluffed his own pillow, double-checked the alarm, and put out the light.

"Can you leave the light on? Please, Dad?"

"No," he said firmly. They weren't going to start that. "I'm right here, Apple Guy. You'll be fine."

"All right," she said drowsily.

Only one thing troubled Brad as he struggled to get back to sleep: the window.

He was absolutely certain he'd closed it. Abbie must have re-opened it. Maybe in her sleep (although she'd never once sleep-walked, not that he was aware) or maybe half asleep, during the initial confusion of her nightmare.

PART TWO
NOISES

CHAPTER TWENTY-THREE

Monday, October 6

CHARLIE MOONLIGHT drove straight from Chicago, stopping only for gas and coffee. It was almost midnight when he pulled into Morgantown. He was beat.

It was going on half a year since he'd been back. Six months that had taken him to Atlantic City, Vegas, Reno. Six months in which his gambling had netted him in excess of $125,000, enough to coast indefinitely, should he hoard it. He was not going to. He was going to buy his sister a new car, his nephew a new bike, his mother whatever she wanted. Most of the rest he was going to donate anonymously to a charity for orphaned Indian children.

He drove, a Hank Williams tape playing. Nothing much had changed in Morgantown. Nothing much ever did, not measured year to year. Town Hall. The school. Main Street, dead at this hour. Zeke's Hardware, owned by a childhood buddy. The *Transcript,* run by a man he didn't yet know, but whose fate would soon be intertwined with his. The Episcopal church. All of it the same.

He left downtown and headed toward Thunder Rise. Past his mother's inn, past Brad and Abbie's place, past milkweed-choked fields that lay dark and forbidding this moonless night. A quarter mile past his sister's house, he stopped his Cherokee. Someone not knowing it was there would never have spotted the wooden gate. It was covered with brambles, much more so than his last stay, and it was brown and rotted, blending easily into the surrounding woods. Charlie dug under his seat for his work gloves and stepped out. His breath came out in clouds; he guessed, accurately, that it was forty degrees. He pulled the briars off the fence and swung it open. He got back in.

The trail was barely passable. One of these years, he supposed, the undergrowth would choke it so completely that a major brush-cutting campaign would be necessary. He would barely make it this time. He drove, his four-wheel-drive bumping and rocking, the branches scraping against the cab with an uncomfortable sound like fingernails across a chalkboard.

In three minutes he was there. He killed the ignition.

The cabin was small, only three rooms and a loft. He'd built it by hand in a single frenetic week more than twenty years ago, shortly after spending his life's savings to buy 325 acres of the only material thing he believed had true value in this world—land. If Charlie Moonlight could call any place home, this building on this spread was it.

He stepped out of his truck, flashlight in hand.

The grass had grown up around the small yard, but in the light he could see it had been trampled recently. He was on guard. Once—only once, miraculously—the place had been vandalized. Completely emptied, his stock of canned goods filched, his lanterns smashed, his kerosene drained, his candles broken, his rifles and tools stolen. Of all the goods he'd so carefully stockpiled before leaving, only the woodpile had been untouched.

He checked for tire tracks. There were none. Whoever had been here this time had been on foot. He went cautiously, silently to the cabin; it was possible someone was still inside. He put his ear to the door, listening for snoring or breathing. He heard nothing, only the hoot of an owl in the distance.

There were no signs of forced entry. He fitted the key into the padlock, opened it, swung the door, and stepped inside.

It was as he had left it—meticulously clean.

But someone had been there. He knew that immediately because of the smell. The cabin did not smell mildewed, as it would have if it had been boarded since April, when he'd left. It smelled fresh and clean, like the early October night outside. And that couldn't have happened by merely opening the door. An effort had been made to air the place out.

He shone the light around. On the table was a vase of wild flowers just beginning to wilt. Next to it was a hand-lettered sign on typing paper that read: WELCOME HOME! He recognized the script as his sister's. Charlie smiled broadly. He'd given Ginny a key to the cabin, told her to use it anytime she wanted. *Thank you, Little Sis,* he thought warmly.

Charlie lit a lantern, went to the sink, pumped the water until it was clear of rust, washed his hands, and splashed it across his face. After the long drive it was cool, good, smelled purer than the stuff from truck stop bubblers. He went to the fireplace and opened the flue. He'd arranged kindling and wood in the wood stove before leaving last spring, and the fire caught with a single match. He slumped down in his favorite chair—a La-Z-Boy recliner—and lit a Marlboro.

The fire crackled cheerfully, perfuming the cabin with birch smoke. Charlie looked at the fireplace mantel, a ponderous creation he'd hand hewn from a single oak. On it was the only article anywhere in the cabin that could pass as decoration: a framed photograph of Charlie and his father when Charlie was fourteen or fifteen years old. Except for the age difference, they could have been twins. Both had long, black, braided hair and sharp, narrow eyes. Both were tall and thin. Both were unsmiling—but were not frowning either. Across each of their faces was written the look of quiet, unassuming intelligence, a look of wisdom and common sense and maturity, even in the young boy.

The power of blood, Charlie thought, and there was no small degree of pride in the thought. *No matter what else you do in this life, no matter where you go, what you profess to believe, you can't escape the power of blood.*

Yes, he was his father's son. Part-time gypsy. Full-time survivor. Like Dad, an educated man with only a high school education. A man whose soul required the outdoors.

He looked at his father, and the memories were strong, good.

George Moonlight had introduced his only son to the woods before Charlie could walk. He'd taught him to hunt, trap, fish, make squirrel stew, skin a deer, build a birchbark canoe, construct a wigwam for shelter, distinguish the edible mushrooms from the poisonous ones, start a blazing fire without matches, find his way through fifty miles of virgin forest without compass or map. He'd taught him to appreciate the sound of a mother quail protecting her babies, the rich smell of a fall day, the crispness of a winter night, the majesty of a hawk soaring across a cloudless sky, the gentle tranquillity and harmony of snow blanketing a field. He'd taught him to respect Mother Earth, drilling into his head the Quidnecks' three commandments: Take only what you need; use all that you take; leave something for tomorrow.

Like George, who had been a merchant mariner, a carpenter, a butcher, a guide, a mechanic, a farmer, a taxidermist ("jack of all trades, master of none," Mrs. Fitzpatrick still said), Charlie knew early on he would never fit comfortably into the white man's world. There could be no nine-to-five desk job with two weeks' vacation and a Rolex watch come retirement.

Charlie needed room. He needed to travel. He needed to be alone. If he'd been another race, he would have been called a free spirit. Another generation, and the word would have been "hippie."

The power of blood.

That had been George's lasting lesson. To illustrate it, to make sure he could never forget, he had told and retold the stories passed down from George's grandfather to George's father to George—told them so many times, and in such vivid detail, that Charlie still knew them by heart almost thirty years after cancer had silenced the father he so desperately loved. Tales of the proud heritage of their people, the Quidnecks, a heritage the white man's bulldozers continued to carve up and destroy in their quest for the only god developers worshiped, the almighty dollar.

There were limits. George had taught him that, too. Unlike some of his tribal brethren, who tried to turn the calendar back three centuries—a hopeless task, a pathetic one—Charlie was not totally scornful. Too many of his people had self-destructed trying to fight the tide of history—a history, granted, rife with loathsome and despicable chapters (George never let him forget how loathsome). Too many had wound up alcoholic, or destitute, or depressed, or chronically ill, with broken families and broken hearts. He himself had learned that lesson bitterly more than a decade ago, when he'd thrown himself into the land suit.

So he would not wage war. Like a scout working enemy territory, he would blend in where he could, quietly retreat when he could not. He would take the white man's dollar, and he would smile while counting his winnings. He would live in the white man's woods—especially since the suit, which had dashed all hope of a Quidneck reservation. He would have white friends if they were worthy. He would indulge himself in what he considered their civilization's greatest contribution to mankind: modern machines. He would own a truck or two, a chain saw, a snowmobile, a power auger for ice fishing, the Honda power generator he'd finally broken down and bought (it was still in the back of his truck). He would own a wide-screen TV and a remote-control VCR and a La-Z-Boy recliner. He would own them and make no apologies.

There was another factor regarding his accommodation—his treason, as some of his brethren considered it. A more important factor.

Blood was blood, and half of his had flowed from County Cork, Ireland. George had always reminded him of that: He was his mother's son, too. Mother, a full-blooded Irish Catholic. He had not embraced her religion, but he had taken to heart her philosophy of life. Mrs. Fitzpatrick believed in judging a man not for the color of his skin, but for what he was; if she hadn't believed that, she never would have married his father, a man her family considered dirt. In her blood flowed kindness and an ample love for children; that blood flowed in Charlie, too, although fate had not seen fit—yet—to send him children of his own.

He stamped out his cigarette. He was exhausted.

But he didn't relish sleep.

Since late August he'd been having dreams. Bad dreams. Long, dark dreams, like tunnels that go on and on interminably toward an unknown end.

Like his ancestors, like his father, Charlie believed that what happened in dreams was as real as what happened awake. If someone spoke to you in a dream, it was that person's way of telling you something he was thinking when awake. If an animal appeared, that animal was real. Spirits inhabited dreams, just as they inhabited the waking world. To them, both states were interchangeable. They could doom a man or help save him. They could guide a man to greatness, could steer him to great trouble.

It meant that lately, when he dreamed of a wolf, an evil wolf, Charlie didn't believe it was a symbol for some unresolved fear lurking in a shadowy corner of his mind. It meant there was a real wolf, and if there were any questions to be answered, it was why this particular wolf was interested in him, and where this wolf could be found in the waking world, and how its evil was going to manifest itself.

The last few weeks had not been happy. He'd thought coming home would change that, but it hadn't. The closer he'd driven to Morgantown, the more disturbed he'd been. He had a headache now. He sensed that whatever was causing his upset—whatever was sending the message to him—was here.

More strongly than ever, he sensed it involved his nephew.

CHAPTER TWENTY-FOUR

Friday, October 10

MAUREEN MCDONALD was appreciably worse.

She was back in Bostwick's office this morning, two weeks and two days after her last visit. Her mother was on the verge of panic. Bostwick didn't blame her. If she'd been his child, he'd have been there, too.

Because things didn't look good. Things didn't look good at all. Maureen's temperature was 103.8, and she was enveloped by a faint, sweaty odor, an odor not dissimilar to garlic—the exact same odor, Bostwick thought with a chill, that terminally ill patients get as their days are winding down. She was still congested, still occasionally experiencing sharp abdominal pains ("like a knife," she said, "stickin' in my stomach."). Every lymph node he touched was swollen and tender.

But he hadn't needed an examination to conclude there was something really frightening going on with this child. He'd sensed that the instant she'd come into his office, shuffling listlessly, her head down, her shoulders hunched, as if the world no longer held any interest for her. A little more than two weeks ago she'd been under the weather, but if you peeled back the aches and pains a bit, you could still see her spirit, alive and well. Now there was barely a hint of that spirit. Now her eyes had a lifeless, distant glaze to them, as if she'd grown tired of seeing. The eyes especially bothered him. He'd learned there was more than a grain of truth to the old adage that eyes were windows to the soul.

If it hadn't developed so quickly, he would have suspected cancer . . . or AIDS.

He hated what he had to subject her to, but there was no choice. It was time to go on a medical fishing expedition.

"Can you be in Pittsfield this afternoon?" he asked Susie when her daughter had shuffled back to the waiting room to claim the lollipop her eyes said she didn't care if she had or not.

"Yes," Susie said.

"Good. I want you at Berkshire Medical Center at one. I'll call and make the arrangements. She's going to need additional tests."

"What kind of tests?" Susie sounded as if she'd just been sentenced.

"Blood tests. X rays. Possibly a liver scan. I'll have a better idea after consulting with Dr. Miller. He's an internist at Berkshire Medical. Also a personal friend. A very capable physician."

"Doctor?"

"Yes?"

"What do you think it is?" Bostwick could tell she was close to losing control. His eyes avoided hers, and the examining room suddenly seemed too small, too quiet, too warm. He'd been here before. Oh, yes. Ordering tests for suspected leukemia cases evoked this mood. Getting positive test results back and delivering that horrible news evoked it, too.

"I don't know," he said. "And I'm being completely candid. I just don't know."

"You don't think it's a cold, do you?" Susie said, allowing herself only the faintest trace of hope. "Like a really long cold?"

"No. Not any more."

"Is it a—a virus?"

"It could be. We'll know better after this afternoon. I'm ordering her work-up stat."

Susie was silent. In the last two minutes Bostwick had seen the color drain from her cheeks. "You don't think it's—you don't think it's *cancer,* do you?" She pronounced that word superstitiously, as if saying it too loudly might jinx her.

"I'd be very surprised if it were. It's very rare that cancer—any kind of cancer—develops so quickly."

"It's been two months almost."

"And that seems like a long time—and it is, in terms of what you've been through—but disease-wise, two months is a snap of the fingers."

"Doctor?"

"Yes?"

"She's going to be all right, isn't she?"

In all his years of medicine—years in which he had had a distressing amount of practice in delivering the grimmest possible news—he'd never learned how to answer this question without feeling like the world's biggest asshole.

"I hope so," he said. "Now I want you to get going. The sooner you're there, the quicker you'll be home."

For two weeks he'd been trying to piece things together.

Something's going on. Something I've never seen in almost a decade of family practice.

That much was indisputable now. This wasn't your basic infection taking the scenic tour through the local youth, a bout of unusually stubborn rhinovirus that sooner or later would be put off the bus by said youths' immune systems. It had gone on too long. On Morgantown's scale, this was as close to a public health crisis as anything in Bostwick's experience.

Because there were too many sick kids out there. Not a townful, or a schoolful, but seventeen kids (he'd counted) with no history of chronic disease or unusual susceptibility who all of a sudden were sick as dogs. Seventeen kids, up from a dozen two weeks ago, all with a common set of symptoms, all with parents getting more uptight by the minute. Some—roughly half, Bostwick calculated—seemed to be getting progressively sicker. A smaller group appeared to be on some kind of strange disease seesaw: flat on their backs one day; chipper as you please the next. A couple, Jimmy Ellis among them, seemed to have recovered and not relapsed—if that was the word. There seemed to be no rhyme or reason.

For two weeks he'd puzzled over it, so intensely that his wife and children had started to comment. For two weeks he'd done his homework. Taken out the case folders each evening and gone over every iota of information with a magnifying glass. He'd done follow-ups on every child, which had meant house calls in a couple of instances. Maureen was the first he'd referred to Berkshire Medical. He knew she would not be the last.

It could be almost anything.

That's what was beginning to give him chills.

It could be bacterium. It could be virus. It could be some kind of obscure but cumulatively lethal poison. It could be something in the water at school. It could be something in the food. Something in the air. Something well documented in the public health texts. Something utterly unprecedented.

It could be the bloody Martians, for all he knew, dropping down to field-test their latest extraterrestrial bug on the unsuspecting inhabitants of Planet Earth.

If he'd been unable to pinpoint the cause, he'd at least uncovered some potentially valuable common denominators. All the children were prepubescent. All except for two preschoolers went to Morgantown Elementary, and both those preschoolers had older siblings who did. All lived on the same side of town, the side near Thunder Rise. There was something else, too, although he wasn't sure how much significance he should attach to it. Nightmares. Each kid had reported frequent nightmares. Probably the fevers would explain that. Kids with temps not only had nightmares but could actually hallucinate.

So could brains poisoned with certain chemicals.

"Will you call me as soon as you get the results?" Susie asked on her way out.

"Immediately," Bostwick promised.

"Thank you, Doctor."

For what? he wanted to say. *For telling you in so many words that your kid's slowly going down the tubes, and I don't have a clue why? For suggesting between the lines that if somebody doesn't come up with something soon, little Maureen McDonald could actually . . . die? And as things stand at this very moment there's not a blessed thing we can do about it?*

"You're welcome," he said, and again he had to avoid eye contact. He felt defeated.

When she had closed the door, he picked up the phone and called the Boston headquarters of the Massachusetts Department of Public Health.

"Epidemiology," he told the operator.

His question was if anything like this had been reported recently anywhere else in the state. The answer was not comforting. The answer was no.

CHAPTER TWENTY-FIVE

Friday, October 10
Evening

ABBIE WAS upstairs in her room, finally asleep. Brad and Thomasine were in the living room. In the kitchen the dishwasher clanged and gurgled as it progressed through its final wash cycle.

They were drinking wine. Earlier there'd been some enthusiasm for watching *Terms of Endearment,* the film Brad had rented, but that idea had gone by the board without a whisper of protest. The cassette was still in its case, which was still unopened on top of the

VCR. A fire burned low but hot in the fireplace. The crackle of burning wood and Brad's and Thomasine's lowered voices were the only sounds in this cavernously comfortable house.

This was the third evening Thomasine had been over for dinner. The first time she'd fabricated some excuse and left shortly after coffee and dessert. The second time, just last weekend, she'd lingered over wine—one glass only, consumed in twenty minutes—she on the couch, he in an armchair. Tonight they were together on the couch. Not touching, although only two or three inches separated them. *Just taking things as they come,* Brad thought.

What had come so far was bowling him over.

Am I falling in love?

He couldn't answer that. He wasn't sure what that meant anymore. He'd known at seventeen, of course, the first time it happened. Her name was Cissy, and just being in the same English class with her had made his whole body tingle, his tongue twist into a dry, sandpapery knot. But now, now, at age thirty-six, bearing the fresh scars of an ugly divorce, in the middle of raising a desperately loved child, swamped by the demands of a high-powered (if low-paying) career . . .

Maybe now he wouldn't know what it felt like, the crazy business of falling off the world for someone. Maybe wouldn't *let himself* know.

He wondered where Thomasine stood. Whether she was going through any of this same soul-searching about the nature and prospects of their relationship. Whether she thought she, too, might be . . . falling. She'd been at the paper a lot lately for her research, and it had been a good common ground for things to happen. And they'd been happening. There had been several lunches, three dinners, and they were getting to know each other pretty well. His divorce, for instance. She knew about that. Just as he knew bits of her past, including the most recent chapter in the romance section, a man from her stockbroker days she'd come within inches of marrying. She wasn't eager to share details, but it didn't take Sally Jessy Raphael to deduce that her relationship with a certain Paul Ingersoll had ended bitterly.

Slow but steady.

That's the ticket.

And if a snail's pace seemed out of character for Bradford Gale, hard-hitting *Transcript* editor, so what? That's how he wanted it with Thomasine. That was his speed. Because he *wasn't* seventeen anymore. No matter how attracted he was to her (and tonight, flush with wine, he was becoming downright horny), he understood his first allegiance was to Abbie. So far Thomasine had complemented that allegiance. Abbie seemed genuinely to like her, possibly was even beginning to regard her as a mother figure, but Brad knew how that could turn. How ugly and convoluted the situation could get. How quickly all three of them could be confronted with decisions none of them wanted to make.

He wanted slow but steady. He sensed Thomasine did, too.

"More wine?" he asked. He'd noticed her glass was empty.

"Sure," she said.

Brad poured. "It's a nice wine," he commented.

"Thank you."

Brad read the label: "Hawk Crest 1985. A California Cabernet Sauvignon."

"Once upon a time, I wouldn't have looked twice at an American wine," she said. "If it wasn't French, it wasn't chic."

"And what changed your mind?"

"I broke up with Paul," she stated flatly. "That opened my eyes to a lot of things, believe me, not just wine."

It was a slightly awkward moment, and Brad moved to break it by getting up and adding another log to the fire. It sent a stream of sparks up the chimney. He stood for a moment, fiddling with the poker.

That's when it hit him, standing by the fire, hit him right between the eyes: a full-blown case of a seventeen-year-old's tingles, light-headedness and all. Thomasine wasn't beautiful in a strictly classic sense, but she wasn't exactly a plain Jane either. Her hair, her eyes, her lips, the swell of her breasts under her white sweater, the fullness of her hips—it was his ideal picture of womanhood. All of a sudden she was making him crazy. He'd fantasized about her being naked, but never so vividly as now. He imagined the softness of her belly, the whiteness of the skin beneath her panties, her nipples, rose-colored and enticingly erect. He imagined the taste of her skin, the warmth, the texture, smooth and perfect as polished marble. He imagined kissing her, her breath intoxicating him, pulling him under, pulling them both under, moving them toward—

The wine was having its effect.

He returned to the couch. His hands were actually shaking.

They sat, not speaking. The awkwardness of the earlier moment had waned; in its place was a more uncertain mood. A mood equal parts anticipation, hesitation.

"Do you mind if I ask you something?" Brad said.

"Of course not."

"Would you be upset if—if I said I wanted to kiss you?"

"No," she said simply.

"I want to kiss you."

"I want to kiss you, too."

He moved toward her, closing that three-inch gap, and their bodies were in contact for the first time. Something passed between them in that instant. Call it a spark, electricity, a jolt. Call it whatever, but it was something they both felt.

His hand brushed her hair, lingered awhile, found her neck. God, it had been so long. So long. She moved closer, arranging herself beneath him. Their lips touching. The slightly sweet aftertaste of white wine. Her breath with his. Her teeth parting and his tongue encountering hers. His body supercharged. His head light. A seventeen-year-old again, goddamn and hallaluia, drowning in a comber of lust.

Hesitantly at first, then more confidently, he moved his other hand along her side, along the outside of her sweater. Up. Around to the front, to where her breast rose in a perfect arc from her chest. She was not wearing a bra. He let one finger be careless. He let it graze the bottom of her breast. He let it pass lightly over the nipple, straining through the fabric. He let it press her nipple and he waited for a response.

"Mmmm," she whispered through their kiss.

Now he felt her hand on his pants. He was hard now. They were kissing deeply now, with more and more abandon, forceful kisses, kisses that could still be tasted years and years later. He brought his hand down, slipped it under her sweater, in contact with her stomach. The skin was smooth, as he had imagined. Warm. He moved upward, toward her breast. She was inviting him. She wanted him.

"Daaaad!"

It was not a scream.

It was not loud. It was pitiful, barely audible, but the depth of Abbie's distress went through Brad like a power drill. He disengaged from Thomasine, almost hurting her, and bounded up the stairs in twos and threes.

He felt the draft before opening her door.

The window was wide open.

This time Abbie was on her bed. Her back to the headboard, clutching her pillow for protection. Her pajamas soaked from her bladder's letting go.

"Oh, Daddy . . ." she sobbed as he embraced her.

"Shhhhh."

"The d-d-dinosaur . . ."

"Shhhhh."

"It s-s-said it's going to t-t-take me."

"Shhhhh."

He smothered her, driving the badness away.

When she was calm, when she was in fresh pajamas and the sheets changed, when she'd had a drink and the window had been closed and locked, they went downstairs. Brad got her settled on the couch, covered her with a blanket, and kissed her. Thomasine kissed her, too. Abbie managed a smile. In a few minutes she was asleep.

"A nightmare," Thomasine said, concerned.

"Yes."

"About what?"

"A *Rhamphorhynchus.*"

"A ram-for-what?"

"*Rhamphorhynchus.* It's a kind of flying dinosaur. Looks like a vulture."

"Does she always have nightmares about them?"

"In the last week or two she's had a couple. I think it's got something to do with the move. Her new school. I guess her mother, too. All of it. I think it's all reached a head."

"But you've been out of New York six weeks. She's been in school almost that long, too."

"I know," Brad admitted. "I think it must be like delayed stress syndrome."

"Maybe tomorrow's weighing heavily on her."

"Maybe."

Tomorrow Abbie was leaving for New York. She was going to visit her mother for the first time since July.

"Is she worried about it?" Thomasine asked.

"No. On the contrary, she seems happy. It's all she's been talking about all week."

"That doesn't mean inside she isn't upset."

"No, it doesn't," he agreed.

Brad and Thomasine chatted awhile longer, but the steam had been taken out of the evening. Both of them felt it plainly.

Thomasine took a final sip of wine and stood.

"Well, I guess this is good night," she said, putting on her coat. Brad was not entirely sorry to see the evening end on this note. Another ten minutes, another half hour on the couch, and it would have been Big Decision time. He wasn't sure he was ready for Big Decisions like that yet. He had the suspicion Thomasine wasn't either. Maybe in another month . . . another couple of weeks. Yes, maybe then.

"Sure you have to go?" Brad said. He was not attempting to sway her. His tone reflected that.

"Unfortunately. I have an interview tomorrow. With Mrs. Fitzpatrick's son, actually."

"That's right," Brad said. "I forgot. He's half Indian, isn't he?"

"Yes. Half Quidneck. Anyway, it was a great dinner. A great evening."

"Let's do it again sometime," Brad joked.

"I'd love to."

They kissed—lightly and chastely—and then Thomasine was out the door.

CHAPTER TWENTY-SIX

Saturday, October 11
Morning

Now that the moment of truth was here, Brad wasn't sure it was such a hot idea.

Abbie taking the bus alone to New York for the Columbus Day weekend.

Even if it was nonstop.

Even if the bus driver had promised to take personal care of her.

Even if Heather had pledged to greet the bus at the Port Authority.

Even if he had asked a friend in New York to greet it, too, just in case Heather screwed up. He expected her to.

Even if Abbie was looking on it as a big adventure.

Even if living in New York had made her quite mature in certain respects, including riding buses.

But Brad had decided he couldn't deliver Abbie for every visit.

It wasn't the drive he minded or the time involved. He could always stay with friends in New York. No, it was seeing Heather. The bus seemed the solution. They had to start somewhere, and it might as well be this visit. That had been Brad's rationale, and he'd been satisfied it was the best of a bad situation.

Until now.

"You're sure you don't mind going alone?" he asked as they sat in the Albany bus station. There were ten minutes until departure.

"Sure," Abbie said cheerfully.

Brad had bought her a small suitcase, and together they'd packed it. She clutched it beside her now, along with a book bag she'd filled with her favorite Barbie dolls and My Little Ponies. Brad looked at her with her luggage, and the emotion he'd been fighting back all morning welled up within him, cutting off his breath. It was emotion he didn't have a word for: a bittersweet combination of pride, and sadness, and an underlying fear.

"You could change your mind, you know," he said shamelessly. "You could—you could go another time."

"Nah," Abbie said. "Mommy's feelings would be hurt." The innocent irony of the statement made Brad angry. *Mommy's feelings. Well, what about Abbie's feelings? What the hell about them?* It was another reminder of the sheer power of motherhood.

Brad bit his tongue. "I guess they would," he said.

"Dad?"

"Apple Guy?"

"Is it OK that I want to see Mommy?"

For the second time he clamped down on his tongue. "Of course it is. She's your mother. The only one you have."

"You don't mind?"

"Not at all." He'd file that one under the white lie category.

"Does Thomasine mind?"

"Why would that matter?"

"Well, because you like her, and you don't like Mommy too much anymore, so I thought . . . well, *I* like Thomasine, too, and I wouldn't want her to be sad."

"She won't be sad, honey," Brad said. "She wants you to do what you want to do."

"Oh, good. Because I *do* want to see Mommy. She said we're going shopping at Macy's and I can get anything I want!" She was quiet a moment. There were fewer than five minutes until departure. "Dad?" she asked.

"Yes?"

"Do you think Mommy wants to see me?"

Try answering that one with a straight face.

"I think so," Brad said. *Sure she does. This week, sure. But just wait another week. Wait till the wind changes direction and see whether she wants to see you* then.

"Good."

The loudspeaker interrupted their conversation.

"OK, Apple Guy," he said, trying to sound brave. "Time to go."

They embraced—until the driver, a friendly, portly sort who'd refused Brad's ten-dollar bill, tapped Brad on the shoulder.

"I'll miss you, Abbie."

"I'll miss you, too, Dad. Remember to feed Maria and bring her in when it gets dark. She doesn't like the dark, you know."

"I know. I love you, Abbie."

"I love you, too, Dad. Millions and millions."

"Don't forget to have your mother call the second you get off that bus."

"I won't."

"Bye!"

"Bye!"

And then she was gone.

What if I never see her again?

The thought was as terrifying as it was paranoid.

What if the bus crashes, killing everyone aboard?

What if Heather kidnaps her?

What if she's murdered?

On the drive home he cried.

CHAPTER TWENTY-SEVEN

Saturday, October 11
Afternoon

BRAD STAYED within earshot of the phone. He tried writing an editorial Dexter wanted for Monday's paper but found he couldn't concentrate. Then he tried reading, with similar results. So he did the only logical thing: He went on a tidying binge. He washed the kitchen and bathroom floors, got caught up on the laundry, cleaned out the vegetable bins in the refrigerator, ran Drano through all the drains, disinfected Maria's food and water bowls, scrubbed the mildew off the shower tiles.

But no matter how he busied himself, no matter how loud he cranked the stereo up—and he pushed it almost all the way—the house this drizzly mid-October afternoon was very large and very lonely.

By two-fifteen, five minutes after scheduled arrival time, he was worried.

By two-thirty he was absolutely convinced something had gone awry.

By two fifty-five he was contemplating calling his friend in New York.

At three-five just as he was about to dial, the phone rang.

He leaped for it.

"Hello?"

"What the hell have you been feeding this kid anyway?"

It was Heather, and she was apeshit. She sounded the way she had so many nights during the final weeks of their marriage: ready to start blowing some fuses. Brad was caught completely off guard.

"Is Abbie there?" he asked. "Is she all right?"

"She's here."

"Is she all right?"

Heather didn't reply.

"Damn it, answer me. Is she all right?"

"Why don't *you* tell *me?* She got off that bus looking like she was going to die, her face white as a sheet. And she was in tears. The bus driver said she'd gotten cramps half an hour after leaving Albany. Started moaning and clutching her stomach. Then she started crying. Cried most of the trip. That's three hours, Jack. The driver didn't know if it was her appendix or what. He said he almost pulled off the highway to a hospital. So you tell me. *Dad.* Is she all right?"

"Oh, God." *I knew it,* he thought. *I never should have let her get on that bus.* "What about now. How is she *now*?"

"She's stopped crying."

"What about her stomach?"

"She says it doesn't hurt anymore."

"Are you sure?"

"Of course I'm sure."

"Does she have a temperature?"

"No."

"Where are you calling from?"

"Mars. I'm calling from Mars, Brad. Surprisingly clear line, isn't it?"

"Don't play games with me, Heather. Where are you?"

"My place. Where the hell did you think I would be?"

"Are you going to take her to a doctor?" The venom was rising. "You'd better take her to a doctor. Take her to a doctor right away."

"On Saturday in New York? Do you know how long the wait would be? Huh! You're dreaming. You've been stuck in the boonies too long, Brad. Lucky for her Dave's here."

The name didn't register immediately. "Who the Christ is Dave?"

"The man I've been seeing, that's who," she said curtly. "He's an M.D. I told you that."

That's right. She'd told him about David Wang, a young doctor whose parents had left China in '49. Brad remembered thinking: *Poor slob, to get hooked up with Heather.*

"What's he say?"

"He seems to think it was indigestion. On top of that, she's probably coming down with a cold. Except for a few sniffles, he says she's fine now. I hope for your sake he's right."

"I want you to watch her carefully all weekend," Brad ordered.

"Thank you, Brad. Thank you very much for the advice."

"I want to be called if she gets sick again. Immediately."

"Yes, *sir.*"

"Now let me speak to Abbie. And, Heather—"

"Yes, dear?"

"Forget the bus home. I'll be picking her up."

Brad expected an argument, but there was none. Whatever points she felt compelled to score were already on the board. The bus had been a grand slam.

"Yes, dear."

"Noon. Monday. Your place. And I don't want any shit. No games. Now put my daughter on."

"*Our* daughter," she said before getting off the line. "No court in the world can change that."

There was a pause and the sounds of muffled voices. Heather had her hand over the phone. Then Abbie came on.

"Hi, Dad." She sounded tired but not gravely ill.

"Apple Guy! How are you, sweetheart? I heard it was a tough ride."

"Yeah. But I'm OK now."

"I'm sorry, hon."

"Why?"

"For putting you on the bus."

"It wasn't your fault, Dad," she said. "I just got sick, that's all. Mommy thinks it was something I ate, but I don't think so. I think maybe it was just the bus. It was awful bumpy and rocky. You know. Like one of the rides at the fair."

"The important thing is you're OK now."

"Yeah. I thought I was going to throw up, but not anymore." She paused. "Dad?"

"Yes, hon?"

"Don't worry. The bus driver took care of me. He said if I got too sick, he would take me to a hospital. Wasn't that nice?"

"It sure was. Now listen to me."

"What?"

He lowered his voice. "Do you want me to come get you? I could leave now and be there in four hours."

It would be a violation of the court order, there certainly would be a thermonuclear exchange with Heather, but he would do it. For Abbie, he would do it. Because he thought he had a pretty good idea about the origin of Abbie's sickness, just as he had a pretty good idea about the origin of her nightmares. It must be Heather.

Abbie hesitated a bit. "Nah," she said.

"You sure?"

"I'm sure."

"OK," he said reluctantly. "But guess what?"

"What?"

"I'll be getting you Monday. You won't have to take the bus home."

"Really?"

"Really!"

"Oh, goody!" she exclaimed. "Can we get an ice cream on the way?"

"Anything you want, honey," he said. "Anything at all."

CHAPTER TWENTY-EIGHT

Tuesday, October 14

BAGGY EYES. Pale skin. A slight but perceptible tic near the left corner of her mouth.

Susie McDonald looked as if she hadn't slept in a month.

That was Brad's impression, anyway, as she sat across from him in the *Transcript*'s conference room. For ten minutes she'd been describing a bout of sickness involving children at Morgantown Elementary, which her daughter attended. Now Brad had turned inquisitor.

"How many kids are we talking total?" he asked.

"At least a dozen that I know of." She cleared her throat. Her throat had needed clearing a lot the last few days.

"Not that I doubt you," Brad said, "but how did you come up with that number?"

"I've been calling mothers. Some I know. Others I heard through the grapevine. You have to understand, Mr. Gale: people are starting to talk. This isn't Albany. Word gets around pretty fast in Morgantown."

"I know."

"I forgot to mention Ginny Ellis. She gave me some names, too. She's a teacher. Lives up on the rise near me. Near you, too, as a matter of fact."

"Sure. I know her. Her son is friends with my daughter."

"Jimmy," she said thoughtfully. "He's one of the ones who's been sick, you know. On and off, like most of them."

An image of Jimmy at the county fair crossed Brad's mind, followed by a distinct memory of Ginny describing the bad stomach that had almost kept them from coming. "Nice kid," Brad remarked. "Seems pretty healthy to me."

"Now. But who knows how he'll be in another week? That's one of the things I don't get. These kids are drifting in and out of it . . . whatever *it* is. My Maureen has been like that. Sick for a while, then better, then sick again. Dr. Bostwick at first thought it was separate sicknesses. Like two colds in a row or something. You know how that happens sometimes."

"What does he think now?"

"That it's probably the same thing. That it has cycles of some kind."

Brad scribbled a few notes on his trademark yellow legal pad. There was a story here, all right. You didn't need Dan Rather to deduce that.

"You said the symptoms are similar?"

"Yes. There's a bunch of them: abdominal pain, congestion, diarrhea, nausea, fevers—especially at night. Flu symptoms."

"Except this isn't flu season."

"No. And tests don't show any flu virus. Another thing that's strange: Not everyone seems to have all the symptoms all the time. I mean, one kid will have fever without cramps, another will have only nausea, and so forth. They can change. The kid who had fevers but no cramps might develop cramps and lose the fever." She knitted her brow. "Am I making sense?" she asked.

"Perfect sense."

"Sometimes you'll even get a kid who has all the symptoms. Maureen's been like that lately. That's why we went back to Dr. Bostwick last week."

"He sent you to Berkshire Medical."

"Yes. Heaven only knows what it'll cost. X rays, blood tests, allergy tests, urine tests, another throat culture. We spent Friday afternoon there. We were back again this morning. It's beginning to feel like we live there. It's hard on Maureen. God, is it ever. On top of not feeling good, she's scared. Scared like I've never seen a kid," she said, her voice weakening.

"Do you have any results yet, Mrs. McDonald?"

"We know a few things it isn't. It isn't mononucleosis. It isn't leukemia, thank the Lord, or hepatitis, or the flu. Beyond that . . . they just can't say yet. All the tests aren't back yet."

"They can take awhile."

For the first time in the interview Susie was close to tears. "That's what's so hard. . . ." She sniffled. "Not knowing."

"I understand," Brad said softly.

He was thinking of Abbie, of course.

Had been thinking of her for an hour, since this woman had called and asked if she could come in immediately, it was that urgent.

And not because of the incident on the bus. He'd already forgotten that. He was thinking of Abbie because she went to the same school as Maureen McDonald. Breathed the same air in the same classrooms and the same halls. Drank the same water from the same bubblers, which were connected through the same mains to the same municipal wells. Ate the same snacks from the same cafeteria. Was in contact with the same children, five days a week, every week.

He remembered the mental note he'd made Abbie's first day of kindergarten. The note to have one of his reporters inquire about lead paint and asbestos that might still be lurking in Morgantown Elementary. He tended to discount asbestos; the symptoms didn't fit. Lead poisoning was something else again. If lead had found its way into food—yes, there was a chance it might be responsible. What he knew of the symptoms more or less fitted what she was describing.

"You don't think these are unrelated cases, do you, Mrs. McDonald." It was a statement.

"No." She was starting to regain her composure.

"Do you have any theory about what it might be?"

"Of course I do. It's all I've been thinking about the last month. Me and my husband. Yes, we have theories. Pick one. One day we think it's something in the water; the next day it's got to be some kind of strange new virus that some kid brought back from his summer vacation in Mexico or wherever. If my daughter had ever had a blood transfusion, I might even think it was AIDS."

"But she hasn't."

"No. There's no way it could be AIDS. I—I don't think so, anyway. Unless she found a needle we didn't know about, and—"

"I think that's absolutely impossible." Brad reassured her.

"I—I suppose you're right. It's just that . . . well, your mind gets to working and . . . you're a father. You understand."

"Of course. Have you been to the principal?"

"Yes. Last week. I had an appointment."

"And what did he say?"

"He just about laughed at me," she said, and the memory of it was making her angry all over again. "Kids are always getting sick, he said. Especially inside a school, with such close contact—kids sneezing, or wiping their noses, or horseplaying around—germs are inevitable, he said. And germs cause sickness. He spoke as if I was one of his students."

"He hadn't noticed an unusual rate of absenteeism."

"No. 'Nothing out of the ordinary,' he said. Those were his

words exactly. So I gave him the list of the names I'd made. He looked at it, counted them up, and handed it back to me. 'This all?' he said. Can you imagine it. 'This all?' I wanted to hit him. I honestly thought I was going to hit him."

"Does Dr. Bostwick know you were coming to talk to me?"

"No. Does that matter?"

"Not really. I'm not an expert on public health, but wouldn't he be the place to start? That doesn't mean we won't do a story because we certainly will. But isn't it his job to do something?"

"To a degree. He can order more tests, and he has. And he can notify the state Health Department. He did that, too, he told me. I got the impression they weren't too interested either. That's why I came to you. I thought an article might . . . you know, get them off their asses. Because I think it's a problem, a really serious problem, and not only because of Susie. I mean, these kids are still sick, and no one seems to know what the hell is causing it. I think it's spreading, and it's only a matter of time before . . ."

Her voice trailed off.

Brad stopped scribbling, stood, and looked out through the glass into the newsroom. Good. Rod was at his desk, reading the paper.

"Do you mind if I have one of my reporters talk to you? Rod Dougherty. He'll be doing the story. He's one of our best, believe me."

"Not at all."

Brad went into the newsroom. He quickly briefed Rod, then told him the story was to be his highest priority. If it took a week to do, fine. If it meant a trip to Boston, fine. Just get to the bottom of this.

"Mrs. McDonald, this is Rod Dougherty," Brad said when they returned. "Rod, Mrs. McDonald. I'll leave you two to get acquainted."

CHAPTER TWENTY-NINE

Saturday, October 18

THEY WERE IN woods a half mile from Charlie's cabin, still on his property, alongside a stream that was sufficiently clean and cold to support a healthy population of native brook trout. It was a brush-choked, trout-filled stream, the existence of which was probably known to only five or six people, including Jimmy and Charlie, whose father had first brought him here.

Charlie wasn't fishing this afternoon. He was teaching his nephew how to make a snare.

Jimmy didn't have a drop of Quidneck blood, or the blood of any other tribe, but since his infancy, his interest in the outdoors, his respect for it had rivaled Charlie's at a similar age. Charlie considered it a sign of the quality person he was surely going to be as an adult.

"Why do we want to put it here, Uncle Charlie?" Jimmy sniffled. His cold had come back about a week ago. Since then he'd been battling a runny nose.

"See these?" Charlie said, pointing to a set of small tracks that ran up to the stream and back into the forest.

"Yeah."

"These are turkey tracks. Turkeys have been drinking here."

"You mean Thanksgiving turkeys?"

Charlie chuckled. "No. Wild turkeys. After becoming almost extinct, they've come back in great numbers. But they're still very, very shy. But that doesn't mean you can't trap them. You just have to know what you're doing. Now watch."

Charlie selected a young sapling about his height. With his knife—a bowie knife with a worn scrimshaw handle, a gift so long ago from his father—he trimmed off the branches. He tested the sapling's flexibility and resistance by pulling it low to the ground. He cautioned Jimmy to stand back. He released it. It shot back into position with a fierce whistle. Perfect.

With his hatchet, he hacked two forearm-length pieces of branch from a nearby maple tree. He carefully sharpened the ends and made notches in each. A third length of maple he whittled into a stake about three feet long. He notched that, pounded it into the earth with the head of his hatchet, then arranged the two other pieces to form a triangle. That was the trigger.

All that was left was the lariat and the bait. His father had taught him to use hemp for the loop, but Charlie had discovered ordinary hardware cord was superior. He tied one end to the sapling. From his coat pocket he withdrew an ear of corn. He pierced it with the point of one arm of the trigger and attached the cord. Gently he released his hold. Snares were delicate, tricky affairs; if you weren't careful, you could be snatched up yourself. This was an expert job.

It had been a year since he'd made a snare, and he was pleased to see he hadn't lost his touch.

"There," Charlie announced, pleased. "We come back tomorrow, and dinner will be waiting. Wild turkey is very good, you know. Roasted on a spit over a slow fire. You eat it like chicken, but it tastes much better."

Jimmy didn't respond.

Over the last half hour he seemed to have become increasingly uninterested. It wasn't like him. Jimmy had always been fascinated by anything Charlie showed him in the woods. He was preoccupied now, but not with the snare. Since that day he'd been playing Rambo . . . had seen the *wolf* . . . Jimmy had not set foot in the woods. Any woods, a fact he wasn't about to admit to his uncle.

Jimmy was remembering that terrible day now. The memory was vivid, too vivid. It was as if it could happen all over again, somehow *had to* happen all over again.

Out of sight a squirrel suddenly chattered.

Jimmy started, looking wildly around, his eyes wide, his mouth open. Charlie could sense his fear.

"W-what was t-that?"

"A squirrel," Charlie explained. "That's the way they usually sound. Angry. Except for jays, they're the angriest animals in the forest."

"Are you . . . sure?"

"Sure I'm sure." He looked his nephew in the eye. Jimmy looked down. "Jimmy?"

"Yes?" he said timidly.

"Is something wrong?"

"No. I just thought it was—"

"You can level with me, you know. Brothers can always level with brothers and know it won't go any farther."

"I just thought it was a—a *squirrel.* Honest."

Charlie placed his hands on Jimmy's shoulders. Jimmy tried to squirm away, but Charlie wouldn't let him. "You can't fool your uncle Charlie," he said firmly. "You didn't think that was a squirrel. I know it, and you know it. Now are you sure you don't want to talk about it?"

"Well . . ."

"Is it wolves?"

"Yes," Jimmy admitted. "I'm afraid of the wolf."

"But there aren't any wolves," Charlie said, "as I've told you.

There haven't been wolves here for hundreds of years. Since the English came and chased them away. Like I've told you, you have to go a thousand miles to find a wolf. Unless it's in a zoo, and there aren't even any zoos around here."

"I know, but . . . the wolf . . . it came back. Last night."

And with that he burst into tears.

Charlie was surprised. Since coming East, he'd seen his sister and her son on several occasions. The nightmares Jimmy had been experiencing in August had ended, and there had been only passing references to the wolf—usually when Ginny wasn't listening and always with the beaming pride of a child who knows he's conquered another of his fears. The wolf simply wasn't an issue any longer; Jimmy, in fact, had forgotten Charlie's promise by phone from Reno to chase it away. And although Charlie's own dreams continued to feature a wolf, he'd almost come to believe it had nothing to do with Jimmy.

"Is it the same wolf?" Charlie asked gently when Jimmy's tears had subsided.

"Yes."

"It was in your room?"

"Yes. It talked again. It said it didn't forget me."

"Then what did it do?"

"It went away again."

"Did you tell your mother?"

"Unh-unh. She doesn't believe me. Do you believe me, Uncle Charlie?"

"Of course, I believe you, pardner."

"Can you make it go away, Uncle Charlie? Please? Can you make it go away so it never comes back again?"

"Sure I can," he said. "No problem. I can take care of it."

It was precisely then, as the words were leaving his mouth, that a blast of wind swept across the tops of the trees, bending them, rattling their leafless branches, producing a moaning sound that reached down into Charlie's bones. The ground shook.

Hobbamock.

The word pierced his consciousness like a sharpened stake.

Hobbamock. Quidneck for the cold northeast wind, the wind that brought the dreaded storms Yankees called nor'easters.

Quidneck, too, for "Great Evil Spirit."

Over their heads the wind intensified. It was suddenly, inexplicably cold, an early blast of winter. Down through the trees it penetrated, deeper, stronger, until it was whipping Charlie's and Jimmy's hair, raising the blood in their cheeks, stinging their eyes. Jimmy clung fiercely to Charlie's legs. Jimmy was crying again. Louder than before. Sunset was a good three hours away, but the woods suddenly were dark, as if a total eclipse were beginning.

With a whipping sound, the sapling snapped erect, closing the snare around an invisible prey.

"Oooooh . . ." Jimmy blabbered.

"Come on," his uncle ordered, forcing calm into his voice. "It's just rain coming, that's all. If we hurry, we might beat it."

He didn't believe it was rain coming. He believed it was Hobbamock.

CHAPTER THIRTY

Wednesday, October 22

AT 1:10 P.M. on Wednesday, October 22, Dr. Henry R. Hough, an epidemiologist from the state Health Department, stepped out of his Toyota Celica and walked briskly into Morgantown Elementary's principal's office. In his briefcase he carried a clipping that had reached his Boston office by express mail.

Rod Dougherty's story had not solved the mystery of what was making so many kids sick, but it had painted in no uncertain strokes a picture with something very wrong in it.

It was the kind of story Brad liked to call an ass kicker:

"MYSTERY DISEASE" WORRIES PARENTS, PROMPTS OFFICIALS TO SEEK STATE HELP

BY RODNEY DOUGHERTY
Staff Writer

MORGANTOWN, Oct. 20—Town and school officials admit they are concerned by a rash of sickness that has hit children at Morgantown Elementary hard this fall. The illness—which causes cramps, vomiting and diarrhea, among other symptoms—is of unknown cause.

Officials say they plan to ask the assistance of the state

Health Department, which has the necessary expertise for an investigation.

"At first we thought we were dealing with some kind of very early flu," said Dorothy Garland, school nurse and also a member of the Morgantown Board of Health, "but now we're not so sure."

"It's a mystery disease and I'm scared," said Susie McDonald, whose daughter, Maureen, a kindergarten student, has been sick on and off since August.

"I want answers, and I want them now," added an angry Justin McLaughlin, father of a second-grade boy who has missed an entire week of school and who remained sick this morning.

Principal Anthony Mancuso said he shares the concerns of parents and will "do what it takes" to get answers.

But early last week, at the start of a special *Transcript* investigation into reports of the sickness, Mancuso repeatedly insisted the school has not had an unusually high absenteeism rate this year. He said the local Health Board, which monitors school illnesses, was likewise unconcerned.

When presented with a list of 16 names of children who have been sick or who continue to be sick, Mancuso continued to maintain that strictly in terms of numbers, the number of children who have been out sick for one or more days this fall is not unusual.

He conceded, however, that the unknown nature of the illness is reason for concern. Joe Rizzi, a spokesman for the Health Board, designed primarily to be a record-keeping and monitoring body, not an agency equipped to solve medical mysteries, agreed.

"I don't mean to downplay parents' fears, but I sincerely doubt we're dealing with any truly life-threatening disease," Mancuso said. But he added: "The fact that we don't know—yet—what is causing this 'bug' certainly means we have to pay attention to this. And I assure you, we are."

Officials with the state Health Department said they were unfamiliar with any outbreak of unusual illness anywhere in western Massachusetts. They had no further comment.

Mrs. McDonald and other parents say they are worried that some agent in the school's water, hot lunch program, or heating and ventilation system might be responsible. Attempts to determine if asbestos or lead paint was used in construction of the building so far have been unsuccessful.

Nurse Garland cautioned, however, that it would be premature to say that the cause is something found at the school.

"These children all attend the same school, true," she said, "but they also live in the same town, ride the same buses, play in the same playgrounds, and probably eat the same food bought at the same one or two stores. It could be almost anything."

Still, she noted: "Morgantown Elementary is as good a place as any to start" looking for the cause.

Dr. Mark Bostwick, a general practitioner who has treated several of the sick children—many of whom he has referred to Pittsfield's Berkshire Medical Center for tests that so far have been inconclusive—said it would be impossible at this stage to pinpoint the location of the agent.

"It would appear from my records that most of these kids live on the same side of town, out toward the rise," he noted, "but that's a very preliminary observation. That could be strictly coincidence. I would say the school is a better shot as a common factor."

Bostwick said he would welcome the involvement of the Health Department. "This could be a virus, a bacterium, or some kind of poison," he said. "The Health Department has the knowledge to deal with any of those."

Dr. Hough, the state epidemiologist, met for two hours with Mancuso, members of the Morgantown Board of Health, and Dr. Bostwick. No parents were invited; none attended. Rod Dougherty was barred from the meeting, but he got a general outline of what had transpired in an interview later with Mancuso. It was sufficient for the lead story in Thursday's paper.

During his two hours in Morgantown, Hough made copies of all available records. He told Bostwick to send any test results from Berkshire Medical to him by express mail. He asked a battery of questions, using a tape recorder and an epidemiological questionnaire to record the answers. After suggesting the school board ap-prove money for asbestos, lead, and water testing, he toured the school, stopping briefly in the cafeteria, rest rooms, boiler room, and nurse's office. He shook hands heartily and promised to be in touch within a week.

Then he left, unconvinced that what was going on in Morgantown Massachusetts was anything worse than a comparatively obscure but ultimately harmless virus making the rounds. A virus that, sooner or later, would be defeated by that mightiest—and cheapest—of disease fighters, the body's immune system.

CHAPTER THIRTY-ONE

Thursday, October 30

ABBIE DIDN'T know what to make of this man Thomasine had convinced Brad to invite over for dinner. She spent most of the meal being alternately awed and itchingly curious.

He was a real live Indian. On that point Thomasine had been emphatic. But except for his long, dark, braided hair (which unquestionably was an Indian touch), Charlie Moonlight didn't look like any pictures she'd ever seen, and during the Indian phase that had preceded dinosaurs more than a year ago, Brad had buried her in books about Native Americans. He didn't wear a loincloth or a deerskin coat; he was dressed in jeans and a flannel shirt. And he wore a watch. A digital watch, the same kind Daddy wore.

Then, again, he did have that name. Who had ever heard of anyone having Moonlight for a last name? Only Indians named themselves after animals and the weather, nature stuff like that. Indians were very clever that way. Much more so than other people, who had last names that didn't mean much of anything. Still, he didn't speak in a funny accent (in fact, his English was as good as Daddy's!). He didn't eat Daddy's roast beef with his fingers. He didn't smoke a peace pipe after dinner. But he did live in the woods, and he did say he liked to hunt. During the meal he'd held her spellbound with the story of the time he'd tamed a wild raccoon, getting it to the point where it would perch on his shoulder and eat corn out of his hand.

To make it even more confusing, he was Jimmy Ellis's uncle. Jimmy and Abbie had become great friends, and she knew for sure *he* wasn't Indian.

"Do you wear feathers?" Abbie burst out when Thomasine and Brad had retreated to the kitchen to scrub plates from the main course. All evening she'd been battling to keep that question in. Despite Brad's predinner admonition to "be polite, I'm sure he won't appreciate some nosy kid's questions about Indians," she could contain it no more.

Charlie laughed—a hearty, benevolent laugh. "Sure I wear feathers," he said. "Sometimes."

Abbie's face lit up—from pleasure, not surprise. Real Indians *had* to wear feathers, at least every once in a while. "When do you wear them?" she asked.

"Oh, at ceremonies sometimes. Indians have powwows every year, usually in summer. Once in a while I go. That's when I might wear a feather headdress, during the dances. Indians love to dance."

Abbie could just picture it, a band of war-painted, feathered Indians circling a totem pole under the stars and moon, whooping and waving tomahawks and beating on their tomtoms. She'd have to get her father to take her to a powwow.

"Wow" was all she could say.

"Oh, yes. Indians like to be happy. You wouldn't know that from a John Wayne movie, but it's true. They like to dance, sing, sit around a fire and exchange stories, feast. At the Wampanoags' powwow, in Mashpee, a town on Cape Cod, they always have a giant clambake. Of course, it's not all fun. Sometimes we're serious. Sometimes we communicate with the spirits."

"*Spirits?*" Abbie asked, absolutely breathless. "Are they like ghosts?"

"Something like ghosts." He chuckled. "Talking to them is like doing magic."

"Can *you* do magic?" Thomasine hadn't mentioned anything about magic.

"Well . . . "

"Could you do any magic now?" The excitement meter was into the red zone.

"Don't pester Mr. Moonlight," Brad said sternly. He was back in the dining room.

"She's not pestering me," Charlie cut in. "She wants to know if I can do magic. That's all."

"Yeah, that's all," Abbie said triumphantly. "I just want to know if he can do magic."

"I don't know if you would really call it magic or not, but . . . sometimes I can guess things I don't already know."

"Really?"

"Yup."

"Could you do it for me?"

"Well . . ."

"Pretty please? With sugar on it?"

"Well, I suppose I could try." It was at times like these that Charlie remembered how soft the spot was he had for kids.

"Let's see," he said, his brow furrowing in deep concentration. "You—you have a special nickname, right?"

"Right."

"And your . . . daddy calls you by it mostly, right?"

"Right." Abbie thought she would explode, the excitement was that strong. This was so much better than that magician guy she'd seen on TV, Doug Henning. Because Charlie was *here,* here in the room with her. It was like her own private magic show. Maybe next trick he could produce a rabbit.

"And it's a special name. A very special name."

"Yes."

So far Brad wasn't impressed. Thomasine, who'd joined Brad by the table, was not so skeptical.

"Is it . . . Poopsie?"

"Noooo! That's silly."

Charlie was struggling. It was rare that he could get plugged in on demand, but it had happened. Usually, when he was eager to gamble, he would wait in the shadows of a casino until he felt it happening spontaneously, then move quickly to the tables. But there had been times—he could count them on one hand—he'd been able to move the mental levers, and it had happened.

Suddenly the first ghosts of an image, like a photograph materializing in the developing tray or a dealer's hand coming up even as that dealer was telling him to bet or hold.

It was an apple.

The image of a red delicious apple, big and juicy and ripe.

It was followed, suddenly—almost painfully—by another image. The image of a man. An odd little man, featureless.

"How about . . . Apple?"

"Yes!"

"Apple *Man*?"

"Almost!"

"Apple *Guy*?"

"Wow-wee!" Abbie said, her excitement bursting around her. "It is! It's Apple Guy! How'd you guess?"

How did he? Brad wondered. *Thomasine must have told him, that's how.*

"Well, like I told you, sometimes I can do magic."

They finished the wine (Charlie did not drink), had dessert; then Brad parked Abbie in front of the TV while the three adults talked.

Brad was getting to like Charlie. Perhaps "like" wasn't exactly the right word. There was something intangible about him that made Brad uncomfortable; he couldn't put his finger on what, exactly. But like Abbie, he was fascinated by this man who so proudly proclaimed his Quidneck ancestry, even if 50 percent of his genes had been imported from Ireland. Thomasine had predicted Brad would be interested. She ought to know. Charlie was the first genuinely cooperative subject she'd found for her thesis—he'd been one of the leaders of the ill-fated land claim—and they'd spent much of the last two weeks in interviews. Already she had six ninety-minute tapes filled, with more ground still to cover. Thomasine had found him to be intelligent, articulate, likable, if highly opinionated and strong-willed. It was a wonder, Thomasine thought, that the tribe had lost the suit with someone like him to lead. It spoke volumes about the Indian's predicament in the white man's world.

As did Brad's ignorance.

Brad had never met a Native American before. In his work he had interviewed Shiite Muslims, Israeli soldiers, an astronaut, a President, several senators, an even greater number of representatives, stars of stage and screen, Bruce Springsteen, mobsters, a hairless woman dying of radiation sickness, the editor of *Pravda,* Oral Roberts, the half of a pair of Siamese twins who had survived a botched separation, a Colombian cocaine king, Saudi Arabian oil ministers—but never an American Indian, *only the people who owned the entire goddamn country once upon a time.* It was an embarrassing cultural void, Brad realized, sitting here in Charlie's company. And it put Thomasine's research into a whole new light. *They really have been made into ghosts,* he thought. *Ghosts in their own land.*

"OK, Apple Guy," Brad said when her tape was over. "Time for bed."

"Can I sleep in your bed?" she begged.

"No," he said firmly.

"Oh, please? Please-oh-please-oh-please."

"Well . . ."

"Thanks, Dad."

"Just one more night," Brad said, trying to put some authority into his voice.

"I can just see it when she's sixteen and wants the keys to the car." Thomasine chided him. "Any bets on how the old marshmallow here will respond?"

Brad shot her a dirty look, but it was in jest. "Come on, Apple Guy," he said, patting Abbie's bottom and heading her toward the staircase. "Say good night to everyone."

"Good night, Thomasine. Good night, Charlie."

"Good night, Abbie," the guests said together.

Brad and Abbie went up the stairs. A few minutes later Brad descended alone.

"She's been having nightmares lately," Brad explained to Charlie. "I've been letting her sleep in my bed."

"Nightmares?" Charlie repeated.

"Nightmares. On and off for a couple of weeks now."

"Tell me about them," Charlie said.

"Just ordinary kids' nightmares, that's all," Brad answered, uncertain why his guest would be so interested.

"About a wolf?"

"No. A dinosaur." Brad was becoming irked. There was something accusatory in Charlie's voice.

"Any particular kind?"

"Yes. A flying dinosaur. A *Rhamphorhynchus,* to be precise."

"What does it look like?"

"An oversize vulture, is as near as I could describe it. Why?"

"Just curious."

"Nightmares are pretty common with kids that age." Brad said, launching into his mini-discourse on Childhood Fears and Their Subconscious Manifestation. He wasn't about to tell this stranger what he believed the real cause of Abbie's sleep disturbances was: Heather. "Kids are full of fears, which find their subconscious expression in bad dreams. It's actually a healthy process, from what little I've read. Sort of the mind's pressure-relief valve. Harmless, if momentarily scary."

"That's one explanation," Charlie said.

"And what's another explanation?" Brad shot back, more angrily than he intended. He wasn't sure he wanted Charlie to answer. Was it possible he'd found out about Heather, the way he'd found Abbie's nickname?

"Sometimes dreams have greater meaning," Charlie said. "Meaning that we may not at first understand, may never understand, especially if we don't *try* to understand. And not everyone wants to try. I think Thomasine, whose work in anthropology has opened her mind to how other races and peoples see dreams, would have to agree."

"I would," she said. She thought of *Primitive Culture,* the 1871 book by Edward B. Tylor, one of the great classics in the field. Dreams and visions were eloquently, if chauvinistically, discussed in it.

"Sometimes dreams can be warnings," Charlie went on. "Sometimes dreams can be real events that we may misinterpret as wanderings of the sleeping mind. Adults especially may be prone to that mistake."

Since Jimmy's snare lesson, Charlie had been preoccupied with an old story his father had told him. He couldn't seem to get it out of his mind. (And yet it was nothing like the obsession it would soon become.)

"Let me give you an example," Charlie continued. "There's an old legend that many years ago, before the white man came—at a time when only Quidnecks and Mahicans and Pocumtucs walked these woods—the children of a certain Quidneck village began to be sick. By day they were fevered and complained of aches and chills. Sleep brought no relief; at night, they said, they were visited by spirits that took the form of bears, wolves, giant vultures, flying snakes. Their natural interest in the woods vanished, and they became tired and listless, preferring instead to remain by the village fires, or the corn patches, or in their wigwams and longhouses.

"At first the mothers thought little of it. They knew that children are always getting sick, just as they are always getting better again very quickly. The natural order of things. But these children did not get better, and when, after days and days, when the children were so sick the mothers began to fear they would die if something were not done, they called in the village powwow."

Brad had heard the term, but only in the context of annual gatherings of Indians—what he considered tourist attractions. The kind of event he'd been telling Abbie about.

"Not that," Charlie said, as if he'd been able to reach into Brad's mind again and pluck the thought lying on the surface. Unconsciously Brad swallowed. "I mean what you would call a medicine man or a priest."

"Shaman, to an anthropologist," Thomasine added.

"Correct. The powwow examined the children, and he spent nights with them in their wigwams, days with them by their mothers' sides. He listened to them tell of their dreams. He took notice of other omens. The weather, which had turned sour, destroying crops. Animals acting strangely. Finally, he withdrew into the mountains to ponder what he had seen. While he was gone, the earth shook and the clouds opened and the thunder came. All of the children of the village—there must have been twenty-five or thirty—were sick, and none was getting better. The whole village was frightened. By now it was very clear that some terrible evil spirit was at work.

"The powwow emerged two days later, very shaken and upset. During his time on the mountain—the mountain we today call Thunder Rise—he had seen both Cautantowwit, the Great God of Good, and Hobbamock, the Great Evil Spirit. It was Hobbamock, and spirits under Hobbamock's control, that were making the children so sick. And it was those spirits taking the forms of wolves and flying serpents that were visiting the children at night. The powwow did not see them—they showed themselves only to children—but he sensed their presence. That's what reminded me of this whole tale, the fact that they were not nightmares, but actual spirits."

"So what did they do?" Thomasine asked. She was fascinated by Charlie's tale. At Brown she had read similar tales of illness among the New England Indians, who, on the whole, were rarely sick. Until the English arrived, that is. The English brought smallpox, measles, diphtheria, other new diseases against which the Indians had very little natural resistance. Some whole tribes had been wiped out; others were nearly destroyed. It was during this period, the 1600's, that a whole new body of Indian legends had arisen, including, she suspected, the one Charlie was relating.

"From what the powwow had seen and heard"—Charlie picked up the story—"it was obvious that the 'sickness' was a threat to the whole tribe, not just that one village closest to the mountain where Hobbamock had his home. The chief sachem called a meeting of the tribal council, and it was decided that there was no choice: The evil spirit must be fought, and he must be defeated, or soon all the children would die. Cautantowwit himself pledged to join in battle. So they gathered the warriors, and they armed themselves with spears and hatchets and bows and arrows, and one day, one thousand strong, they marched to the top of the mountain.

"The battle went on for two weeks, day and night. Hobbamock was very cunning, and his spirits were very fearsome, and hundreds of warriors were lost, despite the intervention of Cautantowwit. As far away as the ocean the screams of the confrontation could be heard. But in the end Hobbamock was driven back underground, into the cave where he lived, and the entrance to the cave was sealed with rocks, too many for even the god—a badly wounded god now—to move. Hobbamock could not be killed, but he could be injured, and he could be weakened, and ultimately he could be contained."

"And the children recovered," Brad said.

"The children recovered. Hobbamock, being immortal, lived. Legend has it that it is he, still feeling his wounds, still trapped inside his cave, who is sometimes heard as low thunder."

"The noises," Thomasine said. "One of Brad's reporters wrote a story about them in the *Transcript.*"

"According to the legend," Charlie said, "Hobbamock can never forget his defeat, no matter how much time goes by. He is angry, and he is eager for another chance in battle. He is eager for more children, who give him strength. But my people never gave him that chance. The memory of that dreadful fight lingered in their minds. That is the reason they would never enter any of the caves on Thunder Rise."

"Well, it's an interesting legend, Charlie," Brad said. "As Thomasine mentioned, we had a story awhile back about the noises, and we mentioned something about an old Indian legend in it. Too bad my reporter didn't talk to you. He could have fleshed that part of the story out a little. It was pretty sketchy in spots."

Brad wondered if actually Charlie believed any of what he had said or considered it folklore. As Brad did.

There was no answer in Charlie's silence.

After Charlie was gone, Brad and Thomasine made love for the first time.

"Would you like to stay the night?" Brad asked simply.

"Yes" was Thomasine's equally simple answer.

Arms around each other, carrying half a bottle of wine, they went upstairs to Brad's room. Brad moved Abbie to her own bed and returned to Thomasine. They fell on his bed, tangled in embrace, lost in deep kisses.

CHAPTER THIRTY-TWO

Friday, October 31
Halloween

DESPITE HERSELF, Thomasine giggled the next day when she saw his cabin. When it was seen through her eyes, Charlie had to agree, there *were* comical elements.

"Eclectic," Thomasine pronounced when she'd finished laughing.

"That's not the word you were really thinking," he said good-naturedly.

But it really was.

How else to describe the disparate elements of his environment? The collision of old and new, synthetic and natural, traditional Quidneck and contemporary American? What else but eclectic? What a wealth of detail for her thesis. There was a book in Charlie Moonlight, a book that would not only educate but entertain. *Yes,* she thought, thrilled once again at having discovered him. *A more valuable subject you'd be hard pressed to find.*

Next to the wood stove there was a twenty-five-inch floor-model color TV. On top of the TV, a videocassette recorder and a library of early Woody Allen films, which were next to a pile of books on Indian culture. In the kitchen, cabinets full of canned goods, over a counter with fresh vegetables and three skinned rabbits, which he would soon make into stew. Outside the front door, his Honda generator, whose cord ran through the kitchen, past the sink and the old-fashioned handle pump, and into the living room. In the living room, a Naugahyde reclining chair, surrounded by birchwood chairs he had built.

"Who's this?" Thomasine said, examining the only photograph, a picture of a boy—obviously the young Charlie—and an older man.

"Can't you tell?"

"Your father?"

"Yes. He's been dead a long time."

Thomasine picked up the photo for a closer look. "You look happy. Both of you."

"We were," Charlie said respectfully. "I loved the man. He was good, strong, gentle. He respected nature. He loved his wife and his son with all his heart. You can't ask for more."

"No, you can't," Thomasine agreed.

She replaced the photograph on the mantel. For some reason, hearing Charlie mention his father had reminded her of the dinner at Brad's.

"That was a pretty intriguing story you told last night," she said. "About the legend of Thunder Rise and the Great Evil Spirit."

"Intriguing?"

"I mean, it's a marvelous legend. It shows a lot of imagination. There certainly were easier ways to explain the noises in Thunder Rise. I mean, look what the white settlers decided they were: thunder. You Quidnecks came up with an evil god trapped inside a cave after a gargantuan battle. It's, well, highly creative."

Charlie didn't respond. Thomasine was learning not to take offense at his silences. He wasn't brooding, he'd let her know early on. Wasn't offended, wasn't trying to insult or put off. His silences meant he was thinking.

"You think it's more than a story, don't you?" she finally said. "More than a folktale."

Charlie sidestepped the question. "Stories about Hobbamock have been with the tribe for centuries," he answered. "This is but one of many."

"And you've told me a couple of the others." Thomasine persisted. "None with the conviction of last night. Hearing about Abbie's nightmares really bothered you. I could tell."

Charlie wondered if Thomasine knew Abbie wasn't the only child in Morgantown who had been having nightmares the last several weeks. And he didn't just mean Jimmy. Ginny had told him that several of her students had been experiencing recurring bad dreams, apparently quite vivid and forceful. Bad dreams, their parents had related, with common animal themes. Bears . . . wolves . . . snakes . . . a flying creature some said was a dinosaur, others said was a vulture, almost never seen in the Northeast anymore. Dreams that sounded disturbingly similar to Charlie's own. No one, not the doctors, not the parents, not Ginny, not Brad or Thomasine last night, appeared to have drawn a strong connection between the nightmares and the sickness . . . and maybe there wasn't a strong connection. Maybe it was too incredibly farfetched.

Probably it was.

"I've been having dreams of my own," Charlie stated.

"Nightmares?"

"You would call them that. I would say I have been visited by spirits."

"What kinds of spirits?"

"I don't know. Dark spirits. Animals."

"Are they evil?"

He hesitated before saying: "Yes."

"Does that worry you?" She was trying to draw him out.

"It doesn't leave me happy. Would it you?"

Charlie lit up a Marlboro and drew deeply into his lungs. It was a curious relationship that was developing between him and Thomasine. The woman was a stranger—funny, well spoken, smart as a whip, but still a stranger. She claimed to be a scholar, a breed of people he'd always distrusted for their arrogance and contempt. It would have been easy to dismiss her as someone who had tiptoed down from her ivory tower to mingle momentarily with the savages. Someone who soon enough would retreat back to academia, where, over cocktails, or an afternoon tea, she could regale her upper-crust friends with amusing tales of the tall half Indian with the funny habits and the long ponytail.

But Charlie had always trusted his instincts, been a good judge of character. And he liked this woman with the brown hair and excitable eyes. He'd liked her within five minutes of meeting her; that was why he had agreed to be her subject. There was a bonus. She seemed to have genuine empathy for the modern Indian's plight. Seemed to *believe* in the virtue of the old ways, even if recognizing, as did he, the impracticality of many of them today. It seemed more than academic onanism, this thesis of hers. More than once he'd insisted she had to have Indian blood. She swore she didn't.

"Could Hobbamock return?" Thomasine asked. "I mean, could he get out of his cave?"

"No. At least I never heard he could. Not on his own. But he could be let out. Someone could release him—intentionally or by accident. It happened once, my father said. Lucky for the tribe, he was returned."

"Do you think he's out now? Is that what you're leading up to?"

"I don't know." It was a truthful answer. It seemed he didn't know a lot lately.

"But you believe in Hobbamock?"

"Yes."

"And you believe he's behind the sickness?"

"I—I can't answer that. I'm inclined to, I suppose, yes."

"You know about the noises being louder than usual this summer and fall, of course."

"Yes. I've heard them myself, here in this cabin. As recently as last week."

"And you know about the children being sick."

"My nephew's one of them."

"Abbie's nightmares would fit into the legend, wouldn't they?"

"Yes. Jimmy's, too. He sees a wolf. And there are other children who've been having nightmares, if that's the right word—how many, I don't have any idea. Ginny says there's been talk about them at school. Of course, the dreams have been overshadowed by the sickness. I would expect that. Quidneck beliefs aren't on the curriculum, last I checked," he said.

"Do any of these people know of the legend?"

"I don't think so."

"Ginny?"

"No. The old stories have pretty much died away. You know that."

Outside darkness was gathering. In town the children would soon be trick-or-treating. They would have to dress warmly, Charlie thought. The afternoon high had only been about forty, and now the temperature was approaching freezing. When he came home, the air had had the certain feel of snow. Before the clouds had obscured it completely, he'd seen a ring around the moon.

Charlie stoked the wood stove, sending a blizzard of sparks up the chimney. Ordinarily it was the kind of evening he would have felt at peace. Ordinarily he would have stoked the fire, sat by it, and either read or watched one of his movies as he drifted off to sleep. But sleep would be difficult tonight, he knew, and when it came, it would be tortured.

"He doesn't put much stock in such beliefs, does he?" Charlie said.

"Who?"

"Your friend."

"Brad has a more clinical mind," she said, not disparagingly. "I think it comes from being in journalism so long. There's very little room for gray; it's mostly blacks and whites."

She remembered how Brad had politely dismissed Charlie's story after the Indian had left. Charlie was right: Brad did put very little stock in Indian legends or any other kind of legend. "Very interesting," he'd said, careful not to mention how unnerving Charlie's "guess" about Abbie's nickname had been.

Thomasine hadn't exactly embraced the legend of Thunder Rise, either. If an anthropologist swallowed every story she came across, the contradictions would mount until ultimately she would be left with nothing to credit. Still, she had a rule of always keeping her mind open. Her professors had taught her that there was usually a kernel of truth in even the most bizarre legend or myth, not to mention the possible insights into the culture that had spawned them. Unlike Brad, who put his money on technology and science, Thomasine believed that man did not have all the answers. Likely never would.

"That's why I left so much out," Charlie said. "Because of Brad."

"What did you leave out?"

Charlie's eyes roamed around the room, as if what he were about to say were hidden up there on a wall. "The part about the souls," he said.

"What souls?" She was mystified.

"The children's. According to the legend, Hobbamock stole them. *Collected* them, to be more correct, the way one might collect seashells or pretty rocks. That's what caused the sickness—his theft of souls. That's what killed the children before we were victorious on Thunder Rise. Slowly, bit by bit, day by day, he separated their souls from them."

Thomasine had read of such beliefs—among other places, in a tribe tucked away in a remote corner of the Amazon rain forest. But as far as she knew, the concept of soul theft was rare and even more rarely documented. Which made it all the more interesting.

"But why torture them so?" she asked. "Why not trick the children? Bribe them somehow, like the Pied Piper of Hamelin?"

"Because he derives great pleasure from making them sick. This is an evil god, Thomasine. Vile. The closest thing Christianity has to him is Satan."

"Did Hobbamock steal adult souls, too?"

"No," Charlie said firmly.

"Why not?"

"Who would want them? The innocence is gone. A grown-up soul is a hardened thing, damaged goods. But children . . . the souls of children are still pure. Still sparkling clean and virtuous—Abbie or my Jimmy, for example. If you wanted to, you could look at it like honeybees, seeking nectar. Instinctively Hobbamock knows to pass by the dried-up flower in favor of the fresh bloom.

"Perhaps in time, having exhausted the children within his reach—the children around Thunder Rise—he might turn to adults. Or perhaps he'd extend past Thunder Rise for more children. There's a world of children. Having consumed what was at his doorstep, he might go in search of others. Might leave Thunder Rise and go on some kind of world hunt. I don't know. I have no idea of his appetite or the limits of his powers. I don't know they've ever been tested. He has never been allowed to get that far."

"But you believe he is gaining strength."

"Yes."

"With every soul he takes," Thomasine ventured.

"Exactly. Like an animal feeding. Like—like a bear in March, breaking its hibernation. Yes," he said solemnly, "I think I believe that. And I think I believe there would come a point where it would be extraordinarily difficult—I hesitate to say impossible—to stop him."

"What point is that?"

"I have no idea."

The conversation changed soon after that. But the echo of it lingered while Charlie made a quick rabbit stew, and the two of them prepared to eat.

"I want to be an Indian," Abbie announced as the last light of the day drained from the sky over Thunder Rise.

"But I thought you were going to be a ballerina," said Brad, who'd scrounged the necessary ingredients of the costume from Mrs. Fitzpatrick when he'd picked up Abbie on the way home from work.

"Yeah, but I changed my mind," Abbie said. "Can't I, Daddy? *Please*?"

"But we don't have the right costume."

"We can *make* it, silly. Mrs. Fitzpatrick taught me how to cut feathers from construction paper. They look real neat."

"What about the rest of it?"

"You use finger paints on your face. A skirt for the skirt, which is supposed to be from a deer. And black knee socks for the leggings. That's what girl Indians put on their legs. And, oh—my old slippers look just like moccasins."

"Has Mrs. F. been talking to you about the Quidnecks again?"

"Yup. Plus Charlie, last night. Remember?"

"OK. I give in." He looked at the kitchen clock. "But let's get a move on. It's almost six-thirty."

"Thank you, Daddy."

They drove—there was no other way to trick-or-treat in their neck of the woods, Brad had been advised—but by eight o'clock they'd still only managed to make a dozen stops, including the Ellises, the McDonalds, Thomasine, and Mrs. Fitzpatrick.

"You look like a real Indian," said Dexter, opening his door and depositing a fistful of Milky Ways into her shopping bag. The publisher was their last stop.

"Thanks." Abbie beamed.

"And you look like you would appreciate a beer," Dexter said to his editor. "Do you have time for one? If I get this young Indian a can of Coke?"

"It's really past her bedtime," Brad protested.

"A quick one."

"Yeah, a quick one, Dad. Don't be a poop."

"Well, I can see I'm outnumbered. A beer and a Coke it is," Brad said, closing the door behind them.

CHAPTER THIRTY-THREE

Saturday, November 1

OVERNIGHT IT had snowed. Old-timers couldn't recall ever seeing snow this early, and they would marvel about it through the weekend and well into next week. Almost two inches blanketed Morgantown—not quite enough to bring out the plows, but more than ample to make driving treacherous.

Or hair-raising, if you were a little nutty behind the wheel. Brad was this morning, the first day of November, as he and Abbie headed for the market.

"Ooooohhhhh!" Abbie shrieked in pure pleasure as Brad fishtailed the Mustang down Thunder Rise Road.

"If I ever catch you doing this when *you* drive, I'll ground you for a year," Brad warned hypocritically.

Abbie just continued to shriek.

"Heck, if *I* get caught, they'll be grounding *me* for a year. I can just hear the police now: 'And *you're* the editor of that rag? Make my day! You have the right to remain silent. . . .' "

Brad laughed. Let them catch him. The radio was on, his daughter was happy, and he felt good. No, he felt *great.* Two months into their new life, and everything was under control—and some things were better than merely under control. Thomasine Lyons, as Exhibit Number One. He still didn't know if they were falling in love, but they were falling somewhere, that was for goddamn sure. Twice now they'd made love—ambrosian, honey love. And they were seeing each other almost every day. Going steady, he would've said back when he was seventeen.

Even the damn dog wasn't such a pain in the ass anymore. Yes, Brad concluded, life was sweet. After Hurricane Heather, they deserved some smooth sailing.

"OK," Brad announced as he turned the radio up. "You ready?"

"Ready!" Abbie responded, not knowing or caring what it was she was ready for. With Daddy in this kind of mood, it had to be good.

"This one's a classic. Here we go!"

It was "Under My Thumb," the great Rolling Stones tune. How many years old—and it still sounded incredible.

Brad cranked the volume until the speakers were shaking the door panels. He rolled the window down. The air was invigorating. Not yet eleven, and the mercury had already shot up to fifty. The sun was breaking through the cloud cover. Crazy weather up here in New England, Brad thought again. Who knew what tomorrow would bring? Maybe a heat wave or a solar eclipse.

The Mustang hurtled on down the road, only her seat belt keeping Abbie from flopping side to side, Brad intent on hugging that fine line between cheap thrills and accident. Soon they were nearing the center of town. Brad brought the speed down a bit and stopped the fishtailing—over Abbie's loud protest. They were passing houses now, and every one of them seemed to have a yard full of children, amazed at how their world had been transformed while they'd been sleeping. It was an odd juxtaposition: snowmen and snow forts next to trees draped with wet toilet paper, leftover from last night's Halloween naughtiness.

"This is the only way to listen to rock 'n' roll," he shouted over the chorus. "Real loud!"

He looked over at his daughter and exulted. Yes, the frosting on the cake was Abbie's happiness.

Except for her occasional nightmares—Brad could think of nothing but to let them run their course—she was as happy as she'd ever been. She'd made plenty of friends, including a very good one, Jimmy. Her teacher praised her kindergarten performance. Mrs. Fitzpatrick couldn't imagine a better afternoon helper. And seeing her mother Columbus Day weekend apparently had sated whatever desire she had for Heather's company, at least for the time being; since the visit Abbie hadn't once mentioned her. Visitation rights or no visitation rights, Brad had decided that unless Abbie demanded it, she would not be paying a visit to New York for a few weeks. The court could go fuck itself, as far as he was concerned.

Then there was Thomasine. Unless his daughter had become incredibly skilled at hiding her emotions, it seemed to Brad that not only did Abbie not resent her, but she had become genuinely fond of Thomasine, as Thomasine was of her. Of course, it helped that Thomasine made a point of bringing a treat (Barbie dolls were the favorites) on her every visit. And she'd certainly scored big points this week by bringing over a real live Indian.

Yes, it was a good spell for the Gales, Brad thought as he pulled into the IGA parking lot for their weekly shopping.

At the McDonalds', life had become hell.

Over the last few days Susie and Hank had convinced themselves their little girl was dying.

They were right.

CHAPTER THIRTY-FOUR

Monday, November 3

MAUREEN WAS too sick to be scared when she was admitted to Berkshire Medical Center. Bundled in a blanket and clutching her Cabbage Patch doll, she sat stonelike on her father's lap while Susie mindlessly signed forms and answered the admission secretary's questions. Dr. Bostwick, who had ordered Maureen in, was due any minute.

It was 8:15 A.M.

Only five days ago the McDonalds had dared hope that things were looking up. An endless ordeal of tests had not disclosed what was making their daughter sick, but a solid week of bed rest and antibiotics had had an effect. On Tuesday her temperature was normal and she ate three healthy meals. On Wednesday she returned to school. She was in school again Thursday and felt so good Friday afternoon that Susie dressed her like Raggedy Ann (unlike last year, when she'd been the Wicked Witch of the West; Maureen went hysterical at the mention of a scary costume again) and drove her trick-or-treating to a couple of houses, including the Gales'.

Midnight Friday her fever returned with the force of a fire storm. Overnight she vomited three times. By sunrise Saturday her sheets were soaked with sweat. Some color had returned to her cheeks during the week, but now her face was gaunt, her eyes sunken and glazed again. She had no appetite, and it was only with patient coaxing that her parents were able to get orange juice into her. It did not stay down, and when her body had finally, agonizingly rejected every last drop of it, she continued on for another ten minutes with dry heaves. Saturday night saw no improvement; during the one short period she was alone in her room, a terrible nightmare awakened her, leaving her quaking. By Sunday morning she was slipping in and out of delirium (she thought at one point that Susie was her grandmother, dead two years) and her temperature was 105. Tylenol didn't touch it, and on Sunday night, when Susie called, Bostwick said he wanted her admitted first thing the next morning, immediately if her condition worsened overnight.

He arrived at the hospital as Susie was fumbling in her purse for their Blue Cross card.

"How's our favorite little girl?" he asked Maureen, but he knew, looking at her, just how bad she was: dying, in fact.

The terrible weight of that thought chilled him, and for the first time this whole nightmarish fall, he felt fear—real, gut-clawing fear. In his years of practice he'd lost only one child to disease: Justin Rosenberg, who'd been wasted by an extremely rare case of eastern equine encephalitis. He'd never forgotten Justin, never forgiven himself, even though he knew in his heart of hearts he'd played it by the book, and there wasn't a damn thing he could have done to save the kid. Unless . . .

. . . "unless maybe you'd diagnosed it a day or two earlier." Those had been the medical examiner's words, and they hadn't been an accusation. They'd simply been a single offhanded comment delivered when the ME had come to the hospital to collect the body for autopsy. Bostwick had never forgotten those words. He heard them in his head now, as stinging as when they'd been delivered.

"Don't feel like talking, honey?" he continued. "Well, that's all right," he said, smoothing Maureen's brow. "You don't have to. You just be quiet, and we'll take care of everything."

Bostwick opened his briefcase and took out a pad on which he'd written orders: an IV; fifteen-minute observation; a private room. He'd hand delivered a copy at midnight to the hospital so it could be ready for her.

"How long have you been here?" he asked Hank.

"Half an hour."

"Half an hour?" He was astounded. "Nurse?" he called to the nurses' station, where two white-uniformed people, a man and a woman, were sitting at a desk, having coffee.

"Yes?" the male nurse answered.

"This is Maureen McDonald," Bostwick said, gesturing toward the child.

"I know."

"She's supposed to have been admitted," Bostwick snapped.

"I know."

"Then why the hell is she still sitting here?"

"Because she hasn't been assigned a room yet, Doctor," the nurse said brusquely. It was obvious he didn't like being challenged.

"Really?" Bostwick said. Hank and Susie, as preoccupied as

they were, could feel the anger in his voice, cold and dagger-sharp. "Maybe I'm not making my point, my friend. Let me put it this way: I'll give you two minutes to get her one, and then I'm going to that phone there and call the administrator of this hospital. Believe me when I say Mort Silverman's a personal friend . . . who shares my views about incompetents." He pulled back his sleeve to expose his watch. "Clock's running," he said, turning his back.

In fewer than ninety seconds an orderly appeared with a wheelchair. "She'll be in room two-two-four," the young man said quietly.

"That's a private?"

"Yes."

The orderly helped Maureen into the chair. She made the move without protest or reaction, so limply that it raised the hairs on the back of his neck. Justin Rosenberg had behaved like that the morning he'd been admitted to Berkshire Med, right in this very room.

"You go on up with her," Bostwick said to her parents. "I have a couple of things to attend to. I'll be up in a minute."

"OK," Hank and Susie said, speaking together. They made no effort to disguise their fear.

Bostwick went down the corridor, through the cafeteria, and into the front lobby, where there was a more private pay phone. He took his calling card out of his wallet. Seeing Maureen had convinced him; he'd waited too long already.

"Atlanta," he told the long-distance directory assistance operator. "Centers for Disease Control."

"One moment, please."

Over the last three weeks there had been tests. So many tests. They'd tested blood, sputum, urine, feces, skin, hair, spinal fluid—every conceivable specimen, short of biopsy. And not just from Maureen McDonald, who'd been picked at like a holiday turkey, but the other children, too, none of whom, no credit to him, was as sick as the girl being admitted this morning . . . yet. If narrowing the possibilities could be considered progress, he had made some. They could conclude now it almost certainly wasn't any of the streptoccal or staphylococcal infections. Wasn't salmonella. Or shigella. Or mononucleosis. Wasn't influenza or any recognizable cold virus. Wasn't meningitis or encephalitis. Wasn't any of the long shots they'd tested for: hepatitis, diphtheria, dysentery, dengue fever, trichinosis, malaria, for God's sake. Wasn't the really long shot: AIDS.

So what the hell is it?

Bostwick was haunted. So was the Berkshire Medical Center internist who'd been working in tandem with him, Dr. Miller.

Just what the hell?

How many times had they gone over the symptoms? The epidemiology? How many hours had they pondered the age of the children, where they lived, where they went to school, into what toilets they moved their bowels—anything, everything they might have in common? Only recently he'd gotten around to reading Randy Shilts's awesome account of the early days of the AIDS epidemic, *And the Band Played On.* The terrible frustration of the initial researchers—the frustration of *not knowing what it was*—had left Bostwick with a haunted feeling. Like those early doctors, he and Miller were grasping at straws. Sucking wind royally.

Desperate. That was why Bostwick recently was wondering if nightmares might not be a more important piece of the puzzle than they'd assumed.

Every one of the children, as best they could determine, had been experiencing terrible dreams. That fact had come to Bostwick's attention early on, when he'd started interviewing the children and their parents, almost all of whom were willing, eager, to divulge the most intimate details of their families' lives in the hope of turning up some crucial clue. As concern had risen, taboos had fallen away. With Bostwick—and later Miller—they'd gone over sexual practices, the proximity of diaper pails to beds, the defecation patterns of household pets, the amount of time leftovers stayed in the refrigerator, whether toothbrushes were shared, how often laundry was done, and on and on and on. Gosselin, the epidemiologist in Atlanta he was trying to reach now, would have been proud of him.

But neither doctor had put much weight in nightmares.

Now Bostwick wondered if they should.

He knew precious little about sleep disorders, or mass hysteria, or mass trances. He seemed to recall from his med school days reading about mushrooms that many years ago had poisoned a French village, causing the entire populace to hallucinate. Whether or not anything like that could cause all of the other symptoms, too, and whether any natural or synthetic hallucinogen could somehow have gotten into food or water, affecting only kids, not adults, were questions he couldn't answer.

Nor, he sincerely believed now, should he be expected to. Whatever they were dealing with, it was beyond the skills of an ordinary physician to decipher. Beyond the skills even of a talented and educated physician, which is what he'd always prided himself in being.

This was a matter for the Health Department. And the Health Department wasn't doing its job.

True, its staffers had done testing. Obligatory, cover-your-ass-in-a-class-action-lawsuit testing. They'd tested for lead paint (and they'd found it, under too many coats of latex to be highly hazardous), asbestos (none), salmonella (negative), shigella (ditto). They'd taken samples of water back to Boston to see if they could detect traces of carcinogens (no results yet, but it didn't matter; any dummy could see these weren't cancer symptoms).

The truth was, this Doc Hough from the Health Department was a clown. The truth was, Morgantown was too small, too far from Boston to matter yet. The brutal reality, Bostwick suspected—it made him angry enough to keep him awake nights—was that not one of these kids was sick enough for the red lights to start flashing. At best they were a blip on a monthly morbidity report. *Christ,* he thought, *tell it like it is. No one's died. The bastards need a death, don't they, before they take the hicks seriously? A goddamn sacrifice to the Almighty Public Health God before the dollars can be authorized, isn't that what we're talking about here, folks?*

Well, he'd make the bastards pay. Before this was all over, he was going to spill his guts to TV, newspapers, the wire services. He swore.

A computer voice enunciated the number for the Centers for Disease Control.

"Thank you," Bostwick said reflexively. He was concentrating too hard to notice, or care, that a machine had just spoken.

He dialed, gave his calling card number, and the receptionist came on the line. "Good mornin', this is the CDC," she said with a drawl that any other day would have been pleasant. Today Georgia Peach was annoying.

"Dr. Raymond Gosselin," Bostwick said.

"Thank you. That extension, for future reference, is six-one-two-one. I'll connect you now."

Saying his name brought the memories back in a flood tide. *Raymond Gosselin.* A Wisconsin boy, thrown together by fate with Bostwick as a roommate freshman year at Tufts Medical School in Boston. A brilliant kid, one with a sense of humor and a way with women that Bostwick to this day wasn't sure he really understood. Gosselin defined homely, what with oversize ears, bad skin, and not an iota of talent for dressing. And the ladies loved him. Couldn't get enough of him. At a stage of his own development when Bostwick was struggling for a night at the movies with someone, anyone, Gosselin kept a sexual assembly line in full-scale operation. The first year a different partner every weekend, and precious few of them as nerdy-looking as Gosselin himself. Eventually he'd settled down and married one of those women, a classmate Bostwick once coveted.

If forced to give a reason, Bostwick would've had to say it was Gosselin's brilliance that attracted such a crowd of such fine ladies. He was one of these rare people who seemed to come by knowledge supernaturally; he barely ever cracked a book, yet always scored an A. But it wasn't innate knowledge that was his mark. In the lab, and later in the clinic, Gosselin was possessed of rare skills. No one Bostwick had ever met had such an instinctive feel for how the human body worked, how its parts fitted together in such perfect harmony . . . until illness interfered. The day of graduation the dean personally told Gosselin he'd never once in almost a quarter century at the school seen such promise.

Gosselin knew that. Gosselin intended to be a star. He had an ego to match his genius, and he intended to leave his imprint on medical history. He wanted prizes, including the Nobel. He wanted to go coast-to-coast lecturing, and eventually he wanted to write his autobiography. Epidemiology, the study of diseases, seemed the perfect specialty to take him there. You could attract great attention, in and out of medicine, by mastering epidemics. In America you could join civilization's greatest disease-fighting team, maybe even captain it someday. You could make great contributions to mankind, and while they'd had their arguments, Bostwick never doubted that noble notion was also part of the strange mechanism that made Gosselin tick.

He waited what seemed an eternity. "Dr. Gosselin's office," a secretary finally said.

"Is he there?"

"I'm afraid not. May I ask who's calling?"

"Bostwick. Dr. Mark Bostwick. I'm an old—an old classmate of Ray's."

"I see," the secretary said, thoroughly unimpressed. In Gosselin's rarefied world, Bostwick could see, old classmates didn't count for doodly-squat. "May I leave Dr. Gosselin a message?" the secretary asked.

"Can you tell me when he'll be back?"

"Not until the end of the month," she said, and now she was beginning to sound annoyed. "Thanksgiving week."

"Is there a number where I can reach him now?"

"I'm afraid not," she said curtly. "He's in Haiti. In the *field.*" She pronounced the word as if it were sacred.

"Well, please have him call me," Bostwick said, giving his number. "And please tell him it's urgent. Let me give you my number."

Thanksgiving.

He wondered if it would be too late.

Invisible, the bear watched and waited.

It was patient, as patient as the centuries had taught it to be. It waited until Susie, unable to sleep, went down to the cafeteria for another cup of vending machine coffee. Her daughter was asleep, if uneasily. Susie and Hank had agreed to rotate nights on the cot the hospital let them set up in Maureen's room. Hank had missed too many days from work, so Susie had taken the first night. Already it was endless.

It was 1:45 A.M.

At the other end of the corridor a plump, middle-aged woman sat behind the nurses' station desk. Nurse McGibney was reading a Sidney Sheldon novel and smoking a nonfilter cigarette. That was against regulations, but who was going to care? The night watchman? He was in the boiler room, getting sloshed. The night supervisor? She smoked, too. Pediatrics was only half full tonight, and only one child, that McDonald kid, had orders for fifteen-minute checks. She'd just looked in, and everything had been fine. Tonight was going to be a skate, McGibney could just tell.

Maureen smelled the bear before she saw it, before she was awake.

A rotted vegetable odor, like potatoes left too long in a root cellar. It filled her sleep, not warning her, just quietly—but with a growing insistence—announcing its presence. After more than a week the bear was back. She didn't have to see it to know that it was back, just as it had promised it would be.

What unsatisfying sleep there had been evaporated. Her eyes snapped open, and there it was, its black fur completely filling the room, its teeth shiny and white and oh, so sharp.

It had followed her here.

"Well, of course I did," it said, knowing, as it always did, what she was thinking. "I will follow you no matter where you go, didn't I tell you? Didn't I tell you there's nowhere to hide, not in your room, not in the hospital, not anywhere? Why, they could take you to a police station or a church, and I would still come. I gave you my word, and real bears *always* keep their word."

It spoke, but not in words. Not words you could hear. Maureen had learned that the bear always got inside her head when it had something to say. It could do that, it had told her, because it could do anything. It had to do that, it had said, so none of these pesky grown-ups would hear it. *Because grown-ups don't believe in talking bears, do they, Maureen?*

"Go 'way," Maureen said, and her words were audible, but only barely; her body was too drained to be forceful. At her station Nurse McGibney turned the page of her book, tamped out her cigarette, and immediately lit another.

"Go 'way."

"Goodness, we seem to be unusually out of sorts tonight, don't we?" the bear said, feeling her resistance, recoiling from it. So the little creep still had some fight left in her after all. It wasn't turning out to be as easy as He had predicted it would be. But the day would come. Soon. Very soon. The bear smelled it in the air. They would have to endure only a little longer, and she, the first, would be theirs. The floodgates would open wide, and the torrent that would be unleashed would bring them souls without end.

"Go 'way," Maureen repeated, concentrating what tiny bit of strength she had in the command. The disease had sapped her, but it had not defeated her. Not yet.

"But don't you want to come with me, Maureen? You'll like it where I take you. I've told you that. You'll like it *very* much."

"No," she shouted at the monster. "*Nooo!*"

"Shhhh," the bear urged. "They'll hear you. And you know what Mommy and Daddy think when you start in like that. They think you're being naughty. They think you're *making things up*—or even worse, that you're having some kind of head problem. Goodness. You wouldn't want Mommy upset again, would you? She's already so upset. And imagine what the nurse would think! Just imagine, Maureen. They only *talk* nice. Underneath they're terrible meanies. Oh, yes, they really are. They *like* sticking little girls with needles. *Big giant* needles that they twist around!"

The bear breathed fire. A small lick of blue flame, as much as the cramped hospital room would permit. It shot toward Maureen. She pulled the sheet over her head so she didn't have to see.

"No," she whimpered. "No . . . please . . . go 'way . . ."

She was not afraid. Not as much as the first few times, anyway, when the bear had been such a shock. Then she had panicked. Wet the bed. Screamed every time until her mother or father or both had come running in. The normal range of reactions. But after the fifth time, or the sixth, or the seventh, she had started to wonder. The bear breathed fire, but the fire had never harmed her. The bear talked of taking her away somewhere, but it had never tried to kidnap her, although it was certainly powerful and clever enough to make off with her if it was really serious, she knew.

No, she didn't know what to think anymore. She knew the bear was for real, no matter what any grown-up said, and she knew it was very familiar with her and everything about her, but beyond that . . . she just didn't know. She did not connect her illness with the bear's appearance because no one had ever made that connection for her. She did not know anything about an evil spirit named Hobbamock because the bear had been explicitly instructed never to mention its master's name. She did not know that the crazy old neighbor who'd been killed in the fire had unwittingly unleashed the bear, pursuing his fool's dream for gold inside Thunder Rise.

All she knew was she wanted the bear to go away forever.

"Go 'way," she whimpered.

"But wouldn't you like to come with me?"

"No! Just go 'way. Please go 'way. Please, please, please . . ."

"I will," the bear said smugly. "Because there is other business to attend to tonight. Other little boys and girls I must see. Boys and girls who are glad to see me."

Maureen heard the sound of her mother's footsteps in the corridor. They stopped at the nurses' station. A muffled conversation, punctuated by weary laughter, drifted her way. Then the footsteps started again.

"I will be back," the bear promised before slipping away. "You can count on it, Maureen. And maybe next time you'll be coming with me. I'll have to think that one over. Now good-bye."

In the blink of an eye it was gone.

"You're awake, honey," Susie said, slipping into the room. Susie sniffed the air. There was a foul odor she hadn't detected before. It was laced with another smell, an industrial kind of smell that reminded her of Hank soldering pipes. Perhaps a sewer line had backed up in the basement somewhere, and an emergency crew was working on it. If it lingered, she'd have to complain to the nurse.

"How do you feel, sweetheart?" she said, running cold water on a facecloth and pressing it to her daughter's brow, pale and hot. "Would you like a cold drink?"

Maureen shook her head and started to cry, more from an overwhelming sensation of futility than from fright.

CHAPTER THIRTY-FIVE

Wednesday, November 5

CHARLIE SAT in his favorite chair, the lantern light casting restless shadows across his face. He had a cigarette in one hand. The fingers of the other were curled tightly around a coffee mug containing half an inch of a colorless, odorless liquid. The wood stove was full of wood, the damper closed to a crack; the fire would burn all night. Outside, the wind moaned under a sky studded with stars. Frost patterns were forming on the window.

He was about to take a drink.

And he was scared. He did not want to begin the ceremony of the *pniese.*

His father had outlined the ritual, but Charlie had never attempted it. There'd never been any situation to justify such a risk. George had told him of men, some very wise and mighty men included, who'd been permanently changed by it. Gone away somewhere, and never come all the way back, the way some hippies in the sixties had dropped too much acid and never returned to themselves.

But the time was past when Charlie had any choice. He had to have truth—for the children's sake as well as his own.

Two nights ago he'd been to dinner at his sister's. He'd driven over in the brand-new car he'd promised her (a black Oldsmobile Cutlass), and for perhaps fifteen minutes she and Jimmy had been beside themselves. They'd run their fingers over the upholstery, inhaled that leathery new-car smell, marveled at the air conditioning and cruise control, fiddled with the ultra-electronic radio and the power windows and locks. Ginny had taken them all for a cushioned, sinfully comfortable ride. Her Escort couldn't compare, she bubbled. It was like the difference between a hang glider and the Concorde.

Within half an hour the Ellises' excitement had trailed away, exposing an underlying, unyielding anxiety that deeply disturbed Charlie.

These were two people on the verge of breakdown. People with fears that were never more than a few feet outside the door, no matter what they did. Neither Jimmy nor Ginny mentioned nightmares, but Charlie knew instinctively he was having them. Worse was the low-grade fever Jimmy'd been running for two weeks. No vomiting or night sweats, just a stubborn 100.8 degree fever. The same beginning signs as the last time he really turned sick. Just like Maureen McDonald, who was in her third day at the hospital, according to Ginny. Just like the other kids Ginny knew about from school.

Charlie looked at his nephew and sister, and he saw two people convinced the sky was about to fall.

He believed in Hobbamock. That much he was sure of.

But could Hobbamock really be loose?

The possibility had been gnawing at him since the incident with Jimmy and the snare, worming and boring into his head until it occupied the meridian of his thoughts. Night or day he couldn't shake it. He'd lost his own interest in hunting, fishing, being in the woods, all the normal pursuits. In Morgantown what was normal anymore anyway? Too much was happening too fast. The kids' nightmares. The sickness. Strange twists and turns in the weather. Stories the old-timers downtown were telling about animals acting queerly. His own dreams . . . He had come to dread the night.

Did he believe Hobbamock was responsible?

In the days when his ancestors ruled the land, there would have been no such thing as a crisis of faith, and in his darkest moments he prayed that's all this was. Then there could have been only one interpretation: Somehow Hobbamock had been released, perhaps even busted free on his own, a quantum leap in possibility that Charlie would not allow himself to entertain.

Did he really believe?

Modern Man wouldn't. People like Brad Gale, so arrogant in their rationalism and orderly lives. People who worshiped science and technology, and held the smug belief that the Creator had intended his greatest creation to be master of his universe. People who dwelt in a world of blacks and whites, but precious few grays, the predominant color of Quidneck philosophy.

Charlie lived in that world, too. Mrs. Fitzpatrick had tried her darnedest to raise her only son in the purified faith of the motherland, Ireland, but the seeds of his father's beliefs ultimately had found more fertile ground. As a teenager Charlie had consciously embraced Quidneck pantheism, in which spirits and gods were everywhere, in the trees, the birds, the snow, the sun and the moon and the stars. He chose to believe that the good god, Cautantowwit, had created man, and that the bad god, Hobbamock, ceaselessly sought to destroy him. He believed that when he died, a man's soul made a great journey into the spirit world—like the Christian afterlife, potentially a world of great punishment, but also great promise. A world a man might enter, but only at great risk, while he was still alive.

Charlie believed as the Quidnecks had . . . or rather, wanted to believe.

Was Hobbamock loose?

He needed an answer.

The *pniese*—a Quidneck word that translated roughly as "journey past the spirit barrier"—might provide one.

And it might transport him somewhere only to strand him there forever.

Charlie contemplated the clear liquid in the cup, waiting for the final impulse to swallow it.

This afternoon, as the day was fading, he'd pressed it from a plant whose name—to his knowledge—was known only to the Quidneck. His father said it grew only on Thunder Rise, and it was true Charlie had never seen it anywhere else. Nor had he found it in botany books, although he had looked more than once. It was a delicate, tiny plant, similar in appearance to a lady's slipper, although it apparently did not flower. George had called it Eagle's Beak, a name whose origin was lost in time.

Charlie took a deep breath and drank.

He recoiled from the acid taste, which was like biting into a fresh-cut lemon. Charlie fought the impulse to spit it out. In one gulp the cup was empty.

In preparation Charlie had fasted for two days, and his stomach churned in one vast, queasy wave as the liquid trickled down into it. He was instantly nauseated, and it was all he could do not to vomit. *It's too late now to turn back,* he thought, but he was not remorseful or even upset. He was, instead, almost relieved that he had finally taken the plunge.

The initial jolt was the worst; within five minutes, as the liquid circulated, his stomach had settled down, and the aftertaste had begun to moderate. Charlie arranged himself cross-legged in his La-Z-Boy and closed his eyes.

There was no particular trick to meditation. In the old days a Quidneck attempting the *pniese* would have worn ceremonial garb, and his brothers might have built a blazing fire and surrounded it and him with dance and whooping; but George had told him those were mere accessories, more show than substance. The key was not gaudy exuberance, but blind concentration. As if it were some kind of spiritual sluice, the mind had to be forced open. It had to be cleansed of its skepticism and worldliness. Like a child, it had to be prepared to accept—no, intuit—things unimaginable.

Charlie concentrated on a clear sky in summer, focusing in on the depthless blue, finding there an endless variety of textures and shades.

If he had had any expectations, they were of muffled voices, shadows taking form and then losing form again, colors being distorted, sounds echoing and reverberating off the inside of his skull. Once, on one of his swings through the Southwest, he'd gone up into the New Mexico mountains with a Navajo brother and ingested peyote for a solid day and night. Their hallucinations, simultaneously beautiful and terrifying, had left an indelible mark on Charlie. They'd encountered spirits on that occasion, there was no question. For twenty-four hours their bodies and souls had been abuzz with energy and revelations he'd never been able to explain to anyone else.

So he did not expect to sleep.

But that's what happened. All evening, as he'd contemplated the *pniese,* his muscles had been knotted and stiff, and there had been a tension-induced pressure in his chest and head. With surprising quickness, his muscles began to relax. The pressure began to lift inside his head, and he was suddenly, completely drowsy, as if he'd run a great distance and finally found a warm and welcome spot to drop. He fought the drowsiness, but even at the start his fight was halfhearted. Soon he was unable to keep his eyes open.

Not fifteen minutes after drinking the potion, Charlie Moonlight was snoring.

When he awoke—*if* he awoke—the television was on. The generator wasn't running, but he understood subliminally that it didn't have to now.

At first there was only static on the screen and no sound. Charlie pulled himself up in his recliner, the way moviegoers come to attention when the popcorn commercials have ended and the main feature is about to begin. It did not occur to him that he had not meant to watch TV, had not turned it on. He did not remember anything called Eagle's Beak. He did not know what time or day it was, or care. He only vaguely sensed it was dark, that the lantern had gone out, that the wood stove was still throwing heat.

As he watched, the TV static began to change. It got brighter, and then the million electronic pinpoints began to assemble themselves into a pattern. The pattern was the rough outline of a face, which took on finer and finer detail: sharp eyes; black hair; sun-toughened skin; a strong chin.

It was his father.

"Son," George said.

"Dad," Charlie replied. He spoke perfectly naturally, as if the last time he'd seen his father were yesterday out in the woods he so loved, not three decades ago laid out in a casket in the parlor of the Boar's Head Inn.

"You should go back," George said. "There is too much danger where you want to go."

"I have no choice."

"There are things you should not see."

"I must."

"I cannot change your mind?"

"No."

"I will lead you as far as I dare. Then you will be on your own."

Charlie stood and crossed the room to the TV. On top of it was his videocassette collection, the VCR, a box of matches, a flashlight. Perhaps he might need the flashlight and matches. He placed them in his shirt pocket and glanced again at his father.

"Here," George said, extending his hand through the TV into the room.

Charlie took his hand. His father's grip was warm, firm. Charlie bent down and walked into the TV.

They were outside. The sky was cloudless. The sun was scorching, the landscape treeless and flat. Like Kansas prairie, it stretched toward infinity in every direction.

Only one object disturbed the monotony of the scene: a spear, lying on the desert near Charlie's feet.

It was a painstakingly crafted weapon, with a pink granite tip, carefully sharpened, and a handle of ash that had been painted with bright colors: red, orange, green. No ordinary warrior had ever carried such a spear. This had belonged to a war chief, probably one victorious in battle. More than one enemy's head had been carried home on this spear.

Instinctively Charlie picked it up. For an instant he felt a surge of energy through his body. It dissipated as fast as it had come on.

"Let's go," George said.

They walked silently across the red clay soil, baked to hardness by days, weeks, probably months of sun and no rain. Past shriveled cactus plants, the only evidence of life, they moved, their feet following a path that had been worn by the passage of unknown others. They both were soon sweating. The sweat plastered their hair, soaked their clothes, came off their faces in streams. Charlie shed his wool shirt, continuing along in dungarees and boots.

On and on they plodded, numbed by the featureless landscape until their legs and feet seemed disconnected from them, separate entities carrying them relentlessly forward. Charlie did not ask where they were headed. He did not ask if, in fact, his father really knew. He was a stranger in this new land, which he assumed must be one of the Lands of the Dead, one of many in which Quidnecks believed. An interloper who did not have the status to ask questions, he sensed he was being allowed to continue only by the grace of some spirit, whose presence once or twice he thought he fleetingly felt. But he could not be sure. He only knew he was not in control of this scene; how it played out was in someone else's hands entirely.

Charlie could not guess how long they had been walking when he observed an irregularity on the horizon.

Since they had started out, his eyes had been fixed to that horizon—in part because he needed focus or risked losing perspective altogether in this vastness, in part because he knew instinctively something eventually would appear on it. At first it was only a speck, shimmering in heat that rose in waves from the baked earth. Charlie thought it might be a bird, closer to them than this sea of parched flatness made it appear. But it was not a bird. As they got closer, he saw that it was a mesa, flat top resting on chalk-covered cliffs. He had a vague memory of having seen a similar promontory; a blurred image of a Navajo brother glimmered in his head and was gone.

"We must not go much closer," George said, speaking for the first time.

They continued awhile, the father trying to slow the son's eager progress. Soon Charlie could discern figures, a swarm of people, including one almost twice the size of the others.

"Close enough," George said, restraining his son.

They stopped. Behind the mesa Charlie could make out mountains, over which storm clouds were breaking. The sun still baked them, but there was a whisper of a breeze now, the promise of rain . . . a deluge of rain . . . cleansing, devastating rain.

Charlie squinted, but he could make out no more detail on the mesa.

"Here," George said, withdrawing a pocket telescope from inside his shirt. "Use this. I do not want to see any more."

Charlie looked through the telescope.

The giant's back was to Charlie, but he did not need to see his front to know he was naked. His skin was bronze-colored, his muscles sharply defined, his neck trunklike, his head shaved. He was not painted, did not have earrings or other jewelry that Charlie could see. Gathered around him were what appeared to be his followers, more than a hundred in all, men and women, as naked as the leader himself.

The giant turned.

Charlie was overcome with disgust.

In one hand he was clutching his penis—an enormous organ that was fully, frighteningly erect. He displayed it for the spectators, whose roars of approval came drifting across the desert.

"Hobbamock," George said.

Charlie moved his binoculars off the giant to an earthern mound that seemed to function as some sort of stage or altar. On it was a row of people, spread-eagled and tied with leather to stakes. Not adults, Charlie realized with building rage. Children. About a dozen of them, split roughly equally between the sexes. The girls were on their backs, the boys on their stomachs. Each had been painted with one red stripe, almost like an arrow, that ran down their torsos to their loins. Charlie could not be sure it wasn't blood, let with a single slice of a sharp knife.

His anger, already at fever pitch, rose even further with the shock of recognition. Abbie Gale was one of the children. Susie and Hank McDonald's daughter. Several children he did not recognize. One other he did: Jimmy, his nephew. Jimmy, who appeared to be first in line.

Hobbamock pranced before the crowd. Charlie strained to hear the cries of the children, but he could detect none. Perhaps they'd been drugged. If they were saying anything, it was being drowned out by a rhythmic drumbeat the onlookers were sending up.

"I warned you," George whispered, his voice shaking.

"No!" Charlie protested, his voice escalating. "Nooooo!"

"Quiet," George implored.

"Noooooo!" Charlie gripped the spear he'd found. His knuckles were white.

"We must go now."

"He must be stopped!" Charlie screamed.

"We are powerless." Charlie had never seen his father so afraid. "We are unarmed and overwhelmed. It would be crazy."

"We have this," Charlie said, lifting the spear.

"It is useless in your hands."

"We must try."

"It would be suicide."

"Jimmy is one of them!" Charlie said savagely. "My sister's son!"

The old man looked down, ashamed. But there was nothing he could do any longer; in his Land of the Dead, there was peace—great, endless, soothing peace—but there was no power. All power had been stripped on the passage over. The most George could do was guide, and that had been accomplished now.

"Come, before it is too late," he said, retreating.

Charlie ignored him.

Spear in hand, he ran madly—blindly—toward the mesa. He was bellowing. His rage filled the flat landscape, catching the attention of the spectators, then Hobbamock himself. Hobbamock stopped his ritual. The spectators were immobilized. Silence settled over them like drowning.

As Charlie watched, the spectators began to be transmogrified. Their size did not change, but their features began to. Fur grew on some; scales, on others. Their faces melted into liquidy pools, and then the pools began to re-form themselves into new shapes. Limbs contorted. Hands became paws; fingers, claws. The end product was an assembly of wolves, bears, snakes, vultures.

Hobbamock's agents. Charlie remembered meeting them in his dreams.

It was almost dark now. The storm clouds had cascaded in like stallions stampeding, and now they were broiling angrily overhead. The sky was spitting rain, and the wind had whipped itself into a howl. As the darkness enveloped him, the mesa and the spectacle on it began to fade. George had disappeared. The realization brought tears to his son's eyes. Desperately, irrationally, Charlie groped for his flashlight. He found it, pushed the switch, but the batteries seemed to have gone dead. He did not bother with the matches.

The last thing he saw as the blackness was complete was Hobbamock, his face radiant, his lips locked into a sneer. The last thing Charlie heard as consciousness dimmed was Hobbamock's cackle—owllike, painful, ascending in pitch until it was past painful, until only a dog could have heard it.

CHAPTER THIRTY-SIX

Saturday, November 8.

"WHAT DO YOU want to play?" Jimmy asked Abbie when they had reached the attic. With a few curtains and streamers and some old furniture (including the giant dollhouse they'd picked up for a song at the flea market), Brad had transformed the attic into a children's wonderland. It was Abbie's favorite place.

"Wanna color? I've got lots of books. *Rainbow Brite, Winnie-the-Pooh, She-Ra, Princess of Power, Big Bird—*"

"Nah," he said.

"Want to go down and watch TV?"

"Nah. Got any GoBots?"

"Nope."

"G.I. Joe?"

"Unh-unh."

"Boy. You don't have *anything.*"

"I have fourteen Barbies," she said proudly.

"That's girl stuff. How about we play dinosaurs?" Three months ago Jimmy would have suggested Rambo. But he didn't play Rambo anymore. An awful thing had happened playing Rambo—a thing that was still going on.

"I don't want to play dinosaurs," Abbie said, squirming.

"Why not?"

"Just because, that's all."

"Well"—Jimmy coaxed—"you could be a caveman and I could be a *Tyrannosaurus rex.*"

"No."

Jimmy didn't get it. They'd played dinosaurs before, lots of times, and Abbie had loved it. Maybe it was the roles.

"OK," he offered, "you could be *Tyrannosaurus rex,* and I'll be the caveman."

"No!" Abbie shouted, and burst into tears.

Jimmy's first thought was: *Oh, boy. Mr. Gale's gonna hear her, and then I'll be in for it. And I didn't even do anything.* But Abbie's sobbing wasn't that loud, and soon that fear had passed. Jimmy's second thought was to comfort her. Yes, that's what he should do. Because Abbie was a friend. Not a girl friend or anything serious like that, just a *special friend,* as his mother, who liked Abbie tremendously, called her. Almost as good as his best boy friends—even if she didn't have Trans Formers or GoBots.

Abbie had retreated to the attic window, where she sat on the floor, looking forlornly outside. Tears trickled in two streams down her peach-tinged cheeks. Without hesitation, Jimmy did what Ginny had always demonstrated you do when someone close to you is very, very upset: He went over and hugged her. Abbie accepted his embrace. Framed by the anemic light of November, they comforted each other.

"I'm sorry," Jimmy said, not knowing what he'd done to be sorry about but figuring it was best to apologize anyway. "I thought you liked dinosaurs."

"I used to," Abbie admitted. She was getting a hold on herself.

"But not anymore," Jimmy concluded.

"No. They're . . . too scary, that's all."

"Scary? But dinosaurs have been dead millions and millions and millions of years." He reassured her.

"No, they haven't."

"Yes, they have."

"No."

"Yes."

"Well, I'm still scared of them."

Jimmy wasn't sure he got it. He had never been afraid of dinosaurs; neither, he assumed, had Abbie. How else could they have played them the last time without something like this happening? His mind skittered over the various fears in his life. Losing Mommy.

That fear, probably the granddaddy of all his fears, had been there as long as he could remember. It ranked just above Charlie Going Away for Good. Being Late for Kindergarten was another fear. That was a new one, but no longer a very significant one; he'd been late once, and his teacher hadn't yelled at all. Liver for Dinner. That wasn't exactly a fear, but it was sure bad. Wolves. Until the incident in the woods—until THE NIGHTMARES—he'd *liked* wolves, at least pictures he'd seen in *National Geographic.* Now, just thinking about wolves gave him a sick feeling in his stomach. Sometimes the thought was so bad he got a sharp pain in his head, as if he'd fallen while ice skating. Maybe something like that had happened to Abbie to make her dislike dinosaurs. He didn't want to ask. It wasn't something you'd run around telling everybody.

"Like wolves are scary," Jimmy blurted out.

"Yeah. Like wolves."

Abbie looked at her friend, her very best friend of all the people she'd met since coming to Morgantown. There were a lot of reasons to like Jimmy: He was very nice, and he lived pretty close, and they liked a lot of the same games, and his uncle was Charlie, the Indian. But the biggest thing was how brave Jimmy was. One recess, way back at the beginning of kindergarten, he'd stuck up for her when Amy Wallace had started kidding her about what she'd brought in for show-and-tell: a milk bottle. ("A *milk bottle's* a *stupid* thing for show-'n'-tell," Amy had said, teasing her. Abbie had tried to explain that in New York they didn't have milk that came around by a milkman, but tears had gotten in the way. That was when Jimmy had butted in. "Amy, you're just jealous 'cause Abbie's *prettier* than you." It had reduced Amy to tears.) Yes, come to think of it, the time with the milk bottle had been the thing that had really made them special friends.

Discovering that someone so brave could actually be . . .

. . . afraid of something the way she was . . .

. . . well, that made him even nicer.

"Jimmy?" she said.

"Yeah?"

"Have you ever had nightmares?"

Nightmares. The word sliced through him like a razor blade. It felt like the time he'd had to have a tooth pulled, the electric feeling from the Novocain needle as it entered the gum. Jimmy swallowed.

"Have you?" Abbie repeated.

Should he tell the truth? He'd never mentioned the nightmares to any kids. Only adults, and only a very few of them: Mom and Uncle Charlie and Dr. Bostwick, the time he was sick back then before the fair. But Abbie was his friend. His *special friend.* She was having nightmares, too. He knew, because she'd told him one morning on the bus. If anyone could understand, it was Abbie.

"Only a couple of times," he said. It was a white lie.

"Really?"

"Really. You, too, right?"

"Sometimes," she said. "About dinosaurs."

"All kinds of dinosaurs?"

"Oh, no." Abbie corrected him. "Only one kind. *Rhamphorhynchus.*"

"Which one is that?"

"That's one of the flying ones. It's got a long tail and lots of teeth. Like a vulture. Have you ever seen a vulture?"

"Only in a book about birds. My mom bought it for me."

"What's your nightmare about, Jimmy?"

"A—*a wolf.*" There. He'd finally said it.

"Wow," Abbie said in awe. "Was it big?"

"Gi-gan-ic."

"Can he talk?"

"Yes, he can."

"So can my rhamphorhynchus!" Abbie exclaimed. "Is he a *mean* talking wolf?"

"*Very* mean," Jimmy said, then added, with no small degree of drama: "He wants to eat me."

"Boy," Abbie said, her voice equal parts wonderment and tingly fear, "that's like the dinosaur. I think it wants to eat me, too. I told my dad, but he doesn't believe me. He says it's all make-believe."

"That's what my mom says, too."

"But how could it be make-believe?" Abbie reasoned. "It comes right into my room."

"Like my wolf."

"I could touch it if it weren't so scary and it didn't make me cry." The memory of it made Abbie shudder. Maybe she wasn't so keen to talk about this, after all, although in the broad light of day, the nightmare never, ever seemed quite so bad.

"Does it smell?"

"Like BO?" Abbie said.

"Yeah, like that. I can smell the wolf. It's wicked gross. Like farts," he added, giggling.

"So they must be real," Abbie concluded.

"Right," Jimmy agreed.

They locked glances. Something—so real they almost could have reached out and touched it—flickered back and forth between them. Something they did not really comprehend, something at once unsettling and strangely comforting. For the very first time they were sharing darkest secrets, and the unburdening of them was a relief.

"My dad says the dinosaurs will go away," Abbie said, "that it's just nightmares 'cause of us moving from New York to a new place and everything, and it always goes away. I wish he was right," she said dubiously. "Do you think your wolf will go away, Jimmy?"

"I don't know," he answered, the creepy sensation crawling back into his spine again.

"I don't know either. I wish I could chase it away, instead of waiting for my mind to do it itself. I don't think my mind really wants to."

"My uncle Charlie promised he has a way to keep the wolf away," Jimmy boasted.

"Does it work?"

"I think he forgot his promise," Jimmy lamented. " 'Cause the wolf still comes sometimes."

"Maybe if you had a gun," Abbie suggested, almost without meaning to. Guns were outlawed from the Gale household. But how many times on TV had Abbie seen problems taken care of with guns? Lots and lots of times.

"Yeah," Jimmy said. "A gun." Once he had hold of the idea, he wondered why it hadn't occurred to him before.

A gun. Better than a camera. Better than anything even.

That's what Rambo would do, he started to think, catching himself before he was too far into the thought.

In another few minutes their talk had moved on to more innocuous subjects. Another few minutes after that, and they were absorbed—silently, happily—in a jigsaw puzzle.

In the second-floor study Maria had been listening to the sounds from upstairs.

Children sounds.

Every once in a while a low growl escaped the dog, so low that a person on the other side of the study couldn't have heard it.

Lately Maria had been reacting to her human masters strangely.

Brad had the vague sensation that something was wrong with the dog. She didn't—didn't what? Didn't *like* them quite as much anymore? That was silly. Dogs were dumb brutes, incapable of intellectual functioning much beyond the level of chewing shoes and napping. It was hard to articulate. There hadn't been any single incident with Maria, but on a couple of occasions Brad swore he saw a mean look in the animal's eyes that had never been there. Crazy, but it seemed as if the dog were watching them now, wary of them, where before her face had been full of nothing but brainless good humor.

Upstairs Abbie and Jimmy were jumping. Maria could feel the vibrations through the floor.

The Big Dog voice whispered:

(Don't trust them. They'll stop feeding you, you know. It's only a matter of time. That big one . . . the way he whacks you with that newspaper, orders you around, calls you names. Who's in charge here anyway? And that little one, isn't she mean? Knocking you about the way she does. No, it's not a pretty picture for a dog. And it's going to get worse before it gets better.)

CHAPTER THIRTY-SEVEN

Thursday, November 13

PNIESE and the *Transcript* story about Harry Whipple combined to lead Thomasine and Charlie to where they stood now: the entrance to an old mine up Thunder Rise.

"You knew it was here?" Thomasine said.

"Yes," Charlie answered, "but I thought it had been closed down years ago. Before I was born. Until that article I had no idea it had been worked recently."

"I'm not sure I'd use the word 'work.' 'Farted around in' might be a better way to describe it. Apparently he thought he'd strike it rich in here. From what Brad said, Whipple was crazy as a bedbug."

"I know," Charlie said. "His drinking didn't help things."

"Was Whipple right?"

"About what?"

"Gold."

"Let's just say"—Charlie smiled—"that the Quidneck was not above a little practical joke or two when the white man first settled the area. Now come on. Let's go inside."

Thomasine was not eager, but she followed him. Instinctively Charlie went in, inching toward the side shaft that Whipple had opened but not resealed months ago. He moved slowly, deliberately; it had been a week since the ordeal of *pniese,* and he still had not fully recovered. It would be another week, he guessed, before he had his strength back. At least he no longer was nauseated and diarrheic, as he'd been the first three days.

Charlie was drawn toward the rock pile. "Someone's been digging through here recently," he said after examining it.

"Whipple?"

"I assume so."

Charlie started climbing toward the top of the heap.

"Be careful," Thomasine cautioned, training her flashlight on him.

"I am," he said, feeling carefully with each step before placing his full weight into it. His caution was rewarded: He got to the top without falling or dislodging any of the larger rocks, some of which were big enough to crush a person. Charlie found a rock that would support him and sat down, out of breath. With his flashlight he explored the void in front of him.

"Holy shit," he exclaimed. "Holy shit."

"What?" Thomasine said, her words bouncing and clanging off rock.

"A cave."

"Is it big?"

"Huge. My light won't penetrate to the end."

"You're not going in, are you?" she said worriedly.

"Are you crazy?" He spit back. Thomasine remembered a conversation they'd had about the Quidnecks' natural aversion to caves—an aversion, Charlie'd explained, stemming from their belief in Hobbamock.

"Please don't," she begged.

"Even if I wanted to, I couldn't. The bottom must be a seventy-five-foot drop. No way."

Suddenly, a rumbling like late-summer thunder. They could feel the vibration through their feet. Dust showered down on them, powdering their hair. The thunder crescendoed, then slowly subsided, as if a subway had just rumbled through beneath them.

"The noises?" Thomasine asked. She had never heard them.

"Yes." Charlie nodded.

"I didn't think they were that loud."

"They're usually not."

They were still contemplating what they had heard when there was another sound, distinct from the first. A cackling. A crowlike cackling, full of mockery and scorn. Like the thunder, it rose in intensity, then faded away.

"Hear that?" Charlie said, as if to reassure himself it wasn't only in his head. Ever since the *pniese,* his head had been filled with sounds—rustlings and whispers punctuated by occasional outbursts, like a baseball crowd overheard from afar. Echoes of the experience, he supposed, trickling back somehow from the Land of the Dead. He'd been helpless to ward them off.

"Yes," Thomasine replied nervously. "I heard it. Is that the noises, too?"

"I don't know."

"It sounds like . . . laughter."

"I know."

"You don't think there's someone here, do you?"

"I don't know what to think," Charlie said, backing down, "except I've seen and heard more than I want to. Let's get out of here."

CHAPTER THIRTY-EIGHT

Monday, November 17

THE MONDAY, November 17, *Transcript* had an unusual feature, an editorial signed by the publisher, Paul Dexter. It appeared on the front page, signaling real urgency:

> Will someone have to die before the Commonwealth of Massachusetts finally is convinced it has a public health problem of crisis proportion in Morgantown?

That would seem to be the case, wouldn't it, Department of Health? Because for a month you have known about our children being sick. You have received urgent calls from our local physicians—competent, compassionate healers who simply do not have the expertise to handle this situation any longer. You have seen copies of several stories this newspaper has written about a concern that is coming to dominate all talk here. You know that three children have been hospitalized. You know that two dozen have been sick to one degree or another. You must know—and if you do not, you should not be entrusted with the public's health—that the numbers are growing steadily.

And yet you have done nothing.

Unfair, you will howl. Strictly speaking, you are right. Some preliminary testing has indeed been done, but you might as well have spent your time and money golfing for what the results are worth. One month after it was reported to you, Department of Health, the origin and treatment of this disease—if, in fact, it is a disease and not some form of poisoning, or something else entirely—remain unknown. You cannot tell us what it is, only a few things that it is not. This is a form of deliberate neglect that borders on the criminal.

People living at this end of the state traditionally complain that they are ignored by state government, the center of which is situated 120 miles away in Boston, and we candidly admit there sometimes is precious little substance to such complaints. This is not one of these times. This is a medical crisis. The lives of young children are at stake. We, the parents and citizens of Morgantown, demand answers, and we demand them now.

Will it take a lawsuit—or, unthinkably, the death of an innocent child—before we have them?

We sincerely hope not.

—Paul Dexter, Publisher

Bostwick, whose call had prompted Dexter, read the editorial at Berkshire Medical Center, where Maureen McDonald had just been readmitted.

He had not wanted to bring her back. Her initial stay had been three days, and she not only had stabilized during that time but had improved to the point where Bostwick thought she'd be better off at home. At home her improvement had continued, and just four days ago there had been the first renewed talk of maybe letting her try school again.

Last weekend was a repeat of two weeks ago.

By this morning he'd had no choice but to readmit her.

Now there were four children hospitalized.

CHAPTER THIRTY-NINE

Tuesday, November 18

AFTER THE CAVE experience Thomasine had insisted Brad listen again to Charlie. That's why the three of them were having lunch today at Paul's Diner.

It was not going well. Thomasine had suspected it might not.

She and Brad had already been through one minor little tiff over Charlie. It was the morning after he'd come to dinner and they'd been recounting the events of the evening before. Yes, Charlie was a likable enough sort, if highly opinionated, Brad had agreed. Yes, he was intelligent, and well spoken, and a real hit with Abbie, and nothing to scoff at in the looks department, as Thomasine seemed to have taken pains to point out. So what was the caveat? Thomasine had wanted to know, sensing the skepticism in Brad's voice. That story about that alleged Indian god, Brad had finally admitted. Didn't she think it crossed the line into fantasy? Just the slightest bit? And wasn't he, Brad Gale, being a "cultural chauvinist" for so readily dismissing Charlie's ancestry? Thomasine had countered. Was he really so closed-minded? That was when Brad had good-naturedly suggested that maybe Thomasine was "a bit naive, like most grad students." The exchange had ended there, but not Thomasine's suspicion that Brad was jealous. It was an insane notion that Brad saw Charlie as a threat, but the irrational, Thomasine had learned the hard way, was the worm in the center of all jealousy.

Now, as the three of them picked at the remnants of their meal, there was silence. Charlie had just finished retelling the legend of Hobbamock, this time emphasizing those details that corresponded to contemporary Morgantown. He'd told for the first time two chapters of the legend he'd remembered only recently: a spear which had finally turned the tide in the initial battle against Hobbamock, and Hobbamock's brief escape more than a hundred years ago, an incident about which his father had been sketchy. Together he and Thomasine had recounted their visit to the cave. Thomasine still wasn't sure what had happened there. She only knew that in the aftermath Charlie's legend had taken a troubling step closer to believability. As biased as it would be, she wanted Brad's opinion. Maybe secretly she wanted a dose of his skepticism to balance this disturbing new feeling she couldn't shake on her own.

Brad had listened, and now he was expected to speak.

"Very interesting" was his response.

Charlie looked coldly at him and then, somewhat less coldly, at Thomasine. He should have heeded his instincts when she'd asked him to come today. The last thing he'd needed was another exposure to Brad Gale's skepticism. But Thomasine had begged.

Thomasine shot Brad a dark glance of her own.

"I mean," he added, "it's certainly something to ponder."

"You think you have all the answers, don't you?"

Brad was caught off guard. "No," he said clumsily.

"Most of them. You think you have most of them."

"They don't pay me to be stupid, if that's what you're driving at."

"What I'm driving at is kids. There are some very sick kids out there."

"Thank you for letting me know."

Charlie ignored the sarcasm. "More and more sick kids and not one of your doctors and public health people knows what's causing it."

"If you'd been reading the paper—"

"I have. Some of us Indians are literate, believe it or not."

"Then you know that there's a question of gross incompetence here. Off the record, I'd say it's not stretching it to think there's potential for some kind of class-action lawsuit."

"Off the record, I'd be very worried if I were you."

"What's that mean?"

"It means you have a kid."

Brad was well aware of that. He and Thomasine had discussed the risk to Abbie more than once, and he was keeping an eagle eye on his daughter's health, trying desperately not to succumb to hypochondria. Abbie added urgency to the *Transcript*'s daily coverage.

"Is that supposed to be some kind of scare tactic?" Brad said, his voice moving toward anger.

"Let me answer that with another question," Charlie said. "You've heard of David Berkowitz?"

"Of course. Son of Sam."

"Do you know what made him kill all those people?"

"He was mentally ill. A paranoid schizophrenic with criminally dangerous delusions, if you want to get clinical about it." He remembered Berkowitz well. For more than a year he'd called in all sorts of favors in an unsuccessful bid to get permission from the authorities to interview him. During his reporting career at *The New York Times* he'd been fascinated by Berkowitz. He still was.

"What if I told you I believed he was possessed?"

"I'd respect your opinion. But it wouldn't be mine."

"Why?"

"Because there's no such thing as possession."

"Can you *prove* it?"

"That's like asking me to prove there's no such thing as Santa Claus."

Charlie was nonplussed. "How would you explain Hitler?" he continued.

"I wouldn't try to."

"You don't think he was crazy?"

"It depends on how you define crazy. To the Jews he was a monster. To the Nazis he was a military and political genius. At least for a few years."

"You've never believed he was Satan, to use the Christian word?"

"I've never thought of him in that light, no."

"Maybe he and Son of Sam were *both* Satan."

"Sure, and I'm the Easter Bunny." Thomasine shot Brad a look. "Just kidding," he added lamely.

"Let me ask you another question." Charlie continued. "Can you tell me what guides salmon back to the place of their birth after swimming through so many thousands of miles of ocean? Or how birds can migrate from one continent to another, returning the next spring to the same nest in the same tree where they had last year's brood?"

"What's the point, Charlie?"

"The point is your culture. It's like you—so smug and self-satisfied, thinking science and medicine and technology have all the answers."

"On that count, at least, I think we've done a better job than your people," Brad said gently. "For an awful lot of the questions, we *have* found the answers. Your people have benefited, too. Not in every way, not that there hasn't been great injustice, but there's been some good, too. Surely you see that."

"I don't think there's any need to continue this," Charlie said.

"Fine. I make a point, and you want to end the discussion. Have it your way."

Charlie stood, reached into his wallet, and withdrew a twenty-dollar bill. He slapped it onto the table. "This will cover everything," he said.

"Charlie . . ." Thomasine said.

"Look at him," Charlie said, gesturing toward Brad, slumped back into his chair, as if cosmically bored. "He thinks I'm crazy."

"I think your stories are interesting," Brad said.

"You think they're bullshit," Charlie said, spitting the word out. "Bullshit your lady friend made you sit and listen to."

"I didn't say that."

"You didn't have to. I can read it on your face: 'Dumb Indian,' it says. Something like that." He was standing behind Brad now, his bulk towering over him.

"You're being ridiculous."

"I've seen it too many times not to recognize it when I see it."

"Well, what do you expect me to say? That I believe in the big bad god Hobbamock? This isn't your everyday story, you know. Even you have to concede that."

"And you're not your everyday mortal, are you?"

"If not automatically believing some fruitcake story puts me a cut above, then, no, I guess I'd have to say I'm not."

All of a sudden Charlie was at the flash point. Thomasine could feel the tension, heavy in the air.

"Charlie . . ." she pleaded. "Brad . . ."

"*Brad?*" he said incredulously. "Speak to your friend here!"

"No, *you* speak to me," Charlie thundered.

"I have nothing more to say."

"What?" Charlie mimicked. "The Great White Father is speechless? No more advice, Mighty One?"

"Yeah. Trade the loincloth for a pair of Levi's," Brad snapped, so snidely he surprised himself. "It's the twentieth century out here."

"You arrogant son of a bitch."

Unknowingly Brad had pressed the wrong button.

A man named Jason Donahue—Charlie would never forget him—had been the assistant DA for Massachusetts in the land claim suit, and for three days he had cross-examined Charlie. Donahue was not a brilliant litigator, but he did have one talent: baiting witnesses. John Freeman, the Quidnecks' attorney, had warned his clients about him. The best strategy, he said, was to stay cool. A jury might appreciate coolness; it might not. But it definitely would not award points for temper.

For two days on the stand Charlie had been unflappable. Donahue simply couldn't rattle him, no matter how big an asshole he became, and he'd been out there on the frontiers of assholeism. The third day was different. By now Charlie'd had just about enough of Donahue's insinuation that the Quidnecks were nothing but cultural charlatans made suddenly greedy by a string of successful suits in other states. It really wasn't anything as subtle as insinuation. For two days he'd peppered his questions with references to "firewater," "high-stakes bingo," "unemployment," "massacres of Puritans," "scalping," "warpath." He'd even managed to mention John Wayne, a comment that elicited an open chuckle from one potbellied member of the jury. The judge, despite a string of objections from Freeman, had allowed Donahue to continue merrily on. Taunting, waiting.

Now Donahue was questioning him on the Quidnecks' animist beliefs. No one living in the twentieth century could possibly believe there actually were spirits living in rocks and plants, could they, he'd taunted, unless it was one of those weird little tribes the *National Geographic* turns up from time to time in the Amazon? You know, Donahue said, the ones where the women don't cover their breasts and the men stick twigs through their noses.

Charlie was at last getting flustered. He was still astounded by the fact that only the lawyers could ask the questions. According to the rules, you had to sit there politely while some arrogant bastard pulled down your pants and lit into your bare hide with a rod. You were not allowed to defend yourself. You could not fire back. To think they called this justice . . .

Charlie felt the anger building, the greatest he had ever known.

"Got the loincloth on?" Donahue quipped. He slipped it in quickly, before the judge could rule him out of order.

That was it. Charlie snapped. Bellowing, he rose from the witness stand and went for Donahue, who'd been parading like a rooster before the jury. Charlie would have gotten to him if the bailiffs hadn't been agile, hadn't seen Charlie tensing in the moment before he exploded. He was hauled from the courtroom in handcuffs. A picture of him had wound up in *The New York Times.*

Charlie looked down on Brad, still sitting. Their eyes locked.

For one crazy moment Brad's mind was flooded with jealousy. He wondered if Charlie had ever lusted after Thomasine. For the very first time he wondered insanely if the two of them had slept together, if that's what they'd really been doing, holed up in the Indian's cabin up there in the woods of Thunder Rise.

Charlie's eyes had narrowed to cat's slits.

There was something more than anger in them. Brad had seen it before, that night Charlie had guessed Abbie's nickname. It was as if those eyes were an open doorway to somewhere. A threshold to somewhere Brad had never gone, would never want to go. Brad broke eye contact. He had no choice. Charlie's gaze was too intense. It almost burned.

Charlie later would feel tremendous guilt over what happened next, happened in lightning-quick fashion. He would chastise himself, and he would come very close to apologizing to Brad—although he would not. But now, his anger exploding as it had that day in court, there was no insight, only instinct.

Charlie reached down and grabbed Brad by the shoulders. His fingers dug in, causing Brad to wince with the sudden pain.

"What the fuck are you—"

He did not finish. Letting out a tremendous whoop, Charlie lifted him out of his seat.

Thomasine watched, horrified. She knew how fatigued Charlie still was—the *pniese* seemed to have aged him five years—and she knew the toll his nightmares and insomnia continued to take. This wasn't the first time she'd sensed that this was a man on the edge.

But it was the first time she thought he might go over.

"Charlie!" she screamed.

Charlie had Brad over his head now. The veins in his neck looked ready to burst. His skin was suddenly flushed. Charlie felt nothing. No exertion. No pain. His mind was strangely empty, as if the outburst had temporarily drained it. He didn't have a plan or a next move. He hadn't come here with any intention of throwing a man through a window or across a floor, although he clearly had the strength.

It seemed surreal—this crazed, ponytailed man lofting this smaller, but not small, man with the glasses and button-down shirt. Brad tried to yell, but a strangled gurgle was all that came out. He was too startled to be afraid, but he was embarrassed. And enraged, more so than at any time since his fury with Heather. When this was all over—it would soon be over, wouldn't it?—Tonto here was going to pay in a big way. The red man might not have a concept of civil liberties, but the white man sure as hell did.

"You're going to hurt him!" Thomasine shouted. She looked around wildly for help. Except for the waitress, a busboy, and the cook, who seemed to have disappeared into the kitchen, the diner was deserted.

"Charlie! Put him down goddamn it!"

Thomasine's words penetrated. As quickly as it had sprung up, the storm was over. Charlie returned Brad to his chair, putting him down almost gently. It reminded Thomasine of a parent returning a slumbering infant to its crib. Brad immediately set about fixing his collar, settling his hair, preening himself, as if that might restore some measure of dignity.

"Maniac." He swore at Charlie. "Let's go," he said to Thomasine, rising.

Silently they went to the door. For several minutes Charlie did not move. Then he, too, left.

CHAPTER FORTY

Wednesday, November 19

LATE THE DAY before, Dexter's editorial had landed on the desk of the director of the state Department of Health. It was the first Morton C. Smith, M.D., had heard of Morgantown or the goings-on out way out there somewhere at the opposite end of the Massachusetts Turnpike. He was livid. He threatened firings. He made no secret that epidemiologist Dr. Henry R. Hough, a man whose competence had never impressed him, was in greatest danger.

Hough arrived back at Morgantown Elementary before the students this morning, accompanied by one of the Health Department's young, and competent, epidemiologists.

This time they did more than review files. They had a nurse draw blood from every child at the school—sick or not. They took samples of food, paint, water, soil, sending all of them, along with the blood, by Federal Express to the department's Boston laboratories. They made plans to stay the remainder of the week, so they could interview every parent of every sick child. Per deliberate instruction by the boss, they made themselves extremely accessible to the media (including a paper and radio station from Pittsfield), and they hand delivered an urgent letter from Smith to Dexter. The letter committed the "full resources" of the department "until this situation is settled once and for all." Without meaning to panic, it hinted at calling in the Centers for Disease Control "the instant it is deemed necessary by a full and thorough review at the highest levels of the Health Department."

CHAPTER FORTY-ONE

Sunday, November 23

TOM, OF TOM'S Turkey Farm, liked Abbie so much that he climbed into the pen and waded through about a million terrified birds until he'd captured the one she had her eye on. He had a hell of a time corralling it. This year, he explained, the birds had been unusually skittish.

"There," he said after she'd petted the dumb creature to her heart's content. From his coat pocket he withdrew a length of twine. "I'll tie this around it so you'll be sure to get it on the big day."

"Does it hurt when you kill them?" Abbie asked.

"Oh, no," Tom lied as he released the turkey, which, along with its brethren, had three days left to live.

"Honest?"

"Honest." He turned to Brad. "Let's see." He mused. "It's Sunday today. You want to pick it up Tuesday or Wednesday?"

"Wednesday."

"Tastiest bird you'll ever have," he said, heading back to the farmhouse. "And that's my personal guarantee."

Brad and Abbie lingered by the pens after he had disappeared into the house. Abbie had eaten turkey before, of course, but this, Brad thought, was a heck of a lot better than plucking a plastic-wrapped carcass out of the freezer case. This was what living in the country was all about.

"Mommy's not coming, is she?" Abbie still didn't understand—not completely—that Heather and Brad hated each other.

"No, honey," Brad said.

"And I'm not going there, am I?"

"Not unless you want to. You don't want to, do you?" he prodded.

"Nah. I didn't have much fun last time. She was out with her doctor friend mostly."

"I know," Brad said, incensed again.

"I don't think she'll miss me."

"Well . . ."

"Well, it's true," Abbie said, her tone clipped and cold. Two months ago, when she spoke about her mother, Abbie's sentences often were laced with emotion: sorrow; perhaps guilt; maybe a twinge or two of dark, smoldering anger. Now, nothing. She could as easily have been talking about what vegetables they were going to serve with their turkey. Brad decided it was another positive sign. Time, the great healer. Knock on wood, her nightmares had been slacking off lately. It had been a week since her last one. Prohibiting dinosaur books at bedtime, he reasoned, had been the smartest move he'd made in a long time. He didn't know why he hadn't put his foot down sooner.

"We'll have Thanksgiving here," he said.

"You mean at Mrs. Fitzpatrick's?"

"I think she sees enough of you, young lady, during the week," he said good-humoredly. "Dig me, pygmy?"

"Is Thomasine coming?"

"No, she's going to her parents," Brad said. Since the—what would you call it, *altercation? Comedy? Absurdity?*—with Charlie, things had been cool with Thomasine. Although she wouldn't say it, he knew she blamed him for what had happened. Brad was convinced no permanent damage had been done in their relationship, but he acknowledged that a few days apart could do no harm.

"Can Jimmy come?"

"I think he'll be at his house," Brad said.

"You mean it's gonna be just you and me?"

Brad was crushed. "Is that so bad?"

"Of course not, Dad," she said enthusiastically. "That's *good*!"

"I was beginning to wonder."

"Can I help with the dressing?"

"Sure," Brad said. "You can help with everything."

"Oh, goody!" she bubbled.

Behind them the turkeys kept up their mindless gobbling.

CHAPTER FORTY-TWO

Thursday, November 27
Thanksgiving

STARTING AT DAWN, it snowed steadily. By nightfall almost a foot had fallen, and the wind had piled the drifts to a yard and deeper. A real corker, showing no signs of letting up. The weatherman had said eighteen inches might get dumped before it broke—sometime after midnight, if they were lucky. Definitely a year for the record books, the old-timers marveled as they dozed, sated, by their wood stoves. No one could remember a crazier one.

As dusk brought shadows to the second floor of Berkshire Medical, Hank and Susie McDonald continued their vigil. Earlier they'd shuffled down to the cafeteria for their only meal of the day. Staff had done its best to put on a home-style feast, but man has yet to find the secret to disguising institutional food, especially when it's served on a fiberglass partitioned tray and the salt and pepper come in tiny paper packets. The McDonalds took only a few bites before abandoning it for overly sugared coffee, the new staple of their diet. Before going back up, they exchanged a few words with parents of two other children hospitalized for the same reason as Maureen. It was mindless talk, something about storms and food, and it ended quickly and awkwardly. Misery loves company, but today . . . today misery wanted to be alone.

What was this, the tenth day of Maureen's second hospital admission? How long had she been sick? The calendar had lost all meaning. Everything now ran into everything else, the minutes into hours, the hours into days, the days into the worst time of all, the nights. They'd read stories about parents with terminally ill children, always wondering where they'd summoned the amazing courage to get through such ordeals. Now they knew it was neither amazing nor courageous. It was purely a matter of survival, of breathing, napping, picking at tasteless food, drinking endless bad coffee, resuming cigarette habits so proudly broken when their daughter had been born. Everything but the hospital seemed to have slowly receded. *Here* was reality, only here. Nothing else seemed to exist. Hank had taken LSD once, in high school. It had been like this, a merciless distortion of both time and space.

They were losing their grip.

At six Bostwick dropped by.

He'd driven his four-wheel-drive Bronco, standard machinery in these parts for a doctor who still believed in house calls. He parked in the deserted doctors' lot, located between the hospital and woods that stretched over the hills all the way back to Morgantown. Preoccupied with thinking about the three children he was here to see, he did not notice a set of tracks leading from the woods, around the Dumpster and up onto the loading dock—oversize, large-clawed tracks, left clumsily in the snow.

It did not matter. In another five minutes the wind had erased them.

He found the family in Maureen's room. Hank was at the foot of the bed, thumbing mindlessly for the fourth or fifth or millionth time through a dog-eared *People* magazine. Michael Jackson, it seems, had taken to sleeping in an oxygen chamber in an attempt to slow aging. Hank had to laugh at that one. They all could use an oxygen chamber; he felt he'd aged ten years this fall. Susie was at the other end of the bed. She was stroking her daughter's brow.

In the last half hour Maureen had crossed that fine line from semiconsciousness into sleep, as Susie called the feverish, moan-punctuated state her daughter had been slipping in and out of for a week. Since Maureen's eyes had shut, Susie had been watching the rise and fall of her chest. Was there something different about that motion—one of the few reassuring signs left in this netherworld?

Or was it only in her mind?

No, it wasn't. She could see it plainly. Maureen's breathing had become more labored. Before, the rise and fall of her chest had been hypnotic. Now it was irregular, disturbing.

"I don't like that," Susie announced to Bostwick.

"What?"

"Her breathing. It seems . . . different." It was not the word on her mind. Susie believed in jinxes.

Bostwick listened through his stethoscope. He heard a familiar wheeze, pneumonia's telltale voiceprint. He was convinced it was a complication of the child's primary disease, not the disease itself, and for two days he'd been flooding her with antibiotics. So far to no effect.

"She's still congested," he said noncommittally.

"This is worse."

Bostwick listened again. "You may be right, but I don't detect a change."

Susie looked at Bostwick and burst into tears. "She's dying, Doctor," she sobbed. "I—I can feel it."

Bostwick said nothing. Because she was right: Maureen was dying. The only question now was when. Over the last week, as her condition had worsened, he'd found himself wondering morbidly how he was going to tell her parents about the autopsy, how they would have no choice about it. Now that the Health Department was fully involved, it would be a long, nasty affair. A real pathologist's dream. They would cut everything open, biopsy every part of her, probably take whole organs—brain and liver would be likely candidates—pack them in formaldehyde and ship them hundreds of miles to specialized laboratories, where even more strangers could pick and slice and stain to their heart's content. It made him sick thinking of it, even though he knew it was the right course, the only course.

Outside, the wind howled and the snow beat against the window. The heat was at hospital level, but Bostwick still felt a draft. Hank threw Michael Jackson onto a chair and went to his wife to put his arms around her, comforting her. "Let's take a break," he suggested when she'd regained a degree of composure. "I think we need one."

She nodded.

All three went downstairs, where a vending machine faithfully dispensed a murky substance, allegedly coffee, twenty-four hours a day.

Eyes still closed, Maureen sensed the room was empty.

She didn't mind.

Recently she'd found a new place to go. A deeper darkness than that place where dreams were so awful. The shadow place. It had been a scary place at first, but once she'd gotten used to it, she'd found it was safer there. There was no pain there. No dry throat or gnawing feeling in your stomach.

The bear materialized at the end of her bed.

"I promised I'd be back," it whispered.

Maureen was not aware at first who had spoken—if anyone.

For longer than it was possible to say—maybe it was her whole life—she had been in the hospital place. A place where there were no pets, no outside, no playmates, no fun, where the smells were all mediciny, and the grown-ups used words you didn't understand, and they stuck so many tubes and needles into so many parts of you so often you didn't even feel it anymore. Sometimes, most times, your parents were there at your side, comforting you, promising you it's going to be all right *(but it's really not, Mommy, is it?),* and it was then, only then, that you might have a fleeting pleasant thought. Other times your parents faded from sight, and it was like being lost in the woods on a moonless summer night, your whole body hot, as if it were on fire, and you wanting to scream, but you couldn't; nothing felt the way it used to.

"Maureen?"

The bear moved closer.

"I'm back. And I have a big surprise."

The voice was beginning to penetrate. At first Maureen thought it must be her mother.

"It's not Mommy." The bear corrected her.

Then it's Daddy. I love you, Daddy.

"It's not him either," the bear said. "You know who it is, Maureen. It's me, your friend."

Maureen opened her eyes. Lately it took effort to open her eyes. Concentrating, she brought the room into focus. She kept hoping that one of these times she would find herself not in a Very Bad Place but in a Very Nice, Very Bright One: like her backyard, with her swing, and the playhouse Daddy had built, and the flower garden she and Mommy planted every year.

She kept hoping, and hoping, and—

She saw the bear. It was grinning, as usual, its fangs bared.

She tried to speak, tried to order it away *(please,* PLEASE, *go away),* but her mouth wouldn't work. The tube they'd inserted—the tube that made her mouth so dry—had robbed her of speech.

"We're going on a trip tonight, Maureen," the bear declared.

No! she wanted to say.

But she was tired of fighting. Tired of fighting the sickness, tired of fighting the bear, the hospital, everything in the Very Bad Place. She only wanted darkness—the new, good, very deep kind. The shadow place.

"Come," the bear invited. "Time's awasting."

She closed her eyes. A crimson froth bubbled on her gums. Pain—a new pain, an all-pervasive pain—stung her entire body.

"I see you're ready," the bear said, touching her forehead in the same place Mommy always did.

Maureen's body instinctively stiffened. An observer might have noticed a tiny spark arcing from the girl's forehead to the bear's claws. It lasted only a second. Her body began to spasm—lurching, electrocutional spasms that rocked the bed so violently the bear was sure that damn code team would come running. They passed quickly. The new pain did, too. Slowly the knots in her muscles loosened. There was a momentary awareness of trying to enter the shadow place, and not being allowed to, and then there was nothing.

Maureen exhaled her final breath. It left her without protest, her lungs slowly collapsing. Her left hand, drawn to her face in a gesture of futile defense, flopped back to the mattress.

Maureen McDonald was dead.

The bear did not linger. It had what it wanted—and knew where to deliver it, while still fresh.

A smile flashed across its chops. It did not have to crawl out a window, of course. Crawling in and out of windows, leaving paw-prints, skulking around after dark were only tricks. Useful tricks where kids were concerned, tricks that were fun to play on adults, but still only tricks.

No, it simply disappeared, leaving nothing but a faint electrical smell, like soldering or an overheated motor.

From Thunder Rise down into the valley and beyond, Morgan-town shook with a fresh round of the noises.

In the cafeteria the McDonalds were too preoccupied to notice. Bostwick heard something but dismissed it as a furnace starting up.

By their wood stoves the old-timers took notice.

The next day, as a cold front pushed the last traces of the nor'easter over the hills toward Boston and the Atlantic, they would venture as to how they were the loudest yet. One particularly old old-timer would remark that they sounded less like thunder than some kind of underground laughter, but his colleagues would dismiss that as the effect of one too many holiday tipples.

CHAPTER FORTY-THREE

Friday, November 28

DEXTER HAD insisted Brad take the day after Thanksgiving off. "You could use a little vacation," he'd said. "I don't want my editor burning himself out."

Abbie and Brad got the show on the road early. Yesterday's storm had blown over, leaving a morning so brilliantly clear it could almost seduce Brad into believing a Berkshire winter might not be so bad after all—even if, by all accounts, it was kicking off a month early. Brad had shoveled the front walk, and an enterprising young man recommended by Mrs. Fitzpatrick had come by with his plow to take care of the drive.

Abbie and Brad were building a snow fort when Rod Dougherty telephoned with the news about Maureen McDonald.

Maria, tethered by a chain, had been watching warily from inside the garage. The golden didn't like this snow, not a bit. Didn't like the cold, too sharp on its nose. Didn't like the happy noises the child and the grown-up were making, either, or the fact that the grown-up continued to chain her up. Maria was almost always tethered now. Brad hadn't decided what he was going to do once real winter set in, but temporarily, at least, the garage was Casa Doggy.

That hadn't been the original intent. This was going to be one of those sleeping-by-the-hearth creatures, Man's Best Friend. The early progress was encouraging. The dog had been house-trained in two weeks. Brad and Abbie had fashioned a cozy little corner for her in the kitchen—complete with muddy quilt and food and water bowls initialed with the letter *M*—and she was perfectly content to sleep there. Like all goldens, this one was terminally stupid, but she had enough functioning neurons to begin learning the commands Brad considered bottom line: Sit; lie down; come; go to hell.

About a month ago the dog had started acting queerly. It was as if she had been lobotomized, leaving those few functioning neurons disconnected from the organism. She stopped coming and lying down on command. She forgot house training; the living-room rug, Brad's shoes, under the kitchen table were as good a place as any nowadays for a crap. She had taken to growling, seemingly without provocation. Brad had the unsettling feeling the dog was constantly watching them, watching and—and what?

Waiting?

Waiting for what, exactly? It was a silly notion, but once it entered his mind, it was wedged tightly there. Brad no longer trusted the animal, especially around his daughter. If there'd been a way to get rid of it . . .

The ringing of the phone was insistent.

"You stay here, sweetie," he said to Abbie, who was working on the snow fort's north wall.

"OK," she said cheerfully.

"Just be careful," he said. "Don't pile it too high."

"OK."

He dashed into the house. "Hello?" he said, winded, when he picked up the phone.

It was Rod Dougherty. In the background Brad could hear standard newsroom sounds: phones; loud voices; the clickety-clack of a nearby terminal. Almost noon. They were coming up on their final deadline.

"The McDonald girl died," Rod said simply. "Late last night. We're scrambling to get something for today's paper."

"Jesus," Brad said, sounding surprised.

But he wasn't really. The mystery disease had been their number one running story since early fall, and as it had developed, it had become increasingly clear where it would end. Someone would die. Maybe many were going to die. Brad had no doubt that eventually (sooner rather than later, he believed) the cause would be found, and treatment and cure would be available. As cruel as it sounded, Brad could see good in Maureen's death. If nothing else, it would jolt the public health bureaucrats. Because by now it wasn't only the *Transcript* interested in the disease. Just Tuesday Brad had fielded a call from AP in Albany. A friend at the *Times* had expressed interest. Word was leaking out. A death could only hasten that process.

Brad gave Rod a few pointers on writing the story, and they discussed a tentative plan for covering the funeral, which would be Monday. Then he talked to his city editor about where the story should be played: on page one, bannered across the top. Did they have a file shot of her? No? He thought of Abbie's kindergarten group photo—Maureen was standing directly behind his daughter; he could see them in his mind's eye—but he couldn't bring himself to offer it. Try the school, he advised. He hung up and went back outside.

Abbie was not at the snow fort.

Abbie was gone.

For a millisecond a string of nightmares flashed through his mind (all on Every Good Parent's List of Standard Nightmares). Abbie was kidnapped. Run off to the river, where she'd drowned. Lying dead in the road, where she'd been hit by a passing truck. Fallen into the old farmer's well out back that he'd vowed a thousand times to seal before calamity struck.

His imagination had gone no farther when he saw her. She was standing just outside the garage, her face a foot from Maria's. The dog was straining against her chain. Her teeth were bared.

From one nightmare to the next: Crazed pet mauls helpless kid.

"Abbie!" Brad screamed.

She didn't respond. He couldn't tell if she'd heard him.

It had started quite innocently. Abbie had tired of snow forts. "Maria?" she called, looking for diversion. "I'm your best friend! Here, puppy!"

As Abbie had approached, the dog had growled, then lunged. Only the chain had prevented contact. Abbie froze. Daddy was right: Maria had been acting a little funny lately. If things continued, he'd said, they probably should take her to a vet to get her all checked out. But she'd never done anything like this, growling and snapping her teeth.

Abbie stood, her legs wobbly. She could feel the tears, very close to the surface. She didn't know what she would have done if the dog hadn't been on the chain . . . or if the chain suddenly snapped. Ever since they'd gotten the dog, she had been growing ("like a weed," Daddy'd said). But until now Abbie didn't realize just how big she had gotten. If Maria stood on her hind legs, she would be taller than Abbie. And now, growling, her teeth glistening, she didn't seem like Maria at all, but more like a wild jungle animal.

Brad reacted instantly, tearing into the dog, screaming bloody murder, driving her back with the snow shovel. "Lie down, you bastard!" he swore. "You ever go at her again like that and I'll—I'll . . ." For Abbie's sake, he didn't finish.

The dog knew when she was bested. She slunk off into a corner and lay down. She would not lift her head, but neither did she take her eyes off either human.

Brad wrapped his arms around Abbie. She seemed frightened but otherwise unharmed. The tears that had been so near the surface were quickly retreating.

"What happened?"

"I don't know, Dad. I was just going to pat her when she started growling. Maybe she . . ." But Abbie couldn't think of any possible explanation for the dog's behavior.

"Maybe she isn't feeling good," Brad finished. He stifled the urge for an "I-told-you-so"—of his often repeated warnings to stay away from the dog until they checked her out with the vet.

"Yeah, maybe that's it."

"Dogs can be like people."

"Yeah. They can."

They walked back toward the fort. Neither was eager to resume the job. So they stood, vaguely admiring their work, daydreaming.

"Who called?" Abbie finally asked.

Brad swallowed. He could not look at his daughter. He gazed out over the fields, so quintessentially New England under their blanket of white. Half a century ago this had been a working farm, and the stone walls remained virtually intact, crisscrossing and dissecting the landscape as far as the eye could see. On the horizon, radiant in the brilliant light, was Thunder Rise. The only clouds in the entire sky hovered over it, halolike, casting gray shadows on the pine trees that stood out starkly against the snow.

Such beauty. It seemed sacrilegious to introduce death.

"Who, Dad?" Abbie repeated.

How do you tell a not-yet-six-year-old one of her friends is dead? He didn't have an answer. He supposed you muddled through as best you could.

"I have some very sad news," he said, embracing his daughter.

"Is it about Mom?" she asked immediately.

Her response surprised him. "No, it's not," he said.

"Mrs. Fitzpatrick?"

"It's Maureen."

"What about her?" she said, faintly alarmed.

"She died, honey." He swallowed again, this time with greater difficulty. "Last night. In her sleep."

Abbie didn't answer. Not initially. A scowl took shape on her face, then deepened, as if she were pondering some great mystery. In his arms Brad could feel her muscles stiffen. He'd felt that before—many times, during the separation and custody battle. It was her body's response to stress or pain or severe rejection.

"Why did she die, Dad?" she asked softly. She felt the tears resurfacing.

"She was very sick, hon."

"Have I ever been that sick?"

"Oh, no. Not you, pumpkin."

"What did she have?" Brad had discussed the disease before, but only fleetingly.

"A bad sickness."

"But why did she die?" Abbie repeated.

"God called her," he blurted out. "She's in heaven now. Very happy." A stock reply—a ghost of childhood Catholicism sprung to life. Considering the circumstance, he thought it was a good answer.

Abbie looked skyward, looked for the moon. It was not out. She pointed up. "God?" she repeated.

"God."

"But why would God do something like that? Maureen was happy *here.* I know because she was my friend." Abbie's scowl softened and dissolved, and the tears finally surfaced. Brad was out of answers. He tightened his hug and said nothing. Abbie's sobs shook her body, but there was an oddly reassuring feeling to them. They were the sobs of a strong, healthy little girl.

Healthy.

For how long? It was an ugly thought, unplanned. But there it was. There was no getting around it. He knew at that moment how much Maureen's death had changed the stakes. For the first time, he wondered if coming to Morgantown hadn't been a colossal mistake.

CHAPTER FORTY-FOUR

Tuesday, December 2

DR. RAYMOND GOSSELIN arrived the day after Maureen's funeral. Bostwick met him at the Albany airport, and for the first part of the drive they talked old times. It really was good to see him, Bostwick thought. He'd aged (hadn't they all?), and he was still homely as sin (floppy ears stay floppy); but he looked healthy and happy in a knocking-on-middle-age kind of way—as if he ate well, had a challenging career, made a lot of money, lived with a wonderful woman in an equally wonderful house, and worked out every other day at the local racquetball club. All of which, Gosselin informed his old roommate, he did.

"That sweet southuuurn clime," Gosselin bantered, using the fake Georgia accent he always sprang on his northern friends. "Heck, you just can't beat it."

"No snow, I bet." The sun had eaten away at it, but there was still plenty left from last week's surprise storm.

"No snow. Heck, it was seventy-two at Hartsfield when I left."

"Can't beat that."

"No, sirree."

The talk soon enough turned to the disease. It wasn't only friendship that had brought Gosselin to Morgantown: The state Health Department had finally requested the official involvement of the CDC. Gosselin, high up on the centers' Public Health Services' seniority list, wore enough medals to get the assignment when he volunteered. Yesterday he'd read the summary staff had prepared for him, and he'd talked an hour on the phone to Boston. By the time he'd gone to bed last night, he had his theories.

Diseases turned Gosselin on. Especially offbeat diseases, the ones found only in some godforsaken tribal village once every hundred years. And the mystery killers—those were the *crème de la crème.* Before the *Legionella* bacterium had been identified, Legionnaires' disease had been like that. A total mystery, and deadly as hell. Gosselin's first big CDC assignment had been a support position on the Legionnaires' task force, and it was there, as he liked to pun, "that I got the bug for good." His hero was Dr. Daniel Gajdusek, the American virologist whose work solving the Polynesian killer virus kuru won him the 1976 Nobel Prize in medicine. Such an honor for Gosselin, Bostwick would have agreed, probably was in the cards. Although they had not corresponded since their residency days, Bostwick for years had come across his name in the literature—either as author or subject. Gosselin was the doc who had cracked the famous Virgin Islands fever, the disease that had killed four tourists and sent a boatload of millionaires to the hospital. Turned out it was a parasitic worm causing that one; Gosselin had isolated it within three days of coming to St. Thomas. He'd gotten his smiling face in *People* magazine.

"I think you missed your calling," Gosselin said as he removed a bundle of folders from his briefcase and thumbed through them.

"What should my calling have been?"

"Epidemiology. You do excellent backgrounding," he said, ruffling the papers. "The tests you ordered, the sequence—good detective work, every bit. I wouldn't have done any differently myself." A decade ago Bostwick would have been insulted, but now he felt something akin to pride, considering Gosselin's reputation.

"I had no choice, really," Bostwick said. "My kids were getting worse. The state was doing doodly-squat."

"Typical," Gosselin said, sounding personally peeved. "Massachusetts or Montana, my experience has been the same: Health departments sit on their asses until it's so hot they have no choice but to jump."

"The paper here's given them a few good jolts. I know the editor personally. He's got a kid of his own."

"Good. I'm sure they needed a little roughing up in the press. I don't think it's deliberate neglect in these cases, by the way. I think it's inexperience. The local yokel syndrome, we call it, and we see it in health departments in even the biggest jurisdictions. There's a real tendency to believe that if you cross your fingers and hold your breath, it'll go away.

"The funny thing is, in nine out of ten cases, it does. If we blitzed every time we heard the word 'epidemic,' we'd need the Pentagon's budget, for heck's sake. Not that I wouldn't take that kind of dough." He smiled. "Combat pay for some of the crap we have to take working with the locals."

"You'll be working *with* them?" Bostwick asked.

"No choice. That's how we operate, in concert with the local authorities—in most instances, state health departments. In fact, that's about the *only* way we can get involved, by official request. Most people don't know that."

"I must confess I didn't."

"Did you know your state Health Department called Atlanta? Late last week?"

"No."

"Not that there wouldn't have been ways of finagling an invitation if they hadn't. But in this case, the request was generated—quite unilaterally and before my input—in Boston. Maybe they knew what you were up to." Gosselin smiled.

"It wouldn't surprise me. I've made enough noise."

"Before I left, I spoke extensively to Smith."

"He's the director."

"Right. Seems slick, in a positive sort of way. He put me in touch with this doc, Hough, who's been handling the nuts and bolts of the thing. Tell me. Is he as stupid as he sounds?"

"Worse." Bostwick laughed.

"If it's any comfort, we'll be in the driver's seat all the way on this one."

"It *is* a comfort."

They were over the line now, heading through downtown Pittsfield. Berkshire Medical was only a couple of blocks away. Tomorrow Bostwick would take him there to see the four children who were still hospitalized.

"Any preliminary ideas?" Bostwick asked.

"Of course," Gosselin said. "Three, to be precise."

"*Legionella?* I tried to get them to test for that. They just about laughed."

"Ah, *Legionella pneumophila,*" Gosselin said, as if merely pronouncing the name gave him a secret thrill. "I doubt it, although I'll be screening for it as a matter of course. There's a lot of stuff I'll be screening for, even though I am virtually certain it isn't any of them. Parrot fever, toxoplasmosis, Q fever, Weil's disease, even smallpox, which, of course, has been extinct since 1977 but which all of us remain instinctively fearful of. No, I have other, more likely candidates."

He went on to describe them. Heading his list was babesiosis, caused by a protozoan parasite. The disease was unusually difficult to diagnose and even harder to treat, Gosselin said; antibiotics did not touch it. Transmitted by tick. Incubation period of one to twelve months, which would explain the appearance of new cases once tick season had passed. Worldwide occurrence, with cases reported in U.S. in Nantucket, Massachusetts, Long Island, and Wisconsin. Extremely rare. Frequently fatal.

Suspect Number Two was brucellosis, a bacterial infection. Nickname: Bang's fever. Worldwide occurrence. Reported annual incidence in USA: 150 to 250 cases. Transmitted by cattle. Fatal in 2 to 5 percent of cases. Usually responsive to tetracycline plus streptomycin or other aminoglycosides.

"Untreated, either can last months, a year," Gosselin said. "Don't you remember them? We studied them in med school."

"Vaguely," Bostwick said. "They're not exactly your garden-variety disease."

"No. In fact, they're quite rare. Still, I can't believe no one's tested for them. Heck, not with all these dairy farms."

"Like I said, they're not your average diseases," Bostwick said. He felt Gosselin was pointing a finger of blame at him.

"I don't fault you," Gosselin said quickly. "I doubt there are five family practitioners in the entire country who have ever seen them—except perhaps in the big cattle states, which Massachusetts definitely is not. Even out West it's almost unheard of today. The vets have done a damn good job cleaning it up. But I *would* fault somebody in your health department for not testing for it. At least they hadn't in the reports I have. It should have been one of their first candidates."

"What's your third possibility?"

"A nasty little bugger called relapsing fever, spread by lice and ticks. It's an appropriate name. *Borrelia recurrentis* knocks you on your ass for a week, lets you up the next week, knocks you down, lets you up, on and on like that through as many as ten cycles. The epidemiology is *very* unusual. To a layman, it appears to have no logic, no order, no clear progression even."

"Sounds like what we have here," Bostwick said hopefully.

"Yes, except there hasn't been a documented case in the U.S. for fifteen years, and that one was somewhere out West. But diseases sometimes have a way of popping up when and where you least expect them," he said, that excited tone back in his voice. "I keep waiting for the day smallpox returns."

"Well," Bostwick said softly, "I hope you find it, whatever it is. And fast. I was at the little girl's funeral yesterday and—and—" His voice was suddenly choked. A part of Bostwick—a very private, very personal part buried somewhere under layers of logic and common sense and professional judgment—blamed Bostwick. It was a blame he knew would only get worse with the passage of time, just as it had with Justin Rosenberg.

Bostwick's sudden emotion made Gosselin uneasy.

"Oh, we'll find it, all right," he promised. "Heck. Don't you worry about that. No, sirree."

CHAPTER FORTY-FIVE

Wednesday, December 3

THE NURSING HOME was a cinch to find. Up Route 7 to Williamstown, across the Vermont border into Pownal, then west across the New York line into Hoosick Falls, whose major claim to fame was the gin mills that operated there so flagrantly during Prohibition. The home stood at the entrance to town, on a bluff overlooking the Hoosac River, not far from a valley where Quidneck Indians once had their largest village.

At the front desk Charlie asked for Ben Wilcox. He wasn't even sure Ben was still alive. The Quidneck who'd tracked him down for Charlie hadn't been up in years, and Ben had no family. None that Charlie could find, anyway. It was a long shot, but that's what Charlie was down to now. Rolls of the dice.

"Ben Wilcox?" the nurse said, evidently surprised.

So he is *dead,* Charlie thought.

"Yes," he answered.

"Are you a relative?"

"No," Charlie admitted.

"Then who are you?"

"A friend," he said, fudging.

"He can't have visitors. He's a very sick old man."

At least he's alive, Charlie thought, relieved. *I'll take my chances.*

"Just five minutes," he pleaded. "I've driven a very long way."

"And he's very sick," she snapped.

The nurse scrutinized the stranger, Ben's first visitor since she'd started at the home two years ago. It was obvious from his ponytail and dark, chiseled features that he was an Indian, like Ben. Probably here for some crazy reason only Indians would understand, maybe a secret tribal ritual associated with dying. There was no doubt Ben was nearing his end. Although mentally he still had moments of sharpness, physically his house had crumbled. Staff's only question now was could he possibly hang on to his hundredth birthday, July 13 of next year. The latest line was that he could not.

"Please," Charlie implored.

"I'm not sure he'd be able to talk."

"I only want him to listen. To know I'm there."

"I can't guarantee he would. He's very sick."

"Please. I may not have another chance."

"Are you a *good* friend?" She was softening.

"A best friend."

"Room one-twelve," the nurse finally said. "First floor, fourth door on the right. And keep it to five minutes. I'll be watching the clock."

"I will. Thank you."

Charlie walked down the corridor. Suddenly he was in no hurry. He'd always hated hospitals, convalescent homes, doctors' offices—any place where sickness was so comfortable. Every one smelled the same: sickly sweet, as if there were a law that said institutional disinfectants all had to have a certain scent. Nursing home sounds were even worse: a cacophony of babbling and snoring, even at midday. Despite the flower prints that adorned every wall, and the Muzak overhead, and all the other phony cheeriness, there was no way to gloss over what a nursing home was: a place to die. In Quidneck times there had been a place like that. A much more honest place—situated in the very heart of nature, the only place a Quidneck could die with dignity. His father had described it as a grove of pine trees beside a tranquil, trout-filled lake where old warriors and powwows would travel, alone, when they were ready. The Going-Away Place had long since disappeared; even its location had been lost. Bitterly Charlie supposed it was a white man's development now, covered over with a shopping mall.

Room 112 was a triple. Medicaid country. The man in the first bed was asleep or comatose; it was impossible to tell. What was left of his body was hidden by a sheet, but the folds and creases could not hide the fetal shape he was locked into. The second man's eyes were open, but nothing registered on them when Charlie went by.

Both of his legs had been amputated above the knee. The stubs seemed to stare out at the world, fish-belly white, lifeless.

Charlie read the adhesive-tape label at the foot of the third bed. WILCOX, BENJAMIN, it said.

Ben's eyes were closed, his hands folded peacefully over his belly. Once, Charlie could see, his deeply creased face had been handsome; even now it was not unpleasant to look at. Wisdom and serenity were written on it, but also a tiredness that was not from age alone. *This is a man in the process of letting go,* Charlie surmised. How much more comfortable he would have been in the Going-Away Place. How much easier to make peace than here, in these soulless twentieth-century surroundings. Charlie wished he could take Ben there.

"Ben," he said, bending down, his voice a calm, motherly thing.

There was no response, not even a fluttering of eyelids.

"Ben. It's Charlie Moonlight."

Nothing.

"Your Quidneck brother."

Nothing.

"George Moonlight's son."

The old man drew a deeper breath but did not open his eyes.

"George said you were a very wise man." Actually his father had mentioned him only once, in passing, but there was nothing to be gained by saying that. "Like your father, and his father before him, Running Fox."

Ben's hands twitched. Charlie brushed the old man's forehead with his hand. Ben's skin felt like old newspaper.

"Hobbamock," Charlie said.

Ben's hands twitched again.

"Hobbamock is free. I need your help."

The old man took a deep breath, then another, and another. He seemed to be struggling with something. Perhaps it was the decision to respond to this stranger or to stay where it was quiet and warm.

"The children are dying," Charlie whispered.

Ben opened his eyes. Charlie was surprised to find them clear, blue, intense. Even so far gone, fire still smoldered in them.

"I need your help," Charlie said.

The old man nodded.

Charlie had not remembered Ben's Christian name. He'd had to ask around before learning that. But once he'd remembered the old tale his father had told—of Hobbamock's momentary escape when Thunder Rise was first being mined—he remembered the Quidneck who had stopped the evil. He had been an illustrious powwow, this Quidneck. In fact, that was the context in which he'd come up. George Moonlight had been telling his son, who was eternally fascinated by such things, about some of their people's distinguished leaders. Running Fox had been one of the greatest, and not only for his role in reimprisoning Hobbamock. Running Fox had been the last powwow to also hold the title of chief sachem, a rare distinction in Quidneck history.

Ben Wilcox was his grandson.

"I undertook *pniese,*" Charlie told Ben.

Since the ordeal Charlie had been obsessed with divining its lessons. He'd concluded that it would be possible—even simple—to seal off the evil god's cave. A few well-placed sticks of dynamite would take care of that. That probably would stop Hobbamock's advance; if his strength had not grown to the point where he could break out—a big if—that would be the end of him. (He could not, at this point, let himself consider another possibility: that Hobbamock had left his home and now roamed free.)

But the children already under attack—*and Jimmy's one of them, there's no doubt of that*—what of them? *Get them away from here,* had been Charlie's first idea. *Send them all to California.* With Jimmy, it might be possible. He might somehow be able to convince his sister to pack her bags and go. Then, again, he might not. And what of the other kids? Could he just forget them? No. Not and be able to live with himself. So how do you get all of *them* out of town? Kidnapping? What were the chances of getting away with that? No, parents would have to be persuaded; the *Transcript,* prime media outlet for the area, would be the logical place to sound the alarm. Right. He could just hear Brad Gale now: "You want to do *what?* Oh, certainly, Charlie. Let me introduce you to Rod Dougherty, our ace reporter. He'll get all the facts for a page one story. And by the way, thanks. Thanks for doing us all a great public service."

Even if there were some feasible scheme to banish an entire town, instinct told Charlie that it was already too late. That once Hobbamock had his claws into a child, it would take more than mere relocation to save them. Charlie had returned, time and time again, to the legend. In it the Indian children had somehow been freed of

Hobbamock's hold. Cured, as it were. Years ago, in telling the story of the great battle with Hobbamock, his father had said that what had finally tipped the balance was a spear.

"In the *pniese* there was a spear," Charlie whispered into Ben Wilcox's ear.

With effort the old man nodded. It was as if Charlie had stated something obvious, like the fact the sun rose in the east this morning and likely would set in the west.

"In the *pniese* I thought I could kill him with it. I was certain that was why it was there, for me, to use against him. But it was useless in my hands. I . . . must have been lacking something. Maybe it's an incantation. Or a dance. A cry. Something. Something to supplement the spear. Or maybe it's not the spear at all. Maybe I've been misled. Please. Please help me."

With one curled finger, he motioned for Charlie to come closer. When Charlie's ear was inches away, he spoke a single word: "Child."

Charlie thought a moment. "A child must be sacrificed?" he said doubtfully.

Ben shook his head. He spoke another word: "Spear."

Charlie was baffled. Then it hit him. "A child must use it. A child must use the spear."

Ben nodded.

"A child must use it against Hobbamock."

He nodded.

"Can it be any child?"

Ben shook his head and uttered another word: "Sick."

"It must be one of the sick children."

Again, a nod.

"And if this does not happen?"

Ben closed his eyes.

"They will die?"

Ben's eyes flitted open. He nodded.

"All of them?"

"All," Ben said hoarsely. Even one-word answers were exhausting him.

Charlie sensed that. "Ben" he said gently, "I have one more question. Only one. Where is the spear? Please. Did your grandfather ever say?"

Ben tried to push himself up in the bed, but the effort was too much. He would have to answer as he was. With obvious pain, he completed four sentences—the last sentences he would speak on this earth. He told Charlie that the spear had passed into the hands of a Quidneck who lived in New York, that this was long before Charlie was born, that the man's name was Brown, and that he had been very, very rich.

Ben closed his eyes again, and this time he did not reopen them. He was done.

"You'll have to go now," an irked voice from behind Charlie said. He turned. It was the nurse. He had not heard her enter.

"I'm done," he said.

"I said five minutes. It's way past that."

"I'm done," Charlie repeated. His voice had a threatening tone that the nurse did not like one bit. She was very glad he was leaving voluntarily.

"Good-bye, Ben," Charlie said softly. "Thank you."

The old man did not respond.

On the drive home Charlie reflected. Now there were two tasks facing him.

Finding the spear. And a child to wield it.

CHAPTER FORTY-SIX

Thursday, December 4

Rational people do not, perhaps, do such things. But Justin McLaughlin was not a rational man the morning his eight-year-old son died at Berkshire Medical. He was an angry, saddened, frustrated, scared-shitless powder keg of a man who still had two live and seemingly healthy children to think about.

So he called the press.

McLaughlin knew what he was doing. He was a partner in an advertising firm in Pittsfield, and he'd dealt with the media before, understood their power. Even in his rage and grief he was able, through several phone calls, to orchestrate an impressive turnout. A network-affiliated TV station from Albany joined the *Transcript,* the

Berkshire *Eagle,* a stringer from the Boston *Globe,* two Pittsfield radio stations, and the AP at his conference, which he held on the front steps of the hospital.

He hoped to hell the Health Department tuned in that night.

"Jay's dead," he said, weeping from the outset. "I can't bring him back. I know that."

Rod Dougherty's tape recorder was running.

"But there are four other kids inside there with the same thing, and four other sets of parents, and maybe a dozen other kids just a step or two away from being hospitalized, and . . . and . . . *nobody knows, damn it*! No one knows what is killing these children. No one knows how to make them better.

"This—this *thing*. . . we want answers, and we want them now! Before anyone else . . . dies."

McLaughlin fumbled for his wallet, found the snapshots he wanted, and held them up for the cameras.

"These are my children," he said, pointing to three smiling faces gathered around a birthday cake.

"Jay's in the middle," he said, his voice breaking. "He's the one wearing the party hat. This is Becky. She's nine now, in third grade, at Morgantown Elementary. Peter's four, and still at home. Both of them, thank the Lord, aren't sick. But they've watched their brother . . . die . . . these last few weeks. Watched him go from . . . God, he could throw a baseball like you wouldn't believe, boy, could he ever . . . to go from all that to the hospital.

"And now—now, what's happened is giving Becky and Peter nightmares. They can't sleep, they see monsters, they wake up crying and sweaty, and it's because of Jay. They're scared it might happen to them, too, can't you see? Can't you?"

His wife could not bring herself to join him, so he'd faced the press alone. He looked particularly vulnerable now, Rod thought, standing alone in the sun, the cold breeze ruffling the lapels of his coat.

"We live over near the rise," he continued when he'd composed himself again. "On mornings like this Jay liked nothing better than to play in those woods. He would come home, his cheeks red, all out of breath, so—so happy. Maybe after lunch we'd go outside together. I'd have my catcher's glove and he'd throw . . ."

He paused, remembering, sniffling.

Someone ought to stop him, Rod thought, *before we're all crying, too.*

It wasn't necessary.

McLaughlin waved the snapshots of his children and said: "It's too late for Jay, but for their sake . . . for the sake of all the other children . . . I beg you, please . . . please . . ."

He did not finish his sentence but turned and walked back inside the hospital, where his wife was waiting. The reporters, trained since Journalism 101 to toss questions as naturally as drawing breaths, didn't say a word.

"You sound frustrated," Brad said.

"Perhaps a bit," Gosselin conceded. "But heck, all that means is we'll just have to work harder."

They were in the *Transcript*'s conference room. Bostwick, who'd arranged the meeting at Brad's insistence, was with them. So was Rod Dougherty. Gosselin ordinarily didn't talk to the media—no matter how carefully you explained something, he believed, they always got it wrong—but for his old college buddy, he'd made an exception, provided it was strictly for background.

"So what's next?" Brad asked, absently drumming his pen.

"Atlanta, of course," Gosselin said. "There's all that lab work to be run. Half the blood probably hasn't even arrived there yet."

"Mark says you leave this afternoon."

"Right after this."

"Will you be back?"

"Depends. Sometimes we solve these things at home. You'd be amazed at how much the computers can help. I don't know how they ever did investigations without them."

"Doc?" Brad asked in a more somber voice.

"Yes, Mr. Gale?"

"Do you have any idea how much worse it's going to get? How many more kids are going to be affected?"

"He has a personal interest in this," Bostwick explained. "I think I mentioned that."

"A daughter," Brad said. "She's not six yet."

And you better believe I'm going to do everything in my power to make sure she sees six . . . and seven, and eight, and right on up till I'm walking her down the aisle.

"Are we off the record, Mr. Gale?"

"I already said we were."

"You understand we're off the record?" Gosselin said to Rod.

"Yes."

"Off the record, I don't have the foggiest notion how widespread this will become. Until we know what it is, there's no way I could even guess. I would say, however, that the absolute worst epidemic ever in any way accurately documented—the Black Death, in the fourteenth century—only claimed a third of its possible victims. Thirty-three percent. A terrible, toll, granted—especially if you had the misfortune to be in that percentile—but two thirds *did* survive. That fact is often lost."

"It's still not much consolation." *In fact,* Brad thought, *that's the most insensitive, arrogant thing I ever heard.*

"I realize that, Mr. Gale. And were I a betting man, I would bet the house that whatever we're dealing with will pale by comparison with the plague."

Good! Brad thought. *Great! I can see the headline now:* MORGANTOWN MYSTERY DISEASE FELLS ALL CHILDREN, BUT TOLL PALES IN COMPARISON WITH BLACK DEATH. CDC OFFICIALS GREATLY RELIEVED!

"If this ultimately affected even five percent of the people in this area," Gosselin said, "we'd be talking a public health problem of historic and catastrophic proportions. You'd have the President personally intervening.

"More than that, I just can't say yet. Heck, I admit that I came here suspecting three specific diseases, and there was very good reason to. While I can't rule them out entirely until I get some lab results, I've seen enough to cast serious doubt on all three. Certain information I've gleaned here was not, ah, in the preliminary reports."

"Such as?" Rod asked.

"Such as the sleep disorders. Such as the apparent concentration of cases on one side of town, the side near the mountain. Such as some other factors I'm not at liberty to disclose at this moment, not even to you, Mark. I'm sorry."

"So what is it, Doc?" Brad demanded. "What the hell is it? Some bug escaped from an army lab?"

Gosselin laughed—inappropriately, Bostwick and Brad both thought. This week Bostwick had had ample time to rediscover all those reasons he'd fallen out with his med school roommate. The guy, basically, was a jerk. *Brilliant,* but still a jerk. There was no way around it.

"There are those who believe that's where AIDS came from, you know." Gosselin went on more sternly. "Bad novelists and starving free-lance writers, mostly. What are we dealing with, Mr. Gale? I'd put my money on infection, as opposed to poisoning or some kind of mass hysteria. I'm leaning toward bacterial cause, as opposed to viral, although I wouldn't rule a virus out just yet. In some respects, it reminds me of *Legionella.* Heck, no one at first knew what was killing American Legion conventioneers in Philadelphia that summer of 1976. And while the responsible bacterium was not absolutely one hundred percent unknown—most people don't know that—for all intents and purposes, it was a brand-new disease. Why did it pop up that summer in that hotel's air-conditioning system at the exact time that group of people, most somewhat elderly and disease-susceptible, were there? That, I suppose, is a question for a higher power.

"The point is that whatever we're dealing with here seems, at the moment, quite mysterious. And three years from now when we look back at the Morgantown cases, we'll wonder how we ever could have missed it. We'll wonder what the fuss was all about."

You arrogant shit, Brad wanted to say. *All we are for you is your next paper.*

But he didn't say that. Instead, he remarked: "There are all kinds of theories going around, you know."

"I imagine there are," Gosselin said uninterestedly. "Probably some pretty wild ones."

"I made mention of an army bug—that's one popular theory."

"Here and everywhere else."

"Others think it's something in the groundwater," Rod added. "Some chemical, leaching from a hazardous waste dump."

"At this stage, water as the mode of transmission is doubtful, but I couldn't entirely rule it out. I think we can rule out hazardous waste. Tests of well water have turned up nothing. Neither does the EPA have a record of such a dump anywhere near here."

"A few people think it's radiation—like radon."

"Those people obviously are even more ignorant than the norm. Nothing here even remotely resembles radiation sickness. And radon's only known hazard is lung cancer, which invariably takes years, decades to be seen. Not to mention an entirely different range of symptoms."

"The Indians even have a theory," Brad said.

"*American* Indians?"

"Yes. Quidnecks. The area around Thunder Rise was theirs. There are still a few left. They say the disease is caused by an angry god. They—at least one of them—believe this god is stealing kids' souls. Apparently that's a slow and painful process. When they're finally stolen, the kids die."

"Charming, aren't they, these Indians?" Gosselin said.

Brad and Rod nodded in agreement.

But Bostwick didn't think it was so charming. He'd heard the old legend—was it from Brad's friend, Thomasine, who'd also told Rod?—and he'd found it fascinating, in a morbid kind of way.

Now, for reasons he could not explain, he found it disturbing.

CHAPTER FORTY-SEVEN

Friday, December 5

GINNY ELLIS didn't like the change in her half brother. Not one bit.

Charlie had always been intense, if that was the word. Always a nonconformist (that was Mrs. Fitzpatrick's description), a man who placed his stock in the old Indian ways. She had always admired him for that—for the way in which he rejected the shallowness and greed of the late twentieth century for a set of simpler, more honest values. She'd fancied Charlie as something of a modern-day Thoreau, wandering the countryside in search of deeper truths.

Now, as he sat at her kitchen table, she didn't think those values were so very noble anymore. She thought Charlie had gone over some philosophical precipice into a dangerous abyss. Or maybe it was simpler than that.

Maybe he'd just cracked.

His proposal . . . it was *insane.*

He was insane.

Charlie's thoughts about Ginny were similar. He'd come over for dinner this evening and found the Ellis family in full-blown crisis. Making his bed this morning, Ginny had found a gun under Jimmy's mattress. And not just any gun. It was her late husband's over-under shotgun, a weapon capable of taking down a circus elephant. And it had been loaded. *Jesus.* Not only had Jimmy found the gun (that wasn't too hard; Ginny had stored it in the garage loft), but he'd broken the lock on the trunk where the ammunition was stored and loaded it. When Ginny had found it, the goddamn safety wasn't even on.

The gun had done it. Pushed Ginny over the edge. When Jimmy returned from kindergarten, she'd presented him with the weapon and asked him in a voice seething with rage just what the hell was going on. What the hell was this, his idea of a real-life Rambo? Hadn't she made it clear he was never to play that again? Hadn't the incident in the woods last summer been enough?

It wasn't Rambo, he'd answered, quivering with the response. "I don't play Rambo anymore. It was the wolf. I wanted protection against the wolf. Please, Mommy. I told you, it's back."

Ginny was not into corporeal punishment. She'd never more than slapped Jimmy before—once or twice, and then only lightly on his bottom—but now she lit into him with a belt, raising welts on his back and buttocks and the backs of his legs. She was immediately overwhelmed with guilt. If she possibly needed more proof that her son was experiencing serious emotional difficulty, the discovery of the gun had been it. And what had she done? Whacked the shit out of him. She was so angry with herself it felt as if she might explode.

Upstairs Jimmy finally was asleep.

For how long, Ginny couldn't answer. The nightmares had been especially bad the last two nights. On top of that, his damn cold had returned, making his sleep restive and sweat-filled, despite the Tylenol with codeine she'd been pumping into him. A knot re-formed in her stomach as she thought of what might have happened if he had fumbled for that gun in the middle of one of his nightmares. The knot tightened as she remembered how she'd handled the discovery.

"I blame you," she said angrily to her brother.

"Me?"

"*You.* With all this . . . *crap* about wolves. I know you mean well, Charlie, I know how much you love him, but you're just feeding into things. He told me you were going to help him keep the wolf away. He said you promised."

"I never said anything about a gun."

"Maybe you did. Maybe you didn't. It doesn't matter. Whatever you said, it's been . . . feeding into it." She stopped, her mind seeming to blank.

Charlie looked at the kitchen window. It was open. Listless air rustled the lace curtains Ginny kept so spotless. *December fifth, barely a week after that blizzard, and now it's warm enough to have the windows open,* Charlie thought. *Another bad omen.*

Ginny's attention returned to the argument. "And now you want to use him for this . . . *ritual,*" she said. "It's crazy, Charlie. *You're* crazy. To even think of taking him into a cave and doing . . . whatever the hell it is you want to do. It's nuts. It's more than nuts. It's—it's . . . *illegal*!"

"Things are out of control," Charlie stated.

"And this will bring them back under control? Oh, yes, I can see that, Charlie. That's *easy* to see. I don't know why I didn't see it myself. March my son into a goddamn cave and have him wave a spear around. That's the obvious answer here!"

"You're not being honest with yourself, Little Sis," Charlie said gently, despite his temper rising. The last thing he needed was to lose it, the way he had with Brad Gale.

"Jimmy doesn't have . . . it."

"He's had a fever for a week. You told me so yourself."

"He has a cold."

"He missed school Wednesday."

"Of course he did," she snapped. "I told you, he has a cold. A *bad* cold."

"How many colds this fall?"

"I don't keep track of something like that," she lied.

"What about the nightmares?"

"Every kid has nightmares."

"Not like this. You're denying it, Little Sis."

"I am not denying it!" she said. *"Jimmy doesn't have it, and that's the end of it!"*

Like that, her anger had burned itself out. The tears came, and she slumped into her chair, but not before refilling her glass with wine. Since Maureen McDonald's death, her drinking had picked up considerably. She'd never had more than a glass or two of wine a day, but now she was polishing off an entire bottle before dinner.

"Charlie, I'm afraid," she sobbed. "I've never been more afraid in my whole life. It wasn't this bad even when Jim died."

He sat across from her, his cigarette dangling from his mouth. He pitied her, and if he'd been someone else—a man not afraid to show his emotions—he would have gone over to her, draped his arms around her, smothered her with the blanket of human compassion until the storm had passed. She'd been through hell—and the real shit wasn't even flying yet. That was what scared him most.

When her crying had subsided, he asked her again. He ran through all the reasons, and how it was her son who would be saved, not to mention all the other kids, and how he was convinced more than he had ever been convinced by anything in his life that there was no choice . . . no choice at all.

"For the sake of the kids," he pleaded. "For the sake of the kids."

"No, Charlie," she declared. "I can't let you."

"Jimmy will die." It was a savage thing to say, and he was almost ashamed for letting it pass through his lips. But he was past the point where mincing words was doing anyone any good. They had to deal in *facts* now, even if she didn't see them as that.

"That's . . . so . . . cruel," she said, her eyes moistening again.

"I'm only speaking the truth. Please, Little Sis. I need him. For him."

"No," she repeated, the iron momentarily creeping back into her voice.

CHAPTER FORTY-EIGHT

Saturday, December 6

"WANNA HEAR my part?" Abbie trilled.

"Which part?" Thomasine kidded. "Your hand?"

"Noooo!"

"Your *arm*?"

"You know what I mean," Abbie said. "The part in my Christmas play!"

"Sure," Thomasine said enthusiastically. "I'd love to hear that."

"OK. I'm one of the Three Kings, and I have to sing a song."

Saturday, and the damn weather seesaw had dropped them into the cold again. Only because they were a full week into December was it close to tolerable. Brad had gotten a fire roaring, and he'd cooked dinner, and after dinner Thomasine had insisted on making a holiday punch out of ginger ale, lime juice, oranges, and rum. It was very smooth stuff, and Brad had insisted they not let a drop go to waste. "Cheers," he said every time he refilled their glasses—and there were a lot of those times in the two hours after dinner. "Cheers," Thomasine responded. She was getting sloshed. Brad was getting sloshed. Both of them, happily and cheerfully getting sloshed . . .

. . . and looking forward to when Abbie was finally in bed.

Christmas was less than three weeks off. Jesus. It had crept up on them so fast; it always did. The only reason they were even aware of its approach was this morning, when they'd gone food shopping. Driving through Morgantown Center, they'd seen stores decorated with trees and elf figurines and tinsel and nativity scenes. When they'd gotten home, Abbie, with Brad's help, had made out her Christmas list. Brad had written "MR. S. CLAUS, NORTH POLE" on the envelope, then stashed it by the phone in the kitchen cubbyhole. First thing Monday morning, he promised, he'd have it in the mail. Reindeer would probably carry it on the long journey to Santa, Abbie conjectured. You're probably right, her dad agreed.

"You ready?" Abbie asked, taking center stage in the living room.

"Ready," said Thomasine.

"It's about the kings who came to see Baby Jesus. He was in a manger with Mary and Joseph." Abbie pointed to the couch where Thomasine was. "Pretend that's the manger," she said, "not a couch."

"OK."

Abbie curtsied and began, not at all self-consciously, to sing.

Seeing her standing there, Thomasine was struck again by how pretty Brad's daughter was. She remembered the first time she'd seen her, on Mrs. Fitzpatrick's inn's porch, how impressed she'd been by her curly brown hair and cat green eyes and the way she carried herself, confident but not obnoxious, at once grown-up and little-girlish. She remembered wondering where this striking little girl had gotten her looks, from her mom or from her dad. She remembered learning the answer when she met Brad. There could be no doubt: Abbie was her father's daughter. Physically and in every other way.

And there was nothing whatsoever wrong with that.

Since Thanksgiving Thomasine and Brad had steadily moved forward. She liked to think of their relationship as something living, something sweet and fragrant and sturdy, like wild flowers in late summer. Thomasine found herself savoring what they had at the oddest moments: in front of her computer; in the middle of interviews; on the phone to Brown. *Almost three months we've known each other,* she reflected. *Two months we've been sleeping together. Long enough to find the skeletons in the emotional closets. The big ones, anyway. Except for that bitch ex-wife of his, there don't seem to be any.*

The only blemish on the face of things—Charlie—seemed to have faded. Since returning from her vacation, there had been no mention of him, or his tale, or the scene with him in the restaurant, or the creepy trip Thomasine and Charlie had made into the mine. With the passage of time, it was becoming easier and easier for her to believe that what had happened in there had just been her mind playing tricks. *Brad's right,* she'd conceded after endless pondering. *Good old cold, analytic Brad Gale, whose philosophy about such matters could be summarized: There are fairy tales, things that go bump in the night . . . and then there's the real world. And while Charlie's right, in a purely philosophical sense—all things are* not *as they seem—there are limits. Even an anthropologist has to recognize limits.* Especially *an anthropologist. If that's cultural chauvinism, so be it.*

She smiled, thinking of Brad and watching his daughter sing her Christmas carol. Abbie seemed genuinely to like her. That was good. Very good. In this kind of situation it was almost as crucial as the feelings of the man himself.

"You're a star." Thomasine complimented Abbie.

Abbie smiled and kept on singing. Brad, who'd been out at the woodpile, slipped in the back door in time to watch the end of her performance. He joined with Thomasine in a long round of applause.

"OK, critter," he said, "time for bed."

"Dad . . ." she pleaded.

"No 'dads,' " he said, about as sternly as he ever sounded. "It's way past your bedtime."

"What time is it?"

"Almost nine-thirty. Now you say good night to Thomasine and let's get upstairs."

"All right," she said, trying to sound mortally wounded. And succeeding. "Good night, Thomasine," she said.

"Good night, Abbie."

They kissed, and then Abbie and Brad went upstairs.

Brad brushed his teeth with her. He'd had one of his rare cigars, and he expected to be kissing Thomasine very soon. Brad tucked his daughter in, then read her *One Morning in Maine,* her favorite story since he'd outlawed dinosaur books. He kissed her good night, left the door open "a crack," as Abbie had requested (a crack you could drive an eighteen-wheeler through), and went downstairs to Thomasine, who was tending the fire.

They were barely settled on the couch when the nightmare revisited.

It had been two weeks and one day since Abbie's last one. Brad knew exactly because he'd been crossing his fingers and keeping count. He hadn't admitted it to anyone, not even Thomasine, but the nightmares had made his blood run cold. They were so graphic, so powerful. They could only signal some deep-rooted emotional problem, the kind that could cripple for life.

Two weeks and one day. Almost to the point where he could breathe more easily.

Abbie's screams shattered the quiet.

Brad bolted for the stairs, gesturing Thomasine to stay put. He rounded the corner and exploded into Abbie's room. Her back was to the bedboard, her knees to her chest, her hands clasped over her ears. She was hysterical. Brad took her in his arms.

"Shhhh." He soothed her. "It's all right. All right, Apple Guy. Everything's all right. Daddy's here, and it's all right."

"Rham-fo-ram-for . . ."

"Shhh. It's OK."

"Rhampho . . ."

He dreaded the word. "There are no dinosaurs, honey," he said. "Not here or anywhere. Not for millions of years."

"Rhampho . . ."

"Only in museums."

"Rham-pho-ryn-chus."

"It was only a bad dream."

"But . . . it wasn't." Her sobs were subsiding, but he could feel her heart, hammering away inside her chest. Her whole body seemed to reverberate from the force of it.

"Yes, it was, honey. Only a bad dream."

"No."

It was senseless to argue. "Shhhh," he said. "Shhhh."

But she was compelled to continue. The nightmares—they were real. She knew it, and Jimmy knew it. She couldn't understand why the grown-ups didn't know it, too. Why they didn't believe it when it was so . . . awful.

"It talked again, Daddy."

"See?" he said hopefully. "It had to be a dream. Because dinosaurs don't talk. Even if there were any anymore," he quickly added, "which there aren't."

"It said my letter to Santa was stupid. It said why did I bother, 'cause it was going to get me before Santa could bring me my toys."

"But you've been a *very* good girl, honey," he explained. "You're going to get lots and lots of toys." He was treading water now. Kicking hard and fast to stay afloat. "Santa told me so himself."

Abbie just shook her head. "It said I won't be here because it's—it's . . . going to take me away."

"Oh, honey. Nobody's going to take you away."

"It said it hasn't been around because it's so . . . busy. With all the other kids. The kids who are sick. Kids who are dead. Kids like . . . Maureen . . . and Jay McLaughlin."

And then the tears returned, with more fury than before. Brad held her, saying nothing, until they passed and his daughter had fallen into an uneasy sleep. It took more than an hour, plenty of time for Brad to think. He thought he had never been so powerless in his life.

Or scared.

PART THREE
HOBBAMOCK

CHAPTER FORTY-NINE

December 11 to 15
A Long Weekend

BRAD WAS at his computer terminal. Every few seconds his left index finger would tap the "next story" key. He was flipping through the wire queue, trying to find something to plug a hole that had just popped up on an inside page.

The stories flew by. Brad barely absorbed the datelines, never mind the gist of the pieces.

His thoughts were on Abbie.

He'd known all along, hadn't he?

At least for several weeks, as the sickness had spread and the first two children had died, Brad had known. That's what was giving him his own nightmares, wasn't it? What was making him reconsider his move to Morgantown on an almost hourly basis, what was driving him to bury *Transcript* readers with news of the "Mystery Disease," as his headline writer had taken to calling it, what was . . .

. . . *what was making him wonder how much longer Abbie could tempt fate.*

Because that's really what this horror show was all about, wasn't it? Strip away all the medical jingo and bureaucratic breast-beating, and this is the bare bone you were left with: Every morning Abbie woke up healthy was simply another morning of reprieve. Screw Gosselin's cheery little lecture about the Black Death's striking down only one out of three, or two out of five, or whatever the Christ he'd said. Deep in his heart—a place he didn't dare probe anymore—Brad feared it was only a question of time before . . .

. . . *before Abbie came down with It, too.*

And yet—and yet, when she came home sick from kindergarten two weeks before Christmas, like Ginny Ellis, he denied it had anything to do with the Mystery Disease. A part of his mind—a big, strong, stubborn part—wouldn't let him even consider it, not for more than a fleeting moment.

"Brad?"

It was Rod Dougherty, yelling from across the room, where he'd answered the city desk line.

"Yeah?"

"It's for you," Rod said gravely.

"Who is it?"

"Dorothy Garland."

"Who?"

"The school nurse."

"Jesus," Brad said. "What's she want?"

"I don't know. She said it was an emergency."

These had not been the best of times for Dorothy Garland. She'd wound up several times on the front page of the *Transcript,* a place she hated to be, but that wasn't the worst part of the last two and a half months. The worst part was the kids. Dorothy liked kids—no, *loved* kids, had six of her own to prove it—and to see so many so sick was not only depressing but very frightening. To think that now, with some fifty children sick—fully 15 percent of the school—and the authorities were no closer to solving it than before . . . It was enough to make a school nurse a nervous wreck. And it had. She was seriously considering quitting.

There was something else, too, and Nurse Garland was far from the only one noticing it. Before all this Morgantown had been the very epitome of an elementary school, a Norman Rockwell-ish celebration of learning and eternal youth most graduates recalled tenderly into their dotage. Now it was more like hell. Oh, games still went on, and the sounds of tag and red rover filled the playground at recess, and Principal Mancuso still personally greeted every student getting off the bus; but there was an underlying gloom, as if they all were actors doing the best to read their parts and really not being very convincing at all.

Lately a new act had been added: the concerned call home. Time was long past when Nurse Garland or Mancuso took chances. The slightest complaint from a kid nowadays, and that kid had an automatic ticket home.

That kid's name was also automatically given to Bostwick.

Abbie was in the school sickroom, lying on the antique black-leather examining table. The roll of white paper at the head was crumpled evidence that she'd not been resting easily.

"I'm glad you came," she said to her father when he rushed in, out of breath, but she didn't sound glad. She sounded beat.

"How do you feel, sweetie?" he asked.

"My stomach."

"It hurts?" he said, rubbing her abdomen.

She nodded. "I threw up."

"I know. The nurse told me."

"Maybe I'm going to throw up again."

"Nah. Probably something you ate, that's all. Probably all done throwing up. Why, I bet when we get you home all nicely tucked into bed, by tomorrow I bet you'll feel fine."

"That's what I told her," Nurse Garland said, but there was no more conviction in her voice than in Brad's.

And in fact, Abbie was not better tomorrow. She was worse. She'd had another of her nightmares Thursday night, even though Brad had kept all the lights in her room blazing, and it took her more than two hours to get back to sleep. Two hours of hand-holding, and drinks of water, and endless verses of their favorite song.

My, oh, my, she's my Apple Guy!
Give her a kiss, won't you try?
Give her a monkey, I don't know why.
Take her to a movie, but let's not cry.
Climb on a staircase, way up high.
Along with my favorite little old Apple Guy!

She managed a smile once or twice before finally falling asleep. When she awoke Friday, her eyes were bleary, her voice scratchy from a sore throat. Her face had deep, craggy lines Brad had never seen on a child. Yesterday's nausea seemed to have moderated, but now she had stomach cramps. By noon her temperature had climbed to 101. Except for trips to the bathroom, she did not budge from the living-room couch, where she was huddled under a comforter.

"I think it's my tooth, Dad," she ventured weakly as Brad waited for Mrs. Fitzpatrick to spot him Friday afternoon so he could go to the Transcript for an hour or so.

"Why do you say that, Apple Guy?"

"Because it's loose. See?" She opened her mouth wide and wobbled one of her lower front teeth.

"Does it hurt?"

"Yeah, some. Is it gonna fall out?" she asked anxiously.

"Sooner or later. But a new one will be right behind," he hastened to add. "It's normal. Everyone goes through it. It's called getting your permanent teeth."

"Oh."

"You know what happens when it falls out, don't you?"

"No."

"You put it under your pillow, and while you sleep, the tooth fairy takes it and leaves money."

"Money?"

"Usually a dollar bill." In his day it had been a quarter.

"A whole dollar?" she asked, brightening momentarily.

"A whole dollar."

"Goody!" She sounded excited, interested.

But in another five minutes she'd forgotten about the tooth fairy. Another ten, and she had drifted off to a semisleep.

Does getting new teeth knock the hell out of you like this?

Brad pondered that one, with a desperate hope that was indeed the case. He remembered Abbie as an infant, the holy war he and Heather had gone through when their daughter cut her first set. It really had been the beginning of the end of the married Gales, hadn't it, those awful three or four months when Abbie was awake every night, seemingly all night, bawling uncontrollably? That was the time Heather had been trying to get back into acting and finding out just how few doors were open to her.

Yes, Abbie had been miserable cutting her first set of teeth. He didn't remember ever hearing such a thing happening with the second, but it didn't seem so ridiculous. So why was he avoiding an informed answer? Why wasn't he pulling his Dr. Spock off the bookshelf to see what old reliable had to say? Friday evening, back from the paper, he finally thumbed through Spock. There was, as Brad suspected, a chapter on permanent teeth.

But there was no mention of accompanying sickness. Not like Abbie's.

Saturday morning Thomasine came by with a bag of goodies: ginger ale, orange Crush, lemon sherbet, Campbell's chicken with rice soup, and *Mary Poppins* for the VCR. Abbie managed to keep some soup down, and she actually seemed to enjoy the orange Crush. *Mary Poppins* wasn't such a big hit.

Thomasine didn't need a weatherman to know which way this wind was blowing. Brad was distant and preoccupied—more than she'd ever seen him. Which was saying a lot. Although charming when the situation demanded, Brad would never be accused of being happy-go-lucky. He was intelligent, and like most intelligent people, he could be moody, withdrawn, especially when bothered or . . . Thomasine hesitated to say *scared.* She didn't know if she'd ever seen him scared. She didn't know if that's what she was seeing now. She only knew he didn't want to talk about Abbie. Didn't want to commiserate or armchair-diagnose. Didn't want to acknowledge that his daughter had been sick going on three days and showed no sign of improvement, none at all.

Only once was her sickness really mentioned, when Thomasine came in the door:

"It's probably the flu," Brad said, anticipating her.

"And I'm probably the Virgin Mary," Thomasine almost quipped, but didn't.

"Probably is the flu," she agreed.

Thomasine stayed through lunch, and then walking on eggshells got too much. Fabricating some excuse about an overdue report to Brown, she apologized and left. Driving to her apartment, she wondered how long it would be before Brad had noticed she was gone. She was worried about him.

And Abbie.

Saturday night Brad let Abbie sleep in his bed.

She woke three times crying, but there were no nightmares.

The denial continued into Sunday evening.

That's when Bostwick called.

"I heard Abbie's pretty sick," the doctor said.

"Just a cold or something," Brad said, then added suspiciously: "Who told you?"

"Mrs. Garland," the doctor lied. Thomasine had made Bostwick swear he'd keep her out of this, but it was she who had called, Saturday evening.

"Oh."

"Is she still running a fever, Brad?" he demanded.

"Just a little one."

"What's 'just a little one'?"

"You know, just a little bit hot when you touch her forehead."

"In degrees, Brad. Did you take her temperature? With a thermometer?"

"Yes. It was a hundred and three last time I took it."

"And when was that?"

"This morning."

Bostwick was floored. He didn't pretend to be Brad Gale's bosom buddy, but he thought he'd gotten to know him more than superficially as the Mystery Disease story had unfolded. Someone who did well under pressure, maybe even throve under it. And here he was acting and talking like someone who was borderline retarded.

"This morning?" Bostwick echoed. "Don't you know temperature is lowest in the morning?"

"Is it?"

"Yes, it is," Bostwick snapped. "Now tell me what else is going on."

Brad did—truthfully.

When he was done, Bostwick ordered him to have Abbie at Berkshire Medical Center first thing in the morning.

Brad held Abbie's free arm. The nurse who was about to draw blood promised it would hurt only "a little bit."

Abbie knew better. Two years ago she'd been hospitalized for an operation to straighten a crossed eye. The operation had been a success (you would never know looking at Abbie today that anything had ever been wrong with one of those pretty green eyes), but Abbie had learned a thing or two about hospitals during her three-day stay. She'd learned that when someone said, "This will only hurt a little bit," what he really meant was, "Nothing ever hurt this bad." She'd learned that the steel instruments they touched you with were cold, as if they kept them in the freezer. She'd learned that when you felt well enough for a soda, they brought you too little. She'd learned that there were rules for everything, including when people could come see you, and *who* could come see you, and what you could wear, and what time you had to get up.

She'd learned that people in hospitals could Pass Away.

It was a horrifying concept, Passing Away, one nobody had ever told her about. Discovering it, she was sure, was accidental. Passing Away was obviously the kind of thing kids weren't supposed to know about, one of those things that grown-ups clam up on because "you're too young to understand."

Abbie found out about Passing Away from Gina. Gina was the

girl in the room with her, a pig-tailed, freckled girl who kept her up late the first night, laughing and talking. Abbie liked her, even if she *did* talk too much. She was a couple of years older, and she'd been in hospitals lots and lots of times because something was wrong with her heart. She bravely assured Abbie there was nothing to worry about. An operation was just like going to sleep, recovery just like waking up. Gina's operation was down for early the next morning, and her bed was empty and freshly made when Abbie, scheduled for midafternoon, woke up.

Gina never returned.

Without being able to explain why, Abbie knew she would never see her pig-tailed new friend again.

And she was right. By the time Abbie regained konk-shus-ness the next morning from her own operation, a new girl already had taken Gina's place. Gina, Heather later informed her, had Passed Away, God rest her soul.

That's what they call it, Abbie thought as she waited for the Berkshire Medical nurse to take blood, the memory of Gina terrifying her again. Passing Away. *Maureen Passed Away, too. Daddy said so. She went into the hospital, I know because Daddy took me there to visit, but she didn't come out. I hope I never Pass Away. I don't* ever *want to Pass Away.*

"I want to go home," Abbie sobbed to her father as they sat in Berkshire Medical's hematology clinic. "Please. *Please,* Daddy."

"We will, honey," Brad said, "very soon."

"Ready?" the nurse said cheerfully. Brad wondered how people like her could be so goddamned cheerful, jabbing needles into people for a living.

"Daaaad!" Brad felt his daughter's body tense.

"It's OK, sweetie," he said. "It only lasts a minute."

"Now you're going to feel a little jab, like a mosquito bite," the nurse said, removing the needle from the package.

"Daaaad!"

"No worse than a mosquito bite," the nurse said, thumping Abbie's forearm to make the vein pop out.

"It's OK, honey."

"Here we go," the nurse said.

She stuck it in. It was a clean hit. Abbie's crying picked up several notches, but at least the nurse wouldn't have to do it again. She could draw all the samples she needed—four in all—from the one needle. *Bull's-eye,* Brad thought. *Thank God for that.*

"All done," the nurse announced.

"You were very brave, Apple Guy," Brad said.

Abbie's whimpering was tapering off.

They were in X ray when Bostwick came by. "I'm surprised," he said to Brad while the technician was helping Abbie dress. "She doesn't look too bad. Good color, all her vitals are normal. She even forced a smile."

"She's certainly no worse," Brad agreed. In fact, he thought he'd seen a big improvement this morning. He was aware he wasn't the most objective witness; but her temperature was down, and she seemed a bit more alert today, especially since hitting the hospital. Not happy, but more in touch. It was almost as if her absolute fear of the place had released some magic hormone that already was speeding her down the road toward recovery.

"I don't see any need to keep her," Bostwick said. "Not now."

"Really?"

"Really."

"Thanks, Doctor."

"Nothing to thank me for, I'm just doing my job. But until the tests come back, by tomorrow noon at the latest," he cautioned, "I want her in bed. *In bed,* Brad. Lots of fluids. Lots of Tylenol. Lots of rest."

"Sure, Doctor."

"We'll see where we stand tomorrow."

"It sounds like you think it might be . . . only . . . you know, a cold or the flu or something. It's mid-December. Flu season."

"No predictions, Brad."

"But it *could* be flu."

"Yes, it *could,*" Bostwick said. "But let's wait for the tests to come in before we commit ourselves to a diagnosis."

The fact of the matter was that Bostwick wasn't conceding a thing. The tests weren't just some kind of busywork for the hospital staff, something to keep insurance rates out of sight. If anything, the routine stuff had become more critical with the spread of the Mystery Disease: There were a lot of sick kids in Morgantown, but not all of them were victims of the unknown. Over the last two months Bostwick had found staph and strep infections, one mild case of meningitis, three early cases of the flu, four pneumonias, and one nasty, but not lethal, case of blood poisoning that had started with a parakeet bite.

Bostwick had been thankful for every one. It was bizarre for a doctor to be thinking like that, he realized. But not irrational. And not unkind. It could be reconciled with his interpretation of the Hippocratic Oath.

It was disconcerting how quickly Abbie reverted.

At the hospital she'd been alert, if scared, but now, back home barely an hour, she was listless and feverish, just as she'd been all weekend. *It's as if that magic hormone evaporated the minute we left the hospital,* Brad thought.

She didn't even seem bothered when he told her the bad news about the Christmas play, which was scheduled for that afternoon.

"The doctor says you won't be able to go, Apple Guy," he announced when he had her back in bed. "I'm sorry, but we have to do what he says."

She looked at him *(I don't like that lusterless look in her eyes,* Brad thought) but didn't speak.

"But I'm sure they'll have a spring play," he continued, "and you'll be able to be in that. Maybe you could even play the Easter Bunny!"

"Oh." It wasn't the reaction he'd hoped for.

"Would you like that, hon?" He prodded her. "Dress up in a bunny outfit and sing an Easter song?"

She shook her head yes. Without waiting to see if he was going to continue, she slowly closed her eyes.

CHAPTER FIFTY

Tuesday, December 16

CHARLIE WAS IN the waiting room of Peckham, Bradley & Bradley, Albany auctioneers. The secretary said Mr. Bradley would be with him shortly.

Since leaving Ben Wilcox almost two weeks ago, Charlie had thrown everything into searching for the spear. He'd become a man possessed. There was no guarantee he would find it, probably no way to be absolutely certain he had the right one even if he did, but what choice did he have? None. That was the brutally simple answer. He could find the spear and move on to the next hurdle: finding someone to wield it. Or he could give up, and Hobbamock would continue on the warpath, and children would continue to die, and . . .

. . . he didn't know where things would end.

In the end it was Thomasine who gave him his best lead. Early in her research she'd heard mention of a Quidneck family named Brown, the name on Ben Wilcox's dying lips. A century ago, or so it was rumored, the Browns had been fabulously wealthy. Even by the white man's standards, they had struck it rich. Thomasine's source didn't know where the money had come from, or how many members the family had, or whether any descendants were still in the area, or anything else about them. Only the name of a town: Claverack, New York, some forty-five miles south of Hoosick Falls.

Charlie lucked out in Claverack. He didn't hunt up any Browns with Quidneck blood, but he found a tribal brother whose grandfather, now deceased, had been a grounds keeper for an estate owned by a family named Brown. Actually it wasn't much of a family, Charlie's blood brother explained. Only a father and a son. Both were long since dead, but the brother recalled a niece of Old Man Brown—or was it a great-niece, or a great-great-niece?—who had lived in Claverack until about fifteen years ago, when the wander bug had bitten her and she'd cut loose for Searsburg, Vermont. The brother remembered that explicitly; he had a cousin there himself, and he'd visited once.

And so the trail continued, one tentative path after another. The Browns had been nomadic, like most Quidnecks, and they'd roamed from village to village, drifters subsisting on mill jobs and dishwashing and every other kind of economic potluck the white man could dish out. *Pushed around like the bream is by the bass,* Charlie thought bitterly, *many of them driven to the bottle by despair.* From New York into Vermont and back to Massachusetts Charlie drove, floating questions in bars and gas stations, consulting phone books and town hall records as he passed through a string of one-whistle towns that the twentieth century had left behind.

He hit pay dirt in Readsboro, Vermont. That's where Old Man Brown's great-great-niece was living—alone, in a trailer, and on Social Security. Old Man Brown had died before she was born, she had told Charlie over coffee two mornings ago, but as a child she'd known his son. Young Brown, everybody called him, even though by then he was well into his seventies. Yes, she said, Old Man Brown had been wealthy, the only Quidneck she'd known to be so blessed; he'd made a fortune in quarrying. Yes, he'd spent a lot of his money buying Quidneck art. Yes, there had been a special sword. She was certain. Her great-uncle had seen it, displayed over a fireplace on the estate. As for why it had been special, she didn't know about that. Didn't know if she'd ever known.

"Mr. Bradley will see you now," the secretary said, ushering Charlie into the inner office. She was glad to be rid of him. He was large, and he had a long ponytail, a combination of features she'd only ever seen in motorcycle gangs. He looked perpetually angry, too. She suspected he was a man capable of easy violence. She wasn't eager to confirm her suspicions.

"Morton Bradley," Bradley said, closing the door and extending his hand. Charlie shook it. There was no warmth in either hand.

"Charlie Moonlight."

"Charlie, please sit down," Bradley said, gesturing toward a leather chair. "Charlie, what can I do you for you?"

"I'm interested in a sale you handled."

"How do you know I handled it?" Bradley said suspiciously. He was a fat man, bespectacled, with a whiskey nose. Shyster would be a fitting description for this specimen, Charlie thought. *The lowest kind: a man who's made a fortune off others' misfortune.*

"I saw an old newspaper ad," Charlie said. "In a library."

"Not with the IRS, are you, Charlie?"

"No. I'm trying to track something that might have belonged to my family," he lied. "A distant relative."

"I see. And what was the name of this distant relative?"

"Brown. Peter Brown. He was sometimes known as Young Brown."

"Brown? Do you know how many Browns there are in the Albany phone book alone, Charlie? I'm afraid I'd need more than that. Perhaps you know when we handled the sale?" Bradley sounded irked. Already he regretted the decision to have his secretary send Charlie in. But you never knew what package your business in this business was going to come wrapped in. And it was almost a rule of thumb that the richer a client, the odder he appeared.

"It was thirty-five years ago," Charlie said. "I realize that's a long time."

"That," Bradley said, "is an understatement."

"He was a Quidneck Indian. He collected art. Indian art, especially. He had a mansion. It was in Claverack, overlooking the Housatonic Lake. It burned down some ten years ago, or so I'm told."

"The crazy Indian!" Bradley was suddenly animated. "Why didn't you say so in the first place? The crazy Indian! I've been telling that story for years! Always get a laugh or two out of that one! It was a tax settlement, if I'm not mistaken. The guy apparently didn't believe in giving Uncle Sam his due."

For which he should be honored by having his likeness on a stamp, Charlie thought.

"Yes," Charlie said, reminding himself that this clown was only a shyster. *There's nothing to be gained by taking a stand.* "That's the one."

"Of course, I remember it. My friend, you *never* forget sales like that. It was the most goldarn, offbeat collection of widgets and junk I ever saw. Some very pricey stuff, too. I mean, there were paintings that fetched five, ten grand, and that was no small potatoes back then. No, sirree. But most of it was garbage. Ended up donating half of it to the Salvation Army."

"Was there a spear?"

"Boy, you're really pushing it, my friend." He scratched his head. "Come to think of it, there *was* a spear. There were lots of spears. It's coming back to me now. Yes. Tomahawks, arrowheads, clubs, pipes, funny little straw baskets, a birchbark canoe—the place was full of that Indian junk."

The slur flew past Charlie. He was excited now. "What happened to it?" he asked. "The weapons?"

"Those we were able to sell, if I'm not mistaken."

"To whom?"

"A dealer from Vermont, I believe it was. No . . . wait a minute. . . . It was an art collector. Lived in the Berkshires, if my memory serves me. He was rolling in dough, that much I remember. Paid cash. I suppose you want his name, too."

"If you have it."

"Maybe, but not up here," he said, tapping the side of his head. "I'd have to check the records. Ones that old are in the warehouse, if they're anywhere at all. I'm afraid it would take too long to find them, Charlie. I'm a busy man."

"It's very important."

"I'm sure it is. And I'm sorry, but I can't help you any further."

Bradley stood.

Charlie stood, too, and reached into his wallet. He'd been prepared for this. In fact, he was surprised he hadn't had to resort to bribery sooner. He slipped ten hundred-dollar bills out of his wallet and laid them on Bradley's desk. They were fresh bills, crisp and smelling strongly of brand-new money. Charlie could almost see Bradley's nostrils twitch.

"How about now?" Charlie asked. "Do you think you could dig through your records now?"

"Isn't drug money, is it?"

"It's clean."

"We'll take my car," Bradley said.

CHAPTER FIFTY-ONE

Wednesday, December 17

ON THE SAME MORNING Bostwick insisted on admitting Jimmy Ellis to Berkshire Medical Center, the medical examiner was taking ten-year-old Kristin Rossi out of the hospital in a zippered body bag. Kristin was victim number three of the Mystery Disease. Her death would make the front page of the Boston *Globe.* A copy of the autopsy report would be on Dr. Gosselin's desk by midafternoon tomorrow.

Ginny had fought Bostwick tooth and nail. Jimmy was better this morning, she'd argued. She could see it in his color. She could hear it in his cough, not nearly as bad as yesterday. And just what could they provide in a hospital that she couldn't give him at home anyway? All this kid needed was bed rest and some homemade chicken soup and a mother's TLC. Wasn't this the 1980's, when the idea was to avoid hospitalization whenever possible? "Think of the expense, Doctor," she'd argued. "The effect on insurance premiums. Think of the effect on Jimmy, for God's sake. Does anyone ever think of the patient anymore? Ever since all those tests, he's been *terrified* just thinking about hospitals. Scared out of his mind. Those nightmares . . . worse than they've ever been, and all because of hospitals. You don't want all that on your conscience, do you, Doctor? Do you?"

Her arguments reminded Bostwick of so many others, Brad Gale included. And make no mistake, they were having an impact. It would be ridiculous not to admit he was being affected by the pressure. Christ, he was flesh and blood, too. He dreaded these house calls, these office visits, these anguished, teary telephone conversations in the middle of the night. He was beginning to drink too much, and his relationship with his family had been reduced to farce. He was heading for a crash. He didn't know how much more he could take, but he knew it wasn't a whole hell of a lot.

Jimmy was weepy going into Berkshire Medical, but it was not the waterworks Ginny had expected. He was too sick for that. Too tired, and too hot, and his throat and mouth too dry. His whole body ached. *Maybe he doesn't even know where he is,* Ginny thought, discovering fresh grounds for concern. *Dear God, please help us at this, our time of need.*

The staff couldn't have been nicer, Ginny had to concede. The orderly made a game of the wheelchair ride to his room, and the nurses took great care to point out his TV, and Second Floor East's collection of books, and the Masters of Universe toys, and GI Joe, and Tonka trucks, and lots of goodies like that. They showed him the neat button he could press if wanted assistance with, say, going to the bathroom. They showed him the switch for making his bed go up and down. They were very careful changing him into his johnny, and starting his IV, and taking his blood pressure and pulse, and letting him know everything was going to be all right.

Jimmy said nothing, nothing at all.

The last couple of weeks everything had gotten so confusing. Everything had turned so bad. It wasn't just the nightmares—or whatever they were. He was sick all the time now, worse and longer than he'd ever been sick with a cold or that time he had measles and had to stay in bed almost a week. Mommy kept promising he'd get better, but he wasn't getting better. He was like the other kids. So many of them were sick, too. So many weren't getting any better. Maureen McDonald and another kid had even died, meaning they would never, ever get better. They were dead—the same way raccoons and skunks you found on the side of the road were dead.

Something was happening to the grown-ups, too. They weren't getting sick or dying, but it seemed as if they were going crazy, Jimmy thought. At school the teachers had become nervous and seemed to be watching everyone much more carefully. And there were all those new rules. Don't touch someone else's food. Don't share snacks. You couldn't go to the bathroom alone anymore. A teacher or an aide had to be there with you to make sure you washed your hands with soap afterward. Gym class wasn't being held anymore. And you couldn't drink from the regular water fountains. If you were thirsty, you had to get a drink from the bottled water they'd brought in, and you had to use a paper cup, and you had to crumple that cup and throw it away when you were done, not pass it to the next kid.

But Mom was the craziest. The gun had really sent her into outer space. After finding it, she'd beaten him with a wooden spoon—so hard that he couldn't sit down the rest of the day, only lie on his stomach in bed. She'd never done that before, and he hated her, really hated her, for the very first time in his life. But that wasn't all. Even before the licking, she'd been weird. Making him eat apples and oranges and carrots and lettuce, stuff like that, and no hamburger or ham anymore. All those vitamin pills. All that milk.

Craziest of all, the day after the licking, she'd told him Uncle Charlie wouldn't be visiting for a while—and they wouldn't be going to his cabin either. No reason had been given. She said she didn't want to talk about it. Someday, she said, he'd understand. But he didn't think he ever would.

Once he was settled into his bed, Jimmy dozed off.

When he came to, his mother was gone.

There was light in the window, and Jimmy supposed it was still daytime. In the hall he heard voices and rubber soles scuffing along linoleum. Those were the only sounds. A strange quiet seemed to have settled over the place.

He looked around.

The wolf was in the corner, near the closet. It was grinning, the way it liked to do. All teeth and a glimpse of red tongue. Eyes that seemed to burn.

Jimmy's breath caught in his throat.

"Your mother's gone to get your slippers," the wolf said. "Aren't mothers funny? She marched out of here saying she'd forgotten your slippers, a boy *needed* his slippers, and when you were napping was as good a time as any to go get them. She won't be back for an hour, I bet. Maybe more. It's a good long ride back home. A *good* long ride."

Jimmy didn't respond. He knew he was awake, but he was too groggy to be really shaken, at least initially. *The wolf wasn't kidding,* he thought. *It said it would follow me everywhere, and it did. It must be a very clever wolf, because only Mom and Dr. Bostwick knew where I was coming when I got in the car this morning, and I know neither of them would ever talk to a wolf. They don't believe in wolves.*

He hoped the wolf would go soon. He hoped he could wait until it did without crying or screaming because then he could tell the nurses about the wolf. His mother might not believe him, but here in the hospital, why, they would have to believe him. You couldn't have wolves running around loose in a hospital. No, they wouldn't allow that. Hospitals had rules, and one of them probably was NO WOLVES. That policeman who had waved to him from the little booth out front would take care of the situation. He bet that policeman carried a gun.

"I suppose I should close this," the wolf said, padding noiselessly toward the door. The wolf always moved like that—without a sound, as if its paws never really touched the floor. As if it were somehow able to float from place to place.

The door had been cracked open about a foot. The wolf closed it. It shut without a sound. Jimmy felt the first claw of fear, scratching inside his belly.

"There," the wolf said, turning toward Jimmy. "You know how nosy nurses can be. Always gossiping about this or that. A wolf in one of their rooms—I bet that would be grist for the mill for a very long time."

He hadn't noticed it before, but now Jimmy saw that the wolf was carrying a bag. It was a canvas bag, like what some of the big kids carried their gym clothes in to school when they were still having gym. The wolf reached into it and pulled out a large lock. Jimmy had never seen a lock that big, or that old, except once in a Walt Disney movie. It was one of those steel-plate locks that take huge skeleton keys—a lock you'd find in an old-fashioned prison or a haunted house or a dragon's dungeon.

The lock fitted the door perfectly. Magically.

"And I suppose we should put this on so we aren't surprised. Wolves don't like surprises."

Fear scratched again at Jimmy, deeper.

At home, he'd almost gotten used to the wolf. You never *completely* got used to something so awful, but the wolf had come so faithfully that Jimmy almost expected it. And it wasn't as if the wolf were like needles, or the dentist, or a hornet or a red ant sting, things that really hurt and you really had every reason to be afraid of. The wolf, for all its bad talk and fangs, had never actually done anything. It looked mean and evil, but it was like a ferocious-sounding dog that never bit.

But this—this was new. This was different.

This was the scariest thing that had ever happened to Jimmy.

The wolf turned the key. The lock clicked. The wolf returned the key to his bag.

He locked me in.

I'm all alone in the hospital, and he locked me in.

Jimmy opened his mouth as if to scream, but nothing came out.

"There," the wolf said. "Now we can talk without fear of interruption. That's another thing wolves hate. Being interrupted."

The wolf sauntered to the foot of the bed, its usual post, and took a seat. Jimmy recoiled violently, yanking the IV out of his arm. He did not feel it snap free, did not see the trickle of blood that formed.

"Do you know where you are, Jimmy?" the wolf asked. It didn't seem to have noticed the blood either. "You don't seem sure. You look like—well, like maybe you think you're having a bad dream or something. One of those hallucinations Mommy's been talking about. But it's not, Jimmy. You're wide-awake, and you're in the hospital! Nowadays that's where we prepare little boys and girls for their journey. In the old days, of course, there were no such things as hospitals. We would go right into the villages. Ah, the good old days. I almost feel nostalgic. Do you know what nostalgia is, Jimmy?"

Jimmy could feel his heart beating so hard it actually seemed he'd be able to see it through his johnny if he dared to look. He didn't understand everything the wolf was saying, but he knew instinctively it was very bad. The wolf had never talked like this before.

"This is the exact same room Maureen was in," the wolf continued. "Did you know Maureen? It took a long time to prepare her for coming with us. I think for a long time she didn't want to come. She seemed to be fighting us. Just like you, Jimmy. But children will be children, won't they? Very naive. Innocent. And in the end, you'll come around, just the way Maureen did. Just the way all the others will. Why, you'll have no choice."

Once it had built steam, Jimmy's fear was like a runaway train. It hurtled through his insides, churning his stomach, constricting his throat. His arm hurt where the IV had been, and he'd discovered that he was bleeding. The blood ran down his arm, onto his hand, staining the sheet. He had been groggy, but now he was fully awake. Everything seemed exaggerated: the light; the sound of the wolf's breathing; the terrible pounding of his own heart; the pain in his arm. The room suddenly wasn't a room but an endless, huge cavern in which you could get lost forever and no one would ever know. He thought he might black out. Hoped he might black out. Just go to sleep and be left alone.

The button.

The thought came from nowhere.

"Press the button if you need help," the nurse had said.

"I've brought you a treat," the wolf said. "Because I know how good you're going to be as we get ready to take our journey, I've brought you a very nice treat."

The wolf reached into the bag.

Jimmy inched his right hand down the side of his pillow.

The wolf brought out a camera. Jimmy's mom's camera.

"You can have it back now," the wolf said. "As a reward. In advance of how good I know you're going to be."

Jimmy couldn't find the button.

It has to be here, he pleaded. *Has to.*

The wolf's breath had finally reached Jimmy. It was in his nostrils now, in his hair, his eyes, his mouth, all over him, stinking and stale like a dead animal covered with maggots. Jimmy tried to block it, but he knew he was going to throw up if it lasted much longer.

"I've taken the film out, of course. And I'll take you at your word that you won't find some and put it back in. But it would be fun to play with it for a while, wouldn't it?"

Jimmy's hand found the button. It was plastic, hard, cold.

There was a sudden explosion of light. The camera, the wolf's paw on it.

"See? I've even replaced the flashbulbs. Now *that* would be fun, wouldn't it? Playing with those flashbulbs? I bet Mom would be *amazed* to see that camera again."

Jimmy pushed the button.

The end of his bed began to rise.

The wrong button, Jimmy thought. His fear was galloping.

"What's this?" the wolf said. It seemed momentarily baffled.

Jimmy let go. The bed stopped moving.

"Are we playing tricks, Jimmy?" the wolf said sternly. "Did the wolf say you could play tricks? I don't think so."

Jimmy's fingers were probing frantically. He didn't care if the wolf saw him now or not. He had to find that other button. Had to.

Had to.

"I'm not sure after that that I should give you the camera. But since I'm a nice wolf, I will. Here," it said, laying the camera at Jimmy's feet.

Jimmy had found the other button. He pressed it.

At the nurses' station a light went on and a buzzer sounded.

The wolf heard it. He was puzzled again.

Then he understood.

"Oh, that wasn't very nice," the wolf said. "Not very smart, either, Jimmy. Not very smart at all."

The charge nurse, an overweight woman with a shadow of mustache above her lip, crossed the hall to Jimmy's door.

"Bad boys can get in trouble for things like that. Very, very deep trouble. Boys should remember never, ever to make a wolf angry. Because an angry wolf is a very unpredictable wolf."

The wolf lunged at Jimmy. Jimmy saw the glean of its claws, felt its breath envelop him, heard the clicking of its fangs and the beginning of a howl.

This time Jimmy screamed.

The door opened.

"What is it, James?" the nurse asked.

"W-w-w-w . . ." he stammered.

There was nothing there, of course. No wolf. No lock. No bag.

Only a camera, clearly in sight, and a smell the nurse mistook for flatulence.

Jimmy's tears came freely.

"Dear me, you've pulled your tube out," the nurse said. "No wonder you're crying."

CHAPTER FIFTY-TWO

Wednesday, December 17
Afternoon

THE RECORDS were there, intact and accessible. That surprised Bradley no less than Charlie. In fifteen minutes they had what they were after.

"Ted Wigglesworth," he said. "That's right. Yes. Used to be one of our regulars. Lived over your way, in Lenox. Had a place near Tanglewood. Haven't heard from him in years. Don't even know if he's still alive."

"He is," Charlie stated.

"Do you know him?"

"Not really."

But what Charlie could have said was:

Yes. I know him. Tall, thin man of about seventy. Impeccable dresser. Drives a Jaguar. An arrogant, condescending prick.

Sure, I know him. He testified at the land claim suit. Was an expert witness for the state. Presented himself as a New York banker and patron of the arts, both of which he is. The lawyers had him show the jury slides of his holdings. They were extensive. Filled his Manhattan penthouse and his Lenox summer estate, which is in fact near Tanglewood. What interested the jury was his extraordinary collection of Native American art. He claimed he had the largest holdings outside a museum, and there was no reason to doubt him. Navajo art. Mohawk. Sioux. And yes, Quidneck. He walked the jury through some of it, using those slides. Said it was the least distinguished Indian art he'd ever seen. Said there was no continuity to it, no substance, nothing whatsoever to distinguish it from nearby peoples, the Mahicans or Narragansetts, for instance. In short, nothing to suggest that this group of rabble-rousers here in court, Your Honor, has ever in any way constituted a tribe.

Yes, I know Ted Wigglesworth.

And I despise him as I've despised few men.

Bradley thumbed through the papers, his lips moving as he read through them. " 'Cording to this," he said, "Wigglesworth bought all the Indian junk. Now as to whether that spear you're looking for was part of the lot—or whether he didn't turn around and sell it again; sometimes these big-shot collectors will do just that—I'm afraid I can't help you there, friend."

"You've been very helpful," Charlie said, and left the warehouse while Bradley, engrossed in a trip down memory lane, was still rummaging through boxes.

CHAPTER FIFTY-THREE

Thursday, December 18

"I WANT HER admitted," Bostwick said to Brad. His voice was cold and heavy, like the weather outside.

"But, Doc—"

"Forget it, Brad," Bostwick said, his voice whipsawing. "The girl is sick. Too sick to be home anymore. She needs to be in the hospital."

They were in Brad's kitchen. Bostwick had dropped in unannounced to examine Abbie. She looked worse than three days ago. Languid, like the other ten children currently in Berkshire Medical. Her fever was still dangerously high, 103. She was burning up.

"But you said it might be the flu," Brad persisted.

"I said it *could be* the flu, just as I said it could be a whole bunch of other things. And then I said I wasn't going to predict. I said I was going to wait for test results, and I did. They're not showing anything, Brad. All but the AIDS results are back, and they're not showing a goddamn thing. And you and I both know the AIDS is going to be negative."

"Maybe the tests weren't done right."

"Come on, Brad . . ."

"Maybe you should do them again."

He's starting to lose it, Bostwick thought, and it was only that realization that kept the lid on his anger. *We're all starting to lose it.*

"Some tests, we'll do again," he said. "But I want her in. This morning. It's not negotiable."

Brad stood by the refrigerator, his head down. Everything was only getting worse. It was like a giant snowball heading down an endless mountain, getting faster and bigger as it hurtled on, and no one able to stop it. Everyone in danger of being run over.

"Give it one more day," he pleaded, but it was a dispassionate plea.

"No."

"Twenty-four hours."

"No."

"This afternoon."

"Now."

"All right," Brad finally said. "But I want to bring her."

"Of course," Bostwick said, his tone softening. "I'll meet you there. In admitting. In an hour."

Bostwick let himself out, and Brad went into the living room, where Abbie was on the couch, buried under two afghans. The TV was on, but Brad knew his daughter wasn't watching. She had that same unfocused look she'd had for days, a look that signaled she was drifting again.

"Honey?" he said, caressing her brow. It felt hot as a griddle.

"What, Dad?" she answered feebly.

"We have to go back to the hospital."

"To stay?"

"Maybe a couple of nights. That's all."

She did not protest. Perhaps she'd suspected all along that this was where things were headed, and hearing the formal announcement was anticlimactic. Perhaps she realized the situation was completely beyond her control. Her eyes teared, and she reached for Brad's hand. He took it, tenderly but firmly.

"I know you don't want to," he said, "God, do I ever, Abbie, but I promise it will only be for a short time."

"Will Thomasine visit me?"

"Absolutely."

"Will Mommy?"

"Do you want her to?" he said, struggling to keep his feelings out of it.

"I think I would," Abbie said tentatively.

"Then she will."

"Maybe tomorrow. Or the next day."

"Whatever you want, sweetheart."

"Would *you* ask her for me? 'Cause . . . well, I think it would be better if you did, that's all."

"Of course."

Abbie pulled the afghans tightly around her. Her teeth were chattering. "Will I be in the hospital on Christmas?"

"Oh, God, no," Brad reassured her. "You'll be home long before then."

"But what if I was? Would Santa be able to find me?"

"Santa can find anyone anywhere. That's one of his talents."

"So he'd come?"

"Of course he would, honey."

"The tooth fairy, too?"

"Absolutely." Santa and the progress of the tooth were about the only two topics that interested Abbie anymore. Any day now, Brad kept predicting, the tooth would be out. Any day now.

"Another thing," Brad said. "Jimmy's there. Maybe you two can visit. In fact, I'm sure you can. That would be fun, wouldn't it? Seeing Jimmy?"

Abbie nodded her head, without conviction. It was true that Jimmy had become her best friend since moving to Morgantown. It was true that they'd decided they were going to get married when they grew up, and she was going to be a newspaper editor, and he was going to be a space shuttle astronaut, and they were going to have seven children and three kitties and two dogs just like Maria, and they were going to live in a great big house on the side of Thunder Rise, where they could be near their mommy and daddy, and where the kitties and dogs would be able to run in the woods, and where they would build the biggest swing set ever in the history of the world, and where no wolves or flying dinosaurs would ever dare to go, and . . .

. . . and all that seemed like a hundred years ago. Jimmy was sick now, too, and she hadn't seen him in more than a week. She wasn't sure she wanted to see him right now.

Because none of this was supposed to happen.

Because maybe it means we're all going to Pass Away, she thought. *All the kids, just like Maureen.*

"Dad?" she asked, her voice breaking.

"Yes?"

"Am I going to Pass Away?"

The question stunned Brad. So brutally direct.

"Oh, Apple Guy, of course not," he said. "Hospitals are where you get better."

"Maureen didn't get better," Abbie said.

Brad could not answer. He could only wrap her in his arms and fight his own tears, so close to the surface.

Brad stayed with Abbie in her hospital room until, with the assistance of Demerol ("She needs all the rest we can give her," Bostwick said; "this'll take her to morning"), she fell asleep.

It was nine o'clock.

Emotionally he was an empty vessel, but he was not tired. They'd brought a cot in for him, but there was no way he could sleep now. There was no way he could go back to that empty house either. Just no way he could curl up with a book and try to pretend it was just another night. For one of the few times in his adult life, he understood why so many Type A people become addicted to health clubs. He would kill for a stationary bicycle now, a game of tennis, a heavy-duty session on the Nautilus or Universal. Something to exhaust his body and grind his mind into numbness. A two-hour workout, followed by a sauna, where he could sweat the worry out of him.

But he had not joined a health club, even though there was one in Pittsfield. The *Transcript* would have to do. He drove there without the radio on, the image of Abbie's drugged body haunting him.

Except for the part-time sports copy editor, the newsroom was deserted. Rod, Brad remembered, was at an emergency meeting of the school board, which, advance word had it, would vote to close public schools early for Christmas. Lisa Radeke had gone along with Rod to do a sidebar on parents' reactions; pretty much full-time now, the Mystery Disease was being double-teamed. Brad tried to remember what the rest of his staff was up to, and couldn't. He had the discomfiting feeling that if someone had held a gun to his head and ordered him to *name* the rest of his staff, he'd fail.

Paper work was piled high on his desk in two perfect piles: a stack of pink messages and a higher stack of envelopes. Gracie, the secretary he shared with Dexter, was responsible, God love her. She'd cleaned his phone and the keys of his Atex terminal, too. It all looked very organized, very professional, as if the executive whose domain this was had everything tightly under control. An illusion, but not an unpleasant one, Brad decided. His work station might actually be therapeutic. It might move his brainwaves, if only momentarily, off the painful pattern they had assumed.

He sat. In the old days, when he'd broken into journalism, wire copy still click-clacked its way into newsrooms across America on teletypes. There'd been a certain reassurance to the never-ending chatter of those old black machines, a certain Hollywood-style romanticism no one had appreciated until it was gone—another victim of Technology on the Move. Tonight, as never before, Brad longed for that metallic clang. He fancied that it would remind him somehow that the human experience plodded on and on and on, that his troubles, no matter how they seemed poised to overwhelm him, were overshadowed by someone else's. But newsrooms now had satellite feeds into silent computers that kept silent tabs on humanity around the globe. Except for the never-changing smell of newsprint, modern newsrooms were like the home offices of giant insurance firms: mausoleumlike, windowless environments where so many people piddled their lives away on jobs too trivial to remember five minutes after quitting time.

The contemporary newsroom, he imagined, could be shaped into a respectable metaphor for the human condition if one worked at it hard enough.

He tackled the messages first. Call Reed Berghoff, Pittsburgh *Press,* about story-in-works on Mystery Disease. Call an irate Mr. Driscoll, who claims his yard has the most Christmas lights in Morgantown, "not Harvey Wolcott, as erroneously claimed in today's page three photo." Call Mrs. Pinkerston, who is threatening litigation about "deliberate and illegal conspiracy to keep antivivisection news out of the paper." *Let her sue,* Brad thought. *I'd pay good money for the opportunity to cross-examine one of those animal rights nuts.* One message was from Lisa, who wanted Brad's counsel on a difficult personality profile of a school committeeman.

One was from his ex-wife, with the "urgent," "please call," and "will call again" boxes checked. "She's driving me crazy, Brad!!!" Gracie had penciled in. "P.S. Sounded drunk again."

That's the last thing I need now, he thought bitterly. *A heaping helping of Heather.*

He started into the mail. It was the usual assortment. A brochure of upcoming seminars at the American Press Institute in Reston, Virginia. An entry form for the American Society of Newspaper Editors' annual contest, in which Brad believed the

Transcript had a strong chance of taking a spoı news award for its disease coverage. Several résumés and cover letters, including one that began: "Dear Mr. Gale: My good college buddy Rod Dougherty has told me all the incredibly good things happening at the Transcript since you took over. I am a Boston College graduate and have been working at the Observer, a weekly in Smithfield, R.I., and I am eager to—"

"I was hoping I'd find you here." The voice, deep and assured, startled Brad. It was Dexter. He'd come into the building through the pressroom.

"Oh, hi," Brad said wearily. "Just getting caught up on my mail."

"I wanted to give this to you before I left town. I'm spending Christmas with my oldest. I think I told you. Here." Dexter handed Brad a white envelope with his first and last name typewritten on it.

Brad fumbled with the envelope, finally pulling out five crisp, fresh-smelling bills. Five thousand-dollar bills. "It's five thousand dollars," he said, flabbergasted.

"Now I know why I hired you. Your powers of observation."

"But . . . I don't get it."

"Haven't you ever seen a Christmas bonus?" Dexter laughed. "You've earned it, Brad."

"I don't know what to say . . . except thank you."

"The thanks are all mine. I know you newsmen consider ads beneath you—God forbid we should have to talk about such a banal subject!—but the fact is our ad lineage is up nearly fifteen percent since you came on board, Brad. You've seen last month's circulation figures—or have you? They're in that pile there somewhere. We're selling almost seven hundred more papers a day. We're reaching *Albany,* for heaven's sake. We've never sold papers that far away. And the projections are for us to go nowhere but up. I don't think these developments and your arrival are pure coincidence."

"I've been to the marketing meetings," Brad said. "The carrier contest's been a winner. The classified ad giveaway—you know I think it's a gimmick, but it's worked."

"You can't sell shit, Brad, no matter how you dress it up. It still stinks. You know that and I know that."

"Nothing like an epidemic to boost circulation," Brad said.

"Be that as it may. The bottom line is that envelope is the least

I can do. Buy your little girl something extra-special for Christmas. How is she, by the way?"

"She went into the hospital this morning."

"God, Brad," Dexter said, the authority draining out of his tone. "I'm sorry to hear that. God, am I sorry."

When he returned, Abbie was curled up in the same position as when he'd left her.

"I know it looks uncomfortable, but she's sleeping well," a nurse said. "She won't stir till morning."

It was nearing midnight, and still, Brad was not tired. He kissed Abbie, stood, and went into the hall. The graveyard shift had come on; nurses were making their rounds, addressing each other in insubstantial voices, their rubber-soled shoes squeaking across the overwaxed linoleum floor. At the nurses' station a small artificial Christmas tree had appeared. It was decorated with tinsel and red bulbs. The only thing keeping it from being completely ludicrous, Brad thought, was the absence of any message proclaiming Great Joy! Merry! Happy!

Damn! One week from tonight's Christmas, and I haven't bought a thing!

"Excuse me," he called to one of the nurses, a young, terribly serious sort who seemed far too dour ever to be much of a hit on a pediatric ward.

"Yes?" she said, looking up from her paper work.

"Are there any department stores open at this hour?"

"You mean, like K Mart?"

"Yes. Like that. Places that sell toys. Barbie dolls, to be specific."

"Well, K Mart's open twenty-four hours a day until Christmas. So's Caldor."

"Up here at the mall, right?"

"Right."

"Good. You think Abbie's going to stay sleep for the next hour?"

"She's going to sleep for the next *six* hours."

"Then I could leave for an hour."

"You could do whatever you want, Mr. Gale," she said sourly. "I can assure you that we are on top of the situation here."

CHAPTER FIFTY-FOUR

Friday, December 19

THINGS HAD NOT improved between Charlie and his sister. Twice he'd tried to talk to her; twice she'd turned him away at the door. Not even Mrs. Fitzpatrick's mediation could budge her. If it hadn't been for their mother, if he hadn't been reading the *Transcript,* it might have been days, even weeks, before he found out his nephew had been hospitalized.

But there it was, Jimmy's name on page one in an exclusive interview Rod Dougherty had finagled out of Ginny. With Brad Gale's active encouragement, it had become a formula for Rod: quoting anguished parent on the subject of his or her fears, then providing ample opportunity to lambaste "officials" for their reluctance to do anything. The formula, Brad had explained, was a proven one: Eventually those officials felt the nooses tightening around their necks and were left with no choice but to take real action.

Ginny blamed the CDC people. They were the experts, she said. They had the federal dollars, the federal laboratory, the whole weight of the federal government behind them. And yet "this scourge continues unabated," she said. Obviously someone somewhere had decided Morgantown was too small to count. That was her opinion, and you didn't need to read between the lines to see that it was the newspaper's, too.

Conspicuous by its absence was any mention of the editor's daughter. Charlie knew from Thomasine that Abbie had been hospitalized, but that development hadn't made it into the paper. No quotes from that particular anguished parent, no inside look at their unfolding tragedy, no intimate photographs of the latest young victim. Charlie supposed if he were in Brad's shoes, he would have done the same thing. He could not be critical.

If anything, he had softened toward Brad these last few weeks.

Their altercation in the restaurant was a fading memory now, one that no longer gave a true picture of who had started it, who had been right or wrong, who really believed what, who was the real racist, who had grabbed the bigger share of the asshole quotient. To be truthful, it probably was split fifty-fifty. Through his continued contact with Thomasine, Charlie had learned that all else aside, Brad's credentials as a father were impeccable. Trust me, Thomasine had said, he loves that girl like nothing else. And who could blame him? In a lot of ways Abbie reminded Charlie of his nephew: a quality child who was destined to grow up to be a quality adult. Brad would do anything for his little girl. Kill, if he had to.

Which is why Charlie had been obsessed with an idea since learning Abbie had been hospitalized: *Maybe she could carry the spear.*

A crazy idea, but maybe not quite as crazy as it sounded, at least not as it percolated down through the layers of Charlie's mind.

Because what other choice did he have? Some stranger's child, selected at random from the hospital census, then kidnapped? Even if he had the nerve to attempt it, and for a whole host of reasons he doubted he did, the risk of getting caught was great. Too great. There was a better than even chance he'd wind up in jail, bail denied, whatever slim hopes he'd had dashed for good. Even assuming a miracle and he got away with it, what strange kid would have the frame of mind to perform as he must at the crucial moment? Any kid—never mind one racked by this scourge, away from his parents, and in the company of this Indian stranger—would be scared shitless. Might be scared literally to death.

Jimmy was not an option either. According to Mrs. Fitzpatrick, Ginny was encamped in her son's room, staying with him twenty-four hours of the day. Nothing could budge her. She even had nurses bring the food she nibbled at because she couldn't bear the separation of a ten-minute trip to the cafeteria. Kidnapping Jimmy—pulling it off would be next to impossible. Even if he did, Charlie believed Ginny had so poisoned his nephew that he might freak out, too, at the critical moment—if they got that far. Charlie had little doubt that Ginny would have the police on his trail immediately. And Ginny would know what Charlie was up to.

Abbie.

Has to be Abbie.

Except for Jimmy, she was the only child in Morgantown Charlie knew. He'd contemplated trying it alone, but the *pniese* and Ben Wilcox had been very specific. Alone, even with the right spear— assuming he would get the right spear—he stood no chance of success. It had to be a child. A child under Hobbamock's spell.

He knew what Brad's reaction would be: *Crazy fucking Indian.*

His reaction would make the restaurant scene look like Massasoit embracing the Pilgrims.

Well, maybe he could be convinced.

And if you believe that, I have this bridge I'd like to sell you, he thought.

Still, it was like almost everything now. There were no more options. No more deals, no rabbits to be pulled out of hats, no first-round draft picks or players to be named later. This was sudden-death overtime. This was five-card draw, winner take all, and everyone still in.

He had to try for Abbie.

And he needed Brad's collaboration. There was no way he could get her into that cave, then have her do what she must without Dad at her side every step of the way.

If he had any shot, it was through Thomasine.

CHAPTER FIFTY-FIVE

Saturday, December 20

BOSTWICK STOOD outside his house, not noticing the midnight cold and wind, which were reddening his ears and making his nose run.

He was smoking. After six years, two months, and assorted days of quitting, he'd taken it up again. Nonfilter Luckies, too. It was only one of many danger signs, perhaps the least worrisome. He and his wife hadn't slept together in more than a month. That was a more alarming danger sign. No matter how long his days, he needed several good strong drinks to get to sleep. That was another. On those rare occasions when he was home, his children were treating him with the cold indifference they might show a door-to-door salesman. And for the first time in his life he thought a visit to a shrink might be just what the doctor ordered. At the very least he needed a vacation. A long, quiet cruise to Hawaii, say, gone for a month . . . or never to return, never to practice again.

That was the worst sign, the feeling that he was completely overwhelmed, that he had to get away before the world came crashing in on him.

Because this horror show seemed to have no end. Three kids were dead. Ten—or was it eleven?—hospitalized. Two dozen sick at home, next stop on the disease express Berkshire Medical. Another twenty-five showing first symptoms, although not yet bedbound. On the basis of Gosselin's and state Health's advice, the School Committee had decided to let Morgantown Elementary out three days early for the Christmas holiday; when and under what conditions they'd be back was an open question. Shots of the children boarding buses had made the network news. The *National Enquirer* had done a piece. Back at the office Bostwick had a stack of messages from reporters from as far away as Chicago. He'd returned none of their calls.

He walked across his driveway, past the garage, past last summer's garden into the backyard. The sky was cloudless. A three-quarter moon glared down, bathing the landscape in harsh silvers and whites. Across the field, rising out of the pines, was Thunder Rise. It looked larger than scale tonight, larger than New England, as if a Colorado peak somehow had been picked up, carried across the continent, and plunked down back East. It looked as if you could never get to the top of it, no matter how long or how hard you climbed.

He had never been a superstitious man, never been for or against religion, but as he looked up at the rise (staring down at him so enigmatically, or was it only his imagination?), certain things didn't seem so farfetched anymore. It didn't seem so farfetched that the death toll conceivably could reach ten, twenty, even twenty-five or fifty . . . or more. It didn't seem so farfetched that one of his own children might succumb. It didn't seem so farfetched that this so-called Mystery Disease might cross over into the adult population.

Just before supper Gosselin had called. The CDC remained stumped, he admitted. So stumped that another two physicians had been assigned, starting Monday, full-time to the case. Within a week the team would be coming back to Morgantown. A field office would be established. A county-wide blitz would be under way. And the cause would be found. Sooner or later they would have answers.

But it didn't seem so farfetched that it might take the CDC another month, two months, a half year to nail down the cause, Bostwick thought, *because maybe this is one for the medical sleuth texts. Maybe this is the one that will make Legionnaire's disease, which took months to nail down, look like some kind of parlor game.* And even if they found the cause tomorrow, healing would be another challenge. Like AIDS, it didn't really seem so farfetched anymore that it might be years before a cure or a vaccine or even an effective treatment were found.

If they were even on the right track.

He wasn't so sure they were anymore. This idea Charlie Moonlight was pushing . . .

Who says Western medicine has all the answers? It was a question that had always intrigued him, never enough to do more than read with great curiosity the occasional piece in the literature about Eastern medicine.

Bostwick's last vacation *(oh, to be doing it again)* had been a two-week visit to China arranged by the New England chapter of the American Medical Association. During a train trip through the southern provinces, he'd seen all sorts of wonders performed: acupuncture; herbal cures for cancer; peasant treatments for colds, the flu, diabetes. He'd heard of village shamans who chased evil spirits away, allowing the sick to become well. Through all regimes these practices seemed to thrive—a testimony, perhaps, to their effectiveness. And what of African witch doctors, whose claims were pooh-poohed by the med school profs, but whose tribal clients lived and died by them? What of Haitian voodoo? What of Roman Catholicism, which holds that souls can be possessed by the devil and freed through the officially sanctioned ritual of exorcism? What of Oral Roberts, for God's sake, whose claims to faith healing are gospel to his many followers?

So why not here?

Why shouldn't some Indian whose people have been here a thousand years longer than we have be right? We seem to be exhausting the traditional possibilities pretty goddamn fast, don't we? The star of the show, Mr. Nobel aspirant himself, admits he's stumped, doesn't he? What hope can there be for the rest of us mere mortals?

Meanwhile, kids continue to die. Half of the ones in Berkshire Medical tonight will be lucky if they make it another week.

Merry Christmas, kids. Hope Santa's good to you, naughty or nice.

In some sense, I'm responsible.

And will continue to be, if I leave any stone unturned.

That was the bottom line. These were his kids. Not the Health Department's. Not the CDC's. His.

Bostwick knew where Charlie lived. It was about a mile up the road. He crushed his cigarette under his heel and set off, on foot.

CHAPTER FIFTY-SIX

Sunday, December 21

SINCE ABBIE'S ADMISSION Brad had spent every night in her room, tossing and sweating on a cot, returning home only to shower, change his underwear, and feed the dog.

Three straight nights, and the strain showed. Personal grooming had gone totally by the boards. His face was unshaven; his standard khaki pants and Oxford shirt were wrinkled; his tie was coffee-stained—none of which he seemed to notice. Creases that Thomasine had never seen were firmly etched on his forehead. His eyes were painfully bloodshot. Someone not knowing him might have guessed he was pushing fifty, not still in his mid-thirties.

And so this afternoon of the Sunday before Christmas, Thomasine insisted on spelling him. You need your own bed for a night, she said. Just one night. The way you're going you're headed for a coronary. Bostwick backed her up. It'll do you good, he urged. A world of good.

"She needs me," Brad protested.

"She needs you alive," Thomasine retorted.

"I won't be able to sleep."

"Then get drunk," Thomasine suggested. "Get shit-faced, falling-down drunk. You'll be able to sleep then."

He thought he might like that. Yes, he thought he might like that a lot. A one-night bender, with no one but the walls to talk to, might do the trick. Too bad he didn't have a gram or so of coke. A few lines and about a case of beer would do wonders.

"You'll take care of her?" he asked Thomasine.

"Of course."

"Stay by her side the whole night?"

"The whole night."

"And call me if anything happens—anything at all?"

"Go, Brad," she insisted gently. "Go."

He did. When he got home, the green light was lit on the answering machine. He ignored it. He was going to get drunk, just as Thomasine ordered. There were two six-packs of Beck's in the refrigerator, but he made a last-minute decision against them. Instead, he went to the china closet, pulled out the Tanqueray, and brought it into the kitchen. Did he have quinine water? Yes, he did: an unopened bottle of Schweppes. Lime? He had one of those, too, left over from a dessert Thomasine had made a million years ago, when times were good. Except for a veneer of mold, which wiped right off, it was fine. He filled a juice tumbler with ice and mixed himself a nice cold monster gin and tonic. It was a summer drink, but it was what he wanted, damn it. There were nothing but good, fair-weather thoughts associated with G&Ts. He could use some of those now.

But none came. As he drank his first G&T, and his second, and his third, the one where the buzzing started inside his head, he could think of nothing but Abbie.

The answering machine. On his fourth drink he remembered he hadn't gone through its messages.

Should he?

Of course not. Don't be a fool.

And what if it's Bostwick? Thomasine? What if it's an urgent message from the hospital? What if Abbie woke up wanting me?

What if she's—

He half ran, half stumbled into the front hall. After fumbling with the push-buttons, he got the machine going.

It was Heather.

Pisser.

Yes, this is just what Brad Gale needs, folks. Just when you thought things couldn't possibly get worse, here comes Heather.

How long was it since she'd been in touch? Brad groped around inside his drunkenness for the answer. Since before Thanksgiving, wasn't it? Yes. God bless Heather, loving mother that she was. So terribly concerned for the health and well-being of her daughter, whom she hasn't seen or called or probably devoted a minute's thought to in, oh, only two months.

"What's going on with Abbie?" the tinny voice on the tape demanded. "If I don't hear from you by tonight, I'm calling the state police. Heather. Sunday, December twenty-first, two-thirty P.M."

Police were not a threat Brad took lightly. During the tail end of their marriage, when Brad had moved out with Abbie, she'd called the cops four times on him. Once he'd almost been arrested. He fixed another gin and tonic, doubling up on the gin, and dialed her number.

"Yeah?" the voice answered. With this buzzing in his ears, it was hard to determine from that one word if she was drunk, too.

"Returning your call," he said. He was preparing himself for—for what? An inquisition? Small-megatonnage thermonuclear attack? Or tears in her beers for her poor, sick little girl? Heather was like Berkshire weather, impossible to predict.

"What the fuck's going on up there?" she shouted. *So it's thermonuclear attack,* Brad thought.

"Abbie's in the hospital."

"I know."

"How'd you find out?"

"How do you suppose? It's been all over the news."

"Not Abbie's name."

"I called the paper looking for you. Whoever answered the phone told me. But never mind all that. How's Abbie?"

"She's doing all right," he said. It was a lie. Abbie was terrible—worse than when she'd been admitted. Sleeping most of the time. Disoriented those rare occasions when she was awake. Not eating, not even the ice cream they were plying her with.

"*Doing all right*? You call being in serious condition in the hospital doing all right?"

"They think it's only the flu," he lied.

"Flu? That's not what they're saying on the news. I think you're full of shit."

"What's the purpose of the call, Heather?"

"The purpose of the call, asshole, is my daughter. I'm concerned."

"Please." Brad hooted. "Please don't make me laugh."

"I don't like the care she's getting."

"What the hell do you know about the care she's getting? Your boyfriend been filling that pretty little head with medical gobbledygook, and now all of a sudden you're the expert? Is that it? Abbie's getting the best care money can buy."

"She's being treated at Hooterville Hospital and you have the nerve to say she's getting the best care money can buy?"

That's when he lost it.

"If you're so concerned, what the hell are you doing still in New York?" he shouted. "Why aren't you up here spending the night with her, smoothing her brow, holding a cold facecloth to her forehead for hours on end the way I've been? Why aren't you up here, telling her everything's going to be OK, that she's not going to . . . *pass away,* for God's sake? Who are you to criticize me when all she was to you for four years was a roadblock to your stardom?'"

He went on for several minutes.

At some point (the next day, trying to reconstruct the scene, he would not be able to remember exactly which point) he realized that the line had gone dead. She'd hung up on him, the bitch. He swore, considered throwing the phone, then thought better of it. He stood, phone in one hand, drink in the other, his anger fizzling. It was surprising how quickly it was dissipating, although it was not surprising how quickly it had built. He supposed he was too tired to sustain emotion like that at fever pitch.

Fuck her, he thought. *I'm not going to let her get to me. Not tonight.*

He got a new line, dialed the hospital, and was connected to Thomasine, who told him that everything was under control: Abbie was sleeping, and he ought to be doing the same. He thanked her, promised all three of them a trip to Bermuda during winter vacation, then hung up. Thomasine was right. He'd probably be able to sleep tonight. At least a few hours. At least until dawn. Then he'd get up and try to get some breakfast into his daughter.

The drowsiness he felt now was inviting, welcome. It wasn't that Abbie wasn't on his mind any longer, but her presence there now wasn't as hurtful. The gin had finally cast its summertime spell, and the good memories were cascading over him in waves. Abbie's first day of school, his daughter looking so beautiful it took his breath away. Abbie and Jimmy at the fair. Abbie in the Mustang, trying to find one of her favorite songs on the dash radio. Abbie and Mrs. Fitzpatrick at the Boar's Head Inn. Abbie and Daddy shopping. Abbie and Daddy building a snow fort. Abbie picking out her puppy.

The dog. The goddamn dog.

Oh, Jesus. He'd forgotten to feed it.

"Gotta feed the dog," he muttered. "No choice." Before he could sleep, one last task.

He went out the back. The sky was spitting snow, but the moon peeked from behind clouds that were rolling by at furious speed. Winter was coming all right. It was already here. The old-timers who dropped by the paper every now and again had assured him that once you hit the end of December in the Berkshires, you could expect a solid two months of the deep freeze, not to mention, oh, maybe eight feet of snow in an average season, ten or more in a toughie. And figure, as a rule of thumb, three major blizzards.

Somehow, their dire predictions weren't so frightful anymore. He could handle weather. Weather was a breeze.

Maria was in her usual spot in the garage, the far corner where old tires and some garden tools were piled in a heap. She'd heard his footsteps approach on the frozen ground, the creak of the door opening, his hand groping for the light switch. She watched him now, an intruder. An unwelcome intruder. The cause of this hunger slowly gnawing away at her insides.

"Goddamn mutt," Brad muttered as he picked up an almost empty bag of Alpo. One meal was all that was left. Screw it. If the dog never ate again, it wouldn't be any skin off his back. If only Abbie weren't so attached to her . . .

Maria growled.

Brad heard it.

Halfway across the garage floor, he stopped and stared. In the harsh glow of the one naked ceiling bulb the dog didn't look right. For well over a month she had been acting queerly—he would never forget the day she lunged at Abbie—and he had been wary of her. But the dog had never looked this menacing. Her teeth were bared, her muscles tensed, as if ready to spring. She didn't look like your basic hungry pooch. She looked rabid. Going down the tubes and going fast.

Thank God she's on her chain.

He remembered a story Rod Dougherty had done several weeks ago. It was an interview with Morgantown's animal control officer on the occasion of his twenty-fifth year on the job. At the end of the interview the officer had let slip that he had never seen a year like this year. Never had so many dogs and cats in the pound, left there by owners who said they couldn't control them anymore. Animals that acted rabid, although his careful testing had disclosed not one case of rabies. It was the dangedest thing he'd ever seen, the officer allowed. His own personal theory was it had something to do with sunspots.

Brad approached along the back wall. When he was about five feet from the chain's outer limit, he tossed the food. The pellets showered down around the dog with a sound like hail on a tin roof.

"Here's your food."

He'd turned his back when the dog leaped.

The chain snapped. Brad heard the pop.

Maria hit Brad at hip level, sending him crashing into the wall. He toppled softly to the concrete, his drunkenness cushioning the blow. For a second he couldn't believe what had happened. Then he saw the dog, smelled her, heard her jaws snapping at his sleeve. He was amazed, but he was too drunk to be immediately scared.

"What the hell—"

Maria backed off and stopped in the middle of the garage floor—whether ready to attack again or not, Brad didn't know.

The dog's growling had increased from background static to full-throated aggression.

Brad got to his feet. He couldn't believe what he was seeing. Not Maria—not that lovable, oversize, pick-of-the-litter golden that nice farmer had let Abbie have almost four months ago. Not that faithful, growing-like-a-weed companion to his daughter . . . at least until a month or so ago. This was a forty- or fifty-pound dog, big and strong enough to bust a chain. But it wasn't size that had Brad flipped out. It was those teeth—long, sharp, lethal.

"Easy, pup." Brad edged toward the door, his back scraping rakes and shovels and other tools that were hung from the wall. He felt his testicles tighten. He was suddenly, thoroughly sober.

Maria seemed to sense his fear, seemed to feed on it, seemed to be enraged and emboldened by it. Brad could see saliva, glistening on the dog's bared incisors, dripping down her black gums onto the concrete floor.

The dog's rabid, Brad thought, his fear escalating to terror.

"Easy, now . . ."

He was approaching the door when Maria dropped into a low crouch, her muscles coiled and tense, like a cougar ready to pounce. If the dog sprang, Brad might not be so lucky this time. Might not make it to the door. Might find those teeth clamped down on his hand, or leg . . . or throat.

Brad groped behind him for his ax or the maul he'd used to split half a cord of wood. His hand contacted a garden hose, the lawn mower handle, a spade.

No ax. No maul.

He got a good grip on the spade.

He brought it to chest level.

"Easy, pup," he managed to say, inching toward the door again, wielding the spade like a hockey stick. If he could just get out, close the door, lock it, call the police or the dog officer . . .

Maria attacked.

Brad swung.

It was a direct hit. The sound of spade contacting the dog's skull was like two rocks colliding. Maria went limp at Brad's feet, and blood began gushing from her ear. She convulsed several times and was still.

Brad watched, detached at first, then horrified. Tears began to fill his eyes.

Abbie, I'm so sorry, he thought, even though he knew then he could never tell her the truth. *I'm so sorry I killed your dog. I'm so sorry you had to get sick, and Daddy had to go crazy, and everything had to turn so awful when it was supposed to turn so right. I'll make it up to you, Apple Guy, I promise. Make it up to you a hundred times, a million, make it all better.*

We'll get another puppy, and if you want to name it Maria, too, that's fine. It will be a wonderful puppy, and it will grow into a wonderful dog, and if you want it to sleep at the foot of your bed, well, that's OK, Apple Guy. Really, it is.

As the blood ran in widening rivers across the floor, Brad buried his head in his hands and let the tears come. They came, violently, mercilessly.

CHAPTER FIFTY-SEVEN

Monday, December 22
Morning

BREAKFASTLESS, Brad arrived at the hospital at six-thirty Monday morning. On his way to Abbie's room he stopped at the cafeteria for coffee. He needed something in him, even if it was only caffeine.

Ginny Ellis was at one of the tables, alone, slumped over a Coke. For all Brad knew, she could have been there, frozen like that, all night.

"Hi," Brad said when he'd gone through the line, mostly nurses coming aboard the seven-to-three shift.

"Hi," Ginny said wearily.

"Been here long?"

"I just came down. It's the first time I've left his room since he came in. He was sleeping, and . . . you don't think I'm being awful, do you? I'm going back in five minutes."

"Of course, I don't think you're awful. You need a break. I went home," Brad said, almost guiltily. "They insisted. You should try a night, too. It would do you a world of good." *And if Jimmy's got a favorite pet,* he thought blackly, *you could kill it. That's what I did when I went home. Got shit-faced and went out and clubbed the dog to death.*

"How is she?" Ginny asked. For an instant Brad thought she meant Maria.

"Abbie?"

"Yes."

"She's the same, according to the front desk. I'm just on my way up. How about Jimmy?"

"No different."

"Maybe today's his day."

"Maybe."

Brad nodded understandingly. "Maybe if they both feel better a little later, they could visit."

"Sure."

"It might pick them both up."

"Sure."

Brad finished his coffee and left. Ginny didn't move. Still slumped over her can of Coke. They could drop the Big One, Brad thought, and she wouldn't budge.

When he got to her room, Abbie was asleep. Thomasine was not. She was sitting by the bed, reading the Boston *Globe* and drinking coffee a nurse had brought her. She looked surprisingly fresh, as if she had sneaked home to her own bed last night, not been tortured on a fold-up cot. Surprisingly beautiful. *God, we've come a long way in this relationship,* he thought, *that she would do this for me, and I would let her. I don't know where you came from, Thomasine, or who sent you, or why . . . I only know that right now, you and Abbie are all I have.*

"Good morning," he said, kissing the back of her neck.

"Good morning." She smiled.

"Was it a good night?"

"Yes. She was only up twice. Went right back both times."

"Did she ask for me?"

"Unh-unh."

"And what about you?"

"I slept."

"Tell the truth."

"I did."

"Thanks, Thom. Thanks an awful lot."

"Don't be ridiculous. Did *you* sleep?"

"Without a problem."

Just like I killed Maria: Without a problem. Her bloody corpse is still on the garage floor, should you want to see for yourself.

They chatted, exchanging details of their respective nights—minus Maria. Thomasine had just asked him to join her in the conference room—she had something she wanted him and no one else to hear, she'd said—when Abbie moaned, tossed, then opened her eyes. She looked slowly around the room, seemed to recognize both of them. Seemed to smile, wanly but happily.

Was it only wishful thinking, or did she actually look better?

"Hi, Dad," she said.

"Good morning, Apple Guy. How do you feel, hon?" He sat on the side of her bed and leaned over, kissing her. He was careful not to get tangled in her IV tube or heart monitor leads, a brightly colored bundle of tiny wires that disappeared under her pajama top.

"I'm thirsty, Dad."

"Then let's get you a drink. Would you like ginger ale?"

She nodded. Thomasine handed Brad a Dixie cup of it, and he passed it to Abbie. She drank it in one swallow. *Another good sign,* he dared to think.

"Dad?" she asked when her thirst was slaked.

Involuntarily, Brad tensed. He was convinced she was going to ask about Maria. Convinced she was going to say: *I miss my puppy, Dad. Do you think my puppy could visit me? Do you? If I promised to be good, do you think my puppy could visit? Pretty please? If you brought her in quietly, the nurses wouldn't even have to know she was here.*

"What, sweetheart?" he said anxiously.

"My tooth is out."

"You're kidding."

"Nope. See?" She uncurled her fist, revealing the celebrated incisor.

"The nurse actually gave it the final push," Thomasine explained. "Last night, right after you left."

"Super!" Brad exclaimed. "You know what that means, don't you, Apple Guy?"

Abbie nodded.

"It means the tooth fairy is going to come," Brad said.

Abbie managed a smile. But she very soon lost interest. Within minutes she had slipped back into semiconsciousness. Brad watched her go, the knot in his stomach tightening as she drifted farther and farther from him.

"Come on." Thomasine whispered, motioning toward the door. Brad took a final look at his daughter, making sure she didn't stir, and got up. They left Abbie's room and went down the hall past the stairway to the conference room. It was empty. Thomasine hit the light switch and led Brad inside, closing the door behind them.

"Sit down," she said, her voice thin and unsure. Brad had never heard her this tentative. "Reluctant" and "shy" were not words he would use to describe her, but now they seemed to fit.

"OK, I'm sitting," he said.

"I want you to listen to everything I have to say before you respond."

Already Brad didn't like the direction this was taking.

"And I don't want you to get angry. Promise?"

Brad hesitated.

"Promise," she repeated.

"I promise."

Thomasine paused, as if she'd rehearsed what she was about to say but still wasn't sure where it was best to begin—or if it was best to begin at all. "Remember the legend of Thunder Rise?" she finally asked.

"Yes."

"About children's souls being stolen?"

"Yes." He was getting it now.

"And the children as a result . . . getting very sick."

"You've been talking to that Moonshine character, haven't you?" he said disgustedly.

"Moonlight."

"Moonlight. You've been talking to him."

"Yes," Thomasine admitted. "He was here last night. After you left."

"Here? Here in the hospital?"

"In Abbie's room."

Brad was incredulous. "Are you making that up? You must be making that up!"

Thomasine shook her head. "Bostwick brought him."

"Bostwick?"

"They wanted to talk with me. They did, for over an hour."

"So that's why you wanted me home. So you could—could . . . talk about me behind my back." His anger was fizzling, replaced by a childish sense of hurt.

"Come on, Brad. Don't you know me better than that?" And the truth was, he did know her better than that. The truth was, Thomasine was one of the least devious people he had ever met. "It was coincidental that you were gone," she continued. "If you'd been here, it wouldn't have been any different. They would have said what they said."

"And what was that?" he asked wearily.

"They said things are out of control."

"That's brilliant."

"They said unless something changes, a lot more kids are going to die."

"And?"

"They're desperate, Brad. Bostwick probably more than Charlie, believe it or not."

"Let me guess where this is leading," Brad cut in. "Bostwick believes the Indian now, doesn't he?"

"He doesn't know what he believes anymore."

"But he's at least willing to listen to that crap about Hobbamock."

"Yes."

"And you are now, too."

"I—I don't know what to think, Brad. Honest, I don't."

Brad looked at his hands. "I guess I'm not surprised. It was only a matter of time before that Indian caused more trouble. He—he ought to be locked up. The man's dangerous."

"At least he has a theory, Brad. As farfetched as it is, at least he has one."

"And it's bullshit. *Bullshit.* I can't believe I'm hearing you say this. How's this for a theory—a credible one? We're dealing with a new microbe. Yes, it's a mystery. Yes, it's deadly. But it's still a microbe. Some kind of bacterium or virus. Any idiot can see that."

"Is that what you really believe?"

"Yes," he snapped. "That's what the CDC is saying, isn't it? Bacterium or virus, with more evidence for bacterium? It's been in all the stories lately. That's what Gosselin told me personally. It wouldn't surprise me if he announces this week that they've isolated it and come up with a name for it."

"And a treatment?"

"Only a matter of time."

"Can't you see, Brad? You don't have that kind of time. What if it's like AIDS? What if five years from now there's still no cure? I—I don't want to sound cruel, but you're being blind. You don't want to admit what's happening, and I don't blame you for that, but Abbie's dying, Brad. *Dying.* Like the others have died."

"No, she's not. She's going to pull through. You'll see."

"I hope to God you're right."

"Another couple of weeks she'll be well enough to go home."

"Bostwick doesn't think she'll last a week," Thomasine said softly, breaking eye contact.

Her words were like lasers. "Did he *say* that?"

"In so many words, yes. I'm sorry, Brad."

"But he hasn't told *me* that," Brad protested weakly.

"Because he can't take any more of this," Thomasine said. "Can't you see? He's losing his mind, Brad. It seems everyone is, me included."

There was silence, long and uncomfortable.

"What do they want?"

Thomasine outlined Charlie's proposal. It would mean Abbie, as sick as she was, would have to leave the hospital. Bostwick had already agreed to go along. Thomasine, too. And Charlie. Brad would have to, too, if only for Abbie's sake. The whole trip might take three hours. It could be longer. It could be shorter. Yes, there was a risk. A grave one probably. But what was the alternative?

"What do you think?" she said when she was done.

"I think it's the most preposterous thing I've ever heard," Brad answered, but there was no edge to his voice, no anger, no hostile emotion of any kind that Thomasine could detect. He felt tired. He felt betrayed. Most frightening was how alone he suddenly felt.

"Will you at least think about it?" Thomasine asked.

He nodded yes—not because he intended to but because it was easier that way. He didn't want to fight anymore. "Now, if you'll excuse me, I have to get back to Abbie," he said, leaving.

CHAPTER FIFTY-EIGHT

Monday, December 22
Afternoon

"GOOD AFTERNOON, ABBIE," the rhamphorhynchus said from its hiding spot under her bed. "And how are we feeling today?"

Abbie stirred. In her semisleep, the place where you walked through endless shadows—cool, friendly shadows, like under the big maple on their front lawn—she'd become aware of something different.

A presence . . . the presence of . . .

. . . she didn't know what, exactly.

"The doctors are concerned, did you know that? I've been listening to some of their conversations, and they're *very* concerned. They think you're going to . . . why, they think you're going to Pass Away. My goodness!"

Abbie's eyes flew open. She looked wildly about the room, lit by the dying embers of a cold winter sun. The room was gloomy, like the place of shadows, but there was still sufficient light to make out the closet, the chairs, the empty bed next to hers. There was no one there, not even Daddy.

But she'd heard it. Yes.

The rhamphorhynchus.

It hadn't come since she'd been in the hospital, but now she was hearing it. She was sure she was hearing it. It was talking about Passing Away, just like the last time she'd seen it, at home. Passing Away seemed to be a part of everything now. On everyone's lips or just behind them.

"Do you think you're going to Pass Away, Abbie? You can be

honest with me. I won't tell anyone. I especially won't tell one of those mean nurses. They might—they might give you another needle, is what they might do. Nurses just *love* to give needles, haven't you noticed?"

Abbie figured out where it was.

Not in her mind, which is where Daddy said it lived.

Not next to her, where it usually was. It was under the bed. Afraid it would be seen, so it had gone under the bed.

Abbie began to tremble, the way she had two years ago when she'd fallen off her tricycle, an accident that had sent her whole body into mild shock.

"Daaad," she cried hoarsely.

"Shhhh," the monster whispered. "You know how nosy nurses are. And we wouldn't want to have one of them walk in on us, would we? I have something very important to tell you. *Very* important."

"Daaaad," Abbie cried again.

"He's not here," the rhamphorhynchus said. "He had to go to the paper for a little while. Thomasine's gone, too. I thought they never would! You're a very popular girl. What with these nosy, mean nurses and doctors and all, it's been very hard to get a free moment with you. But soon there will be lots of time. You and I and Maureen and Jimmy and all of our little friends will soon have all the time in the world. Aren't you excited, Abbie? You're not going to Pass Away! You're coming with me on an exciting journey!"

Abbie whimpered. She tried lifting an arm, a leg, a finger . . . and knew even before the attempt that it was impossible. Her body didn't work anymore. Since coming into the hospital, she'd done nothing but lie in bed and be very, very sick. The ability to walk, reach, skip, even eat—they had all gone away. Nothing was right anymore.

That was the most terrifying thought of all, knowing there was no way she could escape.

"There's only one thing that could come in the way of all that fun," the creature continued from under the bed, "and that's the Indian. Do you remember the Indian?"

Abbie did. She hadn't seen him since that night he'd guessed her nickname, but she remembered him very well. Jimmy always talked about him. A very, very nice man. A man who knew magic.

"That Indian is a very, very bad man. He's probably the most bad man there is in the whole world. Do you know what he wants to do, Abbie? To you? He wants to *steal* you. *Kidnap* you, just like those poor children your daddy and your teacher tell you about. Remember those children? You've seen their pictures on milk cartons. The poor things. Kidnapped, and then killed. Yes! That's what happens when you're kidnapped, you know. They kill you, which is much worse than Passing Away. Passing Away . . . well, it usually just happens, and you don't feel anything. But being killed—it's too horrible to describe. Sometimes they make you bleed. Cut you with knives or beat you with baseball bats. Sometimes they do worse things, nasty grown-up things, and then you're dead. That's what the Indian wants to do to you, kidnap and kill you."

No, Abbie protested. *Not Mr. Moonlight. He's too nice.*

"Oh, no, he's not." The rhamphorhynchus disagreed. "He's waiting until you're asleep, and then he's going to sneak in here and take you away. And when he's got you far, far away, he's going to *kill you!*"

Abbie's sobs were audible in the hall now, but there was no one there to hear them.

"And that's not even the worst thing. The worst thing is that Indian is using his evil powers to make Dr. Bostwick go along with him. Thomasine, too. And even your dad. Isn't that awful, Abbie? Everyone ganging up like that on you so that the Indian can *kill you.* Don't you think you should do something about that? Wouldn't you like to be safe, not *killed?*

"Of course you would. Here's what I want you to do."

Between sobs, Abbie listened to the rhamphorhynchus's plan.

CHAPTER FIFTY-NINE

Monday, December 22
Afternoon and Evening

HE'D BECOME a ghost editor, dropping by every day for only a couple of hours. He tried to time his appearance to coincide with the daily budget meetings, dominated now with planning for stories about the Mystery Disease.

Today Brad left at four-thirty. It was dark.

He did not go directly to the hospital. He wanted to shower. He wanted to get the mail, and have a bite to eat in his own kitchen (even if it was only a TV dinner), and make sure the burner was working, the lights on. He wanted to tend to the little details that gave the illusion that at least a few of life's gears still turned.

He had another task. One that had been worming its way into his thoughts all day. One he couldn't put off any longer.

Maria.

I've got to take care of Maria.

It was five-fifteen when he pulled into the drive. It had been dark an hour. The house was black, foreboding; Brad was actually a bit jittery opening the door and going in. He fumbled for the light switch, found it, flicked it. The living room was bathed in light. He checked the thermostat. Checked the answering machine; there were no messages. Opened the mail. It was all bills and flyers. He tossed them onto his study desk. The pile now was several inches thick.

He wasn't hungry. He didn't want to shower yet. Not until . . .

. . . he took care of Maria.

You've been stalling long enough, he said with sudden determination. *Let's get it over with.*

He went upstairs to his room and changed into his oldest jeans and a ratty flannel shirt. Like a murderer destroying incriminating evidence, he would dispose of them when he was done—maybe douse them with lighter fluid and burn them in the fireplace. He rummaged through his closet for an old pair of gloves and went downstairs.

He went out the door and walked toward the garage, his feet crunching on the frozen ground. He had not put the light over the garage door on, or the porch light on, or any outside light. They would be visible from the road. He had the crazy idea that light would draw attention to him, could somehow be a magnet for someone (*who? the cops? the ASPCA? St. Francis of Assisi?*) to discover what he'd done. That was the last thing he needed now.

As his hand contacted the knob to the side door, he had an even crazier thought.

Maria's alive. Last night was all a dream, an ugly, terrible dream fed by too much booze and too much tiredness and too much worry that just goes on and on and on. Maria's alive, and not just alive but well. Stupid bitch that she is, she's going to come bounding toward me, slobbering all over my pants.

He opened the door and turned on the light.

The sight of the dead dog made him gag.

It wasn't the shape of its head, noticeably flattened. It wasn't the brown-yellow mix that ran in a thin drool from the dog's rear. In her death throes, Maria's sphincter and bladder had let go. The evidence could still be smelled.

No, it was the sheer volume of blood. It was going to take a heavy-duty cleaner to get rid of it. He wondered if bleach would do the trick. Maybe followed by motor oil, to disguise the stain.

Brad walked to the far wall. The blanket he used while changing the Mustang's oil was draped over a nail. He lifted it off and placed it in the wheelbarrow. Negotiating his way through the blood puddles, he positioned the wheelbarrow a foot from the corpse. He laid the blanket down next to the dog. Using the same spade that had killed the animal, he pushed Maria onto it. Then he carefully wrapped the blanket around the corpse. With a grunt, he got the dog and blanket off the ground. The body was stiff, as if a taxidermist had been at work. Stiff and much heavier than he had expected. He dropped Maria onto the wheelbarrow.

After checking the street for traffic, Brad opened the garage door and wheeled Maria out. He closed the door and pushed Maria around to the garden, his feet crunching through the final discolored inch of snow that remained from the last storm.

He started digging. The topsoil was iron-hard, and it rejected the spade.

I'll never get through this, he thought.

But he did. Winter had not locked in long enough for more than a couple of inches of topsoil to freeze. Once he'd punctured that, it was easy digging, and he was able to make good time. In under ten minutes he'd gotten as far as he thought necessary to keep the skunks away next spring, a depth of about four feet.

He stood back from the grave, catching his breath, which escaped him like steam. He wanted a cigarette. Wanted one badly. He felt funny, his head light and ready to swim, his torso tingly, as if he had a bad case of pins and needles. And it wasn't the intensity of exercise doing this to him. He didn't know how he knew, but he knew it wasn't that. It wasn't a good exhausted feeling. It wasn't tiredness at all. It was as if . . .

. . . as if he were being watched.

Once the idea was in his head, he couldn't shake it. For the first time tonight he was aware of Thunder Rise, black and brooding under a sky that couldn't decide if it wanted to clear or storm. He'd seen the rise before, of course, while he was digging, but now . . . now he was *aware of it.* Aware of it not as a mountain, but as an entity, a malevolence . . . It was impossible for him to explain, although he suspected the Indian might have a word or two to say. He squinted, trying to see better. Every half minute the clouds would break momentarily, and the mountain would be radiant. It reminded him of the great seal on the back of the dollar bill: a pyramid topped with a human eyeball, a symbol he had always considered incredibly bizarre.

He looked back at the upturned earth, at the wheelbarrow, at the blanket, creased and folded in the unmistakable shape of a large dog.

Get on with it, he scolded himself. *So close. Be done with it.*

But he did not get on with it. The longer he stared at the blanket, the more it seemed different. The more it seemed to change. And not just *seem* to change. It really *was* changing. Brad's breath clogged inside him. If you looked carefully, you could see the folds moving, rearranging themselves in new patterns.

He rubbed his eyes, sure that when he looked again, the blanket would be unstirring.

It wasn't. It was definitely moving.

Dear God, the dog's alive. Somehow, the fucking dog's alive.

Except it wasn't a dog shape anymore. As he watched, his legs paralyzed, the control of his bladder becoming more and more tenuous, the blanket began to unravel. First the end where the dog's legs had been. Peeling itself back, slowly, excruciatingly slowly, to reveal a glimmer of pink. Pink *toes.* That's what they were. Toes. A foot. Another foot. The smooth calf of a leg. The calves of two legs, two small, bony legs. A young child's legs.

"No!" he screamed. "Noooo!"

He didn't need to see more to know who it was.

"No! Stop it!" he screamed, his voice echoing hollowly in the cold.

But the blanket did not stop. It was unraveling—and not on its own mystical power. Brad could see fingers now, the fingers to two hands. The hands were moving the blanket. The hands were unwrapping what was inside the blanket. The hands were freeing whoever was inside.

With sudden force, the hands threw off the rest of the fabric, exposing Abbie, dressed in her favorite blue party dress. Exposing Abbie's face, Abbie's head, grossly misshapen, her hair matted with blood, just like Maria's fur.

"How *could* you, Dad?" she croaked, and he could see crimson spittle, frothing out of her open lips. "My *puppy,* Daddy! My puppy! Mommy might do something awful like that, but how could you? How?"

Brad covered his eyes and dropped to the ground, an insane man mumbling insanities.

The clouds broke again, and for an instant Thunder Rise seemed to smile.

He walked quietly into her room. It was almost ten, far later than he'd ever expected to be. Abbie had been asleep for hours. Her condition was unchanged, the nurses informed him. Brad listened to her breathing, regular but faint. If he wanted to, he could believe some of the power had gone out of her lungs since he'd left her this afternoon. But he did not want to believe that. There were a lot of things he didn't want to believe any longer.

The blanket had been a hallucination, of course. He believed that. A trick a fatigued, guilty mind had played on itself. It had passed as suddenly as it had arrived, and he had buried Maria without further incident.

A hallucination, yes.

But it had shaken him like nothing in his life.

As he slipped a five-dollar bill under Abbie's pillow, wondering vaguely if she would even be aware tomorrow that the tooth fairy had visited, he realized he had made a decision. What Thomasine had called his pigheadedness had dissipated abruptly, completely, leaving only a bland numbness. It might be the wrong decision, but it was the only one to be made. He knew that.

Tomorrow I'll see Moonlight, he thought. *At least let him spell out precisely what he has in mind.*

He pulled a chair next to Abbie's bed. As he pretended to read *People* magazine, hoping it would lull him into sleep that would blot out the last twenty-four hours, Thomasine's words echoed in his head.

. . . *Abbie's dying, Brad.* Dying. *Like the others. . . .*

If he'd heeded his instincts weeks ago, when the disease first appeared—heeded them and not his career, not that fucking career

Heather so rightly criticized—none of this would have happened. He and Abbie would have moved away from Morgantown—far, far away—and everything would be fine now.

It was his fault Abbie was dying. *His.* Silently he began to cry.

CHAPTER SIXTY

Tuesday, December 23
Early Morning

AFTER THE rhamphorhynchus left, Abbie gladly slipped back into the place where you walked through shadows. Cool, comforting shadows, far, far away from this other place, this place of needles and tubes and aches all over and the feeling that you were so hot, so thirsty that you were going to burn up. She slept through the evening and night, not waking until almost eight the next morning. Brad was by her side when she began to stir. Her eyes fluttered open, and she tried unsuccessfully to pull herself up into a sitting position.

"There, there, now," Brad said soothingly. "Easy, hon." He had stopped asking his daughter how she felt. The nurses had said it was best she speak as little as possible. "To conserve her strength," they'd said, and Brad had been struck again by how euphemistic so much of their dialogue with laymen was.

"You know what, Apple Guy?" he said when he'd fluffed her pillow and cooled her forehead with a damp cloth.

She did not respond.

"I think that maybe . . . just maybe . . . the tooth fairy might have visited last night. Want me to check?"

No response.

"Why, look!" he said, reaching under her pillow and speaking with forced excitement. He flashed the five-dollar bill. "A five-dollar bill! I don't think I've ever heard of the tooth fairy leaving a reward that big!"

Still, no response, not a smile or a nod. She was listening, she comprehended—Brad could see that in her eyes—but something was troubling her. And it wasn't only her sickness, the way her body felt.

Something else was written on her face. He could see it there, sketched plainly in the furrows on her brow, in her eyebrows, knitted tightly.

It's something about me, isn't it?

She's afraid of me.

It was a ridiculous thought, and he dismissed it immediately.

But there was no question she was afraid of something. He knew his daughter too well not to recognize fear, even when she was feeling so low. Even when her normal range of emotions was so distorted by sickness.

"What is it, honey?" he asked, ignoring the nurses' admonishment. Abbie's eyes locked with his, and then she turned away, the tears falling.

Brad reached for her hand, but she withdrew it.

In another few minutes she lapsed back into unconsciousness.

On the drive to Charlie's, he puzzled over it.

Maybe she suddenly became afraid of the tooth fairy, he speculated. *Maybe the tooth fairy showed up in one of her nightmares, like the dinosaur, and she woke up afraid of it. That would make sense. Or maybe she's angry at me. Blaming me. Transferring her pain to me. I've read that very sick children will do that. Maybe she's so sick she had no idea what she's doing. Had no idea it was me.* They were terrifying thoughts, and they gave him new conviction in what he had decided to do.

Charlie met him at the door.

Brad had expected a hostile man, but he did not find one. He found a man who'd had too little sleep for too long, a man who'd spent too many hours with too many worries—a man peculiarly like himself.

"Come in," Charlie said, as if he'd been expecting Brad, and he had.

"Thank you."

Brad stepped gingerly into the kitchen. He perused the cabin. Another expectation dashed. Brad had been sure anything reminiscent of the twentieth century would have been banned, and there was, in fact, a preponderance of old-fashioned furnishings. Lanterns and candles. A wood stove, sooty and black and huge and throwing off an incredible amount of heat. A pump sink. Blackened cast-iron pots. Ceramic ware that looked handmade. An oak kitchen table that was probably 150 years old. There also was a VCR and one of the biggest television sets Brad had ever seen. And a chair that was obviously the owner's favorite—a La-Z-Boy recliner. *A genuine Naugahyde La-Z-Boy recliner, for heaven's sake.*

Brad wasn't sure what his environment said about Charlie, only that the machinery that made him tick couldn't possibly be as simple as he'd thought.

"Please, sit. Would you like something to drink?" Charlie offered. "Coffee? Tea? I don't have anything alcoholic."

"No, thanks," Brad said. "I'm fine."

"Something to eat?"

"No. I don't have much of an appetite these days."

"Nor do I," Charlie said, settling his long frame into his recliner.

"Before we talk about . . . why I'm here"—Brad faltered—"I—I owe you an apology. For what happened in the restaurant."

Charlie saw how hard it was for him to say that, and he was impressed that Brad had been able to get it out. "You weren't alone," he replied. "There's an old Quidneck saying about fools: The only thing worse than one of them is two of them. I lost my temper, too. I shouldn't have. But this has been a very difficult period for me, as it has for you . . . for everyone."

There was awkward silence, each man trying to gauge the other's sincerity. *Whether sincere or not,* Brad thought, *he's certainly more civil. Of course, he knows why I'm here. He can justifiably claim victory, if that's the way he wants to play it. Because he* has *won, if you want to look at it in those terms. A complete and total victory.*

Charlie broke the silence: "You're here because of your daughter."

"Yes."

"I'm very sorry for you. I don't have a child of my own, but I have a nephew. I love him like a son."

"Jimmy speaks highly of you."

"I haven't seen him in weeks. My sister won't allow it. I've tried going through our mother, to no avail."

"She mentioned something about a disagreement. She didn't really go into it with me." It was a shade of truth. Mrs. Fitzpatrick had actually given him all the details over coffee in the hospital cafeteria.

"There was an argument. A bad argument. You must think I'm

always arguing." Charlie laughed, a surprisingly contrite, revealing laugh.

"No, I don't. I think Ginny feels very bad about what's happened between you, but she's under a lot of pressure. It's hard being where she is. Believe me. Jimmy's a very, very sick little boy."

"I know. I've been calling the hospital every day. They give a condition update. I've watched his slide from fair to serious but stable."

"That's happened to Abbie, too," Brad said quietly.

"It's only a matter of time before they drop the stable part."

Brad did not respond.

"It's insidious, the stealing of children's souls," Charlie said with new energy, new rage. "Even for the devil—which is what, I suppose, a Christian would call Hobbamock. You see, a child's soul is pure. *Very* pure, like a child's mind, or a child's body, or a child's perspective on the world around him. It is precisely that pureness that makes it so difficult for Hobbamock to work. Pureness makes it so slow. That is why the 'disease,' as people call it, is so prolonged."

Brad could see that Charlie felt compelled to explain, even though no explanation had been sought. He let him continue without interruption.

"I think it would be different if Hobbamock were interested in adults. Adults would be easier prey. Quicker. How many adults have already sold their souls or had them stolen away—stolen by greed, or the love of money, or the pursuit of pleasure?

"So many. So very many. The developers, who have raped the land. The bankers and brokers, whose lives are defined by dollar bills. The generals and admirals with their killing machines. The pimps and pushers and child pornographers. The industrialists, who have polluted the water and earth and air in their blind pursuit of profits. The people I join at the tables in Las Vegas and Reno, the ones who drop twenty-five, fifty, a hundred grand a night—Thomasine has told you, has she not, how I make my living?—these are people without souls or with souls without any value.

"Hobbamock has no interest in damaged goods. He does not want a grown-up's soul—not while there is a child's to be had. That's what I believe, anyway, although, like much of this, I could not prove it. He wants children's souls. And he is greedy."

"Sort of the consummate evil," Brad said lamely.

"Can you imagine anything more evil than destroying children?" Charlie asked, his voice and face suddenly stern.

"No," Brad answered quickly, "I cannot."

"There isn't. But Hobbamock is not the only evil. Christians—you see evil as the devil, a horned creature standing watch over hell. But that evil is more than Beelzebub, Hobbamock, whatever name you use. It comes in an endless variety of shapes and forms, goes by many names, knows every race and ethnic group. It is what makes the generals kill, the pushers sell their crack to grammar school kids. It is what drives the corporations to pollute rivers and oceans, to poison the earth with radioactivity. It is what makes certain foreign leaders let their own people starve while they sit down to ten-course dinners served on the finest china. It is Hitler, and Pinochet, and the ayatollah. It is what this country did in Vietnam, what the Soviets did in Afghanistan, the horrors Idi Amin perpetrated in his own country against his own people. Universal.

"Oh, I can see the questions on your lips: 'What of the Quidneck? Can Charlie Moonlight be so arrogant as to assume his own people are free of evil?' The answer is no. We are not free, not now, not ever. We had our massacres and brutalities. So did many other tribes. We've had our cases of duplicity, and greed, and immorality. There have been those of us—I honestly believe they have been rare, but perhaps that is only wishful thinking—who had as little respect for nature as today's greediest developer. My father often told the story of Mitark, a Quidneck warrior who killed the creatures of the forest wantonly, without regard for his needs. Eventually, when it was discovered who was leaving so many half-eaten carcasses to rot, he was burned to death.

"Can't you see? If we are successful in defeating Hobbamock, who is to say he won't rise again? Not that we should not try to stop him. We should. We *must.* My point is only that evil may be contained, but it can never be eliminated. It may be years, centuries, but there is every chance Hobbamock will rise again. Some other fool will release him—intentionally or not, it does not matter—and people as yet unborn will have to confront him. Can't you see? Where there are people, Brad, there is evil. I've often thought—a thought I've kept to myself—that if fate had reversed our roles and the white man had been the Native American, the red man might have done the same thing to your people."

Charlie stopped. Brad had been listening earnestly, impressed by Charlie's philosophy. The Indian was not a highly educated man, but he was intelligent, probably well read. He had done what so many never do: He'd taken the time to contemplate how the world around him worked. Brad respected that. He wondered if he could explain his own philosophy of good and bad so eloquently.

"I must sound like some senile old theology professor." Charlie smiled.

"No," Brad said. "No, you don't."

"Thank you. You're kind."

"I have questions."

"Of course."

"A lot of questions."

"I still have many myself."

"You don't believe Hobbamock is invincible?"

"No. My people centuries ago proved that. He is powerful—and gaining strength with each new child. But I do not think he is invincible . . . yet. Could he become invincible? Could he gain so much strength that nothing could stop him? This is a question that has kept me up nights."

"But you're convinced he can be defeated?"

"Absolutely."

"By a kid carrying some kind of magic spear."

"Yes," Charlie said softly. "I had . . . an experience, what Quidnecks call *pniese.* What your Bible calls a revelation or apocalypse. The *pniese* made everything clear."

"You think . . ." Brad could not pronounce his daughter's name. "You think the kid carrying that spear will survive."

"I do."

"And get better."

"Along with all the others."

"And Hobbamock will be reincarcerated in his cave."

"Yes."

"I have trouble with that, Charlie. With all of that. I mean, I suppose on some mystical level I could buy into your soul theory. The concept of a soul is very strong in Christianity, and don't some of us, at least, believe you can sell your soul to the devil? I guess maybe I could even force myself to believe that the sword has some type of curative powers. Again, the history of Christianity—especially Catholicism—is crowded with stories of holy icons, shrouds, crucifixes, candles, you name it, all believed by some to have amazing powers."

Charlie understood how great Brad's concession was.

"But if Hobbamock has the power to steal souls," Brad continued, "a frightening, incredible power, how could a few rocks piled up against the opening to his cave be anything more than a mere annoyance to him? Why couldn't he just throw them aside, order them out of his way? Why would he have to wait for some fool to release him again, the way you say Whipple did?"

"Because those rocks will be piled after he has been lanced with the spear. I have already described how the sword does not kill, only weaken, how the evil never can be eradicated, and the best we can hope for is to contain it. I cannot tell you how the sword works. I could speculate that it taps into a child's intrinsic purity and goodness, and that goodness, like the goodness of your god Jesus is greater than evil.

"But I could not prove this. I take the spear's ability to stop Hobbamock—to suck from him even the power to move rocks—on faith. Just as you Christians take on faith that a man named Jesus of Nazareth died on a cross and three days later rose from the dead. You cannot demonstrate to me scientifically how Jesus was resurrected, can you?"

"No," Brad admitted.

"But as a believer you take it on faith. Faith—is it not the very essence of Christianity? Of any religion, white man's or red man's or yellow man's?"

"I suppose it is."

"And so it is with Hobbamock. I *believe* these things to be so."

Another quiet—a deeper one—settled over the cabin. Each man was lost in his thoughts. Decision time was near.

"There's a very strong logic to what you say." Brad broke the silence.

He believed that—believed that, at least from Charlie's context, there was only one road to take.

"But I have to be honest with you, Charlie," Brad continued, using the Indian's first name for the first time this morning. "I'm still not sure I believe any of it."

"No one can force you to believe."

"No."

"Faith comes from inside. It cannot be willed."

Brad found that he was wringing his hands. Avoiding eye contact with Charlie.

"As far as my daughter goes, I—I can't do it."

Charlie was not surprised. He was disappointed but not surprised. "You will do me one favor?" he asked when Brad had stood to leave.

"Just ask."

"You will think again about these matters?"

"I will."

"You will not close your mind?"

"No."

"That is all I can ask."

Brad did not get far. Did not even get back to the hospital. He got as far as his house, where he stopped, got out of his car, and went inside. Driving from Charlie's, he'd remembered that they didn't have a Christmas tree yet.

Two days till Christmas, he'd thought, marveling at how fast time can fly. *Better get moving, or there'll be nothing left.*

He walked into the house, uncomfortably empty, and made his way into the living room. The four shopping bags full of Barbie dolls and accessories were still piled in a corner, untouched and unwrapped.

There. Where that couch is. That's where we'll have our tree. I'll set the alarm to be up before her, and I'll be waiting here, a fire going, camera ready, to catch the look on her face!

Except there was not going to be any Christmas morn here in their house. Wasn't going to be any ecstatic look on Abbie's face. Abbie's face was a study in sickness. Abbie was dying. Reality roared up again on Brad and this time refused to let him go.

Charlie was waiting. "Come in," he said.

Brad did not sit. He launched right in to what he had to say: "I've thought about it, just like you asked. And I've decided that I . . . that I don't have too many choices anymore. I guess the truth is I don't have any. Abbie is going to—to . . ."

He could not bring himself to pronounce that word, even now.

"Abbie's going to get sicker and sicker unless something happens soon. Unless someone comes up with an answer."

"You are right."

"I don't believe anymore that the doctors are going to be in time."

"No."

"This one is beyond them."

"I wish it were otherwise."

"I guess you could say I've lost faith." Brad smiled weakly. "Anyone would, wouldn't they? After all this?"

"Yes, they would."

"I love her, Charlie," Brad said, tears in his eyes, "more than I have ever loved anything or anyone. She's all I have. You—you don't have any children. I'm not trying to denigrate you, but it's impossible for you to know exactly how I feel.

"I don't know if every parent is like me, but my love for Abbie—it *hurts,* for God's sake. Even when things are going great, when that great wheel of life is turning without a squeak, I can feel it—a numbness down inside me somewhere. It's frightening, the strength and depth of that love. The love between a man and a woman—it's different. No less real, but different. God," Brad said, wiping his eyes, "listen to me blubber."

"It's not blubbering," Charlie said. "It's a father in great pain, pouring his heart out. You have nothing to be ashamed of. On the contrary, you should be proud of your love."

Brad looked at Charlie, and for one microsecond the irony of this whole scene was revealed to him. Not two months ago Charlie was set to kill him. Brad would gladly have returned the favor. Now—now he was baring his soul to him.

"I guess it's up to you," Brad said. "I—I'll do whatever you want. You have my full cooperation."

Charlie was not gloating. If the Indian felt any sense of vindication, he didn't let on. He seemed . . .

. . . *genuinely concerned about the children.*

He seemed . . .

. . . *genuinely concerned about the parents, Brad in particular.*

He seemed . . .

. . . *to feel as if this were his chance to take a stand against evil. Almost as if he believed he'd been anointed.*

"You understand in detail what I am proposing?" Charlie said.

"Thomasine has gone over everything with me."

"And you understand?" he repeated.

"Yes."

"You're absolutely certain you're willing to go ahead with this?"

"Do I have any other options?"

"No," Charlie said gravely. "You don't."

"When should we begin?"

"As soon as possible."

"Today?"

"That would not be too soon. Before we start, it will be necessary for all of us to meet. To plan."

"Of course."

"I'll supply the vehicle and whatever other equipment we will need."

"Yes."

"And I'll bring the spear. I know where it is. It's only a question now of . . . *getting* it."

"Yes."

"All you will have to do is bring your daughter. Dr. Bostwick can assist you with that."

On and on Brad listened, replying mechanically. What he was hearing was madness, but it was past the point where it seemed mad. Once he had taken the initial leap—once he'd agreed that Abbie was going to participate—the rest really wasn't so crazy.

The rest really was only detail.

But as he drove back to the hospital, doubt began to creep back into his head again.

Am I doing the right thing? Last-gasp, desperate—but still the right thing, the only thing?

Or have I lost my mind?

He didn't know if he could distinguish anymore between madness and desperation. All he knew was that he loved his daughter with a brilliance and intensity that could make him do anything.

CHAPTER SIXTY-ONE

Tuesday, December 23
Late Morning

BRAD STOPPED at the paper for five minutes and was back at the hospital by noon. He had been away a little more than three hours.

Abbie was gone.

Her bed, like the one next to it, was freshly made and empty. There was no indication anyone would be returning to it: no portable monitor; no IV poles; no personal belongings; no magazines scattered about; no flowers; no get-well cards. This obviously was a room awaiting a new patient.

I must have the wrong room.

That was his first thought, and there was a welcome sense of relief in it. He knew all three stories of Abbie's wing had roughly the same floor plan; he must have pushed the wrong button on the elevator. That was exactly the kind of stupid thing he'd been doing with disturbing regularity lately.

Except he hadn't pressed the wrong button. There it was: the correct room number, 223, on a tag over the door.

He thought: *Charlie's taken her.*

But that made no sense. That was sheer lunacy. Hadn't he and Charlie come to an agreement just an hour ago? Weren't they in the same life raft now, rowing together, not pulling apart?

She's dead.

Passed Away.

And they've already taken her body.

The thought stunned him.

"I imagined you'd be in New York by now, Mr. Gale." A female voice interrupted him. Brad pivoted. A middle-aged nurse he'd seen only once before was standing in the hall, smiling but seeming a bit perplexed, as if she hadn't expected to find him here. She was a floater, employed throughout the hospital to fill in for vacations and sick days.

The first mention of New York blew by Brad. "Where . . . is . . . she?" he asked.

A look of substantial bewilderment crept across the nurse's face. "I—I . . . suppose she's halfway to New York by now."

"New York? New York *City?*"

"That's right."

"Then she's . . . *alive?*"

"Of course she's alive."

Brad was overjoyed—and dumbfounded. "What—who took her to New York?"

"Your wife."

"Heather?" The word exited him like a curse.

"Yes."

"Holy Jesus," Brad moaned. In a flash he understood. Heather had taken Abbie. Heather had cooked up some crackbrained scheme, driven to Massachusetts, marched into Berkshire Medical, and now she had their daughter, to do with as she pleased. The realization hit him like a punch, dead center in the gut.

"She said you two had decided to have Abbie treated in New

York," the nurse chirped, "and you had already left—to get there ahead of time, that is, to take care of some arrangements, you know, like admission and everything I guess. She was a very attractive woman, and she had a doctor with her—"

"Chinese?"

"Yes, and they had an ambulance and a set of signed doctor's orders, signed by you, too . . . at least that's what it seemed . . . and, well, I—"

"I'm not married." Brad interrupted.

"You're . . . not married?" the nurse repeated dumbly. Her face had the unmistakable look of someone realizing she's committed a colossal error.

"No. That was my ex-wife. I have sole custody of our child."

"Oh, Lord!" the nurse exclaimed. "Oh, Lord!"

"My daughter was kidnapped."

"Oh, Lord!"

"You let her be kidnapped." Brad's relief was rapidly giving way to rage.

"Oh, Lord! I'm terribly sorry."

"Why wasn't Bostwick called?" Brad thundered. "Didn't anyone wonder why her mother was showing up only now, after so long?"

"We called Dr. Bostwick," the nurse stammered, tears forming, cowering. She was honestly afraid Brad was going to strike her. "He was . . . on a house call. And we—I . . . usually don't work this floor. She seemed very concerned, Mrs. . . . Heather . . . this woman . . . We . . ."

Brad didn't wait for her to finish. He raved down the hall, shouting and swearing, completely out of control. He ran down the stairs, stormed into the lobby, passed a pay phone, considered using it, and realized she wouldn't be back in New York yet . . . if that's even where she and her M.D. sidekick were heading. He ran to the parking lot.

He sat in the Mustang, trying to control his anger before his brain exploded out of his skull.

Now what?

It was the most important question he'd ever asked, and he didn't have a clue to the answer.

Now what?

His anger was rapidly fading to another emotion—an empty, scared feeling, as if the last reason he'd had for living had been stolen away. There was no telling what Heather was up to. No telling how far she might go.

Now what?

He didn't have a clue.

Despairing, he drove for home.

CHAPTER SIXTY-TWO

Tuesday, December 23
Evening

AFTER TRYING every ten minutes, he finally reached Heather. It was six o'clock.

"Where is she?" he demanded.

"Why, it must be Brad, my heroic ex-husband!" she exclaimed. "Sherlock Holmes, tracking the Dragon Lady to her lair! Congratulations! You found me!" She sounded incredibly overjoyed. She sounded incredibly drunk.

"Where is she?"

"Now, who could you mean, Mr. Big-time Editor? Who on earth could you mean?"

The conversation was an ironic reversal from their last one, Brad thought—a thought that angered and frustrated him beyond containment. *And she can put you up shit's creek simply by hanging up,* he reminded himself. *Don't take the bait. Do what the cops do to when the local psycho's on the top of the bridge, threatening to jump: Be firm but calm. Sympathetic, if that's what it takes.*

"Where's Abbie, Heather?" he repeated.

"Abbie? You mean our daughter? *Our* daughter?"

"Where is she, Heather?"

"She needed quality medical care, and she wasn't getting it in Hooterville Hospital. To quote you, everything's taken care of."

Brad stifled the impulse to rage. "I can understand your concern," he said calmly. "We're all concerned about Abbie."

"Oh, bullshit. You're too wrapped up in your goddamn career to be concerned." "I never believed all that shit about you and bonding with your offspring and crap that came out in court, you know. Not one lousy bit of it. I saw that for what it was: a chance to get at me through her. You're transparent, my friend. You care about you, and that's it. *You.* Y-O-U. If that weren't the case, you never would have given her such second-rate care, watching while she—she *rots.* All because your career was there. I think it's criminal, what you've done! So does my boyfriend, and he's a *doctor.*"

"Where is she, Heather?" Brad repeated, amazed at how deeply her words cut. She was reopening too many old wounds, ripping the scabs off, exposing raw tissue.

"Where is she?" She snickered. "Safe and sound."

"Is she there?"

"Here? *In my apartment*? See what I mean about your judgment? It's worse than I thought."

"Is she in the hospital?"

"Maybe, maybe not."

"I hope to God it's a hospital, Heather, or I'll—I'll . . ."

"You'll what?"

"I'll have police at your apartment in ten minutes," he raged. "I mean it. I can do it. I still have friends on the force."

"Well, whoop-de-doo. And what are your friends going to charge me with?"

"How's kidnapping?"

"Please, Brad," she said. "That doesn't scare me. You know how much New York police like to get involved in a domestic dispute. We found that out through our own personal experience, now, didn't we? Or have you forgotten?"

"I'll ask one more time politely, and then I'll—"

"What? Scream? Throw a tantrum? Let me save you the trouble," she said.

Brad heard the click on the other end. He still had the phone to his ear when the dial tone returned.

Brad had always collected phone books. He found his Manhattan yellow pages at the bottom of a bookcase, turned to hospitals, and began calling each one, asking for patient information, and giving Abbie's name.

Abbie didn't turn up anywhere.

He would not let himself panic. Not yet. Although there was an outside possibility that Heather had dropped Abbie off somewhere outside New York, he seriously doubted it. She was too much a city animal to do that. Too much even to know about a hospital outside

New York—at least one where she could arrange admission without a flurry of questions from a very suspicious staff.

No, in the absence of better information, he had to assume Abbie was in New York. He had to assume she was in a hospital, not a clinic or trauma center. He couldn't imagine any place but a hospital that would accept responsibility for a child so sick.

He had tried unsuccessfully to reach the *Times* medical writer, an old colleague, when he decided to look at a map of Manhattan. Maybe that would help. He laid the map on the kitchen table and ran his finger over it, matching the neighborhoods with a mental picture of the prominent buildings.

His finger was rubbing through Chinatown when it hit him: *Of course. New York Infirmary-Beekman Downtown Hospital. Right around the corner from City Hall. The* Times *profiled it a couple of years back. Small institution, probably not hip enough to consider advertising in the yellow pages, but big enough and good enough to have a growing reputation. Serves a mostly, but not exclusively, Asian population.*

Of course. Her boyfriend is Chinese. He's probably on the staff. That would make admission a breeze.

How could it have taken so long to think of it?

He reached Manhattan information, got Beekman's number, and dialed it. He could feel his heart inside his chest.

"Patient information," he said.

"Patient's name," the operator droned.

"Gale. Abigail."

"One moment."

"Thank you."

"Critical," the voice said perfunctorily.

Brad took a shot. "Is she still in intensive care?"

"Yes."

And another: "Can you tell me what's wrong?"

"Are you a family member?" the operator said suspiciously.

I'm her father, he wanted to say, but didn't. There was no telling if Heather's friend had slipped him a ten or a twenty to call him the second any "relatives" inquired.

"No," Brad said.

"Any further information will have to come from the patient's physician," the operator said. "Thank you for calling Beekman."

Brad replaced the phone. For a moment, he was ecstatic. *I've found her,* he thought jubilantly. *Fuck you, Heather, and the horse you rode in on. I've found her!*

But a darker thought soon edged his joy aside.

Her condition was critical. Wasn't that what the operator said? It had been serious at Berkshire Medical, and now it was critical. Had it worsened from the ride? Or would it have worsened anyway?

The distinction didn't matter.

If she dies, he vowed, *I'll kill you, Heather.*

It was a vow he intended to keep.

The four of them, huddled over Brad's kitchen table. The four of them, drinking terrible black coffee and tracing routes on maps of New York and Morgantown. The four of them, compiling lists. The four of them, consulting phone books and a library book on spelunking that Charlie had borrowed. The four of them, unsmiling, too exhausted to care. They could not have been more somber if the fate of the world had been in their hands.

Only once was there a moment of levity. It came when Charlie suggested that for authenticity's sake, Brad and Thomasine dress in white uniforms.

"If you're going to drive an ambulance, you ought to look like ambulance drivers," Charlie said.

"Then if you're going to be a shaman, you should dress like one, too," Thomasine said.

"Yes. How about a stick through your nose?" Brad said, and everyone laughed, Charlie included.

The planning dragged on until well after midnight. Despite the lunacy of what they were mapping out, Charlie and Bostwick were both sticklers for detail. They did not want to leave anything to chance.

"Merry Christmas Eve," Thomasine said to Brad when Charlie and Bostwick had left. "For what it's worth."

He hadn't noticed the calendar until now. The idea that it was almost Christmas was too cruel to contemplate, so he did not contemplate it.

"Merry Christmas Eve," Brad replied. "For what it's worth. Now we should sleep. It's going to be a long day tomorrow. A very long day."

"*Today.*" She corrected him gently.

"Today."

CHAPTER SIXTY-THREE

Wednesday, December 24
Early Morning

CHRISTMAS EVE dawned with a leaden sky that looked heavy enough to come crashing down on Morgantown. Snow was forecast. A storm that had buried Michigan and Ohio was roaring eastward, and it was expected to arrive by nightfall, according to the radio weatherman's artificially cheerful dawn report—ensuring the Berkshires' first white Christmas in three years.

According to plan, Thomasine and Brad waited for Bostwick at Brad's. Bostwick had been very firm on this arrangement. He'd ridden on the ambulance they were going to steal a dozen times. Knew the owner. Knew the office. Knew where the keys hung. One rock through the door window, one hand inside to the doorknob, and he was home free. There really was no need of three or four people doing the work of one, not when the work was this simple.

Brad cooked sausage and eggs. Neither he nor Thomasine was able to eat any of it, although both agreed it would be in their best interests to start the day with a few calories. The best they managed was orange juice and coffee. Again, Brad's desire for a smoke was intense. At six thirty-five, five minutes after the doctor's scheduled arrival, he was a wreck. He was convinced Bostwick had been caught, or hadn't been able to start the ambulance, or had started it and the engine had crapped out five minutes later, or had blown a tire in downtown Morgantown, or had run out of gas outside the state police barracks . . . on and on and on, a treadmill of nightmare possibilities.

"Relax," Thomasine said, although exactly the same scenarios were running through her mind at triple speed, too.

"What if he got caught?" Brad mused. "One little slipup and the whole house of cards comes crashing down around us."

"He didn't."

"What if the owner of the ambulance company was there?"

"At six in the morning?"

"What if there was an emergency? Those guys are on call around the clock."

"He'll be here," Thomasine said, struggling to believe herself.

And he was. At six thirty-seven they saw the ambulance moving up Thunder Rise Road, its headlights still on. It pulled into Brad's drive and stopped, engine racing. Bostwick tooted the horn, and Thomasine and Brad bounded out. There was a moment of confusion while they figured out how to get on board, then Bostwick gestured toward the rear doors. They hopped inside.

"We start with grand larceny," Bostwick joked, "then move on to the big ones."

"The big ones?" Thomasine said.

"Kidnapping, trespassing, attempted murder . . . whatever the hell they choose to throw at us in New York if we get caught. Just think of the headlines in the *Post,* Brad: DOC AND NUTS JAILED FOR KIDDIE SNATCH!"

Everyone laughed. Nervous laughter, preferable to silence. Last night, huddled over Brad's table, they'd calculated the odds. Considering all the elements of the operation—the ambulance theft, taking Abbie from the hospital (no one had used the word "kidnapping" because no one could decide if returning her was, in fact, criminal), the return trip, the breaking and entering jobs Charlie would have to perform to get both dynamite and the spear—they'd concluded they had about a 50 percent chance of getting caught.

Considering the circumstances, Brad decided those were pretty good odds.

Bostwick turned onto the Massachusetts Turnpike, and the ambulance headed toward the Taconic Parkway, which would take them south, into New York.

At the same time Bostwick was fiddling with the choke of a twelve-year-old ambulance in the parking lot of On-Call Services, Inc., Charlie Moonlight was trying unsuccessfully to pick the lock to a warehouse of the Western Mass. Sand and Gravel Company, three miles east. After fifteen seconds he gave up. He just didn't have a burglar's skills, a fact which did not shame him in the least. He backed off a few feet, put his shoulder down like a guard executing a block, and threw his weight against the door. It flew open with a crash. Glass from the window sprayed inside, shattering on the floor with a loud tinkle. No matter. It would be another hour before the fellow with their Dunkin' Donuts coffees trickled into work.

Charlie knew precisely what he wanted, even if he didn't know precisely where he would find it. Once—an entire summer he'd been unable to get plugged in at the casinos, the worst dry spell he'd ever experienced—he'd taken a job as a common laborer on a dam being built outside Las Vegas on the Nevada-Arizona border. Because of a booming economy, good, reliable help had been hard to find that summer, and Charlie was rewarded for his responsibility and smarts by being apprenticed to not one but three trades: bulldozer operator; pile driver; welder. He'd gotten close enough to blasting to get the basic elements down, although in the decade since, he'd never once had occasion to put that knowledge to use.

(For some reason that had struck him as strange even then, he'd kept his manual for the safe handling of dynamite, plastic explosives, gasoline, propane, solvents, and a slew of other hazardous materials. Last night at Brad's, reviewing the book to refresh his ten-year-old memory, he finally understood the reason.)

The explosives locker wasn't hard to find. It was at the back of the warehouse, by itself, unsurrounded by machinery or fuse boxes or electrical wires or anything else that had the remotest chance of producing an errant spark. The locker had been covered with skulls and crossbones and the word "DANGER," spelled in fluorescent orange letters as tall as a man's forearm. A giant padlock protected the contents. Charlie scrutinized it. Contrary to popular belief, modern dynamite wasn't particularly unstable—provided it was handled properly. He could still hear the damn foreman's warning: "Respect it and it'll respect you."

With a claw hammer he pilfered from the workbench, Charlie went to work. The locker was made of old, dry wood, and the clasp separated from it with ridiculous ease.

Charlie helped himself to a plunger, a set of keys to operate it, a fresh battery, a two-hundred-foot length of wire, caps, and a dozen sticks of dynamite. He placed everything carefully in a cardboard box, cradled the box in his forearms, and went out the door to his Cherokee. He'd lined the back with several blankets, and he arranged the box on top of them, then tied the box down so it could not shift while the vehicle was in motion. Driving slowly, but not so slowly as to arouse suspicion, he made it to his cabin.

At the cabin he hid the dynamite in a small shed, far from wood stove sparks. He went inside the cabin for a moment, lifted the floorboard over where he kept his cash, and pulled out a thick wad of hundred-dollar bills. Then he drove to Springfield, where he was reasonably sure he could shop without being recognized.

In less than two hours he had purchased a trailer hitch, a John Deere snowmobile, a trailer to tow it, two hardwood toboggans, an Echo chain saw, and a pair of snowshoes to go with the three pairs he already owned. He paid cash for everything. As a precaution, he gave an alias and a phony address when clerks were filling out receipts and warranty cards.

He was back in Morgantown by noon, at the end of Thunder Rise Road by twelve-twenty. He backed the snowmobile off the road, unhitched it, and covered it with spruce bows. Chain saw in one hand, a can of gas and a carton of bar lubricant in the other, he disappeared into the woods. The snow, which had been diddling around most of the morning, seemed ready to come down in earnest.

CHAPTER SIXTY-FOUR

Wednesday, December 24
Late Morning

THE STORM TEASED Manhattan, slicking streets and frosting skyscrapers with a sugarcoating of snow. It was not enough to activate the plows and sanders yet, but it was more than ample to make driving treacherous for Bostwick, who'd volunteered to take the wheel. The Henry Hudson Parkway, clogged by construction and fender benders, was itself almost a two-hour nightmare. If Bostwick and Thomasine hadn't been with him, Brad would have been a candidate for the forensic ward. The last time he'd been on this road, it had been summer, and Abbie had been with him, and Abbie had been healthy, and their new beginning had stretched out in front of them like the Yellow Brick Road, and . . .

. . . and he couldn't keep punishing himself like that, Thomasine and Bostwick implored him. It wasn't his fault. Wasn't anybody's.

It was almost noon when they wended their way through Wall Street traffic and reached the hospital, an eight-story brick building that took up part of a block next to Pace University. They circled it once to review their strategy.

"The critical thing," Bostwick reminded them, "is to look as if we know where we're going. As if we belong. I've spent enough time in hospitals to realize that if you act as if you know what you're doing, no one will question you. We're going to blend right in, believe me. Hospitals are like bus stations, a million people always coming and going."

"I wish one of us had been in the place before," Brad lamented, "or seen a floor plan. It would make me feel a hell of a lot better."

"That's exactly what you shouldn't let show," Bostwick said sternly. "The fact that you're uptight."

"It'll be over in ten minutes," Thomasine said. "Then we'll be going home."

"OK," Bostwick said, stopping the ambulance when they were around the corner from Beekman. "Your turn, Brad. It wouldn't look kosher for the doc to be behind the wheel." He and Brad exchanged seats. Brad put the ambulance in gear, and they proceeded slowly down Gold to the ambulance bay. Brad backed them in. He had never been more nervous behind the wheel. One little accident, and the game would be over.

The second the ambulance stopped, Bostwick threw open the doors. Clutching his black medical bag, he jumped onto the platform. He looked determined, preoccupied, professional. Thomasine followed. Brad killed the ignition and joined them on the dock.

"The stretcher," Bostwick exhorted.

"Oh, yeah," Brad said. He and Thomasine went back into the ambulance, rolled the stretcher out, then extended its folding legs. They'd practiced on the ride down, and the procedure went off like clockwork.

"Give 'em hell," Bostwick muttered under his breath as he headed through the swinging doors.

A blue-uniformed guard carrying a sidearm met them immediately. They had expected to see security somewhere in the hospital, but his instant appearance unsettled Brad. Bostwick seemed unperturbed.

"Transfer," the doctor barked convincingly. *He ought to do TV,* Thomasine thought with a mixture of bemusement and admiration.

The guard eyed them suspiciously, as if something weren't quite right, but he'd be goddamned if he could put his finger on what it was. Maybe it was the number of them. You almost never saw three people to an ambulance. One doc and one EMT, or two EMTs, or one RN and one EMT . . . but a doc and *two* EMTs . . . or whatever these other two were supposed to be?

"Where you from?" the guard demanded.

"Pittsfield," Brad replied.

"Where's that?"

"Massachusetts."

"Who's the patient?"

"Abigail Gale."

"You got papers?"

"Yes," Bostwick said coolly. He opened his bag and withdrew a set of documents. "BERKSHIRE MEDICAL CENTER ADMISSION," the form read. Bostwick had forged them last night. The guard scanned them without digesting what they said. They looked official enough. He handed them back.

"You got the room number?"

"No. But she's in intensive care."

The guard eyeballed them again. It wasn't the number that was wrong. It was rare, but once in a while you'd see three to a meat wagon; usually, it was one of the rich folks who were going for a ride. No, there was something else fishy about this group. Not the doc. He seemed legit. But the two with him . . . yeah, it was them. They had the right uniforms, all white and starchy and everything, even had their names stitched on there above their breast pockets. But the way they stood there, their thumbs just about stuck up their assholes . . . especially the guy, the way he was fidgeting, like he was late for his own wedding . . .

"You got any ID you can show me?" the guard said in a surly voice.

"Certainly," Bostwick said, reaching smoothly for his wallet. He showed the guard his driver's license, his AMA card, a slew of other papers.

"How about you two?" the guard said, gesturing toward Bostwick's companions.

Brad sputtered: "We—"

"We don't carry wallets when we're working," Thomasine said indignantly, "and as far as I know, there's no law in this or any other state that says we have to. What is this, anyway, an interrogation? We've got a sick girl to move, pal. A very sick little girl. And if you'd like to be responsible for holding her up, well, then I'm sure your supervisor would be happy to hear all about it. In fact, why don't you get on the horn there and ring him up? Go ahead. We'll wait."

Oh, Jesus, Brad thought. *Now we're dead.*

But the gamble paid off. "I guess you're OK," the guard said reluctantly. "It's just that in New York City—man, you never know what kind of crap people's gonna pull. ICU's on the third floor. Down this corridor, take a right through the ER, then around the corner. Elevator's there on the left."

"Thank you," Bostwick said, and they were off.

"I thought we were done for," Brad whispered across the stretcher to Thomasine as they passed through the commotion of the emergency room. No one seemed to notice them. Except for the guard, it was as Bostwick had predicted.

"Mention 'boss,' and types like that always back down," Thomasine said.

They found the elevator without a snag. Brad pressed 3, and they were whisked up. The doors opened, discharging them into a hall where the fluorescent lights were too bright, the floor so clean and overpolished that it looked slippery. The entrance to intensive care was on the right. Bostwick pushed the hold button on the elevator, then led them through the doors, through a small, empty waiting room, and into the inner sanctum of the ICU. They stopped, reconnoitering. From her station the nurse acknowledged their presence and motioned that she would be free momentarily. She was on the phone. No one else was visible. Bostwick supposed her colleagues were busy with patients.

Brad's body was supercharged—his nerves and muscles like a computerized weapons system, activated and standing by to engage the enemy. It wasn't only the risk of their mission, although that was a substantial contributor. He wanted desperately to see his daughter, to touch her, kiss her... *confirm that she's still alive.* The whole drive down, this morbid premonition that they were already too late had been churning inside him.

"May I help you?" the nurse said, hanging up the phone.

"We're here for Abigail Gale," Bostwick said coolly. He looked at the nurse's name tag. "R. JONES," it said. "If you can show us which room, Miss Jones, we'll get on with it."

"Room three," she said, indicating the room at the end. "But are you sure you're supposed to get Abbie?"

"Oh, yes. She's going back to Pittsfield. I have all the paper work here." He took the documents out of his bag and handed them over.

Miss Jones perused them. Her face went momentarily blank; then her look of concern deepened. "I'm afraid I don't have any order to that effect from *this* end," she said.

"Well, there must be some kind of mistake," Bostwick politely replied. "An oversight."

"I don't think so. Her physician, Dr. Chou, just left—it couldn't have been ten minutes ago. He didn't mention anything about any transport. Not a word. And I believe he would have. He's a very conscientious physician." Suddenly Miss Jones was very uneasy. *Does she know anything about how Abbie got here?* Brad wondered. *Is she a co-conspirator?*

Bostwick had anticipated this reaction. He still hoped he would be able to talk his way through it instead of resorting to force.

"I know Dr. Chou personally," Bostwick said, "and as far as . . ."

While they quibbled, Brad slipped past them into room 3. Abbie was there, alone, looking little different from the way she had at Berkshire Medical. Her eyes were closed, and she was breathing with difficulty.

Thank God, she's alive.

He leaned over her, brushing her hair with his hand. Her forehead was burning. "Apple Guy," he whispered, "it's me. Dad. I love you, honey. Oh, God, how I love you. And I'm going to take you home. Right now."

His words registered somewhere, and her eyes flitted open. A second later they shut. There was no sign she had recognized him.

"It's going to be all right," he whispered, straightening up. "Going to be all right, pumpkin."

In the hall Bostwick was getting nowhere. Miss Jones was a young woman of great common sense, and now she was also panicked. Although it was a tiny intensive care unit—perhaps four beds in all—Bostwick knew she could not be alone. It was probably only a matter of minutes before another nurse or an orderly reappeared. Much sooner if Miss Jones started screaming.

They'd just have to take their chances.

"Come on," Bostwick said. "Enough of this. Let's get her." Thomasine started down the hall with the stretcher.

"I can't let you go in there," the nurse shouted.

"Miss Jones, you no longer have a choice."

"I'll call security!" she shouted, her voice rising.

She did not hear Brad pad up behind her. During last night's planning session, they had considered bringing guns—Bostwick had even briefly discussed needles loaded with a quick-acting sedative—and had finally decided against any weapons. It would have been too easy for someone to get hurt, to get killed. Frankly, they'd prayed that returning Abbie would be as easy as Heather's taking her—without any resistance at all.

It wasn't working out like that.

Brad put his hands over Miss Jones's mouth, pulling her tightly toward him, locking her in a clumsy embrace. She felt surprisingly small.

"One word," he whispered, "and I'll kill you."

Still joined, they crab-walked toward the medicine closet. Bostwick had predicted there would be one—hospitals were very security-conscious these days when it came to drugs, he'd said—and Brad had spotted it on the way toward Abbie's room.

"Open it."

"But I don't have the—"

"Open it!"

She reached into her pocket and withdrew the key. Hand shaking, she fitted it into the lock and opened the door.

Brad snatched the key from her and shoved her inside. She toppled to the floor, too scared to cry. "One word," Brad repeated before locking the door, "and I'll slit your throat." It was an unnecessary warning. Miss Jones would have stayed in that closet overnight if the police hadn't found her there, shaking uncontrollably, a half hour later.

With Bostwick in command, they transferred Abbie quickly but gently from her bed to stretcher. She did not seem to know she was being moved. Back through the unit they went, into the hall. The elevator was waiting.

On the way out they passed the security guard.

"You all have a good day, you hear?" he said, considerably more cheerfully than on the way in.

"Thanks," Bostwick said.

They pulled out onto Gold Street, no lights flashing, and were on the FDR Drive in minutes.

Just to be safe, the guard had memorized their license plate.

Brad knew that years later he would still remember Thomasine's drive through midtown Manhattan and the incident that followed at a gas station on the Taconic Parkway, halfway home to Morgantown.

They had not expected to travel through midtown Manhattan. They had expected to get onto the FDR Drive near the Brooklyn Bridge, as they did. They had expected to head north along the East River, as they did. They had expected to continue north on the FDR Drive to the Harlem River Parkway.

As they could not because of an overturned tractor-trailer.

Thomasine was behind the wheel. "Oh, shit," she swore when she saw the traffic ahead thickening and slowing.

"What?" shouted Brad from the back of the ambulance. Thomasine was driving so that Bostwick could tend to Abbie and Brad could be there to comfort her in case she woke up. So far she hadn't.

"A slowdown. I can't tell what's causing it. Wait . . . I can see it . . . Jesus! It's a truck. Turned over. Looks like it just happened . . . aren't even any cops there yet."

Brad left Abbie, crawled forward, and took the seat next to Thomasine. "Damn thing is blocking the whole road," he said.

"Murphy's Law," Bostwick said softly as he adjusted the flow of Abbie's IV and prepared to take her blood pressure.

"Here they come," Thomasine said. In her rearview mirror she saw flashing blue lights.

"Who?"

"The cops."

Cops, Brad thought with alarm. *Last thing we need is cops. Even if there's no kidnapping report out yet, there's an accident up ahead. Someone may be hurt. And we're in a bloody* ambulance!

"Turn off here," Brad said frantically.

"Here?"

"Yes. Thirty-fourth. We can cut across midtown."

Thomasine slid off the road at the Thirty-fourth Street exit just as the cruiser whizzed past. They crossed Second Avenue, Third, Lexington Park, Madison, uneventfully. Brad was beginning to think the detour might not prove so costly after all when, a block from Herald Square, traffic stopped altogether.

The snow wasn't responsible, although it was no longer just a tease, but a pelting, driving storm that had the potential for real accumulation. It was the shoppers. A thousand shoppers. Ten thousand. A hundred thousand, coursing through the streets and sidewalks and in and out of stores like an army of insects on a suicide march. These were not your garden-variety shoppers, Thomasine realized with instant frustration. They were the most desperate breed of all—last-minute Christmas shoppers engaged in the final countdown. This was do-or-die. And if they were spilling into the streets, trapping cars, creating a traffic jam that was monstrous even by New York City standards, well, that was just too bad.

"We're screwed." Thomasine cursed.

"These things sometimes have a way of breaking up quickly," Brad said hopefully.

"Are you kidding? Look ahead. Gridlock, as far as you can see."

Ten minutes passed, and they had moved four car lengths.

Fifteen minutes, and they'd gone a quarter of a block.

Twenty-five minutes, and they were only to Herald Square. The gridlock showed no sign of loosening. If anything, fed by the shoppers' frenzy, it had intensified.

Ahead to their right was Macy's. THE WORLD'S LARGEST STORE, the giant sign proclaimed.

It's almost Christmas, Brad thought once again. No matter how often he was reminded of it today, that fact struck him as impossibly cruel.

Every year of her life he'd come to Macy's with Abbie. Every single Christmas, starting with her first, when she was a six-month-old bundled in a cocoon of blankets and wedged comfortably into her collapsible stroller. Even when he and Heather had been civil—when, conceivably, she might have wanted to join them—Macy's had always been the quintessential father-daughter treat, deliberately off limits to all but Abbie and Dad. This was to become *a tradition* in the grand tradition of the circus, trips to the ball park, the Staten Island Ferry. And it had. Brad remembered each and every one of their holiday visits with incredible sharpness of detail, as if they'd been written in bold type in the Absolute Best Times chapter of his life's book.

He looked at Abbie, strapped into a stretcher, and he wiped a tear from his eye. "How's she doing, Doc?" he asked.

"The same," Bostwick answered.

But Thomasine was not the same.

Not the calm, take-charge person she'd been in the hospital, or driving up the FDR Drive, or even trapped in gridlock half a block back. Thomasine was getting very, very uptight. Her knuckles were white from gripping the wheel, and she was actually sweating, even though she had the window cracked. Normally the coolest of human beings, she liked to joke about how she'd been known to blow a valve on occasion. Her reaction to Charlie's and Brad's altercation had been one of those occasions. Even caught up in the madness of that moment, Brad had been able to feel her fury, shimmering from her in waves, like heat rising from a summer sidewalk.

Going on half an hour they'd been stranded, Thomasine thought. *Damn!* Thousands of people had been passing within sight of the ambulance—*that's right, the old-fashioned one with the out-of-state plates*—and all it would take was one of them to be an off-duty cop *(or an on-duty one, for Christ's sake)* and their gig would be up. Surely by now the hospital had reported Abbie's disappearance. Surely by now reports of it were crackling out of dashboards of a hundred cruisers from Staten Island to Queens.

Besides, the weather was deteriorating. By the time they got to Massachusetts, there could easily be a foot of snow, and then they would be at the mercy of DPW crews. God forbid. Abbie seemed stable, but Bostwick had been very emphatic on one point: There was absolutely no way of predicting how long she would remain like that. Moving her once already had apparently shocked her system; Bostwick read that in her vital signs, her pulse and blood pressure, both lower than when he'd seen her last at Berkshire Medical. A second move, no matter how careful, was risky. Not to mention what lay ahead of Abbie once they got to Thunder Rise.

It was in the middle of these ruminations that it hit Thomasine.

Siren.

Flashing lights.

The ambulance had both.

This whole thing is such a gamble anyway, she decided.

I'm going for it.

Thomasine reached for the dash and flicked two switches. He couldn't see the lights, but the siren startled Brad. "What are you doing?" he yelled.

"Getting us out of here," she answered, and he could hear it plainly, the derangement in her voice.

"You're crazy! You'll draw attention to us!"

"That's the idea," she answered wickedly. "That's why we'll be on our way in no time."

Thomasine prepared to move out. Incredibly, nothing happened. The siren was not meek; Bostwick knew that from experience. Thomasine had expected Thirty-fourth to open like the Red Sea parting for Moses—the traffic dividing, the cars and cabs slinking to opposite sides of the street—but the most they got was the car directly in front of them to begin tooting its horn. Pedestrians stared briefly, then let their thoughts return to their last-minute shopping. The street-corner preacher who'd been yelling *"Jesus saves souls!"* through a bullhorn stopped momentarily, then resumed his crusade.

"I don't believe it," Thomasine shouted.

"Would you knock it off?" Brad said, panicked.

Thomasine looked at the sidewalk, calculating distances. It was certainly wide enough. The Macy's marquee looked high enough. There was only the question of the people.

"Hold on," she said, cutting the wheel and giving the ambulance gas. It jumped the curb with a lurch that toppled Bostwick. A blue-haired lady screamed. A second lady screamed and dropped her Macy's bags. They crunched under the ambulance's tire. A chestnut vendor fled from his cart. Thomasine inched forward. More people screamed, scrambling to get away. The message rippled with amazing speed through the crowd, more effective than any siren or lights. Thomasine could almost hear it buzzing through their brains: *Crazy person on the loose! In an ambulance! On the sidewalk! Run for your lives!*

And run they did.

"You're going to kill someone!" Brad shouted. "You're going to hit a hydrant! You're going to lose control!"

But she didn't. In under a minute they found themselves with an empty sidewalk. Thomasine put the pedal down and roared past the store, into the open street beyond.

CHAPTER SIXTY-FIVE

Wednesday, December 24
Afternoon

CHARLIE CLEARED as many deadfalls as he could in the time they'd allotted. At two-thirty he silenced his chain saw, even though he was still several hundred yards from the entrance to the mine. Maybe it was wishful thinking, but the rest of the old access road didn't seem as overgrown as the half mile or so he'd hacked his way through. With luck, they'd be able to get the snowmobile right up to the entrance.

It was luck they'd surely need now because the ambulance was probably no more than two hours from Morgantown and Charlie did not have the spear. It was time to get it.

He had turned his back on Thunder Rise, was trudging down through the storm and wind and the growing drifts toward his Cherokee, when he felt it—a light touch, as if someone had gently laid a hand on his shoulder. Charlie pivoted, knowing even as he turned that there would be nothing behind him, just as there had been nothing there that autumn day with Jimmy. He understood immediately: Hobbamock, making his presence known. On fast forward, a succession of images passed through his mind: a wolf; a bear; a vulture; a snake. Denizens of the *pniese.* Hobbamock's warriors, a band of soul deliverers. Perhaps passing by even now, on their way to deliver another.

You know, don't you, you bastard? Charlie thought, not with fear, but with a vicious hatred he could barely control. *You know what we're up to, and you'd stop us if you could, wouldn't you?*

But you can't, can you?

You can only touch the children. Only children, you fucking coward.

He turned again, and this time he ran.

Abetted by the weather, evening already was eating into the afternoon as Charlie proceeded through downtown Lenox and on up West Street toward Eagletop, Ted Wigglesworth's summer mansion. Charlie had his window down for a smoke, and he heard the strains of Christmas carols—Bing Crosby and Andy Williams, crooning about exactly the kind of holiday shaping up this year for the Berkshires, a white one—from an outside speaker one of the shop owners had mounted over his door. Main Street was choked with people, but it was a good-natured crowd, a partly tipsy crowd, a mixture of shoppers and folks let out early from work and red-cheeked kids rediscovering that after they had waited all year for Santa, the last few hours were by far the longest.

Charlie drove past Tanglewood, its summer song muted until a more inviting season. The road twisting, climbing higher, past meadows into pine-smothered hills, passing estates in the million-and two-million-dollar range. The road narrowing, disappearing in woods, reemerging by what in good weather should be a breathtaking vista of town. The entrance to Eagletop was across the street from that vista, between elaborate stone pillars. Charlie stopped before he reached them, scanning up and down the road to be sure he was alone. He was. He turned into the drive, which wound between two meticulously landscaped rows of towering blue spruce. The drive had been plowed, but since the last pass the storm had deposited another four inches of virgin snow. This was the only entrance to Eagletop; behind the estate were woods frequented only by squirrels and deer. No one had passed in or out for hours.

Since discovering the spear was here, Charlie had learned several facts about Eagletop. He'd learned them from the caretaker, Pat Foley, a reliable, amiable, but not terribly bright or ambitious bachelor Charlie knew from high school. Foley's Achilles' heel was booze, and once Charlie had determined where Foley did his major drinking, and when—Mondays and Tuesdays, his days off, at a pub in Lee—it had simply been a matter of showing up with a wad of cash and a professed desire to toast old times.

Sitting in that pub two Tuesdays ago, matching Foley's scotch ("the old man, that son of a bitch, gave me my taste for it") with Cokes, Charlie had learned that Wigglesworth did, in fact, have an unusual spear—one of a kind, or so Wigglesworth liked to brag to his multimillionaire friends. He'd learned that the spear was kept in a glass case in a cavernous, oak-paneled room that Wigglesworth called the library but that was really the mansion's main art gallery. He'd learned that the library was off the front sitting room, which was off the dining room, which in turn was off the kitchen. He'd learned that Foley's "chambers"—a three-room suite—were on the second floor. He'd learned that Eagletop had an elaborate alarm system, said system being activated usually only at night. He'd learned that Foley's boss no longer used the estate as a summer residence; now, as Wigglesworth hobbled into old age, a victim of arthritis and a bum heart, he was there most of the year. Christmas, however, he still spent in New York. He'd left for the city Sunday, taking with him his two bodyguards, servant, cook, and chauffeur, leaving Foley in charge, and alone, until his return shortly after New Year's Day.

Charlie parked halfway up the drive, on a curve where he was not visible from the street or the mansion. He inhaled deeply, savoring the smell of spruce, his favorite outdoor scent. It was beautiful up here. Peaceful and quiet, except for the wind, which bore down from the hilltop in angry blasts that stung his face. Putting his head down, staying among the trees, Charlie continued up the hill on foot. Cushioned by the snow, his boots were noiseless as he approached.

Eagletop—granite, megatherian, inhospitable—loomed out of the storm.

Foley's beat-up '74 Duster was the only car parked in the drive. Charlie had expected that. The drifts sloped up and over it in great, sweeping angles; Foley, the poor slob, was going to have one hell of a time shoveling it out when this blew over.

He's alone, Charlie reckoned with a certainty that did not surprise him. *He's alone, and ten to one he's been drinking all afternoon because it's Christmas Eve. A lovely, fine, wintry Christmas Eve and the cat's away . . . Time for this pathetic little mouse to play.*

Charlie circled the house, peering in through cathedral-height windows as he dodged from hedge to stone wall to gaudy cement bird feeder. He did not see Foley anywhere. Concentrating again—feeling in his fingers and toes the same low-current voltage he felt when plugged in at the tables—he had a fleeting impression of Foley in a small room. *On the second floor. His chambers, as he called them.*

Charlie removed his work gloves, pocketed them, then pulled a pair of surgical gloves over his fingers. He did not want to leave fingerprints. He felt for his burglar tools, but the kitchen door, which faced the woods lapping the estate out back, was unlocked. Charlie held his breath and nudged it open. Foley had said the alarm was activated only at night, but as for holidays, well, that depended on . . .

The door swung inward without a creak of protest. No buzzers or bells. On tiptoe Charlie stepped into the kitchen and closed the door behind him. The insistent wind faded to an unfriendly murmur. He let his breath out, inhaled, exhaled again, and strained to hear any sign that Foley was about.

Charlie froze.

People were talking. Two people.

Probably upstairs—their voices were barely audible, and it was impossible to determine what they were saying. Occasionally one or the other voice would rise in volume. It appeared to be a man and a woman, but it did not sound as if Foley were the man—unless his voice had inexplicably deepened over the last two weeks. His intuition had been wrong. Foley was not alone. He had company, at least two other people, and possibly more.

Charlie crept through the kitchen—like all of the rooms in this gaudy monstrosity, an oversize, overornate room that belonged in a medieval castle. From the dining room he moved noiselessly to the front sitting room, which he recognized from Foley's drunken description. It was huge, easily the floor space of an average ranch house, and it was filled—absolutely *filled*—with furniture and Indian art. Charlie was overwhelmed. If what he was seeing was any indication, Wigglesworth hadn't been exaggerating when he'd claimed to be one of the foremost private collectors in the country. Pottery, ceramics, wall rugs, figurines, headdresses, canoes, tomahawks, clubs . . . on and on, a treasure trove of Indian culture. Charlie recognized some of the styles. Sioux. Chippewa. Seneca. Cheyenne. Nothing Quidneck that he could see.

Why?

It was a question he'd pondered frequently during the trial. *Why would a man so scornful of the culture be so taken with its art?* Money could be only part of the answer; if art was his ticket to the big time, surely there was more money to be made in Renoirs or Picassos. Surely there was more prestige in the art-collecting world than Native American art. *It must be the ultimate form of contempt. Like enslaving your enemy's wife and children after defeating him in battle.*

On the far side of the sitting room was a massive door leading to the library. Before heading toward it, Charlie strained to listen. He could hear the voices, marginally louder. Definitely from upstairs. And not two live people. There was an echoic quality that now identified them as TV voices. Good. They should help mask his movements.

Charlie glided across the sitting room to the library door. It was locked. "Son of a bitch," he cursed. Wigglesworth supposedly kept his most valued collections in the room.

Foley must have the key.

Charlie went back through the sitting room to the mansion's main staircase and ascended to the second floor. With the TV sounds as his guide, Charlie walked on cat feet down a corridor, around a corner into a smaller hall at the rear of the house. At the end of the hall a door was ajar, and Charlie could see the flicker of a TV. He could hear the sound track distinctly now. It was a man and a woman. A man and a woman talking dirty. A porn film.

Oh, God. He spit, sickened by the sight.

Foley was slumped into a stuffed chair, asleep—or passed out. On an end table was a pack of cigarettes, an overflowing ashtray, an empty crystal tumbler, a half-full bottle of Glenfiddich scotch, and a ring of keys with a clip to attach to a belt. Several dozen keys in all. Keys to every lock and every door and every alarm system in the house. Charlie reached for them. They jingled softly, but it was going to take a lot more than keys to rouse the caretaker. Keys in hand, Charlie went downstairs.

CHAPTER SIXTY-SIX

Wednesday, December 24
Late Afternoon

IT WAS LONG SINCE DARK when Thomasine announced: "We need gas."

Since Macy's the trip had been uneventful. The snow had not abated; but the highway crews seemed to have gotten a good jump on the storm, and so far they'd managed to keep the Taconic down to pavement. The ambulance was perhaps an hour from Morgantown when Thomasine, who'd been monitoring the gas gauge (and keeping her observations to herself), realized they wouldn't make it without filling up somewhere.

"How low are we?" Brad asked from in back, where he was holding Abbie's hand. Abbie had moaned several times but was still unconscious. Bostwick was becoming alarmed, although, like Thomasine, he'd been keeping a lid on his thoughts. If she did not wake soon, then what? *Push on, knowing that the exposure, the mine, will almost certainly kill her? Readmit her to Berkshire Medical, hoping her condition improves, and if it does, try tomorrow? Abort everything, essentially throwing our last chance away?* He did not have an answer.

"We're almost on E," Thomasine replied.

"Maybe we better turn off," Brad said. "If we run out of gas . . . I guess I don't have to state the obvious."

"No," Bostwick said, "you don't."

At the next exit—for a place called West Taghkanic—Thomasine left the highway. They were in luck. They'd gone barely a mile when they came up on a station. Miraculously it was still open. Not doing any business, but definitely open. Thomasine pulled in.

The jockey, a kid of about twenty, was alone. They saw him—in outline only—through the window, steamed by heat high enough to make him strip down to T-shirt and jeans. He heard the bell announcing a customer and swore. This was his idea of Nothingsville, working Christmas Eve.

He looked out into the storm to see who it was. Of all goddamn things, an ambulance. One of those old-fashioned kinds that look like a customized Cadillac hearse. Long, low hood, back big enough to hang curtains and hold a bed—might not be too tough to take, owning one of those suckers himself.

An ambulance.

He swallowed. His throat was suddenly dry.

The ambulance.

During the last two hours he'd been sneaking joints (how many, anyway? three? four? a Merry Christmas five?) and pondering the issue of the week: whether his girlfriend would be putting out this holiday eve. He'd forgotten his ghetto blaster, his usual company, and to take the edge of his loneliness, he'd kept his boss Schmidt's Bearcat scanner on. Since about one, the state police channel had been broadcasting intermittent reports of a stolen ambulance with a kidnapped kid inside. It was not known, the dispatcher had emphasized, if the kidnappers were armed, but it was presumed they were dangerous. They'd left a hospital in New York City around noon and it was believed they were headed north to Pittsfield, Massachusetts, where the ambulance had been stolen early that morning.

Just great, the jockey thought. *I shoulda closed at three.*

But that was immaterial now. It was slowly dawning on him that they weren't going away. They'd seen him, he'd seen them, and obviously they needed gas . . . must need it desperately. The jockey would not go down in history as one of God's most gifted children, but he had enough smarts to understand that his ass very quickly could be grass.

The urge to run was suddenly overwhelming. He could feel his pulse, like thunder boomers building behind his temples.

What if they do *have a gun?*

They'll put a bullet in my back, that's what.

The phone.

He could call for help.

And it's in the garage, out of their sight.

He waved at the ambulance to let them know he'd be right with them, then disappeared around the corner. If only there was a back door . . . But there wasn't a back door. Only a john. A smelly, dirty, windowless john.

"What's he doing," Brad said impatiently, "playing with himself?"

"He was just there," Thomasine said. She leaned on the horn.

In the garage the jockey was fumbling in his pocket for change. Schmidt, the cheap son of a bitch, didn't even have a free phone. He finally found one grease-smeared quarter, rammed it down the machine, and dialed the state police barracks. Schmidt, who'd been held up a couple of years ago, had penciled the number over the phone. The jockey was sweating, and his tongue felt like a cork wedged between his teeth by the time his call went through.

"I don't like this," Bostwick said.

Thomasine leaned on the horn again. And again. She was getting pissed. The Macy's incident had left her raw; looking at her the wrong way now would be enough to set her off. She was about to hunt the idiot down when he stumbled out the door, struggling to get into his jacket, and crossed the lot to the ambulance.

"What'll it be?" he asked, trying to mask his nervousness.

"Fill it," Thomasine barked.

The jockey cringed. "Don't do anything out of the ordinary; they may be armed," the police dispatcher had advised. "We'll have a car there in five minutes."

"Premium?" he asked, as politely as he could.

"I don't care. Just fill the damn thing."

"Yes, ma'am."

The jockey walked to the rear of the ambulance, stood dumbly a moment, then pried the license plate open. There was the clang of metal on metal as he shoved the nozzle in, then a low-pitched, steady whoosh as the gas flowed.

"If you'll excuse me," Thomasine said to no one in particular, "I have to use the bathroom."

No one in particular answered. She climbed out of the ambulance. "Rest room locked?" she asked the jockey.

"No, ma'am."

"Where is it?"

"Inside, ma'am."

"Where inside?" she demanded. The jockey looked at her face, but he did not see beauty. He saw beast—a beast ready to pounce. His eyes traveled to her coat, a down-filled parka billowy enough to hide a shotgun. *Probably exactly what she's carrying, too,* he thought, the dryness in his throat almost crippling now. *A sawed-off shotgun, itching for business.*

"Through—through the d-d-door and over there on the r-r-right," he blabbered. "Behind the cash r-r-register, m-m-ma'am."

Thomasine stormed off. *Stupid,* she thought. She found the bathroom and went inside, locking the door behind her. It was predictably filthy.

It was the jockey who saw the cruiser first. It came down the road and slipped quietly into the station several car lengths behind the ambulance. The trooper parked at the rear of the service area, near a half dozen junked cars. He spoke quickly into his microphone, then stepped out into the cold. He slipped the safety off his revolver and moved cautiously toward the ambulance. He was a young man, even younger-looking than his twenty-six years. A rookie, pulling all the holiday shifts this year, and not complaining.

Thank the Lord, the jockey thought. All of a sudden the urge to take a leak was tremendous.

The trooper motioned for the jockey to move away from the ambulance. He did, gladly, backing up until he was behind the cruiser, where he figured he'd be safe once the firing started—and he had no doubt that firing was going to start. Crouching down, he unzipped his fly and took a long, satisfying whiz that turned the snow an off-yellow. The trooper approached the window where Brad was now sitting and rapped on it.

The chain of events that followed was fragmented, staccato, stitched together against a surreal backdrop: a stormy evening at a BestGas station, lights glaring phosphorescently into the darkness like the nighttime set of *Close Encounters of the Third Kind.*

These were the primary elements:

Trooper asking for the license of the man in front, Brad. Trooper checking license with flashlight. Brad anxious, then angry, then verging on violence. Bostwick feeling suddenly, totally depleted, as if he'd gotten this far on sheer adrenaline, and now it had run out. Abbie lying on the stretcher, oblivious, lost in the place of shadows. Trooper ordering Brad and Bostwick out of the ambulance, hands over their heads. Brad prepared for violence, stopping only when he sees trooper's gun drawn and trained dead center at his heart. Bostwick protesting that he cannot leave a sick child's side. Trooper responding that another ambulance already has been requested and that the child will be fine, she is the least of their problems now, please step outside before someone gets hurt, no one wants anyone to get hurt. Jockey daring to poke his head over the cruiser, thinking this might not turn out to be such a bad Christmas Eve, after all. What a story to tell his friends, his girl, his family. A little embellishment, and he could come out the hometown hero. Yes, he could.

And Thomasine, unnoticed by all, forgotten, watching the drama unfold from inside the station. Thomasine, finding a package of distress flares, taking one, creeping outside toward the innermost island.

Thomasine lifting the nozzle to the high octane, starting the pump, hearing the motor whir, spraying gasoline all around her feet, all over the pumps, as close to the ambulance as she can before she is spotted.

The trooper, seeing her, not processing what he is seeing, finally processing and ordering her to stop.

Thomasine lighting the flare on first try and brandishing it over her head while the trooper, Brad, Bostwick, and the jockey watch, flabbergasted.

"Anyone moves and I drop it!" she shouts.

"You'll go up, too," the trooper says, his voice squeaky.

"I don't fucking care! Drop the gun! Drop it!" Her voice demonic, touching a primal part of his brain, the part where the circuits for fear and cowardice and man's million-year-old survival instinct all merge. A part far, far away from the cool techniques espoused in his police academy SWAT team class.

Bostwick numb.

Brad thinking in the insanity of the moment: *Remind me never to cross her. Never, ever to say "boo" when her mind's made up. This, neighbors and friends, is one woman you don't want to mess with.*

"Thomasine!" he shouts, purely reflexively. "Please!"

"Shut up, Brad! You! Trooper! Drop the gun! Or I drop the flare!"

Trooper knowing if he shoots her, the flare will drop, anyway.

Gun tossed uncomplainingly into snow.

The jockey, meanwhile, watching, his legs and whole body jellylike, not heroic. Calculating how large the fireball will be, how far he would have to run before he would be out of harm's way. And remembering the tanker this morning topping every tank off, five thousand gallons of gasoline, give or take a few hundred, waiting to blow a hole clear through to China.

"Into the station," Thomasine orders the trooper.

"Think about what you're doing," the trooper says, his last shred of authority dribbling away. "You stop now, and everybody's going to be OK."

"In or everybody's going to be dead!"

The trooper, looking at the growing ash at the end of the flare, only a question of time now before gravity pulls it off into the gas, thinking of his newlywed wife, and the fireside dinner she has planned for coming off his shift, and his $18,500 starting salary. And complying, walking as calmly as he can into the station, wondering how long it will take the backups he's requested to make it here through the storm.

Thomasine stepping back from the gas she's poured. "Take his gun, Brad," she orders, "and shoot his tires out."

Brad obeying. Stooping to get the gun, and walking toward the cruiser. "Please, no!" the jockey shouts, cowering. Brad ignores him. He puts two bullets in each of the front tires and comes back to the ambulance.

The nozzle into the ambulance the jockey had set clicks off. In the thick silence that has settled back over the scene, everyone hears it. The tank is full. It has been approximately four minutes since the trooper arrived. Thomasine tosses the flare into the snow.

"Tank's full," she says in an eerily calm voice. She drops the nozzle and strolls toward the driver's side of the ambulance, the trooper watching the way goldfish watch the world from inside their bowl. Brad is convinced that Thomasine has been possessed, that the spirit of a long-dead buccaneer or mercenary or French Legionnaire or . . .

. . . Quidneck warrior has taken over her body.

"Ready?" she asks, settling behind the wheel. "I'm sure Charlie's already waiting."

CHAPTER SIXTY-SEVEN

Wednesday, December 24
Early Evening

HEADLIGHTS. Coming up Thunder Rise Road toward him. Charlie flicked his cigarette out the window of his Cherokee. The snow sizzled it dead. The headlights bounced, and there was the screech of tires spinning at the end of Brad's drive. The ambulance regained traction and lurched ahead. It stopped next to the Cherokee. With so much time on his hands, Charlie had been able to keep the drive clear.

He jumped out to greet them.

"Three hours late," he said. "I was afraid something happened."

"Something did," Thomasine answered. "We'll tell you about it later. How'd you make out here?"

"Everything's as set as it's ever going to be."

"What's the road like from here on up?" Brad asked.

"Iffy. We'll have to take the Cherokee."

"Then let's transfer her," Bostwick said. "Now." He opened the ambulance doors and went inside. Brad followed.

"How is she?" Charlie whispered to Thomasine.

"Not good."

"Is he still going ahead with it?"

"He hasn't said no."

"I would understand if he did."

"I don't think he will."

Brad bent over his daughter, his head next to hers. He could feel her breath, labored but not alarmingly so, sweet-smelling . . . *like an angel's.* How long had he been watching her face like this? Every night at the hospital. Every day. Except for the gas station, the whole trip from New York. Watching for a sign—any sign—that she had turned the corner. Watching, hypnotized, at once hopeful and terrified, as if she might slip from his grasp forever if he took his eyes off her for too long. Watching, whispering, "I love you," and, "Everything's going to be all right," and, "I'm right here, honey," because he'd always been told that even deeply comatose patients retain their hearing when all other senses have been lost. Watching, and praying with an intensity and blind faith that had deserted him along about the time, in eighth grade, that he'd stopped being an altar boy.

"We're almost home, Apple Guy," he whispered as he tucked blankets around her and Bostwick disconnected her IVs and monitor and rechecked the contents of his bag. "Almost home."

She heard his voice—or did she?

Felt cold—or did she?

Her breathing clogged momentarily, making a sound like snoring. Her eyeballs rolled, as if she were emerging from REM sleep, but her eyelids did not open.

She'd been in the shadow place for an unknown period now.

Long enough to appreciate how much she liked it, how little she ever wanted to leave. The shadow place was not just comfortably shady. It was warm, the way perfect days in early fall are warm—no humidity, and only a lick of a breeze, enough to barely ruffle leaves on the trees. There were no needles in the shadow place, no sore throats, no nurses or doctors or technicians. No friendly people, either, but the longer she stayed, the less that seemed to matter. She had her memories, but they were very far off, like teeny-weeny clouds that scoot across the sky on those perfect early-fall days. Even Dad, whose voice still sometimes was carried in on the breeze, was getting farther away.

But now—now something was happening. The shadow place was suddenly less comfortable. That perfect temperature was changing. Plunging. Dad's voice—closer, clearer, more real than memory. Other voices, too, familiar.

She opened her eyes and saw her father and Bostwick leaning over her. From farther away she heard Charlie Moonlight's voice. Thomasine's, too. She could not tell where she was—being lifted out of bed? out of a car? an ambulance? was she outside?—only that she did not want to be here. Did not want to be taken wherever she was being taken.

The rhamphorhynchus had warned: "*The worst thing is that Indian is using his evil powers to make Dr. Bostwick go along with him. Thomasine, too. Even your dad. Isn't that awful, Abbie? Everyone ganging up like that on you so that the Indian can* kill you. *Don't you think you should do something about that? Wouldn't you like to be safe, not* killed?

"*Fight them,*" the creature had urged.

But she could not fight. Not Dad. Dad did not want to *kill* her, and he wouldn't let the Indian either. Dad was *good,* she remembered that now. It was the rhamphorhynchus that was *bad.* Deceitful. A liar. It had visited her once in the shadow place, and it'd told her how she could not stay there—how where it was going to take her was so much better. But that was a lie. She didn't know how she knew—perhaps because the creature had never been her friend, as it tried to make her believe, but her nightmare. No, where it wanted her to go was the worst bad of all. Dad had often talked to her about lying, about deceit, about how they were two of the most dee-spickable qualities a person, young or old, could have. Well that went for rhamphorhynchuses, too.

"D-d-dad," she struggled to say.

"Apple Guy!" He got no further; the tears came too fast and hard. He kissed her cheek, found her hand under the blankets, and squeezed it. She smiled weakly. But it was a smile. *A smile, for God's sake!*

"Dad?"

"What, sweetheart?"

"Is today Christmas?"

"Almost, honey."

Bostwick watched, relieved. There was a potential way to bring Abbie out of her state: a powerful stimulant known as methamphetamine hydrochloride. In his bag, he had five vials of a solution he'd concocted, but he had been hoping to use it only in the cave, if at all. It might still be necessary to use it later, but the fact that she had independently awakened encouraged him. Her condition was poor, but it was not critical. Even stepping back from the madness he was involved in, he could truthfully state, as a doctor, that Abbie should be able to survive the next hour.

And past that . . .

. . . that depended on whether Charlie had been right.

The doctor let Brad comfort his daughter for a few moments before gently insisting: "We should go, Brad. After—after the next hour, you'll have all the time in the world."

Brad nodded. "One more stop, honey," he told his daughter, "and then we're going home. I promise."

Charlie folded down the back seats of the Cherokee, and they slid Abbie on her stretcher inside. The adults piled in, and they started up Thunder Rise Road. Overhead the clouds were breaking. A thin moon was revealed, bathing the landscape in shades of silver and gray.

CHAPTER SIXTY-EIGHT

Wednesday, December 24
Evening

SINCE NINE IN the morning they'd tried to reach Bostwick. He did not show up at the office, although he was not expected; appointments were never scheduled for Christmas Eve. He did not show up at the hospital. Nor did he answer his page or inform his answering service of a number where he could be reached. And his wife had no idea where he was or when he would return, only that he was up and out before dawn.

The staff at Berkshire Medical had tried to reach him because one of his patients had only hours to live.

They did not expect Bostwick to perform a miracle—why start now? one particularly belligerent nurse thought—but they knew him well enough to know he'd want to be there, if only to console the family.

Now, a few minutes before seven, it is too late.

Polly McDermott, a fourth-grader, is dead.

She was pronounced as being in that state by the medical examiner at 5:07 P.M. after an afternoon in which her fever topped 110 degrees and her heartbeat became wildly irregular, refusing to respond to any of the half dozen medications an increasingly pessimistic trauma team pumped into her wasted body. Her last words, spoken in an almost unintelligible croak in the presence of her mother, father, and favorite granny, were enigmatic, chilling, and they will haunt them for years and years: "Please . . . Mommy . . . please, Daddy. I don't want to . . . go away. Not . . . with . . . *it.* Please . . . oh . . . please. Not . . . *it.*"

Now her body is in the back of a hearse.

The hearse, driven by a middle-aged man who would much prefer to be relaxing with his family than toiling in the embalming room this wintry holiday eve, pulls away from Berkshire Medical into the dying storm. Jake Cabot heads over the mountain and comes into Morgantown just in time to pass carolers, gathered in the town square. It is a smaller group than usual. Cabot is not surprised. Morgantown is reeling. There are few conversations now that do not get around to the Mystery Disease. Some of the rumors seem downright laughable. There's the one started by an elderly spinster who lives with a house full of cats over Pittsfield way. Edna McCabe believes it is the work of the devil, just as she believes AIDS and communism are works of the devil. There's the one about sunspots being responsible. Or Soviet agents. Less laughable is the one about an escapee virus from a hush-hush military laboratory. No one seems to know where the laboratory that hatched the Army Bug, as it's called, might be—or how its prize germ might have made it to Morgantown and nowhere else—but that does not bother. Fear is feeding on itself, and logic matters little.

Cabot knows Polly McDermott will only further distill that fear, making it a little more potent.

She will not be the last. As he was removing her body, Cabot was informed by the staff not to be surprised if he is asked to return before dawn. At least two children, James Ellis one of them, are given little chance of making it to tomorrow.

The undertaker is not a coarse or greedy man. He does not rejoice, not even privately, in the fact that the disease is fat city for at least one local business: his. But he is a practical man. He has been advised by the CDC to use gloves while embalming victims of the unknown disease, and as he pulls into the driveway of his funeral home, he is intending to follow that advice strictly.

CHAPTER SIXTY-NINE

Wednesday, December 24
Evening

THEY PROCEEDED like robots, their conversation limited to the exchange of two- and three-word commands.

Shoehorning themselves into the Cherokee. The Cherokee powering through drifts to the end of Thunder Rise Road. Parking. Brushing snow off the toboggans. Gunning the snowmobile's engine to warm it. Loading one toboggan with equipment, including dynamite and a rifle. Transferring Abbie to the second softly and tenderly, as if she might break. Thomasine, Brad, and Bostwick stepping into snowshoes. Charlie driving the snowmobile, the snowmobile hauling the equipment toboggan and Abbie's. The others walking behind in the impressions the toboggans leave. Traveling up the mining trail, expeditiously at first, more slowly along the final stretch Charlie did not have time to clear. Stopping twice while Brad chain-saws through insurmountable deadfalls. Reaching the mine. Glancing one last time at the moon, which has chased nearly all the clouds away, then stepping inside. Flashlights piercing the darkness. Charlie and Brad on opposite ends of Abbie's stretcher. Walking toward the side shaft, their footsteps echoing off the rock walls. Standing at the mouth of the cave, their flashlights stabbing the dark, piercing to the cave floor so far below. Charlie rigging the pulleys and ropes. Charlie testing them. Brad double-lashing Abbie into the stretcher. Bostwick feeling for her pulse. Charlie first to lower himself to the bottom. Charlie climbing back up, catching his wind, delivering a short pep talk. Bostwick rappelling down. Brad. Charlie lowering Abbie, who has drifted back to the shadow place. Lowering Thomasine, who is afraid of heights. Lowering the spear. Finally, Charlie shinning down again. The whole group standing by the edge of a thin stream that meanders serpentinely into the distance.

And not one of them—not even Charlie, who's taken unchallenged command—having any conviction that what they are doing is real and not some wild, drug-induced state that would pass if only they closed their eyes long enough.

It was impossible to gauge how long they stood there, spellbound. Perhaps it was five minutes, perhaps only fifteen or twenty seconds. Except for Brad, whose father had taken him on a boyhood adventure through Howe Caverns in neighboring New York, none had ever been inside a cave. Bit by bit, they explored it with their flashlights—the way a blind man might explore the face of a stranger he has reason to fear. The walls, deeply fissured, like the once-molten skin of an asteroid. The ceiling, vaulted like a Gothic cathedral. Forty- and fifty-foot stalactites, untold centuries in the making, dropping down like oversize icicles. Stalagmites growing up to meet them—like the stalactites, painted in iridescent reds and greens and yellows from copper and iron and manganese in the limestone. Occasional coral-shaped formations Brad remembered were called helictites.

And the only sound the drip-drip-drip of the water that creates them, the passage of a century marked by an inch or two of mineral deposit.

Mother Nature's bowels, moist, hidden from the light of day, Brad thought, almost laughing out loud at the absurdity of it. *The old shrew's large intestine, that's where we are. How's that, Charlie, for being in touch with the old lady? Do I merit honorary Indianship for being so in tune?*

Standing there dwarfed by the cave, Brad couldn't decide if it was eminently reasonable to embrace Charlie's belief . . . or dismiss it as indisputable humbuggery. Once again he realized the distinction was academic.

"How far?" he asked the Quidneck. His words floated upward, seeming to hang by the ceiling before they faded and were gone.

"I have no idea." Another set of circumstances, and that response would have enraged Brad. Now he accepted it unquestioningly.

"Which way?"

Charlie turned and trained his light on the cliff they had descended. Starting at the top, he traveled down to their level, stopping at the small arch water had carved through the rock over the eons. Judging by the direction of eddies that disturbed the surface, the stream was flowing through the arch into some lost chamber. There was room for the stream, nothing else. No walkways on either side, no clearance for a boat. Only a scuba diver might be able to get through into whatever was beyond the wall.

"Can't be that way," Charlie said. "If it is, we may as well call it quits now." He turned back and aimed his light ahead, a few feet above the stream. The beam reflected off the walls, covered with moisture. As high as the cave was, it was unusually narrow; at the base, no wider than a couple of school buses laid end to end, Brad guessed. Still, close to the water's edge, there appeared to be passage wide enough for them. Rocks littered the way, but they could probably get through.

"Has to be that way," Charlie declared.

"I say we get going," said Thomasine, her voice exuding none of the derring-do that had extricated them from the Macy's and gas station jams. The memory of last fall's visit to the cave entrance with Charlie was strong, too strong, and she was fighting a losing battle to purge it from her mind. Brad could only guess Bostwick's thoughts. Since the gas station incident he'd gone into a fog that seemed to clear only when he ministered to Abbie. Brad had the troubling feeling that if Charlie told the doctor to dive into the stream and never come up, he'd do it gladly.

"How is she, Doc?" Charlie asked.

"Stable," he said, his voice barely above a whisper.

"We can go?"

"We can go."

"All right," Charlie said. "Let's."

They started off, Charlie in the lead, Thomasine bringing up the rear, Bostwick and Brad between them, carrying Abbie on her litter. *Like one of Marco Polo's caravans to the Far East,* Brad thought, his mind free-associating again. *Crossing the fabled Pamir plateau on their way to Mongolia and Kublai Khan.* At last night's planning session they had debated hand-carrying Abbie—Thomasine had even suggested fashioning an oversize Snugli—but Bostwick had ruled it out. An aluminum stretcher, he'd explained, was lightweight. From a medical perspective, it would be safer than trying to carry her.

It was warmer than they had expected inside the cave—fifty degrees, Charlie estimated—and they did not get very far before they were forced to strip to their shirts. They dropped their coats where they shed them; they could retrieve them on their return. Brad loosened the straps around Abbie and ruffled the blanket to let air circulate around her. No one spoke. Except for Bostwick, who watched the girl like a hawk, no one let his or her attention wander from his or her feet. They were too preoccupied negotiating fallen rocks and small pools of water and keeping whatever small distance they could from the stream, whose depths they could not judge but whose current appeared capable of whisking one of them away in the blink of an eye.

What's so bizarre, Brad thought, *is there's no bat shit in here. No bats. What cave doesn't have bats? And that's not all. There's no sign of any other form of life, either: spiders, owls, mushrooms, none of those crazy eyeless bugs scientists have found miles inside other caves.* Brad had the uneasy feeling that they could pull a net through that stream and come up empty. *No blind cave fish. No crayfish. As if everything living had been swept away millennia ago and not allowed to return.*

They pushed on, unable to gauge how far they had come—or had to go.

Charlie had demanded silence except in emergency. He did not know what he was waiting for (a sound? an apparition? the appearance of wolves or bears or some more exotic creature?), only that he was confident there would be—had to be—some kind of warning before they reached Hobbamock's lair. It might be as ferocious as the attack of a coyote on newborn lambs or as subtle as a trembling leaf. But it would come.

In his left hand, Charlie carried a shotgun case containing the spear. It could stop Hobbamock because this had been so ordained when Cautantowwit created the world. Without it—or if the weapon he'd tracked down turned out to be an impostor—they had no chance. Abbie would die. The other children would follow, as surely as the new moon follows the full. Maybe only one or two children a week would be lost. Maybe, Hobbamock finding his last obstacle removed, a dozen or two at a whack. Even now, having pondered it endlessly, Charlie shuddered at the logical next questions: When would the god be satisfied? Ever? Or would he continue through the years, moving along to another town when Morgantown had been destroyed, another town after that, and another, the experts eternally puzzled, kids continuing to die . . .?

Because who other than Charlie would even know? How many Quidnecks were there left who would have heard?

But they had a chance.

If there was any reason to be optimistic—and there was, he kept reminding himself, there was—it was because Charlie knew . . . *knew beyond any shadow of a doubt* that he had the right weapon. Finding the spear this afternoon in Wigglesworth's mansion (was it *really* just this afternoon?), removing it from its case oh, so gingerly, like a day-old newborn from its crib, holding it, feeling its power surge up his arm into his torso, the spear and the air around it seeming to blue-spark like a Van de Graaff generator—in that moment of triumph, he'd known instinctively.

This is it. As real as Quidneck blood, proud and potent and beyond the merciless reach of time . . .

Five minutes passed.

The only words spoken, most by Charlie, were "careful," "slippery," "watch it on the left," "easy on the right," "big rock," "need a rest," "put her down here," "ready?" "hot."

Ten minutes.

Fifteen.

Almost half an hour, and the impact of their environment had lessened to the point where they could have been embarked on nothing more dangerous than a grammar school field trip for all Brad cared. His skepticism, suspended for two days, was returning with a vengeance.

What did I expect? he asked himself. *What would Charlie say now?*

(Last night Charlie said: "We'll have to be patient. Hobbamock is very crafty. He could not finagle the souls of children if he were not. Without question, he will try to mislead us. Trick us. How? I don't know how. I only know that he will want to meet us on his terms, not ours.")

("Why wouldn't he just remain invisible until we give up and leave, or go so deep into the cave we could never find him?" Brad asked.)

("Pride," Charlie answered, "the downfall of not just man but deity, too. He will be compelled to confront us. To confront *me.* He will have to defeat me, as he was unable to defeat my forefathers."

(Last night it had seemed a reasonable answer.

(But not now.

(Not now.)

"Don't you think it's taking us an awful long time?" Brad said, breaking the silence. His arms were tired from carrying his side of Abbie's stretcher, and his eyes hurt from focusing so hard in such poor light.

"It's been half an hour," Thomasine said.

"Shouldn't we have seen something by now?"

Charlie did not answer. His brow was furrowed in almost painful concentration. Until just now his own faith had been wavering, an admission he would not make to his companions. But now he felt a pressure behind his temples. A gentle, not unpleasant feeling initially, it was steadily increasing, as if someone were pressing large thumbs into his forehead with greater and greater force. He was getting plugged in. He could feel his heart quicken in his chest. An image started to form . . . and was quickly gone.

But not before Charlie had caught a glimpse of its dark, low profile. *A wolf. Hobbamock's wolf.*

Almost immediately, another image shot through his head. And another. And a third. Three animals, each with almost human features. *A bear. A snake. A vulture, no doubt what Abbie calls the dinosaur. Hobbamock's servants.*

"I'm not sure I can endorse going much further." Bostwick joined in. "Abbie's not—"

"Shhhh!" Charlie hissed, motioning the group to stop. They did. Brad and Bostwick settled Abbie's stretcher down onto a dry spot away from the stream. She did not open her eyes, although Bostwick thought he detected a change in her breathing. Heavier, as if preparing to rouse herself.

"What is it?" Brad whispered.

"Shhh!"

Another image came into Charlie's head, departing as quickly as the last. Again Charlie had a fleeting picture of what it was: a boy. A boy who looked familiar. Who looked like . . .

. . . *Jimmy.*

A shiver ran up Charlie's spine.

"What is it?" Brad repeated. To this point, he had not been scared. Disconnected, numb, increasingly dubious—but not scared. Charlie's crazy tales—they just didn't ring true, not even here traveling down the glistening bowels of this Through-the-Looking-Glass cave. Brad had been more frightened any number of summers listening to ghost stories around a Boy Scout campfire. But now . . . now he had a crushing impulse to retreat. Instinct, the same instinct that a million years earlier had alerted his Neanderthal ancestors to the presence of saber-toothed tigers, was telling him he had to get out, *and fast.* Something that hadn't been there even five minutes ago was in the air, beyond the reach of their flashlights, but he could feel it, palpable, unfriendly. *Mocking.* His mind seized on that word and wouldn't let go.

Thomasine could feel it, too. The exact same feeling as last fall, only stronger, steadier. Like laughter . . . but the joke was on them. She could not tell if it was only inside her head or if there really was laughter . . . hushed but audible.

"Do any of you . . . feel it?" she asked.

"It's just a breeze," Bostwick said.

"Inside a cave?"

"No, I suppose there wouldn't be, now, would there?" the doctor said absently.

Bostwick flashed his light along the stream, up one wall, along the ceiling, down the other wall, and back to their feet. Charlie probed, too. The roof seemed much lower here, as if the cave were some sort of giant funnel, and they were being sucked into the stem. Except for that, there were no differences, no signs that anyone or anything had ever set foot inside here.

Except for that feeling.

"I don't like it," Brad said. "It's like . . . being watched." Instinctively he knelt by his daughter's side to offer himself as protection. Abbie's hair had clumped around her face in a messy tangle; one thin strand disappeared into her mouth. With one hand, he brushed it away. With the other, he clasped her hand. There seemed to be more strength in it than the last time they'd stopped. He didn't know whether to be encouraged or further disconcerted. He didn't dare ask Bostwick what it meant.

"Do you feel it, Charlie?" Thomasine asked.

"Yes."

"Is it him?"

"I don't think so."

"His . . . helpers?"

"Maybe. Maybe a trick. But he knows. He knows we're here."

Charlie focused, hoping for another image, another clue, anything. Silently he invoked the name of his father, not knowing if George Moonlight was along or not. During *pniese* his father had indicated this was a job that only someone who resided in the land of the living could handle. Charlie concentrated, closing his eyes at one point, the way he sometimes did at the blackjack tables when the dealer's cards started drifting out of focus. The image of the boy re-formed. It flickered longer than before, then was extinguished.

There was no doubt this time.

It was Jimmy. Jimmy suspended between the land of the living and someplace else, some place Charlie had seen in *pniese.*

"How long for that medication to take effect?" Charlie asked Bostwick, gesturing toward the doctor's bag.

"Until she's fully conscious?"

"Yes."

"Five minutes. Ten at the outside . . . if it works."

"Go ahead and wake her."

"You know I can do this only once," Bostwick explained. "And it'll last only a few minutes, half an hour at most. If it turns out this isn't—"

"*Wake her,*" Charlie ordered.

Bostwick was past the point where resistance, even the most lukewarm resistance, was possible. He reached obediently into his bag and dug with a surprisingly steady hand for a vial and a needle. Brad watched, transfixed, while he broke the needle out of its package and uncapped the vial. He filled the needle, turned it upside down, tapped it to settle the methamphetamine, and squeezed the excess air out. A cc or two of liquid squirted onto his hand in a tiny fountain. The needle was ready. He held it like a dart he was preparing to throw.

Convulsively Brad reached for the doctor's arm, restraining it. Bostwick stopped uncomplainingly. Brad looked at Charlie, who had moved off several paces. The Indian stood erect, eager, like a bloodhound straining at its leash. He wanted to move. Brad could imagine the muscles of his legs and arms, knotting and unknotting in anticipation of action. *We couldn't stop him now if we tried,* Brad thought. *And if we tried independently to leave, he might . . .*

He would not allow himself to finish. "Are you sure now's the time?" was all he said.

"Positive," Charlie answered.

Brad released Bostwick. Mechanically the doctor reached back into his bag for a foil-wrapped alcohol daub. He dropped to a crouch and freed Abbie's left foot and lower leg from under the blanket and straps. He did not want to inject her arm for fear lingering pain would interfere with her throwing the spear. He explored her calf, found his spot, sterilized it with the alcohol, then plunged the hypodermic deep into the muscle. Abbie's leg stiffened. It relaxed as soon as he withdrew the needle.

"Done," Bostwick announced.

"Then let's go," Charlie ordered.

"Same way?"

"Same way."

They set off again, more slowly this time. They were not exhausted. On the contrary, the feeling that they were no longer alone, momentarily subsided, had left them in a heightened state of alert, a state accompanied by fresh energy. They moved more slowly only because Charlie was moving more slowly. Never in his life had he been so sensitized, not even on his winningest night in Las Vegas. It was as if his entire body had been changed into some sort of ultrasophisticated warning device, tuned in simultaneously to sight, sound, tactile sensation, the more ethereal wavelengths that plugged him in. He *had* to move slowly. Any more quickly, and he might vibrate apart.

They had not gone more than a hundred feet when the methamphetamine had penetrated Abbie's central nervous system. She tossed, as if encountering something unpleasant in a dream, and then her eyes flitted. Bostwick monitored her, anticipating each new level of consciousness. She licked her teeth, and her tongue darted along her lips, which the doctor had kept from drying and cracking with a thin coating of Vaseline. Her eyes opened. Nothing registered in them at first. Then they began to rove, from Bostwick to Brad to the cave, strange and dark and utterly incomprehensible. Perhaps it was a new neighborhood in the shadow place. Perhaps only another dream . . .

She raised her head.

"Easy, honey," Brad said, balancing over her. "Lie back. We're just going on a little trip. A little trip inside a cave. Now lie back."

Abbie complied.

Brad fancied the questions that must be going through her mind: Why are we in a cave, Dad? Will we be home soon? You said we would, and you never lie. You're not lying, are you, Dad? Is it Christmas yet, Dad? Did Santa Claus come? Did I get a Tropical

Barbie? A She-Ra, Princess of Power? Will there be any more needles, Dad?

In truth, she was thinking none of those. In truth, her only question was: Can I go back to the shadow place now?

"Dad . . ." she began, her voice hoarse, inconsequential.

"Apple Guy," he said, comforting her. "You just—"

The rhamphorhynchus burst from the stream.

It landed at Abbie's side, spraying her and everyone with icy water.

"Jesus Christ!" Bostwick exclaimed, uncertain what he was seeing, certain he would faint. His body went suddenly limp. His end of the stretcher crashed to the ground, toppling Abbie.

Brad knew immediately. He froze, his panic flaring like flame inside his skull. *And I kept saying it was a nightmare. Shadows on the wall. An overactive imagination. Oh, God, oh, God, oh, God. Forgive me, Abbie. Forgive me for not believing you all this time. If only I had known. If only . . .*

Thomasine buried her face in her hands and vented her tears.

The rhamphorhynchus did not speak. This was no time for another of its casual chats with the little bitch. This, Hobbamock had made clear, was a different set of stakes. This was war. It snarled, its mouth open impossibly wide, its fangs long and white and viciously sharp. Its head slowly rotated, as if sizing up each of the humans it encountered, one by one by one. As if deciding (Bostwick thought as his bladder threatened to let go) which one to devour first.

Abbie was on the ground. She'd toppled into a small pool, landing on her right side, and she was suddenly wet and cold. The effect was not harsh or unpleasant. On the contrary, it was invigorating. Something that could be called a scream escaped from her mouth, but it was not a scream born of terror. It was a scream of protest, of disgust—of extraordinary anger for a child. She hated the beast. Hated it more than anything she'd ever hated. All those nights the beast had scared her, and then, then, when she was sick, it had tried to be her friend. But it was not her friend. Could never be her friend. It was not nice. It did not tell the truth. It told lies, including that very big one about how nice it would be to go away with it. . . .

The creature advanced on her, beating its wings with a sound like a helicopter rotor.

She struggled to get to her feet—and was amazed to find this time that she had the strength. She rose, wobbly and weak-kneed, unsteady. But she rose. "Nooooo!" she yelled when she was upright, her posture painful and hunched. "I don't want to go with you! I don't want to! You're bad!" With her fists, she began to flail at the creature. It dodged and danced just out of reach, hissing, teasing, mocking, trying to lure Abbie into the water, black and deep and capable of sucking her under for good.

Not five seconds had elapsed since the rhamphorhynchus's appearance. It had taken Charlie most of that time to digest what was going on. Now his mind raced at hyperspeed. He could try the spear, hoping it was effective against the creature, suspecting it was not—that it was potent only against Hobbamock. But he could try. And what if it lodged in the beast and the beast flew off with it? Probably that's what Hobbamock's charge to the creature had been. *Get the spear. Or get the child.*

The rifle.

He'd forgotten his rifle. They'd lashed it to Abbie's stretcher, just in case, along with extra ammunition. Charlie trained his light on the upended stretcher. *Come on, damn it,* he thought frantically. But there was no sign of the rifle. It might be tangled in blankets. For all he knew, it might have skidded across the ground into the stream when Bostwick had dropped Abbie. By the time he found the gun, it would be too late.

With an iron grip, Charlie clasped the shotgun case in his left hand. He would not allow it to be snatched away. Flexing the muscles of his right arm and hand, he advanced. The rhamphorhynchus had abandoned its strategy of trying to lure Abbie into the stream. It was going for the kill. It was on top of her, digging its talons into her shoulders, trying to haul her into the water like a cat dragging a mouse off the killing field for someplace quiet to feast. Only Abbie's frenzied defense prevented it from succeeding.

Thomasine, Bostwick—frozen. Brad—kicking, beating ineffectually on the creature with his flashlight, his fist.

Charlie reached for the rhamphorhynchus's neck, clamping and unclamping his right fist with the brawn to crush stones. "You filthy bastard," he sneered, his jaw muscles rippling the skin of his lower face.

He reached.

The creature disappeared.

Soundlessly.

As if it had never been there, all just a figment of their overburdened imaginations.

Abbie went for her father's arms, but she was not crying—yet. Blood trickled from scratch marks on her shoulder where the creature had tried to get its claws into her. If he hadn't seen them, Brad would have sworn the creature had been a hallucination. But the blood was no illusion. Nor was his daughter's sudden new state of alertness. With his fingers, he wiped the blood away. Bostwick would have to treat her.

So the little bitch thinks she's too good for us, does she? Hobbamock shrieked into Charlie's head. *Gotten bold all of a sudden? How's this, then, Chucky? How do you think she'll do with this one?*

There was a hissing, like steam escaping an antique radiator or a genie being released from a bottle, Brad thought.

In place of the rhamphorhynchus a doctor materialized. He was dressed in a green scrub suit and wore a white surgical cap and mask.

But this was not just any doctor. This one glowed, filling the cave with eerie green luminescence, as if it were some strange denizen of the deep sea. This one was almost as tall as the ceiling—thirty, thirty-five feet. In one hand, he brandished a huge scalpel; in the other, a hypodermic.

"Jesus Christ!" Bostwick exclaimed again. His legs were suddenly energized, and he bolted backward, getting only three strides before he tripped over a small boulder and fell. His flashlight flew out of his hand and skittered across the rocky floor and went out. Bostwick lay in semidarkness, suppressing his moans, rubbing his arm, which was already beginning to swell. The pain radiated into his neck, down to his fingertips. He'd treated enough broken arms to know when he had one himself.

Abbie might be able to handle the rhamphorhynchus. But not this. Not another needle. Not a needle that big. "No," she whimpered, the tears she'd been holding back releasing in a tidal surge. "No . . ."

The rhamphorhynchus reappeared overhead. It circled, its wings fluttering. "Told you so!" it screamed. "Told you so! They're trying to kill you!"

Charlie studied the doctor, towering over them. The flying thing had been real. Charlie had smelled its foul breath, felt the beat of its wings, had come within inches of throttling it. It could appear and vanish at will, but it was real. For all its bulk, this other giant seemed not to have mass. It seemed diaphanous, a clever magician's prop, no more. To prove it to himself, Charlie swept his arm through the giant's leg; it passed without resistance. This wasn't real. This was a trick.

Abbie kicked, attempting to burrow deeper into Brad's chest.

"It can't hurt you, Abbie," Charlie yelled. "It's not real!" He couldn't tell if she'd heard. Again he swept his arm through what should have been solid muscle and bone but was no more substantial than fog. "See?" he shouted. "You can put your hand right through it!" But Abbie was not watching. Not listening. Her face was buried in Brad's chest.

Like Bostwick and Thomasine, who'd found shelter crouching behind a boulder, Brad had been jolted into shock. Not a crippling shock—to lung or heart—but a subtler jolt that could lead to catatonia. "We gotta go," he was intoning, over and over and over. "We gotta go. We gotta go. Gotta go."

"No!" Charlie screamed. "That's what he wants!"

"We gotta go," Brad repeated.

"Gotta go," Thomasine mimicked.

Chickenshit, aren't they, Chucky? Hobbamock gloated inside Charlie's head. *Not mighty and strong like you!*

The giant began to stoop. The needle descended on a trajectory that would take it to the approximate area of Abbie's forehead. As unreal as the ghoul-doctor might have been, the needle it wielded seemed the genuine article. It was one of those old-fashioned stainless steel instruments, with two finger loops and a metal plunger. Brad shielded his daughter, covering her eyes with his hands. Thomasine screamed—a high, haunting scream that drilled into Brad's fear, exacerbating it.

What do you suppose the little bitch is going to make of that, Chucky? I bet that's the biggest needle in the world!

The ghoul-doctor stopped, its needle arm poised over Abbie, as if pinpointing its target. Charlie grabbed for its wrist. His arm passed straight through it.

The rifle.

It was a desperate shot, a wild shot, but it was a shot. If anything could stop it, if anything could restore Charlie's swiftly evaporating authority, that had to be it. He reached for the overturned stretcher, pawed frantically through the blankets Abbie had cast off. It had to be there. *Had* to. But it was not in the first blanket. Not in the second. The needle continued descending, steadily but not impatiently. Brad stumbled backward, but the ghoul-doctor's reach was tremendous. It could reach back to the cave entrance if it had to.

Charlie found the rifle. It was loaded.

He clicked the safety off, raised it to his shoulder, sighted the ghoul-doctor's masked head.

The apparition vanished.

The cave was filled with laughter—mocking gales of laughter.

"Bastard," Charlie swore. How ridiculous to think an ordinary gun would be of any use. He dropped it.

"Come on," he said. "It can't be much farther."

The caravan began to reassemble. Bostwick emerged, only a little punch-drunk, from his boulder hiding place. With his good arm, he began treating Abbie's scratches with a Betadine sponge. Abbie's crying tapered off to sniffles. It was long past the point where she could comprehend what they were doing, or why. She wasn't at all convinced that this wasn't merely another shadow place, one far more violent and dangerous than the other one.

"I'll carry her," Brad said submissively. "In my arms."

"I think my arm is broken," Bostwick stated, fashioning a sling from a piece of blanket.

"Does it hurt?"

"Like a bastard. But not for long," he said, preparing an injection of Demerol, a potent pain-killer.

Thomasine said nothing.

They resumed their trip, heading deeper into the cave, the walls narrowing, the roof lowering until the passageway was tunnel size. They rounded a bend and emerged into a cavern. The sight pulled their breath away. Unlike the rest of the cave, this chamber was white, all white, white as chalk, the purest and softest form of limestone. The walls were smooth and domed, like an igloo. An igloo with a ceiling that must have been a hundred feet at its apex.

But it was not the shape or color of the chamber that was so stunning. It was what was situated in the middle of it: a rock platform, perhaps ten feet in height, flat on top. Like the mesa in the *pniese.* Arranged in a circle around the border were flares, smoky and flickering. Charlie smelled burning pine mixed with an occasional whiff of something more pungent. Cedar perhaps.

At the lip of the ledge, seated on a polished, flattened stone reminiscent of a throne, was a man, a white-haired, ponytailed man who looked to be of great age. He was dressed in the traditional garb of a Quidneck sachem: mantle and leggings, with a colorfully decorated band of hawk feathers around his head. He was alone.

It must be Hobbamock, Charlie thought, with less than certainty. He remembered *pniese,* so grotesquely pornographic. This man—if indeed he was a man—was not the lewd being of *pniese.* The sense of righteousness and omnipotence Charlie'd felt suddenly abandoned him, leaving him strangely anesthetized. Until the moment they'd rounded this bend, he'd been plugged in. A man possessed. Now the lines were down, the circuits dead. *A trick,* he reminded himself. *Another trick. Probably not his last.*

Charlie held up his hand to signal silence. It was an unnecessary gesture. The sight of the cavern, so blindingly white, and the stone table, and especially the figure atop it was mesmeric. The adults stared, slack-jawed. Hesitantly Abbie peered over Brad's shoulder.

"That's him," Charlie whispered.

But it can't be, Brad thought. *This is someone's grandfather, venerable and wise. The good Indian god's grandfather. He's going to tell our fortunes, give us each a lucky charm, and tell us to be on our way. Good luck and God bless.*

The sachem stood and pondered them a moment. A kindly smile blossomed on his face. "Abbie," he said in a sonorous, benign voice, "I have waited a long time to meet you. I have heard so much about you. *So* much."

Abbie clung desperately to her father. As afraid as she'd been of the ghoul-doctor, as hot and prickly and aching as she still was, she was surprisingly alert. Surprisingly curious. The methamphetamine was approaching zenith.

"You look scared," the sachem continued, sounding terribly disappointed. "But *I* won't hurt you, Abbie. I promise. I only want to have a word with you. I want you to come forward, Abbie. And after we talk, I will have something very nice for such a good little girl. Something *very* nice."

The range, Charlie thought. *We don't have the range yet. We've got to get closer.* Gently he tried to pry Abbie from Brad, but she wouldn't be budged.

"Closer," he whispered to Brad. "We have to get her closer."

"What is taking so long?" the sachem asked. "Is there a problem, Charlie?" he asked familiarly.

Charlie did not answer. With Abbie in her father's clutches, he and Brad approached the mesa.

CHAPTER SEVENTY

Wednesday, December 24
Evening

IN THE ROOM at Berkshire Medical Center that had become her home, too, Ginny Ellis sponged sweat off Jimmy's forehead again and bent to kiss him. He did not respond. He had not responded to her or anyone in more than twenty-four hours, not even the flutter of an eyelash to suggest he was there.

"Jimmy," she whispered, desperate for this to be the time she finally got through, "I love you. I'll always love you, big guy."

Breathing. Only breathing, the increasingly irregular heave and fall of his five-and-a-half-year-old chest.

If there was any slim comfort for Ginny this Christmas Eve, it was the presence of her mother. Mrs. Fitzpatrick had shut the Boar's Head for the duration of her family's ordeal and came every morning now at seven-thirty.

The clock over the nurses' station read 10:05 P.M.

"He doesn't seem any worse," Ginny said, with a wistful hopefulness her mother didn't have the heart to contradict. Then she added: "Don't believe everything doctors tell you. Doctors aren't God, you know, Mom."

"No," Mrs. Fitzpatrick said, "they're not."

"He'll come 'round, I know he will."

"I pray that he does, honey. Every minute I pray that he does."

Ginny trailed a hand over her son's distended abdomen. She could feel it through the cotton johnny: an almost blistering heat, the same heat that radiated everywhere she touched, whether his forehead or his wrist or his arm. *Good,* she thought. *A very good sign. He's hot because his body is giving it its all.*

Early in parenthood, her mind had sprung the most terrifying image on her. It was right after her husband had died—probably not more than a month—and Jimmy, barely a toddler, had come down with the croup. Bostwick had urged her to keep a watchful eye on him, and that first night she brought her son into bed with her, settling him in the hollow in the Sealy mattress that his father had dug over the years. Every rasping breath Jimmy took that nightmarish night—every agonizingly endless pause between inhaling and exhaling—brought fresh fear to her throat. *What if this is his last breath?* she wondered, time after time after time. *Or this? Or the next one? How could I ever go on living, knowing I had witnessed it in such lurid detail?*

But that wasn't the most frightening image her mind popped on her, her only child drawing his final breath. It was the image of her son's body cooling, the molecules or whatever they were of his body heat dissipating into the atmosphere, his vitality draining away like ebb tide on a beach. Most dreadful was knowing that long after his last breath, long after his skin had turned purple and cold, ice cold—hours after, even—she could probably turn her dead son over . . . and the mattress and sheet below, insulated by the rigid thickness of his corpse, would still be warm to the touch.

She lightly massaged Jimmy's stomach again.

He's still warm, she reassured herself. *They're wrong, that's all. Jimmy's not dying. He's just . . . very sick.*

But of course, he wasn't just very sick. He was dying, and Mrs. Fitzpatrick sensed it as surely as she sensed the never-never land her daughter resided in these days. It had come as little surprise to her when, just before suppertime, the doctor substituting for Bostwick had shown them the latest test results and gently made his pronouncements about Jimmy's chances for lasting another twenty-four hours. They were not favorable, he was terribly sorry to have to say. If they had a family clergyman, well, they might not be ill advised to seek his solace.

"Charlie would want to know," Mrs. Fitzpatrick said when the doctor was done. "He would want to be here, and you should let him."

Ginny turned that over for a moment. So Mom wanted Charlie here. Charlie, whom Ginny blamed, at least in some measure, for all of this. Charlie, who had betrayed her and Jimmy. Charlie, who . . . she could not go on. The simple truth was it didn't matter about Charlie anymore. If Mom thought he should be here, she would defer to her judgment. She would relent.

"Yes," she said, "I should let him. But not because Jimmy's . . . not because of what the doctor said."

"No," Mrs. Fitzpatrick agreed.

"Just because . . . well, it's almost Christmas. Holidays are for families."

"Yes," Mrs. Fitzpatrick said, "because it's almost Christmas."

"And, well, I suppose I've been a little—a little selfish, too."

"You've been under tremendous pressure, honey," the old woman said.

"Yes," Ginny agreed, "I have. We all have. Charlie can come."

Except Charlie wasn't to be found. He had no phone, of course, but Mrs. Fitzpatrick had managed to convince the Morgantown police chief, an old friend, to send one of his men out to the Quidneck's cabin. He'd returned around seven, reporting that Charlie was not there. Nor, the officer said, did it appear he'd been there in quite some time. His Cherokee was gone, and there was a foot of virgin snow in his drive, untouched by foot or tire.

Mrs. Fitzpatrick asked the chief to have his men be on the lookout for him, although she could give them no definite idea of where he might be. Surely he would not have left town unannounced, as he was sometimes wont to do? Not on Christmas Eve. Not when he'd promised to come for Christmas dinner, and his nephew, his beloved nephew, lying so sick in a hospital bed . . .

She was lost in these ruminations when, at 10:10 P.M., Jimmy's condition suddenly and precipitously deteriorated.

First, his breathing went haywire. It had been irregular, but now, as his mother and grandmother watched in terror, he began to cough. Once, twice, three times, accelerating until his entire body was convulsed. The hacking continued, intensified, until Mrs. Fitzpatrick was terrified that he would flop off his bed onto the floor. She had just pressed the call button when Jimmy's mouth opened and blood-tinged bile surged out in a stream of foam. Vomit frothed onto his chin, down his chin to his neck, from his neck onto the johnny top, discoloring it, fouling the room with a stench that burned their nostrils. Some slid back down his throat, activating the gag reflex. He was choking. He was choking, and he was unaware, unable to help himself.

Ginny screamed. From a waitress job many summers ago she remembered the Heimlich maneuver. She started it on her son.

Mrs. Fitzpatrick recited a silent prayer and tried to prepare herself for the end, knowing what they were about to endure would be replayed in their nightmares as long as she and her daughter lived.

CHAPTER SEVENTY-ONE

Wednesday, December 24
Late

"IT'S ALMOST CHRISTMAS," Hobbamock said to Abbie as she, Charlie, and Brad approached. "Only a little while. Did you give Santa your list? No? Of course not. You were sick this year. I'm so sorry you were sick this year, Abbie. It isn't any fun to be sick, is it, Abbie?"

The girl listened, spellbound.

"I'd like to help make you feel better. I'd like to help you have a merry Christmas after all. How about your puppy? Would seeing your puppy be a nice Christmas gift, Abbie? You haven't seen Maria in a while, I know. They won't let you have puppies in the hospital. Such poor sports. But even if they did, you couldn't have seen her. Do you know why?"

Instinctively Abbie shook her head.

"Because your daddy killed her, that's why. Cracked her skull open with a shovel, right there on the floor of your garage. I know it's very hard to believe, but it's true. Why don't you ask him?"

Abbie looked up at her father, cradling her in his arms, expecting him to deny it. But he did not deny it. A look of guilt spread across his face. A look Abbie plainly saw. Her whole body tensed. She was thinking about lying and what the rhamphorhynchus had said that afternoon at Berkshire Medical.

"I didn't think he'd admit it," Hobbamock continued, "but it doesn't matter now. I can bring Maria back. And if you'd like, I will."

Abbie's eyes brightened.

Suddenly there was the dog, lying contentedly at Hobbamock's feet.

"Maria!" Abbie managed to say.

"Yes, Maria. Would you like to pat your doggy?" the god asked. "I bet you would, after not seeing her all this time. And you can. All you have to do is come up here. If your father and Charlie will lead you around to the left, you'll see a set of stairs. *Very small* stairs, built for all my special visitors. You come up here, and after we have our little talk, I'll let you pat your dog. If you're really good, I'll even let you have your dog back. For good. How's that? I think that's very generous, considering we've just met."

Charlie and Brad plodded forward. Abbie was unbearably heavy in Brad's arms, but Charlie had insisted she not even try to walk; it was necessary for her to save her strength, however low her drug-enhanced reserves of it might be, for the encounter. Brad gritted his teeth and pushed forward. They were not fifty feet from the stone platform now, and the floor here was polished, smooth, free of the rocks that had impeded their progress before. Even the river, which flowed from a grotto to the right, seemed calmer, more ordered.

They advanced, Hobbamock seeming to welcome them with benign expression and arms outstretched.

He doesn't know we have the spear, Charlie thought with an almost uncontrollable exhilaration. It was a completely ridiculous idea, that they could have come this close without the god's somehow divining it, but there was no other conclusion he could draw now. *Why else would he let us approach? He must think he's leading us—her—into a trap. Maybe he's even forgotten the existence of the spear. It has been so long, even by Hobbamock's timeless standards. Decades and decades, sealed inside this cave. Maybe even gods forget. Maybe gods go crazy, too, alone for so long.*

"Would you like to see your mommy now?" Hobbamock asked, and now Charlie heard it distinctly: the sardonic edge to his voice, too subtle for a child to catch.

"No . . ." Abbie whimpered. "I want . . . home."

"I can bring her here, too, if you'd like. And heaven knows you haven't seen her in an awfully long time. An awfully long time, just like Maria. I bet you were probably beginning to think she didn't love you, weren't you, Abbie?"

"I wanna go home, Daddy. I wanna see . . . Maria."

"But Maria's here," Hobbamock continued. "If you went home, why, all you'd see would be the *stains,* dark and still sticky on the garage floor. Isn't that right, Mr. Gale? Wasn't it a terrible time you had trying to erase the traces? And you never were entirely successful. I know. I've had a firsthand report. I'm told the whole affair was very, very shameful. I'm told there was *alcohol* involved. Tsk, tsk."

"It's . . . not . . . true . . . Apple Guy," Brad lied in voice shaking so badly he was sure it would die before he'd spit his sentence out.

"Don't listen to him," Charlie agreed. "He's making it all up."

They kept moving, Charlie slowing the pace, trying to stretch every step out. He was mentally measuring the distance, calculating how far a girl of her age, in her fragile health *(fragile health? without Bostwick's drug, she'd be dead),* might be able to chuck it. Twenty-five feet? Never. Twenty? Too risky. Charlie knew they had only one shot. She had to connect on the first try. A miss—and Hobbamock would grab it, or one of his creatures would grab it, or he would simply leave it lying on the ground, impotent out of the child's hands, while he proceeded to annihilate them all. He had the power to do that, no question. The bear, the rhamphorhynchus, the ghoul-doctor—those had been amusement rides for Hobbamock. Fun and games. When it was time to get serious, Charlie knew, Hobbamock would go for the kill. That had been the point Charlie's father had emphasized every time he'd told the tale.

If only they could make it to the base of the ledge before he caught on, they would be ten feet away, twelve at most. She might be able to throw that far. Would *have to* be able to.

" 'Don't listen to me'?" the god repeated. "Is that what I heard you say, Charlie? What a silly, arrogant thing to tell this poor child. And such a lie. It's *him* you shouldn't listen to, Abbie. *He's* the one who sicced the wolf on Jimmy. Who made you so sick. Who killed Maureen. Who wants to kill you, too. He and your dad, the two of them in league together, just as the rhamphorhynchus kept trying to tell you. If only you'd listened, I don't think you'd be in such a jam now."

"No . . ." Abbie cried.

"I think you'd be a happy girl, not this sad little thing I see in front of me now."

"No."

"But it's true."

They moved closer.

"My dad loves me . . ."

"That's what he says. But he lies, Abbie. Just like your mommy. And Charlie. All the adults—liars. But *I* wouldn't lie to you. I just want to have a little talk with you. Sit you on my lap, like Santa Claus, and have a little talk about where you'd like to live. When you're all better. Because I'm going to do that, too, if you're very good: *make you better.* No more of this sickness, these hospitals and doctors. Not when you're with me."

Closer.

And closer.

They were almost directly beneath him. Almost close enough. Abbie was blinded with tears. Brad tried to soothe her, but she would not accept his kindness. She didn't believe what that nasty old man up there was saying about her dad, or her mom, or Charlie, couldn't tell if that dog by the old man's feet really was Maria (one minute it looked like Maria, and the next it didn't, didn't even look alive). But she didn't know anything anymore. Didn't know if her body was really back in the hospital, and this was just another place for her mind to wander around in, a new place, a parallel place to the place where you walked through endless shadows—a cartoon artist's world where things weren't quiet or dim or cool, but moved too fast, or too slow, or were too crazy or too big. Never the way they were supposed to be.

All she knew was that she didn't want to be here. Was afraid here. In her veins she could feel the sudden strength she'd been given start to sputter. The aching, the pain, the hotness—just outside the door now.

Suddenly Hobbamock turned his attention to the Indian. "What's in the case, Charlie?" he asked, as if noticing only now that he was carrying something. "Another gun, Charlie? It looks like a shotgun case to me. I had a report that you came heavily armed. It appears that report was correct."

Charlie was mute.

Hobbamock cackled. "Rifles are no use here. Why do you suppose I let you in with one? You could shoot a rifle all day and all night, and it wouldn't bother me. You could bring a machine gun in here, and it wouldn't trouble me in the least. Why don't you open that case and let me see your other gun?"

They were almost to the base of the stone platform. Charlie saw the stairs and for one fleeting moment was tempted to plunge madly up them, dragging Abbie behind him, until she was close enough to touch Hobbamock. But there was no way they would make it.

"Come on, Charlie. Shoot."

It has to be now.

"Shoot."

"Put her down!" Charlie ordered Brad. Brad did. Abbie stood, wobbly and weak. The blood rushed from her head, and she was dizzy. Vision swimming, she looked at her father, then Charlie, waiting for one of them to speak.

Has to be.

"What's going on, Charlie?" Hobbamock said. He sounded more curious than perturbed. "Is something not to your liking? Before I talk to Abbie, I'd like to see what's in your case. I've already said that. Please don't keep me waiting."

Now.

Madly Charlie unzipped the case and yanked the spear out. It was exactly as it had appeared in the *pniese:* ash shaft painted red, orange, and green; pink granite tip; the whole weapon perfectly balanced for extraordinarily long and accurate flight. He handed it to Abbie.

Abbie stared at him, befuddled.

"Throw it," he ordered. "At him."

Hobbamock rose from his chair and walked to the edge of the cliff. He looked down. He was only feet away from them, close enough to see details of his face, lined and cracked like the binding on an ancient leather-spined book. Close enough to smell his breath: rhamphorhynchus and wolf breath, like mildewed garlic. He was smiling. Grinning. Sneering.

Entirely unconcerned.

"What have we here?" he asked casually. "A spear?"

"Throw it, Abbie," Charlie demanded, frantic. "*You have to throw it at him!*"

She was paralyzed.

"*He's the devil, Abbie! Do it for your dad! Do it for Jimmy!*"

Frozen.

"He's right," Brad shouted, taking her hand and motioning in Hobbamock's direction. "Throw it. *Throw it!*"

She did.

Charlie's head exploded with a burst of sudden concentration. He was searching his mind for the wire that would plug him in, that might help direct the spear. He found something, felt warmth. He seized on it, dumping all his mental current into it, hoping with all his hope. *His heart,* he willed. *Straight into his heart, the son of a bitch.*

The spear lodged in Hobbamock's side. It drew no blood. Charlie watched with building horror as the god calmly reached down and withdrew it. He held it in his hand, examining it.

"You must take me for the most colossal of fools, Charlie," he stated nonchalantly, "to think I would allow you in here with the very weapon your ancestors used against me. As you can see, this is not that weapon, and thank goodness for that. This is nothing but a fake. A fake I arranged to have planted when I discovered your shenanigans one of those long, sweaty nights I had one of my helpers visit inside your head."

The group listened, terrified, as Hobbamock expounded on Quidneck folly.

This is it, Brad thought. *Dear God, please make it easy on Abbie.*

And then an old man materialized behind Hobbamock. A man carrying a spear identical to the one Abbie had just thrown, with one difference. The tip was all black, black as coal, black as night. And yet it appeared to shine, too, as if it were made of some strange material that alternately gave off and absorbed light.

The second man was almost to Hobbamock's side when he called, "Son."

Charlie heard that voice and knew immediately.

"Dad," he answered, incredulous. *"Dad!"*

"You shamed me into action," George Moonlight said. "I have learned things I did not know about the Land of the Dead. Someday I will tell you. "Here," he said, tossing the new weapon down. "Give it to the girl."

Charlie caught the spear. Like the other one, it throbbed and crackled with blue static. The Wigglesworth weapon had been a perfect imitation, a testimony to Hobbamock's cleverness.

Charlie placed the spear in Abbie's hands.

This time she understood her mission.

She cocked her arm.

Hobbamock had been caught completely off guard. George Moonlight had been nowhere in the plan. He was supposed to stay where he belonged: in the Land of the Already Dead. "When I get through with you," Hobbamock screamed at Charlie's father, "you'll spend eternity in—"

It was too late. Abbie had the spear now.

"Throw it," Charlie ordered.

Abbie drew a deep breath.

"Now," Brad urged. "Now!"

Abbie stopped cold.

It was not Hobbamock up there anymore.

It was Jimmy.

Healthy Jimmy. Jimmy dressed for the first day of school. Jimmy discovering the new girl who lives just down the road. Jimmy saying: "Why do you want to do this to me, Abbie? Why do you want to hurt me? I never hurt you. I thought we were friends."

"Jimmy!" Abbie shrieked.

"Best friends! I thought we were best friends!"

"It's not Jimmy!" Charlie yelled. "It's a trick, like the doctor was a trick! Throw it! *Throw it!*"

Abbie hesitated.

The thing had changed again. It was not Jimmy now.

It was Heather.

"Mom!" Abbie screamed.

"Throw it before it's too late!"

"Abbie," the Heather illusion begged. "Don't listen to them. You know how Daddy has tried to keep us apart."

"She hates you, Abbie," Brad hissed. "Throw it!"

Abbie closed her eyes and complied. Charlie concentrated, willing the new weapon to its target. It flew straight and true, piercing the Heather illusion at heart level.

This time Hobbamock did not calmly retract the weapon. This time the Heather illusion began to yowl. It clawed wildly at the spear, twisting, turning, like a moth pinned to a board. It clawed, but it could not touch the weapon. Every time its hands drew near, the weapon arced, like a broken transmission line. The yowling grew in intensity until it filled the cavern.

As they watched, the Heather illusion was transformed. Jimmy for a second. Then the dog. The rhamphorhynchus. A bear. The ghoul-doctor. All of its manifestations. Its entire bag of tricks, parading across the screen in one final, monstrous blowout.

When it was over, only a skeleton remained.

The skeleton of a snake, long and winding and bleached white.

Charlie looked for his father, but he had gone. Weeping, Charlie mustered the group.

CHAPTER SEVENTY-TWO

Wednesday, December 24
Late

THE CODE TEAM was working feverishly and getting nowhere.

Ginny watched vacantly from the doorway, her mother clasping her hand. The medical lingo was blowing right by her, but she understood too well the mood in the room, a mood of bitter determination tinged with a growing sense of futility. Mrs. Fitzpatrick was praying—the most fervent prayers of a life prayer had never been a stranger to. Praying that if God was going to save Jimmy, he do it soon, because his family couldn't take much more of this. Praying that if he was going to take the boy, he do it painlessly, without her grandson regaining consciousness.

"What is he?" team chief Dr. Jefferson asked the EKG technician.

"Still flat line."

"Shit," the doctor swore. "Continue pumping."

A nurse kept massaging Jimmy's chest, tracing small circles with the heels of her hands over the hairless skin, hoping to coax something—any small response—from his heart muscle. Another nurse kept working the ambu bag, forcing oxygen into his lungs, lungs that had stopped working independently more than five minutes ago.

Jefferson was running out of tricks. "More epi," he barked.

"Epi," the critical care nurse confirmed, injecting another dose of epinephrine into the second IV she'd run into Jimmy's left ankle.

"Anything?"

"Nothing," the EKG tech said.

"Try atropine."

"Atropine in ankle line," the nurse said obediently.

"Come on, Jimmy," the doctor coaxed. "Come on, boy! You can do it! Come on! Respond, goddamn it! Respond!"

Because if you don't in the next few seconds, he thought, *the brain damage will be permanent and irreversible even if you should happen to make it somehow . . . and God only knows how.*

"Flat, doctor," the EKG tech said.

Jefferson was down to one last trick. He'd pulled it only once on a child this small, a child he'd lost as a greenhorn resident working his first Friday night shift at Boston City Hospital. He was never really sure the paddles hadn't actually killed the kid, a girl of seven who'd been shot in the stomach and kidney and bowel one hot August night during a dispute between mother and boyfriend.

But what other choice do I have? The family's already said they want every measure used, no matter how ordinary or extraordinary it is.

"We'll zap him," Jefferson announced.

"How many volts?" the critical care nurse said.

"Two hundred."

"You sure?"

"Do it!"

The nurse pressed the charge button on the defibrillator, then set the dial to two hundred. There was no sound. In four seconds the red light blinked.

"Ready," the nurse said.

"Clear the bed," Jefferson ordered. The team moved back in a wave. Metal-frame beds are fine conductors of electricity, a fact taught in every emergency medicine course.

"Clear," the nurse said. She stood over Jimmy, a plastic-handle paddle in each hand.

"Zap him," Jefferson said.

The nurse reached down, burrowing the smooth stainless steel surface of the paddles into his chest. She pressed the button. Two hundred volts shot through Jimmy. His arms and legs scarecrowed into the air, then flopped back to his side with a thud like meat hitting a floor. It was a muscular response Jefferson had first seen in high school biology, touching battery wires to the exposed leg muscles of a freshly pithed frog. Gruesome. It had not become any more pleasant in all the times since that he'd seen it in humans.

"Good lord," Mrs. Fitzpatrick said. Ginny screamed, unsure if the grisly spectacle meant her son was coming out of it or going under for good.

On the monitor the green line blipped momentarily, then went flat again.

"Zap him," Jefferson said.

The nurse did. This time Jimmy's body seemed to levitate several inches before crashing back down.

"Again."

She did. The green line was as straight as a ruler's edge.

"Once more."

Nothing.

Jefferson was grappling with the hardest question that can be put to a doctor—*when is enough enough?*—when the needle on the EKG machine jumped and then started squiggling. On the monitor the green line fragmented, then reassembled in the anthill-and-tepee shapes of a healthy heart's normal sinus rhythm. Through her fingers, still clasped tightly around the ambu bag, the nurse felt the draw of his breath. His chest rose and fell, rose and fell, reestablishing the familiar pattern as if it had never been interrupted. The purplish tint that had developed in Jimmy's skin was being flushed away by a more normal flesh hue. The team could actually see his color returning.

They were stunned. They'd all seen dramatic turnarounds . . .

. . . but this?

"I'll be damned!" Jefferson exclaimed.

"Looks good," the EKG technician, a normally dour individual, said enthusiastically. "Mighty darn good."

"You're telling me. What's his pressure?"

"Ninety over sixty."

"Pulse?"

"One-ten."

"He breathing on his own?"

"Yes, Doctor."

"You're kidding."

"I'm not."

"His functions look . . . completely normal."

"They certainly do."

"I'll be damned. I'll be goddamned."

The draw of oxygen through the intubation tube into his larynx was regular, reassuring. He was breathing on his own again. Jimmy's eyes did not flutter, but beneath his eyelids there was rapid movement. Jefferson clapped his hands an inch from Jimmy's right ear. His eyes flew open, then shut again. With his thumb and forefinger, the doctor pried Jimmy's left eye open and flashed a flashlight in it. The pupil constricted. It dilated when he shut the light off. Fluid gurgled in Jimmy's throat; the anesthesiologist suctioned it. Jimmy's toes and fingers flinched in protest. The doctor withdrew the tube, and Jimmy coughed. A subdued, purely functional, throat-clearing cough.

"I'll be goddamned." Jefferson whistled, daring at last to hope.

In five minutes the team's work was done; James Ellis was a case for ICU now. A nurse swabbed splotches of blood and saliva off Jimmy and replaced his johnny. An orderly with a broom started to mop up. Jefferson stood by the patient, making notes on his clipboard. It had been a remarkable turnaround, nothing less. One for the books. He'd like his team to get the credit, and it would, tomorrow, when he briefed Bostwick. But he wondered if he'd ever be able to shake the gut feeling that it hadn't really been them, after all, but some outside force. A religious force, stray energy from another galaxy—he couldn't articulate it. He decided he wouldn't try. In emergency medicine it wasn't necessarily how you played the game, but whether you won or lost.

Ginny approached the perimeter of the area around Jimmy's bed the team had claimed. Wrappings for needles and medications littered the floor. Jimmy's old johnny top, scissored from his body by the orderly, was crumpled in a ball. Cords and plastic tubes ran everywhere. The paddles, IV poles, portable monitor, standby suction machine, respirator, oxygen tank—a tangle of technology. Their work had been too urgent for tidiness.

"Can I see him now?" Ginny asked, her voice a hollow tin thing.

"Yes," Jefferson said. "For a moment."

"Me, too?" Mrs. Fitzpatrick asked.

"You, too."

"It's a miracle, isn't it, Doctor?" the grandmother said wondrously.

"I don't think it would be too much of an exaggeration to call it that."

"I could never be able to thank you enough, Doctor," Ginny said.

"He isn't out of the woods yet, Mrs. Ellis. Not by a long shot."

"No, but he's on his way. I know he is."

The women approached. Jimmy sensed their presence almost immediately. His eyes opened, and there was a clear, thankful recognition sparkling in them. He licked his lips and opened and closed his mouth several times, as if making sure it still worked. Then he spoke.

"Mommy" was all he said. But it was enough—more than enough.

"Jimmy," Ginny gushed, "oh, God, I love you. I love you, I love you, I love you!"

"Easy, Mrs. Ellis," the doctor said. "Your son's been through a very tough ordeal."

"I'll be careful," she said obediently. "Can I kiss him?"

"If you're gentle."

"I will be!" She bent over him, placing a kiss on his cheek. It was a surprisingly flush cheek, full of color and new warmth.

Jimmy smiled then.

Smiled, for God's sake.

Smiled!

Ginny wept. She was still weeping a half hour later when word filtered into their room that several other children, also victims of the Mystery Disease, seemed to be improving.

CHAPTER SEVENTY-THREE

Wednesday, December 24
Near Midnight

"I DON'T KNOW," Charlie answered when Brad asked how long it would be before Hobbamock recovered from his injury.

Maybe months. Maybe years. Maybe only a matter of minutes. No one knows because no one ever stuck around to find out. They sealed him back up as fast as they could and prayed to Cautantouwwit no one ever let him out again. Because the next time might be the time he decides to move. To someplace like Chicago or New York or Paris, he thought ridiculously.

"You're sure sealing the cave will contain him?" Brad asked, seeking reassurance.

"It should. If we get out in time."

"We'll make it, won't we?" Thomasine said.

"That's what I'm planning on," Charlie said. Thomasine would have liked more confidence in his voice.

And so they moved as fast as they could, Brad and Charlie taking turns carrying Abbie, Bostwick clutching his broken arm but not complaining, Thomasine leading the way with her light, one of only two that still worked. They moved, exhausted, intent only in *getting the hell out of this place.* Back through the cave, along the banks of the stream, as dark and still and deep-running as always, to where they had come in.

Charlie's pulley-and-rope rig was where they'd left it, dangling from the old mine shaft into the cave like the string to a kite. The Indian hoisted Thomasine up first. Brad went next, to handle Abbie. Bostwick stayed with Charlie. Like Abbie, he was going to need a stretcher ride.

"You ought to warm the snowmobile," Charlie yelled up as he secured the rope around the stretcher for Abbie's turn. "It's been sitting an hour."

"Can't it wait?" Brad rejoined, his question floating down into the cave like words in an empty auditorium.

"It'll take two minutes. I'll need that much time getting her strapped in."

They looked at Abbie—Charlie and Bostwick from a distance of three feet, Brad from his cavetop perch. She was sitting where Brad had gently put her down, on the cave floor, her back to a small boulder, her head propped onto her arms. Bostwick's medical magic had almost completely worn off, and her posture suggested deep sleep was none too far away. But simultaneously a change was under way. Charlie and Bostwick could see it in her face: the glimmer of a smile traced with a delicate touch across her lips; the new luster in the pinpoint pupils of her eyes; the rose tint to her cheeks that had been missing since late autumn. The confusion, that unsettling combination of fear and resignation and pervasive pain, the dying young girl they'd brought into this chamber of horrors had taken their leave. Abbie felt it, too, more powerfully than either man. In her mind, the shadow place was only a memory now, receding fast, like an endless night finally chased away by dawn of a clear day. They had gambled, and they had won. The spell was broken.

"You going to be OK there, Apple Guy?" Brad shouted.

She shook her head and grinned.

"I'll be right back. Charlie will take good care of you."

"And me," Bostwick added.

"And Dr. Bostwick will help out. And then we're going home. Just like I promised."

Brad took one of the two remaining flashlights from Thomasine. He backed away from the cliff and disappeared into the shaft.

"All right," Charlie told Abbie. "Let's get you strapped in here. You want me to carry you?"

"Unh-unh," she answered. "I can walk."

"You sure?"

"Oh, sure," she said, tottering to her feet with the agility of an octogenarian rising from a rocking chair after a Sunday nap.

She was almost to the stretcher, was craning anxiously up at the ledge where Thomasine waited alone, when her father reappeared. Without speaking, he walked to the lip of the mine shaft and looked down at her. Their gazes locked. Abbie's grin re-formed. Brad seemed ready to speak when there was the sound of small stones raining down into the stream. He was losing his footing. His knees buckled. Arms pinwheeling, his fingers clutched frantically at the air. His balance went completely, and he screamed as gravity captured him.

Abbie watched her father free-fall into the stream. He landed with a sound like a slap, and then he was gone, pulled into the blackness.

"Dad!" she yelled. Her grin stiffened, and then it was erased by a new look, the look of depthless fright. "Daddy, please!"

Charlie had watched, unmoving, unwilling to believe. And he *didn't* believe what had happened. Didn't believe because at the exact moment Brad swan-dived he heard the faint but distinct sound of the snowmobile engine finally catching. Didn't believe because even in the tenebrous light of Thomasine's lantern the face on the alleged Brad hadn't looked quite right, had been oddly emotionless, not the bubbling-over man whose daughter had just been brought back from the dead.

Didn't believe because George was talking inside his head, informing him, making him understand that it had been an illusion . . .

. . . a trick.

One final trick. Hobbamock's personal good-bye.

"Dad!" Abbie wailed.

"It's not Dad!" Charlie screamed.

"Daddy!"

The Brad facsimile's head popped out of the water. One arm shot into the air, then the other. The fingers were wriggling madly. The classic pose of a person going down for the third and final time.

"Help me, Abbie!" it begged, but it wasn't Brad's voice. It was an impostor. Hobbamock. "Help me before I drown! Please, Abbie!"

"Don't!" Charlie shouted.

"Give me your hand!" the Brad facsimile begged.

With the last bit of Bostwick's chemical strength, Abbie catapulted onto her feet and stumbled toward the river's edge. She knelt, stretching for the hand. Reaching. Stretching . . .

"Just a little farther!"

She tried.

And fell in.

For one agonizing second she floated. Then she, too, was sucked silently under the black-sheened surface of the Styx-like stream.

They all heard it then: from the deepest bowels of the cave, the unmistakable cackle of a madman's laughter.

"Jesus," Bostwick swore.

The ice went out of Charlie's joints, and he stripped his boots and shirt and plunged into the water after Abbie. He was a strong swimmer, had once swum the five-mile water leg of a triathlon on a bet with a professional gambler, but he was not prepared for the intensity of this current. It pulled and clawed at him, beat against him, buffeting his body like a hurricane-force wind. It was cold, unnaturally so, as if here the laws of physics had been suspended and water could be twenty degrees, ten degrees, and still flow. And it was dark. Dark as pitch. Dark as a blind man's dream.

He discovered nothing on his first submergence, only the startling force and opaqueness and temperature of the water, jetting into the unknown region beneath the side of the cave.

On his second try, struggling, exerting superhumanly, he found bottom. The riverbed was not as deep as he expected: perhaps a dozen feet. Before the air in his lungs was consumed, he had a few seconds to feel with his hands. The bottom was water-worn rocks, a few larger boulders, no gravel.

On his third try he was able to patty-cake along the bottom from side to side and back again. He did not find Abbie. He surfaced, panting, snorting a spray of frigid water in Bostwick's direction. His lungs were shooting shards of pain through his chest, and his skin was numbing fast. In his loins he felt his scrotum tightening uncomfortably.

"Anything?" Bostwick yelled.

"No."

On the fourth try he found her arm.

She was snagged, her head sandwiched between rocks. He ran his hand up her arm until he located her shoulders. He tugged at her, but she refused to budge. The water had wedged her with the force of a hammerblow. He tugged again, planting his feet against the rocks for better leverage. His air was gone. He could see the pain, explosions of light in his head. Desperate, he reached for her head, grabbed a clump of hair, and yanked.

She was free. He swam with her to the surface.

Charlie laid her on the shore. Her heart was still beating. Broken arm and all, Bostwick began CPR.

"We've got to get her to the ambulance," he said shortly. "I can't do any more for her here."

Together, he and Bostwick transferred her to the stretcher. In less than two minutes they had her up. Brad was just returning from the snowmobile.

CHAPTER SEVENTY-FOUR

Christmas

CHARLIE REMAINED behind to set the dynamite.

The others went in the ambulance. The sky had cleared completely, leaving behind a crisp, windless, silvery winter night. They passed snowplows, but no other traffic, on their way over the mountain. The storm had kept everybody in, hanging stockings by the fireplace with care.

The code team of Berkshire Medical was shooting for another miracle, this time with Abbie in the emergency room, when a slight tremor passed through the building. It was barely perceptible, but Thomasine and Brad both felt it through the molded plastic chairs of the hospital lobby.

It was midnight—exactly midnight. Brad knew because he'd couldn't take his eyes off the wall clock.

Thirty seconds later there was another rumbling, deeper, longer lasting.

As if Thunder Rise were in great pain.

EPILOGUE

Tuesday, January 6

THE BERKSHIRE Medical Center staff stabilized Abbie, but they could not crack her coma. On Christmas morning she was transferred by helicopter to Boston's Massachusetts General Hospital. She remained unconscious two days. On the third she opened her eyes and smiled—at her father, who'd not left her side since Pittsfield. The next day she spoke her first words. They were: "I love you, Dad." Brad wept openly, as did Thomasine.

On the fifth day the doctors told Brad they could predict with near certainty that his daughter had not suffered any permanent brain damage. She would need periodic checkups and a fairly lengthy recuperation, but unless something utterly unforeseen cropped up, she was going to be fine. For that, they conjectured, everyone could thank the icy temperature of the water in which she'd very nearly drowned.

A week later Brad bundled Abbie up in a down parka and blanket and drove her home. They stopped once, in downtown Morgantown, where Brad used a pay phone.

By arrangement, everyone had parked his car far enough up the road so that Abbie didn't suspect a thing when she and her father turned into the drive.

"Didn't I promise you I'd get you home, Apple Guy?" he said.

"Thanks, Dad." She beamed.

"You stay put. I'll come around and get you. With all this ice, I wouldn't want you to slip."

"Daddy?" she asked as he carried her, still wrapped in her blanket, across the frozen driveway.

"Yes, hon?"

"Did you remember to feed Maria?"

He'd anticipated the question—or one very like it. "Maria's gone," he said gently.

She looked at him quizzically.

"There was . . . an accident."

"Oh, no." She was close to tears. "She's not—"

"We'll talk about it later, sweetheart," Brad interjected. "But I think when we get inside, you won't be so sad. There's a great big surprise for you."

"What is it?" Abbie brightened a bit.

"You'll just have to wait and see," Brad said, fumbling for the key. He found it, turned it in the lock, and the door opened. The fluffiest puppy Abbie had ever seen bounded out. It was a golden retriever. Brad put Abbie down, and the puppy was all over her.

"She's so *cute!* She's just like Maria!"

"Do you like her, hon?"

"I *love* her!"

"And you'll have plenty of time to get to know her. The doctor says you'll be staying home at least a couple of weeks, regaining your strength. In fact, we should get you to bed soon. But first, come with me." Brad headed into the living room.

Abbie took the dog in her arms and followed. She was too preoccupied with the puppy to see the tree immediately, or the mountain of gifts underneath it, or the small group of people huddled to one side trying desperately to remain quiet.

"Merry Christmas, Abbie!" the group burst out.

Abbie was astonished. "Mrs. Fitzpatrick!" she exclaimed. "Thomasine! Jimmy! Mrs. Ellis! Mr. Moonlight!" The only person she didn't recognize immediately was Rod Dougherty.

"Welcome home!"

"Wow!"

The gift opening lasted fifteen minutes. Abbie couldn't believe how many Barbies and Barbie outfits Santa had left. Why, it was as if he'd read her mind! She loved all the clothes everyone had gotten her. She thought the big stuffed rabbit Jimmy had picked out was "really great," the wooden owl Charlie had carved "really neat."

And then she seemed to run completely out of steam. In the time it took Brad to gather all the wrapping paper and stuff it into a trash bag, Abbie was transformed from little dynamo to pale young patient marooned listlessly on the couch.

"I think a certain young lady needs some rest."

"But, Daddy—"

"No buts. If the doctors knew about even this, I'd be in deep trouble. Come on. Let's get you upstairs." Turning toward their company, Brad said: "Of course, you're all welcome to stay."

"We wouldn't dream of it," Mrs. Fitzpatrick said. Then, in a tone the others could interpret only as strict marching orders, she added: "We're going. Come on, everyone."

"Are you sure?"

"Positive."

"Say good-bye to your guests then, Abbie," Brad said.

"Bye."

They went for their coats.

"I'll see you tomorrow," Brad said to Rod. Brad was still wrestling with how much—if anything—he'd publicly divulge about Hobbamock and what really had gone on up there on Thunder Rise. He was leaning toward letting the facts stand as reported in the *Transcript* so far: that the CDC and Health Department were every bit as mystified by the disease's sudden disappearance as they'd been by its strange emergence. That, to paraphrase Charlie, some of life's greatest enigmas just don't have rational explanations.

On the way out, everyone kissed Abbie and thanked her.

Only Thomasine was left. For one long, awkward moment, Brad stared at her, then his daughter, then back at her. He seemed to be seeking guidance.

"You two need some time alone together," Thomasine said matter-of-factly. "I understand. I'll go."

"Please?" Abbie begged. She was holding her new puppy. "Please stay? Pretty please?"

"How could you turn down a pumpkin like this?" Brad said, as he took Thomasine's coat.

"I couldn't," she said, and started to close the door.

As she did, they all heard it: a rumbling, like trucks on a distant highway or far-off thunder on a summer's eve. A rumbling all three chose to believe was only the wind.